CROSS THE LINE

KINGS OF HEART
BOOK 1

LUCKY HART

Cross the Line

A Kings of Heart Novel

Novel Copyright © 2024 by Lucky Hart

Cover Design by BootyFeather

Editors: Kailey Gillotti & Wynne Archer

Proofreaders: Ken Baldwin & Vix

Sensitivity Readers: Mel Cerna, Abigail

 Created with Vellum

To everyone who has ever felt like you were too much and not enough all at once, I see you.

You are enough.

AUTHOR'S NOTE

A few notes first:

At some points, you may get frustrated with Theo. Untreated childhood trauma and parental abandonment can scar deeply, even when those marks are invisible. Please be patient with Theo; his growth is worth the wait. On the other hand, Alec's tendency towards secrecy may exasperate you at times. He's only 21 years old, dealing with burnout from a life of high-level sports, along with his unmedicated ADHD and broken heart.

Could their problems be solved with one long, vulnerable conversation? Sure. However, **1.** There would be no book, and **2.** As humans, sometimes we struggle to do the one thing that we should do or need to do. This is all to say these two oblivious, pining idiots need some time to get on the same page. I hope you can give them some grace to be flawed, complicated humans and that eventually, maybe you will love them as much as I do (because boy, do I love them!).

Part of Alec's story is his mixed race experience. As someone in an interracial marriage who is raising mixed race children, Alec being Mexican is close to my heart. That said, no matter how much some of this might be based on conversations with my spouse or my own personal history raising our biracial children, I cannot speak for those who have lived experience. This is why I'm eternally grateful for my spouse and sensitivity readers who helped me shape Alec's story. I did my best to authentically represent a nuanced portrayal of being Mexican-American, but Alec's experience will not be representative of everyone.

CONTENT WARNINGS

- parental abandonment (past, off screen)
- parental neglect (past, off screen)
- childhood poverty (past, off screen)
- sexual assault (past, off screen, briefly discussed on screen)
- hit and run (on screen)
- hospitalization of a MC (on screen)
- life-altering injury
- ADHD burnout

1 THEO

"WHY ARE you still in the office? Didn't you get off ten minutes ago?"

"The better question is, why are you in my office?" Theo counters. He clicks save on the report he's nearly finished with before spinning in his chair to face his best friend—and the biggest pain in his ass.

Where Jason King's bulk might be considered intimidating, his smile is anything but. The dimple in his chin is on full display when he flashes that smile at Theo.

"You say that as if everyone in your office doesn't adore me." Jason's grin widens, leaning against the door frame. He's just as massive as he was in high school, and even more handsome if you're into big burly men who look like they could carry you without breaking a sweat. There was a time Theo wished Jason was his type because he loved him more than he loved anyone. Jason being straight aside, Theo never held more than brotherly affection for him, which in hindsight is for the best because it kept things easy, and more importantly, safe. "Steven was delighted to see me in the office. More than you."

Steven, Theo's administrative assistant, was on strict orders not to let anyone into his office today until he finished this report. Apparently there's no one Jason can't sweet talk.

"You brought donuts for him again, didn't you?" Theo asks. It's how he got into Theo's office the first time, and it's become a habit. Sometimes, Theo thinks his coworkers like Jason more than they like him. That might also be because Theo rarely talks to them, despite working here for four years.

"Might have," Jason answers, drawing Theo's attention back to the present. He pushes off the door frame and pulls his other hand out from behind his back. There, wrapped in a napkin, is a single buttermilk knot. "Saved your favorite old man donut for you before the rest of your coworkers get to the box in the break room."

"It's not an old man donut," Theo snorts, snatching the donut. "It's just not covered in sprinkles or frosting."

He can tell just by looking at it that it's from the little donut shop he loves on Main Street. It's got old school red booths and kind of shitty coffee, but their donuts more than make up for it. Unfortunately, Main Street becomes overrun with tourists in the summer. People flock to their coastal town of Santa Leon to escape the inland heat, which means Theo hasn't been there in what feels like months. Unlike Theo, who is an introvert with a capital "I", Jason—whose picture is probably in the dictionary under the word 'gregarious'—is the opposite. Even still, with summer in full swing, it must've taken him a good hour to get across town to get these donuts, which means he probably wants something. He just has to wait for Jason to tell him what it is. Luckily, he can never keep a secret for long.

"I mean, it kind of is, but that's okay. It matches your old man sweater."

Theo's mouth is too full of donut to reply, but he looks down at himself and frowns. He got this sweater last week after getting a quarterly cost of living adjustment. It's brown with little zigzags of cream on the sleeves, which reminded him of the mountain ranges that border the edge of the city where he likes to hike. It's also thick and warm, which is nice since his office is always freezing, especially in the summers. He swallows his bite, not seeing the problem. "What's wrong with my sweater?"

"Nothing, man." Jason laughs, grabbing the chair that's next to the door and spinning it around to sit on it backwards. "It's very you. It's great."

"Sometimes I can't tell if you're insulting me or trying to lift up my confidence," Theo says, chasing the donut with the remainder of his iced coffee from his break an hour ago. It's kind of gross, but the afternoon slump is hitting him hard, so the sugar and caffeine combination is exactly what he needs right now.

"I have to keep you on your toes," Jason says, leaning over the back of the chair. He makes it look like a chair for toddlers, not the full-sized office chair it is. "Speaking of which, Alec is back."

If there's anyone who can keep someone on their toes, it's Alexander King, Jason's baby brother. Well, baby might not be the most accurate description anymore. He'll be twenty-one tomorrow, but sometimes it's hard to reconcile the mental image he still holds of the gawky, freckle-faced kid with braces who chased him and Jason everywhere, desperate to be included, with the confident, athletic guy he is now.

"Why is he back early? I thought he was in Mexico for

another week with his best friend." Theo frowns, positive he'd put the date down in his calendar correctly. The Kings were supposed to have a family dinner to celebrate Alec finally coming home after two months gone, doubling as a belated birthday celebration. As with all King family events, Theo was invited, and unless he got the date wrong—which is highly unlikely given his color-coded calendar app—then Alec is early.

"I don't know what happened, actually," Jason muses. "Mom called me and said he was coming home early, and wanted me to pick him up from the airport since they're out of town. Alec told her he'd catch an Uber home, but Mom had a heart attack about her baby being in a stranger's car, and naturally called me to ensure nothing happened to him because I'm the most trustworthy brother."

Theo arches an eyebrow at that, and Jason doesn't hesitate to flip him off. "Fine, she called Andrew first, but he said with his job being so new he can't take off early, and Charlie wasn't answering the phone. Between you and me, I think he's got the right idea about not having a phone or wifi in his studio. He tells Mom and Dad it helps his creative process, but I think it's so he can't be bothered with bullshit like this."

Even as Jason says it, Theo knows there's nothing bullshit about it. Jason's a family man through and through. Theo is sometimes surprised he hasn't settled down and started his own with how important family is to him and how good he is with other people's kids. Then again, the not settling down thing might be because Jason has the worst luck with relationships and always ends up with people who don't appreciate him.

"Anyways," Jason continues, undeterred by Theo's

silence. "Since I was off today, I took the opportunity to swing by their house to get Alec's room ready."

"What did you do?" Theo asks around a too-big bite of donut.

"I'm kind of offended you're even asking me this. I went out of my way to make Alec's bed and—" Theo levels him with one serious look and Jason cracks. "Fine, I covered his bedroom in blown up condoms instead of balloons and hung a birthday banner with dicks on it."

Theo rolls his eyes. Jason might be nearly thirty but pranking his brothers turns him into his mischievous, pain in the ass, teenage self. He tries to imagine Alec's face when he finds it. Alec is always up for a laugh, so he probably won't be phased, but it still gives Theo secondhand embarrassment to imagine it.

"So what are you thinking for the party? Sunday afternoon or—"

"Tonight," Jason interjects.

"No way, that's not enough time to plan."

"Come on, Theo. It's not every day your baby turns twenty-one," Jason points out. At twenty years old—twenty-one at eleven fifty-nine tonight, technically—Alec is hardly a baby. What he is though, is eight years younger than Jason and Theo and a decade younger than his twin brothers, making him the eternal baby of the family. "I need you, man. Help me out? Please." Jason widens his eyes and bats his long eyelashes, as if he needs to convince Theo.

"What did you need me to do?" Theo sighs, not really all that put out. He likes Alec, even if it feels like it's been forever since he saw him.

Jason whoops. "I knew you'd help me out. You're the best."

"I didn't agree yet," Theo points out, even though they both know Theo can never tell Jason 'no'.

"I just need your help to plan a little party."

"Little like something with the twins?" Theo tries, knowing he's going to be wrong.

"Sure, they can come too. And all of Alec's teammates and his friends in the fraternity and the football team and—"

"Is there anyone Alec isn't friends with?"

"Probably not," Jason answers honestly. "He could make friends with a rock."

As a child, Alec had multiple pet rocks, so this really isn't that far off base. Alec has always had a way of making friends and amusing himself wherever he goes. It'd been adorable when he was a child, a little envy-inducing when he was a teen, and now, well, maybe it's still a little envy-inducing. From the stories Jason tells about Alec in college, he's exceedingly popular, as much for his starting spot as a forward on the soccer team as his status as the big man on campus.

"You're doing that pinched face thing again. What could you possibly be overthinking right now?"

"Do you want a list?" Theo retorts, not at all planning on giving him one if he says yes.

He's not jealous of Alec's ability to make friends with people. He's not. He's probably just hungry. That's the only explanation for the weird swirl of emotions in his gut. Theo gets cranky when he's hungry, and the donut is definitely not hitting the way he needs after skipping lunch.

"Look, you've been working on your big boring report on trash for weeks."

Theo rolls his eyes. "The report isn't about trash. At

least not directly. It's about tracking the indicators used to measure environmental and human health over time while taking into account environmental factors."

"You are so smart. I still can't believe you didn't go into grad school with that big brain of yours."

Theo has no reply to this. While Jason's monetary and familial situation allowed him the freedom to continue his education post-bachelor's degree, Theo hadn't had the same privilege. Not that he really wanted a Masters, but the option would've been nice. It's not something he likes to talk about, though, not even with Jason. It's not his fault Theo had a half-absentee single parent, and needed a job ASAP to pay off the school loans he was drowning in. He knows Jason—and the King family—would've helped him if he asked, which is exactly why he's never said anything, and doesn't plan to.

"So this party," Theo prompts, eager to get the conversation back to more comfortable territory. "What exactly do you need me to do? If you're asking me to get snacks and beer at Costco on a Friday night, I'm just letting you know that it's going to require a substantial bribe."

"I don't need you to go to Costco."

"Decorations?" Theo guesses. He's not sure what Jason might have in mind to go with a dick banner and condom balloons, but he could probably swing something. Decorating isn't his strong suit, but he's not a complete disaster. At least, he doesn't think so. He looks down at his sweater, suddenly unsure.

"Decorations were not exactly what I had in mind," Jason says, pulling out his wallet. He passes Theo forty bucks.

Theo's confusion rises. "What the hell is this for?"

"Alec's gonna be starving when you pick him up from the airport. For someone so small, he can eat a lot."

"You want me to pick up Alec from the airport?" Theo blinks at the money in his hand.

"If I do it, he's gonna ask me too many questions," Jason grumbles. "You know how...persuasive he is."

Persuasive is certainly one way to describe Alec. Theo can't help but be amused by the way he manages to wrap all his siblings around his finger.

"You literally coach 250-pound football players. Are you telling me you can't go toe-to-toe with your baby brother?"

"Fuck, yes that is what I'm saying. Have you seen him? He's fucking scary when he's stubborn. Besides, you know I can't lie for shit. I'm gonna spill the beans the second he starts pestering me, and then the entire surprise will be ruined."

That's not untrue. Jason's good at smooth-talking through bullshit in parent conferences but when it comes to flat-out lying, he's comically terrible. When it comes to denying Alec, he's even worse. He used to get in so much trouble with his parents for constantly letting Alec have ice cream for dinner, just because Alec would ask him instead of their parents.

"Listen, we both know you're the only one who has ever been able to resist Alec. On behalf of all of the King brothers, we need you." Jason makes an exaggerated show of pleading, hands clasped together in front of him as he attempts what is probably supposed to be a puppy face, but just makes him look constipated.

"Fine, I'll pick up Alec from the airport," Theo concedes. He doesn't actually mind. He might not be as close to Alec or the twins as he is to Jason, but he likes them all. "Then what, just bring him to your parents' place?"

"You'll need to give us a few hours to get it all together. Take him out to eat."

"Won't Alec think it's weird if I'm the one to pick him up?" Theo asks. He's hung out with Alec before at almost every King family event and holiday since he was younger, but he's never done anything with Alec or the twins alone.

"No way, Alec loves you, man. Besides, just tell him I'm busy and offer him food. He won't care, and if he does, just make something up. You're good at that."

Theo frowns. "I have no idea if I should be offended or say thank you."

"You're just good at not talking about things you don't want to," Jason hedges, leaving Theo with the succinct impression he's leaving something unsaid. "So will you do it?"

"You know I will."

"I knew I could count on you." Jason claps his hands together and then stands. "I already emailed you Alec's itinerary and flight info."

"When?"

"Uh, before I got here. I just assumed you'd say yes, which to be fair, you did." Before Theo can interject, Jason takes two long strides backwards so he's standing in the open doorway, ready to bolt. "Just remember, nothing about the party or secret plans. You think you can handle keeping him busy for a few hours?"

"I'm sure," Theo answers, laughing when Jason practically runs away.

A quick glance at his email lets him know Alec's arriving via Aeromexico at Terminal 3 at six-thirty. That gives him barely an hour and a half to get through rush hour traffic and find the gate. With a resigned sigh, Theo gulps down the last of his watery coffee and the rest of his donut before logging off for the day. Looks like he's on Alexander King duty for the night.

How hard could it be?

2 THEO

"STUPID FUCKING TRAFFIC," Theo mutters, pushing his glasses up the bridge of his nose.

The city of Santa Leon isn't far from Los Angeles miles wise. Nestled along the coastline, it's a cool reprieve from the traffic and heat of the bigger city.

He's been trying to merge into the correct lane at LAX for ten minutes, but no one will let him over, leaving him to sit halfway in the through traffic lane and cause his anxiety to spike. Theo is beginning to question whether he made the right choice agreeing to pick up Alec. He doesn't mind the driving part, but he's not cut out for the severe lack of traffic-law-following currently happening. Then again, what else did he expect on a Friday night?

He shoots off a text to Alec to let him know he's running late, but when he gets nothing in response, he realizes he's going to have to park if he wants to find him. This is what he gets for letting Jason arrange things.

Eventually, he manages to find a spot at pick up, pulling into the open spot and eyeing every passenger that comes out of the terminal. None of them are Alec, and his eyes start to glaze over. He pushes his glasses up onto the top of his head, rubbing his eyes. He's not sure why he even drinks coffee anymore; he's pretty sure he's becoming immune to the effects of caffeine. That or the lack of sleep. Probably that.

With a yawn, he tips his head back, eyes unfocusing as he stares out the rolled down passenger window, when he catches sight of the most glorious backside he's ever seen. Theo might be bisexual, but his attraction definitely leans more male. Especially when they have an ass you could bounce quarters off.

Sitting up a little straighter, Theo straightens his glasses and leans on his center console eying the man's plump back-side. His thin gray sweats appear to be hanging on for dear life, the material stretched tight over his thighs and the swell of his bubble butt. The way he's bent over, it's impossible to see the rest of him, especially through the group next to him with their mass of luggage. However, Theo doesn't need to see his face to appreciate the beauty of what is, unequivo-cally, one of the nicest asses he's ever seen.

The family with all the luggage moves on, and Theo prepares to appreciate the rest of the guy when he notices his hair—or more specifically his curls. The guy's hair has grown a few inches since Theo last saw him a few months ago, but there's no mistaking the soft, golden brown hue of them. When he stands, he shakes the hair off his face, and Theo whimpers, honest to god whimpers. Since when did Alec have a tan—or an ass—like that?

Unaware he's being watched, Alec stretches his arms overhead, exposing a slim strip of his fit belly and a smat-tering of freckles. Theo's watch beeps, alerting him to a spike in heart rate, and all he can do is tap at it agitatedly. Of course he's having goddamn heart palpitations. He just checked out his best friend's baby brother. He's not sure what happened to the knobby-kneed, big-toothed kid who used to beg Theo to play with him, but the man standing there outside of Terminal 3 is not that kid. Not anymore.

Somewhere along the line, Alexander King grew up, and Theo didn't notice. At least, not in the way he is noticing right now. Theo shifts in the driver seat, ignoring the person waving their hands at him from behind him, while he watches Alec bend himself in half in an impressive stretch—his flexibility makes Theo's tongue feel too big for his mouth.

This is not happening. Theo did not just check out his best friend's baby brother a second time. The first time he could brush aside and ignore with a bit of cognitive dissonance, but the second time there was no mistaking who Theo was checking out.

"Fuck," Theo curses, far louder than he intended, made evident by the handful of people who turn and stare. The only one Theo cares about is the one with the brown eyes. Even after other people look away, Alec's gaze is unrelenting. When Theo doesn't break it, Alec raises one eyebrow at Theo, who gets so flustered he accidentally honks the horn. Alec bursts into laughter before grabbing his luggage and making his way over to Theo's car. He tosses his suitcase and backpack into the car before moving to the front passenger side.

"Where's Jason?" Alec asks by way of greeting.

"Nice to see you, too, Alec."

"It *is* nice to see me, isn't it?" Alec grins, both his dimples on full display. Theo's not sure he ever noticed how much more handsome they make his face. "Is that why you're here? You win a contest and a few hours alone with me was the prize?"

"You're so fucking full of yourself," Theo laughs, his heart rate settling. This is fine. This is just Alec. Little Alexander King, who was afraid of the dark until he was ten and slept with a stuffed teddy until he was thirteen. Theo's seen him get his diaper changed and take his first step. Hell, he even helped Jason and the twins teach Alec how to ride a bike. The ass appreciation was simply a mistake. One that won't ever happen again. Alec is gorgeous but off limits.

"I am, sadly, not full of anything," Alec bemoans.

Given how shameless Alec is, that could either be a sexual innuendo or a plea for food. The only option Theo feels equipped to handle right now is the latter, so he goes with that.

"We could go get tacos. Unless you're sick of Mexican food—"

"No one can be sick of Mexican food," Alec interjects. "I could move to Mexico for the food alone. The land and the people are amazing too, but the food? God, the food— *chilaquiles, enfrijoladas, chile relleno de queso, fresa con crema*, and the *atoles*. I haven't eaten so well since my *abuela* died."

Of all the King brothers, Alec had taken the loss of his *abuela* the hardest. She'd passed during Alec's junior year of high school, and it was the longest Theo has seen him go without smiling.

"Antonio's family always made sure to make meatless stuff for me, too. I ate like a King." He turns his gaze on Theo, waiting for appreciation of his pun, and Theo can't help but laugh at his ridiculousness. "You know what, turn the car around and take me back."

"I take it you had a good time then?" Theo grins.

Alec nods around a yawn. "Antonio's family is really

nice. We ate good food and played soccer with the kids in his small town all day. It was the best."

Theo's met Antonio a few times. As Alec's teammate and best friend, he's been invited to several King family events since he and Alec got close in their freshman year; apparently close enough for Antonio to invite Alec to his family's ranch in Mexico for a month. Theo feels a little foolish for not realizing what must be between them sooner.

"I'm sure they liked you too."

"Hopefully," Alec says.

"I'm sure it was nerve-wracking meeting your boyfriend's family for the first time."

"My what?" Alec splutters.

"Your boyfriend, aren't you and him—" but the rest of Theo's sentence can't be heard over Alec howling like a hyena.

"Oh my god, I'm telling Antonio when he gets home next week, this is great." Alec continues to laugh maniacally. "Like I would date a fucking soccer boy, they're annoying and difficult and—"

"You're a soccer player."

"I'm an anomaly, obviously."

"And I'm confused," Theo admits.

It's not until Alec has stopped laughing, which takes a solid three minutes—Theo times it—that he speaks.

"Antonio proposed to his longtime girlfriend right after we got there. He invited me for moral support and also to distract his family after the announcement. I don't know if you've noticed, but I'm pretty good at garnering attention." Theo has definitely noticed, but he remains quiet, pretty sure that was a rhetorical question.

"So you were a red herring."

"I guess you could say that. Antonio gets a lot of pressure. His parents sacrificed a lot to get him here. But if you bring your really loud, gay best friend to be annoying, then everything you do in comparison seems easier to handle." Alec says it so offhandedly, his tone more serious than self-deprecating that Theo can't help but respond.

"You're not annoying, Alec."

"I'm more than some people can handle, but it's cool. I did what I was supposed to, and then, well—" Alec shrugs, falling silent.

Much as Theo wants to push the conversation it's clear Alec is done, his eyes focused on something outside the window. He lets out a soft sigh before adjusting his seat as far back as it can go then reclining so he can stretch his legs on the dash. At five-foot-eight, he's a good five inches shorter than Theo and manages it easily.

"Comfortable?" Theo asks, merging into the exiting traffic lane. He tries to bite his tongue on his next words but can't. "You know that if we got into an accident that would be very unsafe."

"It's cool. I trust you to drive with all the care and safety befitting the precious cargo you have in the passenger seat." He winks at Theo. "Besides, I need to stretch out my calves. They're killing me. You wouldn't believe how cramped I was. I had the middle seat, Theo. The middle seat! Six hours sandwiched between two guys twice my size. Can you imagine?"

"That's really not that hard to imagine," Theo teases.

"Oh, fuck you," Alec snorts, folding his arms beneath his head. "Just because you and Jason are built like brick houses doesn't mean I'm small. I'm just the perfect size to be underestimated."

"I'm not built like a brick house," Theo mumbles, unsure why the comment makes him blush. Alec has teased him about his size plenty of times. Between the two of them, Jason is definitely built like a brick house—six-foot-five and big in every way. In comparison, Theo's six-foot-one frame is lankier, his bulk from high school football long gone. He's still in pretty decent shape from his love of hiking, but his body has softened with age. He's less a brick house and more of a marshmallow one.

"Fine, Jason is built like a brick house. You're more like —hmmm." Alec reaches over, toying with the edge of Theo's sweater. "You know, it's impossible to tell what you're shaped like beneath these sweaters you always wear."

"I know what you want to say, Jason already told me it was hideous. In my defense, my office is freezing. They really crank the air conditioner in the summer."

"What's your excuse now? It's almost ninety degrees outside."

What Theo doesn't want to say is he's gotten so used to wearing the sweaters, he finds it hard to take them off, even when it gets warm. They're comfortable, safe—and as Alec astutely and unexpectedly pointed out—he can hide in them. Not that he's ever consciously thought about it, but now that Alec's pointed it out, he can't deny what is unequivocally true.

"Anyways, I didn't say anything about it being hideous," Alec continues, smoothing the sweater down over Theo's belly. It quivers, and Theo wonders if Alec can feel it through the knitted material. Probably not. "Maybe you're built like a giraffe."

"I'm not that tall," Theo laughs, perpetually surprised by how easy it is to do it when Alec is around. He hadn't realized how dull and quiet things were the last couple of months until Alec stepped back into the picture in technicolor.

"Maybe you're just Theo-shaped," Alec says softly.

For someone who never takes anything seriously, Alec has a way of throwing out statements that leave Theo feeling surprisingly exposed.

"Hey, would you mind if I put on the radio?" Alec asks, hands hovering over the dial. "Quiet makes me twitchy."

"Sure," Theo agrees, welcoming the distraction.

Alec plugs his phone into the adapter, flipping through his playlist until he finds what he wants. He puts on something loud with a fast beat that Theo would normally never listen to on his own. He finds he doesn't mind, the bass beating in time with his pathetic heart as he steals glances at Alec, and wonders when exactly he turned into a man without Theo realizing.

"Hey, Alec."

Alec's fingers tap a mile a minute on his legs, his eyes turning to Theo when he speaks. "Yeah?"

"Happy birthday."

"Oh." Alec's expression shifts into one of surprise, his dimples showing up when he shoots a toothy grin Theo's way. "Thanks."

Something about the expression punches the air from Theo's lungs. He's looked at Alec smiling thousands of times, and yet somehow this feels like the first. His skin is tanned from weeks spent outside, his hair wind tousled and his body relaxed. There is something about him that is magnetic.

"Why did you pick me up?" Alec asks after several minutes of, well not silence with the radio blaring, but lag in conversation at least.

"Jason was—"

"Busy, yeah, you said. What's the real reason?"

"What makes you think that's not the real reason?"

"Because Mom left me a long voice mail apologizing for her and Dad being out of town on my birthday weekend and promised Jason would pick me up and take me to dinner. She said it was already arranged."

"Would you rather Jason had picked you up?"

"Nah, Jason won't let me put my feet on the dash of his stupid baby. He also has shitty taste in music, but that's besides the point. You didn't answer my question."

"Speaking of questions, why are you home ten days early?" Theo counters, desperately trying to change the subject. Just because he is a good liar doesn't mean he enjoys it.

To his surprise, this makes Alec shift in his seat. There's an air of something unfamiliar, and Theo doesn't like it.

"You don't have to tell me," Theo reminds him.

"I was homesick," Alec admits, his voice quieter than Theo has ever heard it. "I'd planned on being home for a week in between training camp and Mexico, but then Antonio changed his flight and begged me to change mine too, and I couldn't say no when he needed me, you know? But then it meant I didn't get to come home, and I've never been away for two months and—" Alec trails off in a gust, deflating against the seat like a balloon with a hole.

"You missed your family," Theo finishes.

Alec plucks at the fabric of his sweats where it's bunched around his knee. "That was part of it."

"There's nothing wrong with being homesick, you know," Theo says, eyes darting between the road and Alec. Judging by the look on Alec's face, there's something else going on. "It could be a lot to be around someone newly engaged too."

The lines of Alec's face, normally relaxed and happy,

knit together. It's clear Theo hit close with his guess and equally clear Alec doesn't want to talk about it.

"So why did you pick me up anyway?" Alec questions. "Did you lose a bet?"

Despite the way Alec laughs, the juxtaposition in his drop in confidence is sharp. It makes Theo's chest clench uncomfortably. It's not exactly a new feeling to want to protect Alec. Back when Alec came out as gay in fourth grade, he and Jason made a point to drop him off and pick him up every day in their football jerseys. No one had actually given Alec any shit for being gay, but he and Jason weren't gonna give anyone any chances. The protectiveness he'd felt then was the kind you have for a little kid you want to shield before the world has a chance to dull their spirit.

Alec is anything but a little kid now, but Theo sees the same flicker of unease he saw ten years ago. The difference is that this time, Theo isn't some cool high school football player anymore. He can't rock up in a sports jersey and Jason's muscle car and magically fix things just by being there. He can't do much of anything except offer Alec a distraction.

"You act like I can't just have missed you." Judging by the expression on Alec's face, it's clear he's going to need to offer more. "Jason was actually busy, but I also wanted to spend time with you."

It's not a total lie. It's adjacent enough to the truth that Theo doesn't feel too guilty.

"You never spend time with me," Alec points out, and Theo isn't sure if he wants to laugh or scream. If there's one thing you can always count on for Alec, it's that he doesn't make things easy. He calls you on your bullshit every time and never lets you get away with anything. This is usually directed towards Jason or the twins, but apparently Theo has made himself fair game.

"Of course I do. I've known you your entire life."

Saying it out loud is strange but true. He and Jason became instant best friends in first grade when Jason realized Theo's lunch box was sometimes empty, and started sharing half of his turkey sandwich and fruit snacks. Jason's mom was pregnant with Alec and while he hadn't understood or even liked babies, he was around to see Alec grow from a noisy wrinkled baby into an energetic toddler into a headstrong preteen into, well, now a man. It's strange to realize he's been around for Alec's entire life, knows his childhood secrets, and yet in other ways, he hardly knows him.

"Name the last time we hung out," Alec demands, crossing his arms and fixing his gaze on Theo. There's nothing sharp in his tone, but the challenge is clear.

"We hang out all the time," Theo tries, racking his brain for the last time. "Right before you left for training. Charlie and Andrew's birthday."

"No, I meant us, without someone else."

Theo opens his mouth then closes it. He tries to think of even one occasion where he was around Alec without it being because of Jason or his family but can't.

"I was nine," Alec says. "I'd gotten a new soccer ball for Christmas and wanted to play with you and Jason so badly, but Jason wanted to go see his girlfriend. He told me maybe tomorrow, but you looked at me, grabbed the ball and took me into the backyard. You were wearing that same brown hoodie you wore every day, and your hair was longer than it is now—almost to your shoulders. We played for hours until Mom had to drag us inside because dinner was ready.

When Jason got back, you guys went up to his room to play video games."

"I forgot about that," Theo admits. "That was twelve years ago. How do you even remember that much about it?"

Alec is quieter than normal, and an unfamiliar feeling builds in Theo's gut. Alec is rarely quiet.

"Hey look! There's a taco truck down that road," Alec announces. "Pull over."

"There's not even a line, how do you know if it's good?" Theo asks, already switching on his turn signal. He tries to look for a name so he might be able to look up the menu online or any reviews, but sees nothing as he parks on an unfamiliar side street.

"You don't know if it's any good until you try it," Alec replies.

He has a point, but Theo is not quite as adventurous an eater as Alec. Partly because of his own taste buds, but also because growing up below the poverty line meant there was never enough money to waste on food he might not like. He's got enough disposable income to cover eating out now, and Jason is paying for dinner tonight, but old habits are hard to break. The thought makes him frown. He's not twelve anymore, rationing out cereal into baggies to make sure it lasted the entire week in case his dad didn't get paid. He's a grown up with a stable income, and he can try a new food truck. Besides, it's Alec's birthday, and if he wants tacos then he should get them, Theo's stupid issues aside.

"Alright, just let me try and look it up first and—"

"No way," Alec interrupts, stealing Theo's phone from the center console and shoving it into the pocket of his sweats. "We are going in blind. This is my last free weekend before the school nutritionist starts monitoring every damn micronutrient I ingest, and going on and on about how vital it is I hit my protein goals as the only vegetarian on the team. We're going on a culinary adventure."

There's very little about approaching an unmarked food truck in an empty alley that feels like an adventure to Theo, but considering he puts in free time in his calendar, he's probably not the right person to judge.

"Sure." Theo tries to smile, but it feels more like a grimace.

"I'm sure whatever we get they can make without onions." Alec pats his leg. "Come on big guy."

"How do you know I hate onions?"

Alec looks at him like he's stupid, which Theo is starting to feel.

"I do pay attention to things besides soccer, you know," Alec snorts, poking him in the side with one of his bony fingers when Theo makes no move to open his door. "Come on, Theo, live a little."

"Stop poking me and I'll come."

"Yes, sir," Alec crows, opening his door. He's out of the car and using the hood as drums before Theo is opening his own door. He smiles at Theo, the wind ruffling his hair as he watches Theo approach. Behind him, the sky turns orange, streaks of white clouds painting a picture. Alec shakes the curls from his face, the lines of his body sharp against the softening sky, and Theo has the sudden urge to take his picture.

A thought occurs to Theo, unbidden and confusing. Alexander King is beautiful.

"Are you ready?" Alec asks, blissfully unaware of Theo's racing thoughts.

Behind him the sky darkens, orange turning red. Something has changed.

"Ready," Theo lies, anything but.

"DO YOU WANT ANOTHER *TACO*?"

Theo shakes his head, pushing his paper plate away from him before reaching for his Topo Chico and taking a chug. The carbonation burns in the best way possible, soothing the edges of Theo's nerves. He hates how he can be anxious like this even when he's having a good time.

"I don't think I can eat another bite," Theo admits, unsure how Alec even finished his second round. Then again, maybe bean tacos are less filling than *carnitas*.

"I feel like I could do another one," Alec muses.

The plastic creaks as he leans back in his chair, slipping his hand under the hem of his cotton shirt. The sun has set now, the flickering light from the street lamp above them illuminating the many freckles that dot Alec's high cheekbones. There's an undeniable physicality to his body and the way he moves, but his features are delicate—sharp cheekbones, long lashes and full lips. Have his lips always been that full?

"How can you possibly fit any more food in there? You ate nine tacos and a side of chips and guacamole."

"I'm still a growing boy," Alec proclaims, patting his exposed belly. It's supposed to be a joke, but the way he rubs his palm over his stomach draws Theo's eyes to the insanity of Alec's body—his stomach flat and muscled with visible abs, and a soft trail of light brown hair leading from under his belly button to down beneath the waistband of his sweats.

Theo gulps the rest of his drink so fast it burns.

Staring at Alec, it's easy to forget himself and the reasons they're really here. He's supposed to be distracting

Alec for the surprise party awaiting him. He's not supposed to be indulging in wayward thoughts. Then again, Jason did tell him to keep Alec occupied. There's no reason they can't enjoy the time until then.

"You know what, I changed my mind. I don't want more *tacos*," Alec announces. "I want dessert. We should stop and get a cake or something. It is my birthday."

"That it is," Theo agrees.

"So you admit I should get whatever I want," Alec says, tipping forward. His shirt falls down, covering his tummy, and he leans his elbows on the plastic folding table, eyes alight with mischief. "We could go somewhere else? I'm legal for a club now."

He waggles his eyebrows in a way that's so ridiculous Theo can't even focus on the fact that Alec is suggesting they go to a club.

"I'm sure there are more exciting things you'd like to do on your birthday than hang out with your brother's boring best friend."

"You're not boring," Alec says, nose wrinkled.

He says it so seriously, as if Theo even suggesting it is offensive to him. Theo can't imagine why.

"We could probably get a cake or—" but he pauses, his phone buzzing. He flips it over, angling it so Alec can't see the message just in case.

> **Jason**
> party is a go

Theo looks up in time to see Alec avert his gaze, clearly trying to pretend he wasn't staring. He sips his Coke, the line of his throat exposed.

Being alone with Alec is unexpectedly easy, and Theo is loath to have it end. He reminds himself that he's being selfish, that Alec would definitely rather be at a party full of his siblings and friends if he knew it was waiting for them.

> **Theo**
> be there in thirty minutes

Once he's texted Jason, he pockets his phone and returns his attention to Alec. This time, he doesn't pretend not to stare, and an unfamiliar weight settles on his chest. No one has ever looked at him with such unmasked intensity, and the well-crafted excuses Theo mentally rehearsed all night flies out the window as he ends up giving the world's most obvious lie.

"I'm kinda tired. I should probably get you home."

He expects a protest or maybe a plea to stop for dessert on the way, already mentally planning a second text to Jason to explain the delay when Alec stands.

"Alright then, let's go."

Somehow Theo had expected Alec to protest, even hoped for it, which makes no sense at all. Alec agreeing to head back to the party awaiting him is exactly what Theo needed to happen, so he's not sure why he doesn't feel any relief.

Alec stands, collecting both of their trash, tossing it in the bin near the food truck before making his way back to Theo's car. All the while, he's strangely subdued, offering no witty quips at Theo for staring or dramatic requests for his birthday cake. It's a side of Alec that Theo has never seen before.

"You coming, Theo?"

Theo breathes deeply, eyes stuck on the empty folding

table where ten minutes prior Alec's presence had domi-nated. Now it's dulled into something that makes Theo's stomach twist uncomfortably, and he has no idea what that means.

"Coming."

3 ALEC

ALEC LEANS his head against the seat, careful to keep his eyes on the changing landscape outside the car. Looking at Theo right now would be difficult. While Alec has had countless years to master the art of disguising his facial expressions around Theo, he apparently lost them all in one night.

Seeing Theo pull up to the curb at the airport was one of the best and worst birthday surprises of his life. An afternoon with Theo was everything that Alec never dared to let himself hope for. He'd done his best not to make it weird, sure that Theo was just doing Jason a favor, except Theo hadn't acted put out or bored. He indulged Alec's tendency to ramble from one inane topic to another without warning, and even laughed a few times when Alec was being goofy to try and make him smile. The best, or worst part, depending on how you looked at it, was the way Theo kept looking at Alec like he was seeing Alec for the first time.

The attention went to Alec's head and rendered him completely fucking stupid. That was the only explanation for Alec acting like such a fool and trying to get Theo to hang out with him even longer. Hell, Alec doesn't even like cake that much. It's alright, and if offered, he'd take a slice, but he always preferred ice cream, even on his birthday. So why he blurted out that he wanted a birthday cake was beyond him. Well, that's not entirely true. Alec knows why he said it. He said it because he's a pathetic idiot who's had feelings for his big brother's best friend for nearly a decade.

He's not a kid anymore; he's a man, thank you very much. Not that any of his brothers seem to recognize that. They all still treat him like he's sixteen and can't take care of himself. Then there is Theo who treats him, well, like an acquaintance. Not that Alec can blame him. It's all his fault, and Alec's been living with the consequences of making the worst decision of his life when he was fifteen.

He'd gone and told Theo how he felt.

Of course Theo wasn't cruel about the revelation. That wasn't Theo's way. He was nice, so fucking nice that Alec almost wished he had been mean. It might have made it simpler to get over him. Instead, he was sweet and thoughtful and let Alec down easy, while also putting enough distance between them that Alec knew without a shred of doubt that nothing was ever going to happen. Even if Alec can look back and know it was the right choice, that it would've been wrong on so many levels for Theo to be with him, it still hurt Alec's pride and broke his baby gay heart.

A heartache he thought he was over, until Theo drove back into Alec's life in his goddamn plain brown Subaru, in his stupid sweater that made him look gentle and sweet. For an unintended birthday gift, Theo ruined Alec's entire goddamn life by reminding him that Theodore James was the first man Alec had ever loved, and all these years later, he is still not over him. Not at all. Not even a little bit.

"Everything ok?" Theo asks.

It's the first thing he's said to Alec in the twenty-five minutes since they left the food truck, and the words are the emotional equivalent of someone dumping a bucket of ice water over his head. Alec's been too quiet, stuck in his head. It's not often he goes radio silent, but when there's no outlet for his energy or racing thoughts, they all turn inward and his usual happy-go-lucky thoughts spiral into darker places. Places he doesn't like to show anyone.

"I'm good, just tired," Alec lies, plastering on a smile as he stretches his legs out until his socked toes are pressed against the windshield. He can see Theo grip the steering wheel a little tighter, obviously worried about Alec's unsafe seating position, and Alec smiles wider.

They say toddlers can't tell the difference between positive or negative attention when they want it, and that's why they act out. Alec's not a toddler; he works really hard to show people he's mature, but he's also not above resorting to stupid shit when he needs a distraction or more attention. In this case, he prefers a little less attention from Theo since having it directed towards him without Jason as a buffer has ripped the bandaid off the wound he thought was healed.

The best he can do is draw attention to himself on purpose. If there's one thing Alec's learned, it's that sometimes the more people look at you, the less they see.

"Did you know it's almost impossible for most people to lick their own elbow?"

"What?"

"It's almost impossible for most people to lick their own elbow," Alec repeats.

"Not that kind of 'what', I heard you just fine. I just

wasn't sure where that random bit of information came from."

"This baby holds the secrets of the universe," Alec says, tapping his head. "Anyways, back to what we were saying about elbow licking."

"I feel like saying *we* is an exaggeration." Theo snorts.

There's the faintest hint of a smile playing at the corner of his mouth, and Alec's previous tension melts away. This is exactly what he wants: Theo happy and laughing at him, not paying attention to his slip-up in moods.

According to Antonio, Alec is a grade-A attention whore, which isn't untrue. Not that Alec ever asked his opinion, but they both have a tendency to run their mouths while also speaking before thinking, which is probably why they get along so well. Alec likes to blame his ADHD, but since Antonio doesn't have that, it is possible that it's just Alec's personality.

Much as he tries to deny it, he really does like attention, and a hell of a lot of it, too. He learned at an early age the easiest way to get that was by making people happy. It was a bonus that as he'd gotten older he genuinely loved making the people he cared about laugh and smile. But it didn't change the fact that deep down, Alec desperately wants to be seen.

Maybe it's being a Leo, or maybe it's having three successful, attractive and substantially older brothers that leaves him feeling like he has been chasing their shadows his entire life. He loves his brothers, and he knows they love him, but the difference in their ages keeps Alec living life ten steps behind. Whatever he does, they've already done.

Realizing he's going down one of his brain spirals, Alec does his best to recover.

"Well, I was talking about elbow licking, and you joined

the conversation. Therefore, it is definitely *we* now," Alec says, hoping he didn't have enough lag in answering to rouse Theo's suspicions further.

For good measure, he winks at Theo, the last knot of tension in his chest loosening when Theo shakes his head and laughs. In that one little act, the world rights itself. Time has changed a lot, but not everything. He can still make Theo smile.

As much as Alec wants Theo to see how much he's changed and grown, the smartest thing to do right now is play it safe. In Theo's eyes, Alec has always just been Jason's carefree little brother who could pull a smile from Theo with a sick ball trick on the field or a ridiculous joke.

The most heartbreaking part of the distance Theo put between them after Alec's failed confession wasn't even Alec's broken heart; it was feeling like he'd let Theo down. Theo didn't have a lot of people in his life, and the number of people he trusted was even less. Knowing that Alec was the sole cause of the wall Theo put up burned more than anything, and for years, there was nothing he could do to fix it.

Maybe now is his chance. Alec can be that someone for Theo again. He can make sure not to let his too-big feelings show or his tendency to spiral when he has to be still. He can be the fun, breezy guy Theo used to know without letting his traitorous heart get in the way.

"I THINK you're full of bullshit."

"I swear to fucking god, it's true." Alec grins, his stomach muscles sore from laughing. He's recounted the entire story to Theo twice now and it's no less funny the second time, nor less incredulous. "Riley swears it's an honorary frat brother tradition, but I'm still not sure why he did it naked."

For some reason, Theo's smile fades with his last sentence, but when he catches Alec staring, he plasters it on bigger than ever. "I'm glad I wasn't in a frat."

"I don't think I'm the frat type, either," Alec agrees.

"Really?" Theo appears genuinely surprised. "That seems right up your alley."

"The sense of community and service?"

"I was gonna say attention-seeking behavior and parties, but that, too. Though to be fair, I don't know the first thing about what frat life is actually like outside of movies, so it's probably not all doing stupid stuff. I'm sure you'd have fun, though."

"You know I love to have fun." Alec laughs, Theo's words strangely cutting. He can't blame Theo for assuming that's all there is to him. How would he know any different? It's all most people think about Alec.

"Gotta enjoy your youth while you have it," Theo says, gripping the steering wheel with his left hand so he can reach over and ruffle Alec's curls. His fingers are there and gone before Alec can appreciate them, the small bit of contact an unexpected punch to Alec's heart.

There was a time when Theo used to touch him—a clap on the shoulder, a congratulatory hug or ruffle of hair. Back before Alec ruined everything with his confession. This is the first time Theo's touched him like that in six years, and Alec's painfully embarrassed at how much he likes it.

Theo pulls into the driveway, shutting the engine off and turning to grace Alec with one of his rare smiles. "Welcome home, kiddo."

Just like that his heart crashes and burns. *Kiddo.*

"I'm twenty-one, thank you very much," Alec retorts, proud of himself for keeping any petulance out of his tone.

"Sorry, my mistake. Happy birthday, big boy."

"Shut up," Alec huffs, torn between arousal and amusement. Desperate to get out of the car and away from the risk of being touched and making another life-altering mistake, he reaches for the door handle. "Race you to the door."

"Not everything is a race."

"That's what slow people say." Alec bolts from the car and takes the stairs two at a time. He pauses halfway up when he doesn't hear Theo following, realizing he's gone and gotten Alec's luggage from the trunk. He waits until Theo locks his car and can see him again before turning around to take the stairs backwards. "I'm still beating you."

"Yeah, yeah, yeah."

The suitcase clunks on the edge of each of the stone steps as Theo drags it up, his eyes never leaving Alec's. It's far more eye contact than he's used to from Theo, and it makes Alec itch to go for a run or kick something really hard, anything to get rid of the rush of adrenaline coursing through him. He taps his fingers on his thigh and breathes in deeply, trying not to look as out of control as he feels.

"Jason said your parents put the spare key in the planter," Theo says when he reaches the landing at the top of the steps.

"I moved that months ago. Mom and Dad are nuts if they think keeping a key outside is okay. I have seen way too many true crime documentaries to allow that."

"Since when do you watch true crime?"

"There's a whole world of things you don't know about me, Theodore."

"No one calls me Theodore."

"And yet, I just did." Alec winks before squatting down, digging his spare set of house keys out of his suitcase.

"How did you know you'd need a house key if your parents' trip this weekend was last minute?" Theo asks.

"I'm obviously the full package." He bats his long eyelashes at Theo, grinning. "I'm sexy and smart and some other things that are not fit to say in front of polite company."

Theo snorts. "You are definitely something."

"I'm taking that as a compliment." Alec grins before unlocking the front door. He turns the key, hand hovering over the handle before he turns back to look at Theo.

"What's up, kiddo?"

Alec fights off the rush of indignation at hearing that a second time. It doesn't matter how much he desperately wants Theo to see him as a man, to see how much he's grown up and matured. He can't push him. All that matters is that for the first time in years, Theo is really looking at him, and Alec doesn't want him to stop. Problem is, he doesn't want to make a mistake, either. He doesn't want to accidentally freak Theo out with feelings and have him run away again.

"Nothing." Alec sighs, resolved to ignore his own wants. He twists the knob, pushing the door halfway open before abruptly turning back around to face Theo. He isn't ready to let tonight be over. Not yet. Maybe he can have just a little bit more time before whatever this is ends. "Will you come in?"

"Alec."

Theo's gaze darts from Alec to the open doorway behind him, probably weighing the invitation. He knows he's pushing his luck, but Alec always likes to push boundaries.

"Please," Alec whispers in a tone that feels embarrassingly close to begging. "I had fun tonight and I—"

Someone giggles in the house, followed by a loud thud and more stifled laughter. Heart stuttering in his chest, Alec swivels on his heels just in time for the lights to turn on and a house stuffed with people to scream "Happy birthday!"

He turns back around to look at Theo's smile, desperately trying to return the expression. He should be grateful, excited, but all he can feel is a crushing sense of disappointment at the realization that Theo hadn't missed him. Theo was doing Jason a favor.

"Alec, my man!" Riley yells, slinging an arm around Alec's shoulder.

Riley's got a good six inches on Alec, though most of his friends do. When he pulls Alec in for a hug, it shoves Alec's face into his chest, and Alec breathes in a little deeper, always relieved at how much his friends indulge his need for touch, even the straight ones. Well, privately Alec has questions about how straight Riley Reed is, but that's not something Alec can figure out for him.

"Happy birthday, my King." Riley's voice booms through the night, the group of people around them cheering as someone passes Riley a gaudy costume crown with oversized plastic jewels all around it. It's absolutely ridiculous, which means, naturally, Alec loves it. What he doesn't love is the way Riley picks him up and throws him over his shoulder. Just because he's smaller than everyone else doesn't mean he's fair game.

"Put me down, you overgrown caveman."

"Not my fault you're pocket-sized."

"I'm five-foot-eight, asshole."

"Like I said, pocket-sized." Riley slaps his ass. "Enjoy the ride. Onward to debauchery!"

The sole upside to being on Riley's shoulders is that it gives him a perfect view of Theo while people file back into the house. Everyone except Theo, that is. He remains in the shadows, something sad in his smile, and Alec can't stand it. No matter how much it breaks his heart, no matter how much he knows Theo will never return his feelings, what he misses more than anything is being able to call Theo his friend.

"Put me down, fucker!" Alec tries one more time. When that doesn't work, he resorts to desperate measures and slaps Riley's ass to get his attention. It works, perhaps too well, because Riley coughs and Alec cackles. Serves him right.

"What's going on?" Riley asks, setting him down. He turns to follow Alec's gaze towards the front porch and raises his eyebrows.

"Fuck off," Alec grumbles, giving Riley a shove. The fucking giant of a man doesn't even budge as Alec stomps past him until he's standing directly in front of Theo.

"I will not fuck off, but I will stay ten feet away," Riley grudgingly agrees following behind Alec to lean against the door frame. He crosses his arms over his chest like some kind of guard dog, and Alec can't help but shake his head. His friends are the best but also a pain in the ass. Besides Antonio, he's definitely closest to Riley. They met last year and have been thick as thieves ever since. Alongside his brother Charlie, they're the only two people alive who know how Alec feels about Theo.

"Down, puppy." Alec laughs. Riley has been protective of Alec since the day they met. To be fair, it tracks given the way they met. While he appreciates that Riley cares, he can handle himself just fine. He's not fifteen anymore. He's not gonna confess his undying love to Theo, he's not a totally pathetic moron even if he feels like it, walking to Theo with a house full of people staring.

Theo shoves his hands in his pocket, watching Alec's approach with clear confusion. "What are you doing? You know your party is inside, right?"

"Then why are you out here?" Alec counters. Maybe he's not a total moron, but he's definitely a partial one. He can't stay away from Theo even if he tries. Worse, he doesn't want to. "It's a party."

"I can see that." Theo laughs. "That's a very nice crown you've got there."

"I know, right?" Alec adjusts his crown, making sure to pull a few curls out. "I look even more handsome."

Theo doesn't reply, but Alec doesn't expect him to. He just can't turn off the part of his brain that flirts with everyone he likes.

"Come inside."

"Go have fun," Theo counters.

"I won't have fun if I know you're sulking out front in the dark."

"I don't sulk."

"Do too," Alec challenges, closing the distance between them and jabbing his finger into Theo's chest. "Get your ass inside and have fun, Theodore."

"It's your birthday." He shrugs in that casual way of his. "I'm pretty sure you're the one who is supposed to go have fun."

"If it's my birthday, then I'm the boss, right? Or the king. The birthday king."

"I suppose it does," Theo agrees, "though I'm not sure if there are actually birthday rules or parameters."

"Rule number one of birthdays: no arguing about parameters."

"What's rule number two?" Theo asks, licking his lips.

Alec has to bite back his desire to say *'give the birthday boy a kiss'*. He doesn't think that joke would go over well given their history, especially since it's not a joke if it's what he wants. Age has done Theo wonders. If Theo at seventeen had been his gay awakening, and Theo at twenty-two was Alec's first love, then Theo at twenty-eight is something infinitely more beautiful. He's filled out, his baby face gone, his body softer in some places and his heart harder in others.

He's handsome in a way that aches. Alec has spent his entire life comparing other men to him, and not one of them has ever held up. He's not sure they ever will.

"Alec?" Theo whispers.

"Rule number two is have fun," Alec blurts, giving in to his impulses by grabbing Theo's wrist. He gives it a tug, heart thundering in his chest when Theo doesn't resist.

"Alright, Alec, just for you."

Alec pulls Theo to the house, ignoring Riley's furrowed eyebrows. It's Alec's birthday. He can have this one night with Theo before everything goes back to how it was before.

"YOU DONE HIDING YET?"

Alec cocks his head up, eyeing Riley. He's had a fair few drinks now, his hoodie removed to reveal his loose tank and strong arms. He looks relaxed and happy, everything Alec should be. His party has been great so far, filled with good music and good friends and Theo. So much Theo.

Despite the people clamoring for Alec's attention, his eyes were drawn to Theo all night. Half with worry over him drinking more than he normally does, and half with appreciation for the sight of his broad chest when he'd removed his sweater. He also kept popping up everywhere Alec was, and after the third time Theo ruffled Alec's hair, he escaped into the kitchen under the guise of getting a drink, hoping no one would look for him.

"M'not hiding," Alec protests, nursing his red plastic cup like it has the answers to the universe. He dumped the spiked punch out the first chance he got earlier and replaced it with orange juice. With Alec's ADHD, alcohol makes him even more loose-lipped and impulsive, which is the last thing he needs.

"Sure, and you're just hanging out in the kitchen, not getting the attention you love and deserve on your birthday for no reason."

"Fuck off," Alec grumbles.

Riley laughs, grinning. It's one of the reasons Alec loves him so much. He might be a year younger than Alec, but his big brother vibes make him seem older than he is. The oldest of five siblings, nothing ruffles his feathers. Not Alec's boisterous good moods, nor his occasional bad ones. Even Antonio rarely gets to see this side of Alec.

"Dance with me."

"You dance with me, and people are gonna talk."

"Then people can talk, and if they have something rude to say, they can answer to these." He flexes his arms. He's incredibly fit, if you're into that kind of thing. Alec prefers something softer. Or someone.

"You got a permit for those guns?"

"Sure do, sweetheart." Riley puffs out his chest before lifting both arms to show them off, dropping a kiss to each of his massive biceps. "They are only used for good, I promise. Now get your ass into the backyard and dance with me."

The hint of malaise threatening his good mood fades as he lets Riley drag him into the backyard. Jason did a good job. Their Christmas lights are strung up along the fence line, and clusters of rainbow balloons hang from the archways. It looks like a cross between a five-year-old's birthday and a frat party, and it's everything Alec could've wanted.

"Make way for the King," Riley bellows, guiding Alec into the center of the dance floor. Well, dance floor might be a bit of a stretch; it's just a series of gym mats Jason dragged out into the middle of the yard, but with the music blaring, people around them dancing and the stars above them twinkling, it's easy to imagine. The mood is high and Alec can't stop from smiling, grateful to his friend from dragging him out of his hiding spot. If he'd been left alone any longer, his mood would've soured quickly.

When Riley manhandles Alec into the middle of the crowd, his giant hands settle on Alec's hips.

"You sure you're straight?"

"I can appreciate a hottie when I see him."

Alec throws his head back and laughs, focusing on the thrum of music as he begins to move his body. Dancing is a bit like soccer for Alec, the more his body moves, the quieter his mind gets. It's all too easy to close his eyes and focus on the beat as he sways his hips and lets go. The only thing that would make tonight better is having Antonio here, but he won't be back stateside until the day their pre-season training begins next week.

"Damn, King, you got some moves."

It's Alec's turn to puff up his chest. He's a good dancer and he knows it. Spinning on his heels, he comes face to face with Riley, who is definitely a little drunk judging by his pupils.

"You sure you're good? People are staring," Alec says. As close as he and Riley have become this last year, he's still a straight guy being grinded on by his very gay friend in the middle of a nosey crowd. Not that Alec thinks anyone here would care about seeing two guys dancing, but a lifetime of having to be careful in locker rooms has affected how much he relaxes sometimes. The large group that was here when the party started has nearly doubled, and Alec's not even sure he knows everyone here anymore.

Riley blinks twice and then smirks. "If they're watching, we better give them a show."

Alec's smile widens. He loves his friends.

Grabbing a fistful of Riley's loose tank, he tugs him close before a dramatic show of dropping to the floor and then gliding back up Riley's body. Around them people holler and whistle. Delighting in the attention they're garnering, Alec does it again, looping his arms around Riley's neck and practically humping his legs. Riley holds his own, rocking his hips against Alec's without a care in the world.

They continue to dance, the crowd around them getting closer as they shift from observing to dancing. The song changes to something equally fast, and Riley makes no move to step away as Alec continues to dance, his earlier stress all but gone.

"Can I have the next dance?"

"Who you asking, sweetheart?" Riley replies, his hand still on Alec's chest as he comes out of his dancing haze and blinks at the girl in front of him. Audrey. Aubrey. Something like that. He's pretty sure she's friends with Eddie.

"You," she answers, eyes never leaving Riley. "Unless you're taken."

"He's too young for me," Alec replies, earning him a curious look from the girl and a booming bark of laughter from Riley.

"Maybe you should join AARP as a dating pool."

Alec flips him off, biting back a smile at Riley's laughter as he weaves his way through the crowd towards the edge of the dance floor. It's not that he couldn't dance alone, or with one of his other friends, but most of them aren't as cool with the level of contact Alec enjoys while dancing. That or they're also queer, and the last thing Alec needs is to lead someone else on. He's been told too many times that his flirty, tactile personality is teasing. It gets exhausting, and he's not in the mood to play that game tonight.

His sneakers have barely touched grass when strong, warm fingers encircle his wrist and stop him from moving any further.

"Wha—" but the rest of the word dies on his tongue when he catches sight of who it is.

"Hi."

"Hey."

"Happy birthday," Theo whispers, words a little slower than normal.

"You said that already." Alec grins.

"Oh." Theo blushes, the light stain of pink coloring his cheekbones. It's a good look on him. Everything is a good look on him. "You looked like you were having fun."

"I was," Alec says, not entirely sure what's going on or why Theo is still holding on to his wrist.

Theo doesn't answer right away, licking his lips and staring down at where his own hand wraps around Alec's wrist like he's only just noticed. He loosens his grip and pulls his hand back, breathing heavy. The rise and fall of Theo's chest is more noticeable without his usual sweater, especially since his white t-shirt fits him like a second skin. The material clings to the breadth of his wide chest and the small swell of his soft tummy, reminding Alec how much bigger he is. Eyes traveling upward, he takes in the deep V of Theo's shirt, which exposes the light dusting of hair on his chest. Everything about Theo's body screams *man,* and Alec can barely bite back a whimper. He is gay. So very, very gay.

"You danced with a guy."

"Comes with the territory," Alec smirks.

"I'm bi," Theo blurts.

"I know," Alec says, fighting back a laugh. He's never actually seen Theo drink, and it's kind of adorable to see the normally calm, collected man be so awkward. "I've known since you were sixteen, remember?"

"I like men more, though. Men are so sexy."

All the blood in Alec's body rushes to his dick, and he squirms. That he definitely didn't know.

"I was watching you dance."

"Riley's straight," Alec says, hating the bitter tinge of jealousy he feels. Riley might be younger than Alec, but with his stubbled jaw and impressive physique, he doesn't look it. Alec's been cursed with a damn baby face and an inability to grow facial hair. Last week, someone asked him if he was old enough to have his driver's license, and Alec nearly screamed.

"I wasn't—never mind," Theo mumbles. He sighs heavily, scrubbing a hand over his face. The smile that was on his face just a moment ago is gone, replaced with something heavy. It makes Alec want to do anything to put it back. Theo deserves to smile more.

"Will you dance with me?"

"How drunk are you?" Alec asks, positive sober Theo would never dance, especially not with Alec. It's not that he doesn't want to dance with him. He wants to, so much. He just doesn't want to be the thing Theo regrets the next day.

"Drunk enough," Theo laughs, and god, the sound is

like fucking music to his ears. Theo's laughter is a beautiful thing, deep and rumbly and not given freely. "But I do want to dance. With you. Will you dance with me, Alexander?"

Alexander.

No one calls him that. No one. It's what Theo used to call him. Before. But then things changed, and he stopped calling him Alexander. Stopped calling him anything. Soon Theo said Alec like everyone else, and Alec hasn't let anyone call him Alexander since.

Drunk Theo apparently doesn't remember any of that, though. It is such a monumentally cruel joke from the universe to give Alec exactly what he wants for his birthday, without any of it being real.

Saying yes would be one of the stupidest things Alec has ever done, which is saying something. He knows Theo is asking him to dance because he's the only person at this party that Theo knows besides Jason, who is too drunk to dance. And the twins, neither of whom dance. Theo's not asking for any of the reasons Alec wishes. He's drunk and trying to have fun, but Alec should still say no before he gets in too deep.

"Alexander," Theo whispers, and Alec is a fucking goner. He would do anything for this man, including break his own heart.

He falls into Theo's space, molding himself to Theo's side. "Alright then, big guy, show me what you've got."

Whatever he expects to happen, it's not Theo draping himself around Alec before he sways his hips from side to side. While Theo lacks the coordination and confidence Riley showed on the dance floor, he makes up for it by the fact that he's exactly who Alec has always wanted to dance with. This is Alec's teenage fantasy come true, and it takes everything in him not to close his eyes. Instead, he keeps them open, trying to memorize every moment.

Their hips sway, and though Theo can't quite match the tempo, it's clear he's trying. It takes a few minutes before Theo's hands settle along his side, the touch light, almost as if he isn't sure if he's allowed. Alec covers Theo's hands with his own, giving them a squeeze before inching them lower until Theo's hands settle low on Alec's hips. He continues to sway his hips when he stumbles, falling against Alec's back and tightening his grip.

"Sorry," he huffs.

"You're fine." The touch is searing, and Alec needs to close his eyes to conceal his expression. This is everything he's ever wanted, and it hurts more than it has any right to.

"This is fun," Theo says and Alec forces his eyes open.

It's worth it to see the way Theo's face relaxes, the lightest sheen of sweat clinging to his brow as he towers over Alec. He's a horrible fucking dancer, and Alec's heart is in his throat at how much he still loves him after all these years. It's always like this. Whether he goes weeks or months without seeing Theo—trying to get over him—the second he's around him, Alec is reminded that it's always been Theo.

"Are you having fun?" Theo asks, shaking the hair from his eyes. "At your birthday party, I mean. It's your party because you're the birthday boy."

He's so stupidly drunk; it's adorable.

"I am." Alec grins.

Theo loosens his hold but doesn't move his hands.

"This okay?" Theo whispers, breath warm where it ghosts across Alec's cheek. His breath is sweet from the punch, but tinged with the scent of cheap beer, serving as a harsh reminder that Theo wouldn't be holding him if he were sober.

"Yeah, Theo. It's okay."

Across the dance floor, Alec catches sight of Riley watching them and averts his gaze, knowing he isn't doing a good job of hiding his own feelings right now. He's only lucky Theo is behind him, and drunk, so he has no idea. He makes up his mind here and now to do anything necessary to ensure Theo never finds out he's still in love with him.

4 THEO

THEO'S HEAD POUNDS, throbbing so hard it feels like it might split into two. There's also something plastic digging into his back. He groans as he rolls sideways, only to fall onto the cold, hard ground.

With a grunt, he opens his eyes, trying to figure out how he fell off his king-sized bed, only to discover that the rug beneath him is an ugly mismatched design that's always reminded Theo of movie theater carpet. Definitely not in his own house, then. Getting both eyes open is difficult, the sunlight streaming through the massive living room windows enough to have Theo groaning and trying to hide his face. Everything is too bright, and Theo's stomach is churning like he's stuck on an upside-down roller coaster.

"Someone save me," Jason moans. Theo's not sure where Jason is, but judging by the sound of his voice, he'd guess on the floor under the dining room table. "I think I might be dying."

"If you are dying, then it's your fault," Theo says, not moving his head off the ground in case it starts to spin.

"Have some sympathy, Theo." Jason sounds suitably

pathetic, but Theo doesn't have any compassion to spare right now. What he has is a raging headache, a bladder that's so full it hurts, and a gnawing pit of anxiety. He rarely drinks, and when he does it's usually only one or two beers. While he doesn't mind a little buzz, he hates being drunk, and he hates having a hangover even more.

There's something deeply unsettling about the idea that he might have said or done something he normally wouldn't while sober. He wracks his brain, trying to remember specific details about the party, but it's impossible to focus, and his mind is nothing but a hazy blank. He might not have gotten blackout drunk, but whatever was in the birthday punch hit hard.

"Theo, get me Advil," Jason moans.

"This isn't even my house. You get it," Theo retorts. He grabs one of the pillows off the couch to prop his head. Theo doesn't want to move from the floor, but he's also not a martyr. There's no reason for him to get a crick in his neck.

"You lived here for a year, this is basically your house, too." Jason appears at the end of the couch on his hands and knees. Even without his glasses on, Theo can tell he looks like absolute shit. There's marker on his cheek in the shape of what he's pretty sure is a dick. His hair is also sticking up in the front with something questionably gummy in it, and he's dressed in a neon green swimsuit with pizza on it. This would be less weird if the King family had a pool, which they don't.

"Come on Theo," Jason whines. "You're basically family."

The reminder should soothe Theo, but at the moment all it does is make him want to hurl as thoughts about his not at all familial feelings towards Alec and the activities from last night come rushing back.

Last night Alec had been the center of attention with his bright eyes and gorgeous smiles. Yet no matter how Theo tried to hide, Alec always managed to find Theo in the crowd and offered a kind smile. God, Alec was too nice.

Alec was the single sexiest person Theo had ever seen, but the worst part wasn't how Theo constantly sought Alec out in the crowd. The worst part wasn't even how, after too much punch, Theo began to wonder if his own big hands might fit around Alec's tiny waist. Or the way Theo ached for one of Alec's smiles when they were directed at someone else.

The worst part though was the way Theo let himself be pulled into the party and laughed and danced and let himself have fun. Not that Theo never has fun. He reads books. He goes on hikes. He and Jason even have pizza most Friday nights where they watch movies and eat too much, at least during the off season. When Jason is in coach mode during football season, all their normal plans go out the window. Either way, Theo can have fun. But he has safe, calculated and controlled fun. Last night was not controlled. Last night Theo let go, and now he's facing the consequences.

Basically family. Theo's gonna puke.

Curling into the fetal position, Theo closes his eyes and presses his fists against them so hard he sees spots. He's always been the responsible one. The Kings loved Theo because he made sure Jason did his homework and got home safely on school nights. Theo's always been good at knowing what to do to make sure people don't get sick of him. He's supposed to be like a pseudo-big brother to Alec. He should not have the hots for him. Just thinking about what Jason's parents might think if they found out makes Theo want to curl into a ball and die.

The Kings have always been so good to Theo. When his dad had to work late and there was no food, there was always a place at their table. On the weekends when his dad worked doubles and the house was as empty as the fridge, they let Theo have sleepovers with Jason. They came to all of his and Jason's games, and while that's because their son was playing, they used to cheer for Theo, too. In high school, when his dad got a new job at a factory three hours away, they'd turned the guest room into a place for Theo so he could finish his senior year with his best friend and not risk losing his college scholarship. In many ways, the Kings are his family, and now he's gone and done something unforgivable.

"You're doing the hangover spiral, aren't you?"

"I don't spiral," Theo mumbles from behind his hands.

The sound of Jason crawling closer is all the warning he gets before Jason flops down beside him and pulls him into a hug. Theo doesn't breathe, doesn't move, but neither does Jason.

"You know you're allowed to have fun, right?"

"Shut up."

"I'm serious," Jason says, and the worst part is Theo knows it. Jason isn't really a sappy guy, but he notices more than most people give him credit for. Sure, sometimes he's as observant as a toddler, but Theo always liked that because it meant there was no one around to notice when his feelings didn't match his words. Besides, there are other times, like now, when Jason is unexpectedly astute.

"You had fun last night." It's not a question, so Theo doesn't respond. He lets his hands fall away from his eyes, rolling into Jason's hug. There'd been a time back when he was first discovering his sexuality where he wondered if he was in love with Jason. He was the only person Theo let in, the only person allowed to touch him. Was that love? He'd quickly realized that yes, he did love Jason, more than anyone in the world—but not romantically. Luckily for Theo, Jason didn't care that his best friend was queer and had never held back from showing his affection.

"Whatever your brain is saying right now, it's lying."

Theo's jaw wobbles. That's another reason he doesn't drink. It makes the anxiety lessen while he's drinking, but the hangover nerve spike is brutal, something Jason knows firsthand. Except this time Theo's not wallowing in his own feelings of inferiority or fears of abandonment. He's thinking about Alec and all his golden skin and warm freckles; Theo is the actual worst best friend alive.

"Everything is okay, dude." Jason's warm hand is on his cheek, and Theo dares to open his eyes, the well of emotions in him taking a backseat to the up close and personal view of the dick on Jason's cheek, complete with detailed pubes. "I'm serious, Theo."

"It's very hard to take you seriously with the dick on your face." Theo snorts.

"There's a dick on my face?" Jason frowns, slapping his cheek. "Well, that's a first."

He doesn't look remotely bothered, but maybe having a bisexual best friend, twin queer older brothers and a loudly gay baby brother have ensured that there's not an ounce of toxic masculinity in Jason King's body. Hell, the last pride parade they'd all gone to, Jason had worn more rainbow shit than Theo or his brothers combined.

"My head hurts," Theo admits, closing his eyes again.

Jason being Jason is somehow the best and worst thing that could be happening right now, because it's exactly what Theo needs and yet everything he doesn't think he deserves. If Jason knew what he was thinking right now, well, Theo's not sure what would happen. Jason isn't the kind of guy who would punch Theo for lusting after his baby brother, but Theo can't imagine he'd welcome it either. Theo's too old for Alec, for one thing. The big thing. He's almost thirty, and Alec is a fresh faced twenty-one year old with his entire life ahead of him.

"My head hurts too," Jason sighs, tucking Theo's head under his chin. He wraps one of his big arms around Theo's back, offering the kind of tactile reassurance Theo would never in a million years ask for, and Theo's mind finally quiets.

THEY MUST HAVE DRIFTED BACK to sleep because one second Theo's dreaming about miles of bared skin and freckles and the next second there's the god-awful sound of a blender whirring.

"What the fuck, Alec?" Jason bellows. If Theo weren't already awake, the pitch of Jason's voice would've done it. He groans, covering his ears and shoving his face into Jason's shoulder. The whirring is so loud it makes his head feel like it's actually in the blender with whatever Alec is making.

"I need my protein shake," Alec says loudly enough to be heard over the stupid blender.

"Fucking protein shake," Jason mutters. "Eat some real food. Quiet food."

"Quiet food won't have complete protein after a ten mile run, dick face."

"Did you put the dick on my face?" Jason asks.

"Nah, Riley did. But I asked him to." Alec's laughter echoes through the kitchen into the open living room.

Theo tries to keep up with the conversation. He's pretty sure Riley was the frat guy attached to Alec's side all night. Tall, dark hair and handsome with a gorgeous olive complexion and enough confidence to rival Alec's. That's probably the type of guy Alec likes, Theo thinks bitterly, hating how sour the tinge of jealousy tastes. Yet another reason he shouldn't drink; it makes him a morose idiot.

"What a beautiful morning," Alec sing-songs, pulling the blinds open in the kitchen, making the large open room even brighter.

Theo groans miserably, trying to use Jason's body as a shield from the horrifying reality of the day. He doesn't want to deal with anything.

"Why isn't Alec hungover?" Theo mumbles.

"Why aren't you hungover?" Jason yells, rolling onto his back.

The blender whirs and whirs. Theo blinks open his eyes and stares at the ceiling, wondering what the hell Alec could possibly be making that requires running the blender for that long. After another thirty or so seconds it shuts off, though the phantom buzzing lingers in his ears.

"Because I wasn't drunk," Alec answers, the sound of his sneakers squeaking on the hardwood alerts Theo to his impending approach.

There, towering above Theo is Alec, who squats down and lowers something onto Theo's face and, oh, he can see. Everything still hurts, but at least the world isn't blurry anymore.

"You left those in the kitchen," Alec says, brushing the hair off Theo's face. "Take this."

"Take wh—" but his words are cut off when Alec slips pain meds between his parted lips, moving a hand to the back of Theo's neck to help him sit up. A second later, a glass of water is lifted to his lips, and though Theo could do it himself, he pathetically lets Alec hold it for him.

"That should help." Alec lowers a bottle of cucumber melon Gatorade down on the table. Jason reaches for it, but Alec slaps his hand away, pushing it closer to Theo. "That's not for you, that's for Theodore."

"What the fuck, Alec? I'm your brother. Where's my caretaking?"

"You got Theo drunk, you don't get any." Alec levels Jason with an unexpected glare.

"Theo's a big boy. He can make his own decisions."

"Theo doesn't like drinking."

"Theo is right here," he points out, his head hurting way too much to figure out what the hell is happening.

Alec's expression softens as he grabs the Gatorade and puts it in Theo's lap. "Drink this. I'll make breakfast after I shower."

"You gonna cook for me, too?" Jason asks, half-slumped against the couch and looking utterly pathetic.

"Yes, I'll cook for you too, idiot. I don't wanna smell you burning the house down." Alec rises, drawing Theo's attention to what he's wearing. Or not wearing. He's got on a pair of running leggings that are so tight they might actually be painted on, his freckled ankles exposed between the bottom of his pants and the low-cut socks. Over the leggings is a pair of bright purple shorts with cutouts on the side that highlight the curve of Alec's plump backside. His shirt is a slashed black tank, the sides of Alec's stomach on full display, and when he turns, Theo sees how many freckles he's got there, too.

Theo has never considered running clothes sexy, but he is definitely reconsidering that right now.

"I don't burn anything down," Jason objects, his indignation bringing Theo out of his thirst spiral.

"You can't even make toast. You're not allowed in the kitchen." Alec points a menacing finger at Jason.

"I'm still confused why you're not hungover," Theo says, watching Alec's full lips curl around his smoothie straw.

Alec grins. "I told you, I didn't get drunk."

"You danced on the table."

"Uh-huh."

"You ran around in your underwear."

Alec shrugs.

"You did all that sober." Theo is way too hungover to monitor his tone.

Rather than get offended, Alec smirks. "Why not?"

There are a lot of reasons why not. At least for Theo. He keeps them all to himself, not trusting himself to speak right now. That's another thing he hates about hangovers. It makes him say things he'd normally have the common sense not to say out loud.

"There's smoothie on your mouth," Theo points out, eyes drawn to the creamy liquid at the corner of his lips. He really does have a pretty mouth—full, pink lips and *oh no*, Theo is not doing this right in front of Alec and Jason. He can't.

Alec shrugs, reaching up to wipe it away with his thumb. He looks at it for all of two seconds before pressing his thumb into his mouth and sucking on it. If Theo didn't know better, he'd swear Alec was teasing him, but that's impossible. Alec has no idea his older brother's best friend is an asshole thinking about what it might look like to have something else thick and white all over his face, wondering if Alec would suck that off, too.

Theo is a horny, hungover asshole.

With a groan, he drops himself back onto the ground, rolling onto his stomach. He'd rather be embarrassed about being socially awkward than let Alec or Jason notice his half-hard dick. His glasses are smashed into his cheek, and he can't quite breathe, but he can't make himself move.

"Theo's having a hangover spiral."

"Stop talking about me like I'm not here." Theo's biting words have little effect since they're half-garbled by the pillow.

"I'll leave you two to do whatever it was you were doing before."

Theo holds his breath, waiting for Alec to leave. What he's not expecting is to have a blanket draped over his back, or have Alec pull his glasses back off, folding them before setting them on the edge of the couch just in reach in case he needs them again.

"I'll make you coffee after I shower." Alec smooths back Theo's hair. Theo might be a grown man who has taken care of himself since he was old enough to walk, but an ache forms in his throat at the offer.

It's the hangover, it has to be. Theo doesn't let people take care of him. He doesn't want them to, either. He doesn't.

For the second day in a row, Theo lies, only this time to himself.

AT SOME POINT, Theo must have drifted to sleep for a second time, proof of just how hungover he really is. This time when he opens his eyes, it's to see Alec in the kitchen and Jason passed out on the floor snoring. The only reason he doesn't immediately whine and close his eyes again is because the scent of coffee is strong enough to wake the dead, or a very smashed idiot.

Theo opens his mouth to ask for some, but then snaps it shut when he realizes Alec isn't the only person in the kitchen.

"What exactly are you doing?"

Theo's too hungover to tell which one of the twins it is from voice alone—Charlie or Andrew. Back when he was a teenager, he couldn't tell them apart to save his life. The only way he can now is because Charlie's always got paint-stained clothing from his job at the art museum, whereas Andrew wears nothing but polo shirts and loafers. He claims it's to be taken seriously with the job he just got with the hockey league, but he's pretty much always dressed like that, even on his days off, so Theo thinks it's just his personal style. Not that he has any room to judge. He is one of the least stylish people alive.

"I'm cooking, obviously," Alec replies.

"Smart ass. Tell me what you're really doing."

"I'm trying to make breakfast here, Charlie. You're distracting me."

"You can multitask like no one else," Charlie says. "Seriously, we should talk about how you danced with a certain someone last night and what exactly that means."

"I danced with a lot of people." Alec waves a spatula through the air, his tone making no secret that he doesn't want to be having this conversation.

"You know exactly which guy you danced with."

Alec hums. "You're going to have to be more specific. I have no idea what you're talking about."

"Dammit, Alec. You know what I mean." Even without Theo's glasses, the change in Alec's demeanor is noticeable, his entire body stiffening. "Look, I don't want you to get hurt. Again. He's a good guy, but—"

"But he doesn't like me romantically," Alec finishes. "Yes, I know, Charlie. Thank you so much for reminding me how unwanted I am."

"You know I'm just looking out for you. How many times are you gonna get your heart broken by the same guy? You need to move on."

Theo's stomach churns uncomfortably. He hadn't known Alec had feelings for anyone, but then again, why would he? Apart from seeing him at family get-togethers, he and Alec hadn't crossed paths much since he started college. Sure, Alec goes to school in the same city, but he isn't just Jason's baby brother anymore; he's living his own life. Theo has a busy job, and Alec has college and soccer. Theo sighs, knowing that Alec is around the King house enough that Theo could've seen him if he wanted to. These are all nothing but excuses. The one who put distance between them is Theo. Alec had tried over the years. He'd invited Theo to his first college game, or to hang out when Jason was busy. What had started out as a means to protect Alec had turned into a loss of closeness that Theo feels acutely now.

He can't help but wonder if he'd accepted all those invites, if he and Alec could've been friends in their own right. He wonders if they still can now.

"He's not gonna hurt me again, because I know what I'm getting myself into this time," Alec snaps.

Theo can't help but frown. Alec is young, gorgeous and funny, any guy would be lucky to have him. Though from the sounds of it, this idiot Alec likes doesn't know that.

"Things were different last night." Charlie lowers his

voice. "I saw how you kept looking at him. I have eyes. You're going to get your heart broken for real this time."

"It's my heart, and I can do whatever I want with it."

"I know." Charlie's sigh is so deep that Theo feels it in his chest. "That's the worst part. I've protected you since you were a kid, but I can't protect you from this, and I hate it, Ally. I fucking hate it."

No one but Charlie has ever been allowed to use that nickname with Alec. Andrew and Jason tried and learned early on to respect Alec's boundaries.

"I don't need protection. I know he's probably never going to feel the same, but I can't move on. Not yet." Alec sets his spatula down. "Don't look at me like that. I don't need your pity, okay? I'm a big boy. I can handle this."

"Of course you can," Charlie tells him. He pitches his voice low enough Theo can't make out what else is said. Whatever it is has Alec launching himself at his brother, burying his face against his chest as Charlie wraps him up in a tight embrace. Charlie towers over him, not quite as tall as Jason but close. And though he's far lankier, he's still big enough that all that's visible are Alec's arms, which hold on tightly.

Theo squeezes his eyes shut, guilt making his stomach churn. He shouldn't have been listening, and he needs to find a way to alert them to his being awake without making it seem like he was spying. Groaning loudly, he stretches out and bumps the couch with his leg, hoping to make enough noise that it'll look like he just woke up. It works. By the time he's sat up and retrieved his glasses, Charlie is back to sitting on a stool at the kitchen island and Alec is watching the stove.

"He lives," Alec announces, far too loudly. He's showered, his curls a little damp at the ends still. There's a drop of water that's slowly making its way down the back of his neck and in between his shoulder blades. Shoulder blades that Theo has a perfect view of, because for reasons unknown to Theo, Alec decided to start cooking in nothing but a pair of obscenely thin gray sweats and one of his mom's aprons. It's got frills and flowers, cinched at Alec's waist, and the sight of the floral bow tied right at the base of his muscular back is making Theo wish he were drunk again.

"You look too happy considering I feel like I'm dying."

"I'd say sorry but I don't like to lie." Alec says it with a smile that makes it impossible to be bothered by his words. "It's your own fault for drinking so much. You and Jason are idiots, you know."

"It was your big birthday." The excuse is feeble even to his own ears. Theo's pretty sure he didn't even drink that much when he turned twenty-one.

"Yeah, we had to have fun," Jason pipes up from beside Theo. Jason makes his way closer to the kitchen, lured awake by the smell of food.

"Well, we know how much Alec loves a party boy." Charlie snorts.

Alec pales and Theo's stomach sinks. He suspected he wasn't Alec's type anymore, but hearing confirmation still stings more than it has any right to.

"Put something in your mouth and shut up," Alec grumbles, shoving a massive plate of pancakes in front of Charlie.

"Have I told you lately I love you, and you're my favorite brother?" Charlie tells Alec.

"What about me?" Andrew pipes up, descending the stairs two at a time. It never fails to amaze Theo how he somehow manages to look exactly like Charlie and yet nothing like him. Their personalities are so visibly different as adults. Charlie's dark hair is as wild and haphazard as his wrinkled, tie-dyed shirt with paint stains, boxers and mismatched socks. Then there's Andrew, who looks entirely put together, his hair the same length as Charlie's but brushed neatly to the side in an attractive swoop, dressed in a pale blue polo with ironed khakis and sensible brown loafers.

"You can't be my favorite. You hogged the womb."

Andrew flips him off while smiling widely. "Morning everyone."

"Why aren't I the favorite?" Jason frowns, slumping into the barstool next to Charlie.

"You aren't my favorite because you don't cook for me," Charlie points out, waving his fork in Jason's direction. "Plus Alec's cute."

"I'm cute," Jason pouts.

"You're my favorite," Theo points out, unable to stand Jason looking like a dejected puppy.

"Thank you. At least someone in this family loves me. Also, why are Charlie and Andrew here if they're not hungover?" Jason scrubs a hand through his hair, frowning when his fingers get stuck. He drops onto the stool beside Charlie, eying his breakfast. "I want pancakes."

"I made you a vegetable omelet and a protein shake." Alec sets both in front of Jason with an innocent smile.

"We had a sleepover for old times' sake," Andrew offers, always one to be counted on for actually answering the questions asked when Jason and Charlie inevitably dissolve into bickering.

"I don't want a protein shake that tastes like ass." Jason pushes it away petulantly, looking closer to thirteen than thirty. "I want pancakes. Charlie has pancakes."

"As someone who enjoys ass, I can promise you that

Alec's shakes definitely don't taste like that." Charlie smirks, making a show of eating his pancakes with an appreciative groan to annoy Jason.

"Thank you," Alec says. "It's yummy."

"They taste more like play dough than ass," Charlie adds, earning him a glare from Alec.

Jason cackles. "Ass play dough."

Andrew leans over, swiping the protein shake from in front of Jason and taking a drink. He shrugs. "It kind of does taste like ass."

"Whose ass are you eating?" Jason asks at the same time Charlie takes the shake and pushes it towards Theo.

"Taste it."

Too hungover to argue with any of the King boys, he does as instructed. It's not the worst thing he's ever had, but the vanilla is overly sweet and the banana is too, well, banana-y. There's definitely something gritty and chalky about the texture, too.

Aware of everyone watching him, Theo shrugs. "It tastes like play dough."

"We need a tie-breaker. Give it to Alec."

"I drink one of those every day, so I don't need to taste it," Alec points out. "I literally finished my own shake before I showered."

"Then settle the votes," Andrew says plainly, lifting an eyebrow at him. "I don't care if the team nutritionist makes you drink one of these every day to hit your protein goals. Be honest about the taste. Ass or play dough?"

"I couldn't say," Alec answers evasively. Theo's not sure he's ever seen Alec so blatantly deflect a question. His own curiosity is piqued enough for him to butt into the conversation.

"Why not?" Theo asks, blinking when four sets of eyes

swivel towards him. Jason looks delighted, Andrew is as impossible to read as ever, and Charlie looks inquisitive. Alec's reaction is the most confusing of all, though, because he almost looks like he's blushing. Theo has never, ever seen Alexander King blush.

"Alec doesn't have to answer," Charlie says.

"Why—" Jason starts, cut off when Charlie shoves a forkful of pancakes into his mouth.

"What aren't you telling us?" Andrew asks.

"Nothing," Charlie tries, but it's no use. The other two are like dogs after a bone.

"What's going on?" Jason and Andrew ask at the same time.

"Not all of us have eaten ass," Alec mumbles.

"I haven't," Jason pipes up.

"No shame in not liking that," Andrew says. "Sex is kind of overrated anyway, am I right?"

"No," Charlie, Jason and Theo all answer at the exact same time.

Theo laughs, along with Jason, until he notices Charlie isn't laughing and neither is Alec. If anything, Alec looks a little pale.

"So the pancakes are amazing," Charlie tries, but it's no use because Jason clearly hasn't picked up on the tone shift.

"What about you, Alec?" Jason presses. "You didn't vote on the smoothie, so place your vote on sex. Overrated or not?"

"You don't need to answer that," Charlie tells him.

"Why are you being weird? It's not like—" Charlie elbows Andrew so hard in the stomach he wheezes, his eyes darting towards Alec and widening in realization. "Right. Don't answer, Alec."

"Why is everyone being weird?" Jason asks.

"I haven't ever had sex," Alec yells, bits of egg flying off the spatula and through the air when he spins. "And now all of you are going to shut up and eat your breakfast, and I don't want to hear a single word about sex or ass or play dough. You got it?"

All three of the King brothers nod, looking thoroughly chastised. They might all be older, taller and bigger than Alec, but it's clear who is in charge. It's also clear that the topic of conversation has rattled Alec.

"I'm going for a run," Alec mumbles, struggling to undo the bow on his apron.

"Let me," Theo says, unsure why he's the first one across the room to undo the bow. He skims his fingers over Alec's lower back, noticing how soft his bare skin is while the words *I haven't had sex* sear themselves in Theo's brain. Of all the things he expected to hear, learning Alexander King was a virgin was not on the list.

He should hurry and undo Alec's apron but he doesn't, fingering the worn cotton tie before Theo gives the bow a final tug and lets it fall open.

"Thanks," Alec says, cheeks unnaturally pink when he turns to face Theo and pulls the apron off. "There's uh, coffee in the pot and your omelet is on the stove. You've been here a million times so you know where the plates are."

"Thank you, Alec."

"Uh-huh, don't worry about it." Alec turns, slipping his socked feet into his sneakers before pulling on the hoodie thrown over the back of Charlie's chair. It's easily three sizes too big on him and obviously not his.

"You already ran nine miles this morning, Ally. Rest."

Alec ignores him, practically darting out of the room. Judging by the looks on everyone else's faces, they're as confused as Theo. Well, except for Charlie, who just looks sad.

"Does anyone know what just happened?" Jason asks when the front door slams.

Andrew shrugs, taking the unwanted protein shake and sipping at it. "Maybe Alec was embarrassed."

"Alec doesn't get embarrassed," Theo says.

"Or maybe none of you know Alec like you think you do." Charlie's tone might be easy, but there's something sharp in it, too. He's not wrong. Theo doesn't know Alec, not like his brother does. If Andrew or Jason pick up on the double edge, they don't say anything. At least not about that.

"What I want to know is, why did Charlie know Alec was a virgin and we didn't?" Jason asks.

"Because Andrew doesn't like talking about sex, and you have a big mouth," Charlie says.

Andrew nods. "That's true."

"Yeah, I would've told Theo," Jason agrees, using his own fork to sneak a bite off Charlie's plate.

"See," Charlie hisses. "And stop stealing my pancakes, or I'll stab you with my fork."

"No, you won't. You're a pacifist."

"I'm anti-war and anti-capitalist, not anti-stopping my idiot brother from stealing my blueberry pancakes."

"Just make more."

"You make more."

"I can't cook."

"Neither can I."

"Then who taught Alec?" Theo wonders, unprepared for three people to turn and stare at him again.

"*Abuela*," Charlie answers. "When Alec went vegetarian, she was afraid he might starve to death, so she started learning to cook more things without lard and meat for him, and I guess he wanted to learn. You know how hard it was for her the last few years with her weakness. She couldn't cook anymore, so she'd tell Alec what to do, and he did it for her. She even taught him her secret recipe for *mole*."

"I never knew that," Andrew says.

Charlie shrugs. "We were all away at college or work-ing. I think Alec spent a lot of time with her while we were gone. He was lonely."

"Alec was lonely?" Jason frowns like he's been physi-cally wounded. "I would've come home more and visited him. Why didn't he tell me?"

"Because Alec doesn't tell anyone anything if he thinks it's going to inconvenience them," Charlie says, the sharp edge back in his tone. "Alec deserves everything."

"'Course he does," Theo agrees.

"He shouldn't ever be hurt by anyone." Charlie stabs his pancakes so hard that syrup squirts onto the kitchen island.

Jason frowns. "What did the pancakes ever do to you?"

"I'm not hungry anymore," Charlie sighs, sliding the plate of pancakes in front of Jason. "I'm gonna go look for Alec."

"But you don't run," Jason points out, already filling his mouth with food.

"I have a car."

"Oh, duh."

"I'll come," Andrew says, as always seemingly content to follow Charlie.

"Was that weird or is it just me?" Theo asks once the twins have left.

"Charlie and Andrew are always weird. I think it's a twin thing." Jason takes another large bite of pancakes, chewing thoughtfully. "Alec was weirder than usual, but he's probably just tense since he has to move back into the dorms next week for preseason training. He always gets tetchy before a new season."

"He goes back in July? I thought classes usually started in August."

"All the D1 athletes have to move in early. Alec's already got his diet and training schedule up on the fridge."

Theo turns around, whistling when he takes in the color-coded and highlighted schedule listing Alec's every workout, meal, and rest period for the next two weeks. It's far more intense than Theo would've ever imagined. Not that he's ever given that much thought to college athletes, but if asked he would've assumed they worked out and that was it. He obviously knew Alec trained hard and was talented, of course he did, but he'd failed to ever think about what that might look like behind the scenes.

"I didn't realize," Theo says, thinking back to Alec's words the night before about his last night of freedom while eating tacos. He'd thought Alec was being dramatic as always, but as he takes in the schedule on the fridge listing every single meal Alec is supposed to eat with weighed and measured amounts to ensure he hits his protein and calorie goals, it suddenly seems less funny.

"That's exactly why I didn't wanna play football in college," Jason says around a mouthful of pancakes. "Way too much work and not enough fun."

"You weren't scouted for college football."

"Fuck you," Jason laughs. "And then you were and you didn't play."

It'd been a bit of a sore subject for a few weeks. They'd gotten really drunk, talked about too many feelings, then woke up the next morning without mentioning it. Every couple of years Jason likes to remind Theo of his failed chance to become a famous football player and in turn, Theo points out he never had the chance to begin with. It's just how they roll.

"It is what it is, no changing the past." Theo shrugs.

While he'd played football in junior high and high school, the truth was that it was only because Jason did, and whatever his best friend did, Theo followed. It didn't hurt that his dad liked football, and Theo had secretly held out hope of trying to get his dad's approval or attention. It backfired when his dad needed to take on a second job to pay for equipment, team fees, away games, and snack rotation.

More than once, Theo tried to quit for the money alone, but his dad refused to let him, insisting it would take him far in life. All playing football did was awaken his bisexuality, when he realized there was more than one kind of ball he was interested in. Which isn't to say Theo hated playing by any means. He enjoyed the team dynamics and camaraderie but never had the kind of love for the game that it felt like he should've.

Instead, Theo spent his high school glory days longing to join some of the other after school clubs like art or photography, but that was something he'd never wanted to tell anyone, not even Jason, and certainly not his dad. It wasn't that his dad had a problem with Theo being bisexual or less sports-obsessed than him, it was that his dad worked himself to the bone every day working minimum-wage jobs. And Theo wasn't stupid enough to think his hobbies would get him a future.

Years playing football with Jason meant Theo had a decent amount of skills along with the body type for the game, but he didn't have the passion or drive that was required to continue sports past high school. He certainly never had the drive that Alec clearly has for soccer. He also hadn't been nearly as talented as Alec is. While being scouted for a D3 school might have been exciting for someone who lived and breathed football, it meant very little for someone like Theo, who needed a full scholarship to even be able to contemplate attending college. His dad hadn't gone to college. Hell, his grandparents hadn't even graduated high school, and the odds were stacked so high against Theo, they might as well have been a fortress.

All being scouted had done was remind Theo that without a scholarship, he couldn't get a degree, and without a degree he'd be stuck living paycheck to paycheck like his dad. So he declined the offers and went to the same college as Jason, both because the academic scholarship they gave him was enough to cover everything besides housing and because where Jason went, so did he.

"You're doing that lost in your brain thing again. Have some pancakes."

Theo doesn't really want pancakes, but he also doesn't want to be stuck in his brain. Jason's solution to everything is food, probably because as kids Theo had never had enough, and it usually had fixed things. He's got enough now, but he never turns it down, not from Jason. He might not be great with feelings, but it's how he shows he cares.

"Thanks," Theo mumbles, taking a bite. The pancakes are perfect, thick and fluffy with bursts of sweet blueberries in every bite.

"You know I was thinking, maybe I should text some of Alec's buddies. See if they got any photos of last night."

Theo groans. He hadn't even thought of that. "I hope they didn't."

"I just wanna see you dancing with Alec. You never dance."

The bite of pancakes stops halfway to Theo's mouth, which remains open and gaping like a fish. "I what?"

"Danced," Jason repeats. "With Alec. You were so drunk."

"How do you remember? I thought you were drunk, too."

"I was, but I can hold my liquor. You never could. You almost got up on the table, but then Alec did and started stripping, and then you did this moon-eyed thing and—"

Theo shoves his forkful of pancakes into Jason's mouth to stop him from talking as memories from last night flood his brain. He had been dancing, alone and then with Alec. He'd gotten a little handsy and then tried to climb on the table, but then Alec had done it first. Drunk Theo didn't care, but sober Theo recoils at the idea of what kind of attention he would've drawn to himself if he'd actually made it up onto the dining room table. Or worse, that photos might've existed of his lapse in decorum. Thankfully, before he could do what sober Theo would regret, Alec had climbed onto the table and drawn all the attention away from Theo and onto himself.

Suddenly Theo isn't hungry at all.

"Your anxiety gets worse when you don't eat," Jason reminds him, swapping the pancakes for the omelet. "Protein will be better."

"Thanks, Dad," Theo snaps. As soon as it's out, he regrets it. The only thing he hates more than his own brain is when he snaps at Jason. It's like snapping at a puppy, and guilt churns in his belly. "I'm sorry."

"It's fine. You need to eat," Jason says, entirely unperturbed. "I know how you get."

He's right. Theo does get anxious when he hasn't eaten, or when he drinks too much, or when he's just awake.

Anxiety is kind of Theo's baseline, but it's definitely worse when his blood sugar isn't stable. Refusing to risk snapping at his best friend a second time, and praying the food will settle some of the hangover, he takes a massive bite, unprepared for how delicious it is.

"The best cure for a hangover is definitely Alec's food," Jason says, nudging Theo's arm.

"Will he be ok?" Theo asks, barely swallowing before taking another huge bite.

"Yeah, he gets in moods sometimes. The only one who can get him out of it is usually Charlie. He's always known how to handle Alec, especially after his diagnosis. Mom and Dad tried, but they were busy and—" Jason trails off with a shrug.

"What happens when he's in school and not living at home?"

Jason pauses, thinking it over. "Not sure. He's got a lot of friends. I'm sure he's got someone he trusts there. Antonio, maybe? Or that Riley guy. They seemed close last night."

The reminder of Riley sets off a fresh wave of nausea, and Theo can barely choke down his eggs. He has no right to care who Alec is close to or to worry about who he turns to when he isn't okay. Except Theo can't deny that he does care. He cares far more than he should.

5 ALEC

"YOU'RE GOING to wear a hole in the floor like that."

Alec stops pacing, lifting his eyes to meet his mother's. A lot of people joke that Alec is a copy and paste version of her, and they're not wrong. They've got the same loose curls, the same light brown hair, miles of freckles, and the same smile. His brothers take after their dad with their height, darker hair, and lack of freckles. As a kid, it made Alec feel weird to look so different from his siblings, but as an adult, he's come to appreciate the features he shares with her.

"Morning, Mom."

"Morning, love." She smiles, leaning her hip against the kitchen island. She's dressed in her workout gear, a far cry from the suits she wears to the office Monday through Friday. Over the summer, she joined some combination book and walking club where she meets to talk about whatever book they're reading while doing laps at the mall before it opens. It sounds incredibly boring to Alec, who has never been able to enjoy reading. It's too much concentration and sitting still for his taste, even if you add in walking afterward. It makes his mom happy, though, which makes Alec happy.

"You excited for move-in day?"

Alec blows out a breath. He is and he isn't. This is his senior year. His last year hanging out with his friends before some of them move back home or on to new jobs. Or in some cases, like Antonio, to start their families already. It's his last year playing the game he loves before shit gets real. He knows everyone expects him to keep playing, to get scouted for MLS and go professional. It's what people have expected of Alec since he joined the all-star soccer league and started winning championships. He's always been good —really good—and he loves the game. Except lately that love has faded, dwarfed by a suffocating sense of dread. Especially since Alec hasn't told anyone he has no desire to play professionally.

Spending the next decade or two of his life stuck on a specific nutritionist-approved diet plan and workout routine to keep his body in perfect shape isn't exactly exciting. The prospect of knowing that his body belongs to other people before himself makes his chest tight. It's on the tip of his tongue to tell his mother what's been weighing on him when she speaks first.

"It's okay to be emotional," she says, moving past Alec towards the fridge. She pulls out the vanilla creamer she likes, fixing herself a large coffee in one of her favorite travel mugs that says, *"You don't want to argue with me, I'm a lawyer,"* that Jason got her for Christmas last year. "Don't worry, though. I know this won't be the end of your soccer career. You're too good, and the MLS would be idiots to not scoop you up. Your dad and I have known you were meant for big things since the day you first kicked a ball. We're so proud of you."

Alec takes a shuddering breath, schooling his features into what he hopes is an authentic smile. This is exactly why he can't talk to either of his parents. They sacrificed so much for him and while their privilege as an upper middle class family meant the costs of all of Alec's training, gear, and special leagues wasn't a huge monetary sacrifice, the time was. His parents missed family dinners and weekends at home, taking turns traveling with Alec to all-star games out of town. They'd both worked on cases on the sidelines, making sure at least one of them watched every single practice and game Alec ever played.

There was never a doubt in his mind that his parents loved him, and he owes them everything. His mom isn't into sports like his dad, but she's no less supportive, and he sees the look in her eye when she talks about Alec's prospects of going pro. He's just never corrected either of them that it's *their* dream. The opportunities he has are once in a lifetime, the kind his *abuela* used to whisper about in her hushed Spanish when she held his hands at night and prayed over him, promising him he would have a better life ahead than she did. She came to this country for a better life, and the weight of that responsibility isn't lost on Alec.

The MLS combine isn't until January. He's got six months to figure his shit out without burdening the people he loves before the MLS SuperDraft. He just needs to get his head on straight and figure out a way to deal with this.

"Thanks, Mom," Alec mumbles, suddenly. "I'm just, uh—"

"Nervous," she finishes, moving past Alec. She presses a kiss to his cheek, and he breathes in the familiar scent of her perfume.

He's always been a bit of a momma's boy, and the hardest part of living on campus is definitely only seeing her on weekends. That difficulty is exactly the reason he pushed himself to live on campus, despite having parents who offered to let him live at home and commute to classes. Desperate to forge his own path and learn how to live on his own, he'd declined their offer and spent the first two years miserable as fuck. Last year he'd finally got to room with Antonio, which made all the difference, but he still hated the cramped noisy dorms. This year is going to be different, though. He and Antonio were lucky enough to secure one of the senior apartments on campus, meaning they're going to have a shit-ton more space and privacy this year.

"Nervous, yeah," Alec echoes, finding it easy to agree. He just wants to make his parents proud of him.

"I gotta get going. You sure you can handle move-in day on your own? Say the word, and I'll call your dad at the country club."

"You don't need to call Dad," Alec says. "He's playing with a client today. You know how important that is to him."

"You're right," she agrees, kissing Alec on the cheek again. "I don't know how we're all gonna cope when you're off playing for real, and we only see you a few times a year."

The knot in his stomach turns to lead. Yet another reason he doesn't want to play professionally. He doesn't want to leave Santa Leon or his family. He loves his life here, his family, and the idea of moving away from it all makes him physically ill.

"I am playing for real, Mom." His voice sounds small, and he forces a smile on his face.

"Of course you are. You know what I mean, sweetie." She ruffles his hair, making it hard for Alec to be annoyed. He knows she means well, both his parents do. They just think he has so much potential and talent that not pursuing a professional career isn't something that's ever been an option for Alec. He used to think he was okay with the life they'd mapped out for him, but things change. Alec changed. Or maybe, he thinks as his throat tightens, maybe he hasn't changed at all, but no one bothered to look hard enough to see if this was what he really wanted.

"I could cancel my book thing and help you move furniture."

Alec bites back a snort. His mom is even smaller than him, barely five-six in heels, and looks like she could be knocked over by the wind. She might be able to take down guys three times her size in court, but she can't help Alec move furniture up three flights of stairs.

"I told you it's fine, Mom. Someone is gonna help me."

"Someone, huh?"

There's a question in her tone that Alec isn't in the mood to answer. He doesn't want to tell her Theo offered to help, partly because he was drunk when he made the offer and partly because Alec feels embarrassingly possessive about it. It's the first time Theo's agreed to do anything with Alec alone since he was a kid, unless you count his birthday. But Alec doesn't count that, no matter how much fun he had. Especially not since Jason put Theo up to it. Learning that tidbit had stung more than Alec wants to admit. Thankfully, Jason and Theo were too drunk to notice how the jokingly-made confession had nearly made Alec cry. He's pretty sure he would've driven himself across the border and never come home if they'd realized how devastated he was to learn Theo only spent time with him as a favor.

"You're going to be late, Mom." Alec puts his hands on her shoulders and turns her towards the front of the house. "You should leave. Right now."

Her smile grows. "Oh, is this someone helping you a boy?"

"Nope," Alec answers, pleased at his straight face. Usually he can't lie for shit, but this is not technically a lie. Theo isn't a boy, he's a *man*. Alec was raised by two lawyers, and if anyone can argue semantics until they die, it's him.

"Alright, alright. I'll get out of your hair. You know, I am looking forward to book club this week. Minnie picked a steamy book. There's a man without a shirt on the cover and—"

"Stop talking," Alec groans.

"I forgot I'm supposed to be celibate and have my four sons through immaculate conception. My mistake." His mom grins. "I'm going." She laughs, offering him one quick wave before departing.

Alec waits until he hears her BMW pull out of the driveway before he grabs his phone off the charging station in the corner, sighing heavily when he sees there are no missed calls or texts. He's not sure why he's surprised. Theo was pretty drunk at his birthday, and he hasn't mentioned his offer to help Alec move since then. Not that Alec has seen him or anything, but he'd casually tried to weasel Theo's weekend plans out of Jason when he came over for dinner last night, and Jason had been no help at all. It was a crapshoot whether that actually meant Theo had no plans, or whether Jason forgot them. He had the world's best long-term memory, yet the short-term memory of goldfish.

There was also another possibility: maybe Theo still intended to come help Alec and hadn't told Jason about it, but that seems highly unlikely. He's pretty sure they probably tell each other when they take a shit. He's never met a pair of best friends with less boundaries than those two, which had made Alec really fucking jealous when he was younger. There was a period where he was sure Theo and Jason must've privately been fucking. He's pretty sure now that never happened, since Jason has never indicated he isn't straight to any of them, and he's kind of an open book. But maybe they had been together at some point, and Theo asked him to keep it quiet. Maybe Theo's been secretly in love with Jason since he was a teenager.

"Fuck," Alec groans, slumping against the kitchen island. He hates this side of his brain. This is why he doesn't like being alone, why he keeps himself busy and never stops moving, because the second he does, he thinks too much and hurts his own feelings.

Stomach churning uncomfortably with emotions he is not in the mood to examine, he swipes open his group chat with Antonio, Logan and Hunter. Initially, he and Antonio had hoped Riley and Logan might share with them. Logan was on the swim team, and Riley didn't live in the frat house, so it seemed like a no brainer. Last minute, Riley's parents had asked him to stay at home another year to help out with his younger siblings, leaving them one roommate short. Hunter was also a senior and a friend of Logan's, and while Alec had only met him once in passing, he seemed cool. Or at least Alec hoped.

> **Alec**
> anyone want move-in day breakfast burritos

Not a minute later the replies come in.

> **Logan**
> fuck yes

> **Logan**
> fill me up bro

Hunter
thats what she said

Logan
youre an idiot

Hunter
fuck you

Logan
thats what she said

Antonio
cant believe you even asked I always want food

Antonio
im still jet lagged, spice me up alec

Hunter
is that innuendo?

Alec sighs, putting his phone back down on the counter. When it's just Antonio, he's safe from that kind of thing, but most of their other friends are kind of, well, obnoxious about sex. Not that Alec is embarrassed by this kind of talk but it gets tiring after a while, having to hear about sex non-stop. Especially when he's the only openly gay guy on his team, so all he hears about are girls.

The notifications keep coming, but Alec decides to ignore them in favor of pulling out a skillet and a carton of eggs along with the salsa he made yesterday and some left-over tofu and black bean thing he made last night. He's barely got the butter melting in the pan when his phone dings again. Tired of listening to it, he picks it up with the sole intention of silencing the notifications, only to notice the last one isn't from his group chat.

Tapping the notification, the uncomfortable knot in his chest loosens considerably.

> **Theo**
> see you soon

THE SOUND of Theo pulling into the long driveway forty minutes after his first and only text has a smile forming on Alec's face. Even though Theo had messaged him, and Theo is usually the kind of guy to stick to his word, he'd still worried he might not show up. His relief is palpable, and he wastes no time setting the dishwasher and then grabbing the foil-wrapped burritos out of the oven where he was keeping them warm. He packs them tightly into his cooler bag, along with some baggies of oranges he picked off the tree in the backyard, and an extra container of his homemade salsa for Antonio. He's just zipping up the bag when the knock at the front door comes.

"Just a sec," Alec yells, glad there's no one around to witness the way he all but runs to the front door like an overeager puppy. Alec needs to develop some fucking chill around Theo, or he's going to walk away just like he did last time.

There's no second knock, but Alec knows he's still there on the other side of the door, waiting. It ratchets up Alec's heart rate, and he takes a deep breath, willing his body to calm the fuck down. He's not going to make any steps towards getting close to Theo again if he scares him off by being too much, too soon. Usually, he doesn't care if people are turned off by his personality, but he lost Theo once, and the prospect of it happening again might be more heartache than Alec can bear.

He might be determined to be friends with Theo, but that doesn't mean he isn't privately wishing Theo might see him as attractive.

Alec turns to face the mirror over the entryway table. He stares at his reflection, smoothing down his t-shirt. It's hot pink with a tilted crown on the front, his last name and number on the back. Riley had it made for his birthday, and Alec's worn it three times since. He fucking loves pink. It highlights his freckles, something he'd spent years crying about as a kid but over time grew to love.

"You are smart, sexy and capable," Alec says to himself, tousling his curls so they're messier. He goes to great lengths for his hair care routine to make sure his hair is soft and frizz-free, but he also likes when it looks messy, like he was rolling around the grass or a bed. Pleased with the results, he takes a deep breath, repeating his positive affirmations to himself as he opens the door.

"Hey," Theo grins, his smile soft and easy and robbing all thoughts from Alec's brain.

"You're hot," Alec blurts, frozen in horror at his own slip-up. "I mean, uh, aren't you hot?"

Theo shrugs, looking down at himself. He pulls the sweater away from his body, making the knit material puff up before clinging back against the flat of his soft tummy. "It's a thin knit, and I don't have anything underneath it."

Nothing underneath his sweater. Fucking fantastic. That's exactly the mental image Alec needs.

"Can I make a confession?" Theo hovers awkwardly at the front door, like he hasn't been to Alec's house thousands of times, like he didn't live upstairs with Jason for an entire year after his dad moved away. That was the year Alec realized he was definitely gay, gay, gay. Not that he's ever told anyone the impetus for his sexual awakening was Theo. That's another secret he needs to keep locked down.

"You can tell me anything."

Theo takes a deep breath and holds it before blowing it out. For someone so large, he manages to look small sometimes, and Alec wonders if he does it on purpose or if he just subconsciously wants to fade into the cracks.

"I didn't remember this."

"But you're here," Alec frowns.

"Yeah, uh, Jason called this morning and was rambling as usual, but then he mentioned you and uh, you know, you about asking about my plans and—"

A weird buzzing noise fills Alec's ears while Theo talks. It's the party all over again, but Theo isn't drunk and he's going to notice if Alec is weird. He needs to calm down, but he is so goddamn tired of being seen as Jason's baby brother first and foremost to Theo. Jason has such a big fucking mouth, and Alec is going to kill him. This is why he shouldn't talk to Jason about anything important. Ever.

"Earth to Alec."

Alec plasters on a smile that he doesn't feel. "You don't have to help if you don't want to. I can call Antonio and see if one of his *tíos* can help."

"You weren't listening to me at all, were you?" Theo is smiling at Alec, and he isn't sure if that makes things better or worse because Theo is not drunk this time, but he's still looking at Alec like he did the other night. Alec is so confused and so gay for this beautiful man that it physically hurts.

"Sorry, no."

"It's alright, I'm sure you've got a lot on your mind. Jason said you always get nervous before move-in day."

Alec grits his teeth so hard he's surprised he doesn't crack a tooth. Fucking Jason and his big fucking mouth. Having big brothers is the worst sometimes. "It's nothing," Alec shrugs, hoping to brush it off.

"It's a big deal, I get it. I remember being in college and that last year. The pressure of finishing classes and getting ready to go out into the world. It's normal to be nervous."

"I'm not," Alec lies because it's easier than admitting the truth.

"Alright," Theo concedes. "I'm sure you're excited. You're a senior now. Living the dream of being a star athlete and all that. Must be exhausting to be young and talented."

"You forgot gorgeous," Alec reminds him, perking up. This is exactly the kind of teasing he loves, the kind that Theo has never engaged in with him before. It gives Alec hope.

"I don't think anyone would forget you're gorgeous, Alexander."

The praise goes right to Alec's head and heart, but he can't let that show. So he settles for more bravado, which is always the safest option.

"I am the full package," Alec smirks, on cloud fucking nine.

"I'm sure you'll break lots of hearts this year, kiddo."

And there, with one little stupid word, Alec's cloud goes poof and fizzles into nothingness.

"So what's the plan for today?" Theo asks, thankfully unaware of the power he holds.

"Moving," Alec replies, settling into smartass territory where things are safe and familiar.

Theo's mouth turns up at the corner, but he says nothing.

Never able to handle silence unless it's of his own choosing, Alec rambles. "Antonio got the keys from the RA this morning, so he went by to open the place up, air out the rooms. Hunter and Logan are supposed to come over to the apartment and meet us. You and I will make the first car load with the kitchen essentials, and then Riley's going to meet us with his pickup truck to start moving the bigger pieces."

He waits for Theo to ask why Alec needs help from him when there are three fit college guys available but he doesn't, instead shoving his hands into his pockets and rocking on his heels. It's the same way he used to do when he was sixteen and nervous. Alec can't imagine what there is to be nervous about now. Maybe he didn't really want to be here and didn't know how to say it. Theo is the kind of guy who honors commitments, even if he doesn't want to. He's reliable and honest and whether he wants to be here or not, he told Alec he would, so he is.

The thought sparks a wave of guilt. Maybe Alec should push the subject and offer Theo one more chance to get out of this all-day ordeal, but he can't bring himself to do it. Come Monday, he's back in the grind of full-time training. Another two weeks and he's going to have a full course load to manage on top of practice and games. The odds of him running into Theo will be slim to none, and Alec's going to be a selfish asshole, and take this time, knowing it's likely the only one he will get.

Given the chance, Alec will take what he can get from Theo. Not just because he's stupidly in love with him, but because he genuinely likes him as a friend. Everything about Theo's calm, steady demeanor makes Alec feel happy, safe and grounded. It's hard to separate the romantic love from the platonic, all of it twisted together in one inseparable mess. However you want to describe it, all that really matters is that Alec loves Theodore James.

There's been a Theo-shaped hole in Alec's heart since the day Theo started to pull away, and it doesn't matter that his love will never be returned because he doesn't expect it to. He just wants to see Theo happy and spend some time with him. He wants one day. Surely he can have this.

"WHEN YOU SAID everything was in your parents' garage, I didn't realize you meant that literally."

"Mom was very distraught to have to sacrifice parking her baby in the driveway instead of the garage, but once I found out we got the apartment for this year, I started getting ready."

Theo whistles, and Alec tries to look at it from an outsider's point of view. Standing in front of the open garage door, he supposes he can see exactly why it looks overwhelming. There are two love seats that Alec snagged from a senior moving out last year at a killer price—before he even knew whether they'd get this apartment—a fairly large dining table with matching chairs his parents picked up at Ikea and built while he was in Mexico, a still boxed up 70" television—which was Alec's big birthday gift request from his parents—a squashy green armchair of dubious origin, several Ikea bookshelves that also mysteriously appeared while he was gone, and more than half a dozen boxes all packed full and neatly labeled with bathroom and kitchen essentials that Alec finished up last week. There's also all of Alec's personal belongings, including a massive storage tote with all of his soccer gear, two suitcases full of clothing and multiple boxes of bedding and room decor.

"Wait, you bought everything in here?"

Theo's tone is unreadable and Alec hesitates, trying to decide how to answer. He knows this looks like a lot. It is a lot.

"It's not a big deal. Antonio's family is already stretching themselves thin to pay for his schooling since he didn't get a full ride like I did, which is bullshit because he's just as good, you know? So I started getting stuff so he wouldn't need anything besides his clothes. Then once I started, well, I thought Riley would be moving in with us too. Riley's parents have a lot of kids, and Riley already works two jobs plus school, and the last thing he needed to do was spend his savings on this stuff, you know?" Alec cuts himself off, taking a steadying breath and trying not to panic at what he just realized. Antonio and Riley don't know, and he intends to keep it that way. "Look, don't tell them. I don't want them to think it's charity because it's not. As far as everyone knows, my parents spoil me, and that's the way I'd like the story to stay."

"I won't say a word," Theo promises, gaze fixed squarely on Alec, who squirms under the attention. Theo hasn't looked at him like this in so long.

"I know I'm beautiful, it's okay to look," Alec says, hoping he doesn't sound as off-kilter as he feels.

"So humble, too," Theo snorts.

Alec turns his back on Theo, not trusting himself to stare at him head-on. He's like looking at the sun. You crave the warmth, the light, but when you look too long, you get burned. Alec busies himself with moving boxes from one stack to another, hoping Theo doesn't ask what the fuck he's doing since he really doesn't know.

"Being humble is overrated. Like okay, no one wants you to be an asshole, and trust me, we've got a few grade-A dicks on the team. And I don't mean that in a good way, either," Alec mumbles, well aware of how Grady and Dwight seem absolutely positive that Alec has a crush on them just because he's into guys. They're not outwardly homophobic or anything—there's a zero tolerance policy for that on the team—but they're fucking obnoxious and make comments about their dicks. They get away with it by doing it to everyone under the guise of locker room talk, but it doesn't escape Alec's notice that when no one is paying attention, it's directed towards him. They're either heavily closeted or fucking assholes, or both. Either way, they annoy the shit out of him. Alec's not cocky, he's confident, and there's a difference.

"Is someone on the team making you uncomfortable?" Theo asks.

Red warning lights go off in Alec's head. The last thing he needs is Theo talking to Jason, who would likely storm into the fucking Dean's office if he thought something was wrong, or talk to their parents to try and bring a fucking lawsuit or something. Alec appreciates his brothers, he really does. He knows how fucking lucky he is to be so accepted and loved when so many other queer kids aren't, but that doesn't mean he wants his big brother solving all his problems. The world is full of dick bags and Alec can handle himself. He has been for three years.

"Aw, are you worried about me, Theodore?" Alec tips his head back and smiles. If he's hoping Theo will shake his head in exasperation and then move on, he's sorely mistaken.

"You know no one is allowed to make you uncomfortable. There's nothing wrong with virginity if that's what it's about and—"

The box currently poised in Alec's hand falls hard and

heavy on his foot, and Alec lets out a string of expletives that would make his *abuela* roll in her grave. Worse than the stinging pain is the way the packing tape on the top of the box pops when it crashes to the cement floor, sending measuring cups and utensils rolling across. Nursing a sore toe and an even more sore ego, Alec drops to the ground to make a grab for the contents.

"I thought we agreed to never speak of that again," Alec hisses, fingers curling around the end of a spatula. He throws it in the now upturned box, eying the rest of the contents with a sigh. There's something poetic about Alec's perfectly packed box crashing to the floor to create a mess that mirrors this conversation. Alec fucking hates poetry.

"There's nothing to be ashamed about," Theo tries, apparently still very much speaking about it.

"I know there isn't," Alec snaps, crawling on his hands and knees after the little frog-shaped kitchen timer he bought. It seemed cute at the time, but now every time Alec sets a timer while cooking, the little frog is going to serve as a reminder of this mortifying moment.

It's not like he's actually embarrassed about his virginity. Mostly. He knows it's a social construct. He knows there's no magic age or that being a virgin forever is even a bad thing. The problem is that Alec isn't a virgin by choice. Not exactly. He's been propositioned more times than he will ever tell anyone, but every time they'd gotten even close, dread had swirled in the pit of Alec's stomach at the idea of being intimate with someone he didn't love. Maybe he's a romantic, or maybe he's fucking pathetic pining away for the same guy for six years, a guy who will never want him the same way. All he knows is there is one reason and one reason only that Alec is still a virgin at twenty-one and that reason is currently standing behind him.

"Alec."

With that one word, the fight goes out of Alec. He wants to be snarky and cranky, and if it were one of his brothers talking to him right now he would be, but this is Theo. Theo, who has the most unselfish heart of anyone Alec's ever met. Theo, who has no idea that he's the reason no one else has ever been able to get in Alec's pants. Because despite all the evidence to suggest Theo will never feel the same, Alec doesn't know how to switch off his stupid fucking feelings and his stupid fucking heart. None of which is Theo's fault or his responsibility to fix. Alec is the one who needs to get his shit together and handle this.

"It's nothing, okay? Just drop it. Please."

A hand appears in his line of vision. Theo's hand, with his massive, thick fingers wrapped around the little frog timer, which he holds out to Alec like a peace offering.

"Thanks," Alec mumbles, letting his own fingers brush over Theo's for a second longer than necessary.

When he lifts his gaze, he finds Theo smiling at him. A real smile, the kind usually reserved for Jason, and something in Alec heals and breaks all at once. With that radiant smile still in place, Theo reaches out to ruffle Alec's hair before moving on to help collect the rest of the utensils. Alec holds his breath until Theo's back is turned on him before letting out a shuddering breath. He squeezes his eyes shut. Alec has done a lot of hard things in his life, but this might be the hardest.

6 THEO

THEO WOULD VERY MUCH LOVE to say he spends the next few days not thinking about Alec, but unfortunately that would be a lie. He's got a job he can't neglect and a huge report due soon, but in between working and drinking more coffee than is probably smart for someone with a brain like his, he thinks about Alec. About his smile and the sound of his laugh, and the way Alec can get Theo out of his head like no one else.

Every time he stops thinking about Alec, only a few seconds pass before he starts again, as if his brain refuses to move on. He replays the night of the party over and over in his mind like a goddamn movie, unable to forget the way Alec looked dancing. He thinks about helping Alec move in over the weekend a lot too, about what it was like to see Alec in a situation entirely outside the King family. And how much seeing him in his own element with his friends had shaken up the little box in his brain where Alec had always firmly been.

That box where his brain put Alec when he was little, used to have facts about Alec like '*plays soccer, scared of the dark, sucked his thumb, little kid.*' Now the box includes things like '*not a kid anymore, cooks killer breakfast burritos, makes Theo laugh, is beautiful.*' Who knew all it would take was a few tacos, getting drunk off his ass, and a college move-in day to shake up everything Theo thought he knew about Alexander King?

After three days of letting his imagination run wild, he does more than just think about Alec. He puts his internet savvy to good use and starts looking up Alec's various social media accounts. Doing this makes Theo feel a little weird, like he's spying, yet that feeling is apparently not enough to deter him from doing it.

Theo tries to tell himself that the only reason he's doing it is because Alec is gorgeous, but there's a very large part of him that knows this isn't the full truth. When Theo looks at Alec's smile, there's a pang of regret at missing out on the man he's become, but more than that is a feeling he isn't used to: longing.

Looking at Alec's Instagram doesn't feel like crossing any lines because he and Theo are technically mutuals, even if prior to this moment Theo hadn't logged into his own account in over six months and didn't know how active Alec was.

Alec's account is a treasure trove of photos and witty tags that leave Theo smiling, easily able to imagine the one-liners falling from Alec's sarcastic, pretty mouth. He spends so long scrolling, he falls asleep with his phone in his hand. He's slightly out of sorts when he wakes up the next morning to a blaring alarm and the dirty reminder of what he'd done when he unlocks it and sees Alec's face staring back at him.

Despite promising himself not to be a creep and doing the same thing twice, he does it anyway. That night after he finishes cleaning up from dinner and showers, he finds himself once again scrolling social media, only this time he ventures outside of Alec's account. It's not long before he finds a photo of Antonio and Alec together and ends up clicking on Antonio's profile to find new photos of Alec. He's pretty sure resorting to looking for photos of Alec on his best friend's account, a guy who Theo is definitely not friends with, is crossing a line but there's no one to bear witness to Theo's treachery. Especially not Alec or Jason.

Embarrassed by his own actions but unable to stop, Theo turns the lights down low before flipping off the television in his room and ignoring the weird feeling in his chest as he sits on his bed. Surrounded by quiet and dark, Theo retrieves his phone and once again opens the app. Despite his slight misgivings about what the hell he's doing, he spends a good hour scrolling through Antonio's account in the hopes of catching a glimpse of Alec. He's not disappointed, finding almost more photos of Alec's face than there exist on his own account.

There are plenty of pictures of Antonio and Alec with a pretty girl too, enough that even if Alec hadn't assured Theo there was nothing between them, he'd see that now. He ignores the ones of Antonio with his fianceé in favor of seeking out the ones with only Alec in them. There's a particularly striking photo of Alec horseback riding through the fields during their trip to Mexico, a large brimmed hat obscuring his curls, his smile wide and free. There's another one of him flipping off Antonio while eating a mango, the juice running down his delicate fingers, that leaves Theo uncomfortably aware of his own body.

Every time he thinks he can't get luckier, there are more, Antonio's account overflowing with photos from their trip. There's one of him playing soccer with a bunch of kids, one where Alec's cheeks are hollowed from sucking on his straw while he drinks something that looks like *horchata*, and even one of Alec shirtless jumping into a muddy river.

Photo after photo showcases Alec laughing and having fun, looking more relaxed than Theo has ever seen him. Where Alec's personal social media is more cultivated to soccer and food with an occasional thirst trap, the photos from his best friend show off a whole new side to Alec, one that's a lot more up close and personal than Theo was expecting.

Each photo leads to another, and soon Theo is tapping on random names and links. The sheer number of people who tag Alec on Twitter and Instagram is, quite frankly, terrifying for someone like Theo, who would rather die than ever be perceived by so many strangers. While some of them seem like friends or acquaintances, there are a slightly worrying amount of photos, tweets, and accounts mentioning Alec that indicate they don't know him but wish they did.

Some seem to be fans who follow college soccer and are more interested in Alec's player stats than his freckles and abs, but there's plenty of engagement from people thirsting over him with candid photos taken of him all over campus last year. There's even one of Alec sleepy and frowning at a camera, making it clear someone was taking a photo of him in the library without permission. There are accounts of betting on his odds of being scouted to the MLS, and one slightly unhinged faceless account on Twitter that rates the boys of Santa Leon University, which lists Alec as one of the sexiest guys on campus. Scrolling further, he notices Riley's now familiar face plastered along with Alec's and finds himself frowning.

Seeing the way strangers talk about Alec like he's a

commodity, rating everything from his soccer skills to his body, makes Theo's stomach churn. No matter how much he tries to tell himself that he feels some kind of pseudo-older-brother protectiveness about randos perving on Alec, the truth is so much more complicated.

For the second night in a row, Theo finds himself up until one a.m. with thoughts of freckled skin and a cocky smile filling his mind.

It's been a long time since Theo wanted anything. He's spent a lifetime trying to tamper down his expectations, to be realistic and responsible and make choices that will ensure he doesn't jeopardize anything he isn't willing to lose. Yet with every thought of Alec, the longing grows, and he knows that he can't deny the truth; he wants to know the missing parts of Alec, to fill in the blank spaces and the missing pieces and find out exactly who Alexander King is now.

A normal person would text Alec and ask to hang out again, but Theo isn't normal, and he's never been good at that. The only reason he and Jason became best friends is because Jason asked and Theo said yes; the rest was history. Theo doesn't even have any close friends besides Jason, though whether that's because he's incapable of casual social interactions or deeply introverted is debatable. Theo tries not to think too hard about it. He's got a stable job, a group of friendly work acquaintances that are at least friend-adjacent, and he's got Jason. Every couple months when he gets tired of his own hand, he has a casual hookup, and that's all he needs.

Except if that is actually true, then why can't he stop thinking about Alec's smile?

More than once, he opens his contacts and stares at Alec's name. He's got his phone number. After helping

Alec move a few days ago, something had changed. Spending time with Alec alone and with his friends had shown Theo a new side to Alec, one he isn't used to seeing around Jason. His brothers treat him like the baby of the family and it shows. With his friends he's more relaxed, and while his outlandish flirting and joking behavior was there, there'd also been moments of quiet conversation that Theo hadn't known he was capable of.

Before he left the apartment, Alec told Theo he had a good day. The implication that he would be up for hanging out again was there, yet something holds him back. If Alec wanted to hang out again, why didn't he explicitly say so? Alec is always vocal about what he wants. He never holds anything back and can't keep a secret to save his life. Maybe he isn't interested in more than a semi-familial friendship with Theo. Maybe he doesn't want to hang out again.

That small possibility holds Theo back from texting Alec first. Even though Theo is fairly certain his offer to hang out wouldn't be straight out declined, he isn't sure where he stands. He also has no idea how one goes about asking someone to hang out if it's not a work meeting or a dating app hookup. Those both have expectations and parameters. This thing with Alec does not. Hell, all the plans he makes with Jason are made because Jason asks first, because he knows Theo won't. The sad truth is that Theo is shit at initiating anything when there is a potential for rejection, however minuscule.

There's also the little thing about Alec being Jason's little brother, which is maybe not such a little thing after all. Realistically, Jason would probably be thrilled if he thought Theo wanted to include Alec in some of their hangouts. And while Theo wouldn't mind that, what he really wants is something infinitely more complicated: he wants to hang out with Alec alone. Which begs the question, how in the hell is he supposed to hang out with Alec without any of his brothers around?

He can't even imagine how that exchange would go over. *'Hey Jason, I've been noticing your baby brother grew up into one of the most attractive men I've ever seen. I had a wet dream about his freckled back, and by the way, would you be cool if we hung out without you?'* Theo rubs his temples. Jason would be pissed off or get his feelings hurt, and either option makes Theo sick to his stomach. He can't hurt his best friend.

Besides, he knows Alec is over Theo. His little crush was years ago, and Alec's a grown man now. It's just now that they're both adults and on equal playing fields, things are different. Too bad Theo's an idiot who took years too long to realize how sexy and fun Alec is.

With a frustrated sigh, Theo tosses his phone onto the far end of his couch out of reach. What Theo needs to do is get Alec out of his head. Thinking about his blinding smile, warm freckles and the impressive breadth of his muscular soccer thighs, is quite possibly the riskiest thing he's ever done. Even daydreaming about messing around with him feels dangerous; actually doing it would be the biggest mistake of his life. Either Jason would end up hating him or Theo would hate himself. Or both. *Both* is definitely the most likely option.

Of course, there's also the part where Alec is long over his teenage crush on Theo and now has feelings for someone else. Something about a party boy is what Charlie said. Probably someone his own age who is social and funny like Alec. Someone who is probably a dick, since he doesn't like Alec back.

That train of thought makes him think about the day

Alec confessed his feelings, laying his entire heart on the line before Theo had practically run away. He hadn't let himself be in the same room as Alec alone for months, and while it had been the right choice at the time because he was way, way too old for Alec back then and didn't have feelings for him, he probably hurt him. Of course Alec had been nothing but smiles in no time, so getting over his little crush on Theo clearly hadn't been too hard, but he still hates the idea he might've hurt him even a little bit. This other guy Alec likes now could hurt him, judging by the conversation he overheard between Charlie and Alec in the kitchen.

Thinking about Alec with another guy makes Theo's chest tighten uncomfortably. He might not be close to Alec anymore, but he watched him grow up. He knows he's something special and the idea of someone hurting him makes Theo more upset than it probably should. Blowing out a heavy breath, he chalks his state of mind up to protectiveness. He is Jason's brother, after all, so of course Theo doesn't want to see him hurting.

The more he thinks about it, the more certain he feels that all these messy confusing feelings are probably just being dredged up because of the party. The reminder that Alec grew up while Theo was busy avoiding him and becoming a man of his own is bittersweet. He missed out on so much, but that doesn't give him permission to feel possessive about who Alec dates or who thinks about him naked. No matter the reason for his current predicament, it's Theo's alone to deal with, and he's dealt with far worse than a burgeoning crush on someone he can't have. While it's nice to imagine they might have more fun together whenever he does see him, thinking about anything else outside of those parameters is not only ridiculous, but wildly irresponsible.

Theo needs to forget the party, forget Alec and his ridiculous little frog timer, his perfectly organized kitchen and delicious breakfast burritos. He needs to forget how it felt to have Alec's full attention directed his way and get back to his normal life.

Normal. Familiar. That's exactly what Theo needs. Grabbing the remote, he flips through the streaming channels until he finds a new documentary about whales he hasn't seen. As the narrator's monotonous voice fills his living room, he slowly relaxes. This is fine. His life is stable and comfortable, and that's all he could possibly need.

***

"I NEED YOU."

"Who is this?" Theo asks, scrubbing a hand over his face. It's pitch dark in his bedroom, and his glasses are mysteriously absent from his bedside table. He'd squinted at his phone to try and see who it was, but between his sleep-addled brain and poor vision, he couldn't tell and answered the call anyway, assuming it was Jason.

It's definitely not.

"Who is this?" the other person repeats in a high-pitched tone. "I am so offended that you don't have me in your contact list that I'm tempted to hang up on you."

"Alec?"

"Of course it's me, Theodore."

Theo squints at his phone to make sure it's not a dream. He has to bring it very close to his face to see what time it is and confirm that the call is indeed coming from Alec's number.

"Why are you awake at five a.m.?" Theo groans. "This isn't even a real time."

"Why don't you have me in your contact list?" Alec counters, avoiding the question.

"I do," Theo answers around a yawn. "Can't find my glasses."

"You answered a call blindly? What are you, unhinged?"

"I thought it was Jason. He's the only person who calls me besides my boss."

Alec makes a thoughtful noise. "Did I wake you up?"

"At five in the morning?" Theo snorts. "Yes, Alec, you woke me up."

"Oh." Alec's exhale is heavy through the phone. "Are you mad?"

The conversation is so bonkers that Theo finds himself answering far too honestly.

"I'd never be mad at you for calling me." A horrible thought occurs to Theo. "Wait, why are you calling me so early? What's wrong? Fuck, is it Jason?"

He tries to stand too abruptly, feet tangling in the sheets when Alec replies.

"Nothing is wrong." At those three words, Theo collapses on the edge of the bed with a heavy thud, kicking at the sheets. "Jason is probably sleeping like a baby. I didn't call him to check, but you know that man loves to sleep."

Heart beating erratically in his chest, Theo throws his legs over the bed and forces himself to breathe slowly. His brain might know everything is fine, but his body hasn't caught up.

"Charlie didn't answer?" he asks, trying to make sense of why Alec is calling.

"I didn't call him either."

Oh. That's unexpected.

"I need help."

That's even more unexpected. Theo should probably ask more questions, but the truth is no matter what is going on, if Alec is desperate enough to call Theo for help and not his brothers, then he's going to help him.

"Where are you?" Theo asks as he grabs his pants off the edge of the bed and shimmies into them.

"Funny you should ask that."

"Are you in trouble, Alec?" Theo pulls his sweater from yesterday over his head, worst case scenarios running through his head as he grabs one of his spare pair of glasses off the top of his dresser. They're not his favorite frames, but he keeps extras for times like now where he's lost his glasses, something that happens far more often than it should. "You're not in jail, are you?"

"Jail. Honestly, Theodore, what would I do to land myself in jail?"

"Streaking." The answer comes out as half-statement and half-question, which feels appropriate.

"I don't know if I'm flattered or offended that your first thought for why I'd be arrested is nudity."

"Sorry," Theo apologizes.

"Don't be, that's probably accurate," Alec laughs. "But uh, no, I'm not in jail. I'm uh...somewhere closer."

"Your apartment?"

"Your front porch."

Theo startles, stubbing his toe on the bed frame on the way out of his door. He curses, righting himself as he stares into his empty, dark living room. He doesn't bother asking what the hell Alec is doing over the phone, ending the call before half-running to the front door. He flips on the porch light while unlocking the deadbolt, swinging the door open to find Alec is, in fact, standing on his front porch. There's mud on his nose, the side of his cheek is caked with blood and his lip is split. His shirt is also absent, wrapped around something in his arm that meows loudly.

"What the fuck?"

"Not a fuck." He holds his arms out to show off a small black void of fur wrapped inside his t-shirt. "A cat. Well, kitten to be precise."

"A kitten," Theo repeats, unable to keep the incredulity from his tone. He takes a second glance at Alec, his concern growing. Aside from the split lip, there's a reddish mark on Alec's side that looks like it's going to bruise, a gash in his running leggings, and his shoes are soaking wet. "What happened?"

"Can we come in? I'm freezing my nipples off," Alec says in lieu of answering the question. He also doesn't wait for a response before ducking beneath Theo's outstretched arm and stepping inside. "Did you get a new rug? I like it."

"Uh, yeah, like nine months ago."

"Suits you."

The rug is brown with zigzagging stripes, and Theo got a killer deal on a second hand website. He says as much, pleased when Alec smiles at him, and then he snaps his mouth shut. What the hell is happening? Alexander King is shirtless, filthy and bleeding in his living room at five a.m. while Theo's talking about his rug. He's got to be hallucinating.

"Hmm, no, I'm definitely not a hallucination," Alec chirps, leaving Theo no room to be embarrassed that he apparently said that part out loud. "I'm gonna take Rio into the kitchen to clean her up. You can follow."

Theo does follow along, not entirely sure what else to do.

"Where did you get a cat? Are you hurt? Why are you out at five in the morning?"

"That's an awful lot of questions," Alec says, far too calm for someone bleeding and dirty. "I could be persuaded to answer them all if you wanted to bribe me with something hot to drink. Preferably with a lot of cream and sugar. Don't tell the team nutritionist."

"Pretty sure you can just have coffee however you want it."

"You'd be surprised," Alec says, the hint of frustration in his tone. Theo wants to ask about it, but Alec switches to his normal sunny disposition. "Can you give me a washcloth to get her clean?"

"Sure, but—"

"Questions after coffee," Alec interrupts. Theo is too tired to argue with him and hurries to the bathroom to get Alec a stack of clean washcloths, and then sets about brewing the biggest, strongest pot of coffee his machine can handle. It's a win-win for them both, because Theo is going to need at least two cups of coffee before he's coherent enough to make sense of what is happening, and Alec is apparently motivated by bribes.

"Can I at least ask what happened to your face?" Theo says.

While the coffee percolates, the kitchen fills with the occasional mewl of kitten displeasure and the bubbling of brewing coffee. Alec doesn't immediately answer, and Theo takes the opportunity to lean back against the kitchen counter and really get a good look at Alec. The blood on his cheek has dried, which should alleviate any worries, but all Theo can do is stare at the mix of blood and dirt smeared across his freckled cheek. A weight settles over his chest, uncomfortable and unfamiliar.

"It was an unfortunate consequence of rescuing Rio." He says it so cavalier, as if he doesn't care that he's dirty and hurt because of a stray cat.

"Where did you find it, the bottom of the riverbed?"

"Yes, actually."

"Shit, Alec." Theo pushes off the counter. He inches into Alec's personal space, taking in the mark on his side with more scrutiny now. The river bottom runs along the freeway and is bordered by tall fencing meant to keep people out for this exact reason. "Why did you go down to the river bottom? Did you fall?"

"I told you, to find Rio."

"That was dangerous." Theo sighs, skimming his fingers over the angry red skin. Alec sucks in a sharp breath and holds it, his entire body strung as taut as a bow. "Maybe I should take you to urgent care or—"

"No." Alec interrupts. "I see enough medical professionals with the team. I don't want to deal with more of them than I have to. I'm good, I promise." Alec attempts to smile, but it comes out as a grimace because of his split lip, which he certainly won't be able to hide during his practice, but that's not Theo's business. Technically nothing about Alec is his business, yet he can't stop himself from getting involved, consequences be damned.

"I'll put an extra spoonful of sugar in your coffee if you let me clean your wounds."

Alec hisses. "You play dirty, Theodore James."

"Is that a yes?" Theo asks, unsure how to read Alec right now. He's known Alec for most of his life, but he's only now realizing how much he doesn't know about the other man, and there's no doubt in his mind that Alec is definitely a man now.

Guilt prickles at Theo that Alec is standing there hurt,

and he's admiring the flat planes of Alec's stomach and chest. He's strong, but lean, and his skin is so smooth. There's no hair on his chest, and instead freckles cascade across his ribs and curl around his back.

"It's working," Alec admits, the weight of his exhale palpable. "Fuck it, I want extra cream, too. I want that coffee milky and sweet."

"I can definitely manage that." Theo turns to the fridge, pulling out the carton of half and half before taking down the sugar bowl from the cupboard above the coffee pot. He's pulling down two mugs when he turns back to Alec. "Any chance I could get you to take some Advil for the swelling?"

"Don't push your luck, mister," Alec mutters, eyes firmly on the kitten in the sink who seems almost as skittish as Alec. "Pass me another dry wash cloth. Please."

The kitten mews, its little paws on the edge of the sink as Alec carefully cleans the muck and dirt from its fur. Theo tries not to think about the similarities between them. He tries, and he fails because those big, vulnerable eyes make him feel protective. Of the kitten? Maybe. Of Alec? Absolutely.

It's difficult to tell if the silence is awkward or if that's just Theo, but every time he thinks of something to say he closes his mouth, not wanting to ruin the peaceful look in Alec's eyes as he washes the kitten. He makes sure to add extra sugar to Alec's coffee while he watches him work, mesmerized by the gentle way Alec handles the squirming kitten.

"Here's your coffee." He sets Alec's cup on the counter before returning to his previous spot. He sips his coffee, sighing with pleasure at the first drink.

"Still a coffee addict, I see," Alec says. He takes the kitten out of the sink and wraps her in one of the clean dish towels hanging off the cupboard. He holds her close to his chest, her scraggly face peeking out of the towel. With her fur all wet, she looks smaller and more vulnerable, and an unsettled feeling settles in Theo's chest.

"Guess I am," Theo agrees, taking another drink. He watches Alec do the same, unable to keep his questions in any longer when Alec hisses, unable to drink the coffee because of his split lip. "What were you doing at the riverbed in the dark anyway? That's dangerous."

"Thanks, Dad." Alec sticks his tongue out, a sure sign he's not actually mad at Theo's prying. "I was out for a run and—"

"Why were you out for a run so early?"

"Sometimes I can't sleep. It's not a big deal. I won't bore you with the details."

"Why would you think knowing about you would bore me?"

Alec appears to choose his next words carefully. There's nothing accusatory or malicious in his words or tone, yet they sting. "I'm just your best friend's annoying little brother. I know you guys used to try and hide from me when you didn't want me following you."

Guilt hits Theo like a goddamn freight train. There'd been a short time where he and Jason had been idiotic, awkward teenagers doing stupid shit, and they hadn't wanted Alec around to butt in or tell Jason's parents. He just didn't realize Alec ever knew they were hiding from him. Somehow, he and Jason thought they were being subtle. Apparently not.

"Look, it's fine. I was an annoying kid."

"You're not annoying, Alec."

"I said I *was* an annoying kid, not that I'm annoying

now. Anyone would be lucky to spend time with me. I'm a fucking delight."

"They would," Theo agrees.

"Why are you being so nice to me?"

"Why didn't you call Charlie?" Theo counters, trying to deflect.

"Charlie's already got three cats, an elderly hamster no one wanted from the pet store and a dog." Alec's eyes remain on the kitten, something heavy in his tone. "He said if I bring him any more animals, he's gonna send me to the rescue center."

While Theo suspected Charlie's large menagerie of pets was due to Alec, he'd never asked. He's not sure what to make of that.

"Jason?"

"He's got two dogs already, and he doesn't have time for more pets, which is why he told me to stop tempting him with strays."

Theo hums in agreement. Jason probably would cave if Alec called him, but his apartment isn't huge, and he really doesn't have room for more pets.

"Why not Andrew? Your parents?"

"Andrew doesn't want pets right now. You know what a control freak he is. I think he'd have a panic attack if his place got covered in pet hair. And my parents said they're done raising kids and animals. They wanna start doing old people shit, like cruises and bingo nights when they're not working."

"They're not that old."

"That's what I said." Alec snorts, dropping a kiss to the top of the kitten's towel-covered head. "I could maybe sneak Rio into the apartment, but last year I got caught with animals twice, and I've been told in no uncertain terms if I get caught again I'll be in serious trouble, and I can't risk my place on the team. Besides, that would be a dick move to my roommates. I think Logan is allergic anyway. Stupid campus housing rules."

"If you don't like the rules, why don't you live at home?" Theo asks. "Jason told me your parents offered to let you stay home and—"

"Wow, look at the time! I should go," Alec loudly interrupts, making it a whole two steps before Theo stops him, hand curling around Alec's bicep.

"No way, let me clean your wounds first. A deal is a deal."

"I can't even drink the coffee," Alec moans. "You're really going to hold me to that deal?"

"Damn right I am. Now sit down so I can look at you."

"I knew you've secretly been dying to look at me. It's okay. All the boys have, and some of the girls, even if I don't play for that team." Alec grins, wincing immediately. "Fuck, that hurt."

"I meant to look at your injury," Theo says, hoping the warmth he feels in his cheeks isn't noticeable. He does like looking at Alec, far more than he is comfortable admitting, but Alec doesn't need to know that.

"That's not fun," Alec protests, but it doesn't escape Theo's notice how quickly he complies.

"Not everything has to be fun," Theo says, reaching out to skim his fingers over Alec's cheek. The cut isn't deep enough to need stitches, but it definitely looks like it needs to be cleaned and secured with a butterfly bandage. Alec tenses and Theo yanks his hand back. "Sorry, did that hurt?"

"No," Alec answers with the slightest hitch to his breathing.

An image of Alec beneath him, mouth open and wanton as Theo touches him in a different way springs to mind, and it's only a lifetime of self-denial and masking that allows Theo to keep a straight face. Thinking Alec is hot is one thing, imaging him beneath Theo, mouthy and eager, is something Theo shouldn't touch with a ten-foot-pole. Especially not when Alec's clearly hung up on some other guy.

"I'm going to go get the first aid kit, and you're going to stay here like a good boy."

"Boring," Alec whines, but lifts Rio up to kiss her face and doesn't move. It takes Theo a minute to find the first aid kit under the sink in his bathroom, fully stocked out of precaution yet rarely used. He half-expects Alec to have moved by the time he returns, but he's in the same place Theo left him, bouncing his leg while baby-talking to the kitten.

Aware of Alec's eyes following him, Theo drags one of the other chairs around the kitchen table and situates it in front of Alec, setting the first aid kit on the table before grabbing Alec's chair and pulling him between the spread of his legs so that Alec's knees are pressed against the inside of Theo's thighs. The kitten meows between them.

"She's cute."

"Of course she is," Alec agrees, eyes on Theo. "Her name is Rio. You can use it."

"You're going to get attached naming her."

Why don't you ever protect yourself? Theo wonders, holding that thought back.

"Too late, already attached. I think she's like eight or nine weeks old, if I had to guess. Could be a little older."

Theo pops open the first aid kit before digging out the antiseptic wipes, Vaseline and a variety of bandages, unsure which might work best. He uses a wet washcloth to clean the wounds first before ripping open the antiseptic wipe and drawing it over the swell of Alec's high cheekbone. For the first time in Theo's memory, Alec doesn't move, body still as a statue as Theo draws it over the angry skin, careful not to push too hard. The gash is only an inch or so long, just deep enough to bleed, but definitely not deep enough to need stitches.

"Okay?"

"Yeah," Alec croaks.

"Sorry if it stings," Theo apologizes, leaning forward to blow on the cut. Alec makes a choked off sound that could be pain or something else. Theo doesn't want to think about the *something else*. Something else is risky, and Theo doesn't take risks.

He doesn't think about the rise and fall of Alec's chest as he smears a thin layer of petroleum jelly over the wound. He doesn't think about the depth of Alec's stare as he smooths a butterfly bandage over the cut on his cheek. Except he does. He thinks about it, and he aches.

Alec sucks in a sharp breath and Theo frowns. "Did that hurt?"

"No." Alec answers so quickly it's impossible to tell if it's the truth or a lie.

"Alright," Theo replies, dragging the pad of his thumb down the side of Alec's jaw.

It's unnecessary from a first aid perspective, a purely selfish touch, yet Theo can't stop himself. He hones his attention on the way Alec holds his breath. When Theo moves his hands lower to trace the bruise that's forming on his side, the kitten leaps down from Alec's lap to explore the kitchen, giving Theo full access to him. He's careful not to press too hard into Alec's side, drawing a second clean washcloth over the skin to clean off the dirt.

Alec's expression becomes something unreadable. His mouth is half-open, his brown eyes piercing Theo. There's something there, but Theo's not used to having to guess. He's used to Alec running his mouth so much you don't get a second to even think. A quiet Alec is something Theo's never been confronted with, and he's not sure what to make of it.

"Cat got your tongue," Theo teases, drawing a new antiseptic wipe over the scraped skin. There's not too much blood, but Alec definitely fought some concrete and lost. Besides the nasty scrape, there's also a bruise, which is discoloring quickly.

"Fuck you," Alec laughs between a hiss. He playfully kicks at Theo's ankle, and just like that he's back to his usual, mouthy self. Everything is back to normal, whatever the hell that is.

"So, uh, what are you going to do with the cat?" Theo asks, squeezing a bit of petroleum jelly on his pointer finger. He smooths it over the wound before covering it with a gauze pad and a few carefully placed strips of medical tape. It's not until he's finished and packed the first aid kit back up that Alec finally answers.

"I don't know." Alec turns his head to watch the kitten paw at his ankle. With a bitten-off wince, he leans down to pick her up, immediately situating her on his chest. "I know I can't keep her."

The way Alec looks at her like she's something precious has Theo speaking before he can think better of it. "I will."

Alec's eyes snap up. "What?"

"I'll keep her," Theo repeats, with far more confidence than he feels.

"You've never had any pets."

"There's a first time for everything," Theo smiles,

unsure why he feels so desperate to wipe away the uncertainty on Alec's face.

"Are you sure?" He glances between the kitten and Theo, his internal debate obvious. "I don't want you to keep her just because you feel sorry for me or something. I don't need your pity, and a pet is a big deal."

Leave it to Alec to not only parse what's going on in his head, but to call Theo on it. Being called on shit is horrible, but the worst part is how much Theo doesn't actually hate it when it comes from Alec's mouth. The sad truth is he's done a lot of things he didn't want to do in order to help people out or keep the peace. Shit, he played football for so long he even got scouted, and he never even enjoyed playing that much. Theo has always found it easier to not rock the boat, but that's not Alec's way, and it's clear he's not going to let Theo do it now.

"It's not just pity," Theo hedges, unable to explain the entirety of it.

Theo never planned on having a cat. In fact, he's never even given much thought to having a pet—period—but when he looks at the helpless kitten in Alec's arms, he finds himself unable to think about it logically. His house is plenty big, he's got no social life to speak of, and he can afford to take care of it. If he also knows it'll make Alec happy while also giving him an excuse to spend time with him again, well, that's something he doesn't want to think too hard about.

Most of the time Theo's an over-thinker, not a doer, but for once in his life he wants to act first and deal with the consequences later. This alone should terrify him, but he can't stop looking at the hint of a smile on Alec's face long enough to care.

"I want to do this," Theo assures him even if he can't explain why.

When Theo makes a decision, it's usually preceded by weeks or months of research, carefully thought out pros and cons lists, and the conviction that whatever choice he makes is the one with the least amount of risks. This thing with Alec and the kitten is anything but. It's rash and impulsive, the risks high and unknown, which should be making Theo spiral. He has no idea why he isn't freaking out. Maybe it's the way the kitten clearly favors Alec, so far showing no interest in Theo, or maybe it's how attached Alec clearly already is, or maybe it's the fact that Theo knows what it's like to be unwanted and abandoned. Whatever it is, his next words are anything but considered.

"You can come visit her," Theo continues, unsure if he's been taken over by aliens. He's never this rash. "Whenever you want."

Alec smiles so big he winces, but even the pain from his split lip can't wipe the joy off his face as he leans forward, depositing the kitten into Theo's lap.

"If you're going to be her new daddy, you should probably hold her."

The implications of that sentence break through Theo's wall of cognitive dissonance. Some of his panic must show on his face because Alec reaches to stroke her back, drawing his hand across her fur before letting it rest on Theo's forearm.

"She won't bite," Alec tells him. "Well, actually she might since she's scared, but she'll learn to trust you. And you won't have to do this alone. I'll help."

The knot of anxiety around Theo's chest loosens. Alec will help. He isn't doing this alone.

"She can smell fear," Alec teases, grabbing Theo's hand

and laying it on her back. She meows, and Theo's chest does something funny once he realizes exactly what it means to have a pet. He is going to be responsible for keeping something else alive. Even the plants in his house are fake so he doesn't risk killing them, and he pays a guy to come mow and landscape his backyard once a month to ensure nothing dies. Even though he has no plans to move, he doesn't want to depreciate his property value. Theo always thinks ten steps ahead. Except, apparently, when Alec or kittens are involved.

"You know this could be a temporary thing, a foster situation."

"Huh?" Theo looks up, embarrassed at the way his anxiety made him zone out.

"A foster situation," Alec explains. "You look like you're going to crawl out of your skin, and the thing is, that's okay."

"I'm not sure how that's okay," Theo mumbles.

"Because pets are a really big deal, and you shouldn't commit to one unless you're certain. If you're not, that's nothing to be ashamed about."

"I do want to help."

"I know you do," Alec says, his smile softening. Somehow this is more affecting than his happiness. The look in his eyes says he understands Theo's panic, even if Theo isn't verbalizing it, and that level of awareness is something he wasn't expecting from Alec. Fun, carefree, silly. Those are words Theo would've used to describe Alec a week ago. Now added to the list of adjectives that describe him are things like kind and perceptive. Words that lodge themselves in Theo's throat and upend Theo's understanding of the other man in frankly unsettling ways.

"However," Alec continues. "Wanting to help and having good intentions doesn't mean keeping her will be the best thing for either of you. How about if we do a trial run? I can reach out to some people I know, see if anyone is interested. In the meantime you can give her a home, on a trial basis. If it doesn't work out, we can find her the right home."

"Temporary," Theo repeats, watching the kitten try and unstick her paws from his sweater.

"Yeah, temporary."

An out. Alec is giving him an out, and Theo is embarrassed at how fast he takes it.

"Alright."

"Good, it's settled. You'll foster her on a trial basis." Alec continues to talk, launching into a long list of things they're going to need from the pet store, along with talk of vet visits and vaccinations. Things that are tangible and real. Theo tries to listen but his focus is splintered, his attention drawn back and forth from the kitten to Alec.

"When did you become so smart?"

"I have always been smart," Alec retorts. "Some people just never bothered to notice. I bet there's a lot about me you never noticed, Theodore."

Anxiety flutters in Theo's chest, the words easy, though the implications are anything but. Alec launches into a random story about someone on his team. The words hold little meaning, but as Theo continues to breathe in and out while focusing on the sound and cadence of Alec's voice, one thing becomes crystal clear: however temporary, Theo's life is about to change.

7 ALEC

"SO WE NEED to go to the pet store. Soon. Very soon."

Ever since they finished breakfast, Alec's been waiting for Theo to point out that he is still here, technically uninvited. Well, Theo is far too polite for his own good so he would never do that, but Alec knows how to read between the lines of what people do and don't say. Once he's overstayed his welcome it'll be obvious, even if Theo doesn't come out and say it.

The only way to avoid that happening is to keep them occupied. It's also true that they do, in fact, need to go to the store. He just neglects to point out that if Theo preferred, Alec could easily make him a list of things to buy, and he could do it alone. Well, what he really wants is for Theo to want him to help, but since that is unlikely, he settles for making himself needed.

"Do we?" Theo replies, his tone impossible to read.

"Obviously." Alec waves his hand in the air, stray Oreo crumbs falling onto his bare stomach. He brushes them onto the floor before lifting the package up and holding it out towards Theo. "Want one?"

"Those are technically mine, you know.

"Which is exactly why I'm offering." Alec grins. "I'm a very polite boy. Do you want one before I finish the pack off?"

"I thought you were on a strict meal plan from your nutritionist and—"

"Zip it," Alec interrupts.

Theo snaps his mouth shut, and Alec tries not to think too hard about why he likes knowing Theo will listen to him when he's bossy. His brothers never listen, the fuckers.

"Do you really hate it?" Theo asks a moment later.

"Hate what?" Alec asks, popping the second half of his Oreo into his mouth. He's pretty sure he knows what Theo means, but he hopes he's wrong.

"The meal plan? Jason said it's stressful."

"Jason has a big fucking mouth," Alec grumbles.

"He worries about you. You're his baby brother."

The words are probably meant to be comforting, but they're like sandpaper against Alec's heart, a harsh reminder of what he will always be to Theo.

"I can take care of myself just fine, thank you."

"He loves you. You know he'd do anything for you."

"Ugh, don't make me think sappy thoughts about Jason," Alec groans dramatically, dropping his head back on the couch. He really does love his brother, a stupid amount, but he's also a pain in the ass.

"Jason is the best."

A prickle of the same jealousy Alec used to feel when he was fifteen teases at the edge of his mind, and Alec hates that all it takes is a few hours with Theo to turn him back into a pathetic version of himself. He doesn't want to be jealous of Jason.

"We've established you have a giant fucking crush on Jason. Can we move on to the shopping list?"

Theo's thick eyebrows knit together. "I don't have a crush on Jason."

"Uh-huh," Alec says while shoving an Oreo in his mouth to hide the fact that his face is trying to form a smile without his permission. He has to remind himself that just because Theo doesn't have a crush on Jason now doesn't mean he never did, or that they never fooled around. Some people have sex without feelings. If Jason is telling the truth, and he always is, Theo certainly does. Which is fine. Alec's not gonna judge someone. It just makes him jealous as fuck because he doesn't want a one night stand or a meaningless fuck, he wants romance. A fact he intends to take to his grave, possibly with his virginity if he continues to be picky and turn guys down left and right.

Suddenly the cookie in his mouth tastes like concrete, and it's all he can do to choke it down. He doesn't like lying, and he rarely has to because people don't ask if he likes the thing he was born to do. They don't ask if he has fun playing anymore. They don't ask if he's happy with his career path. Everyone looks at Alec and sees a bright future. Alec seems to be the only one worried that future might burn him alive.

The Oreo lodges itself in his throat, and Alec barely manages to swallow it, fighting back a sigh as he reseals the package and tosses it onto the coffee table, no longer in the mood for cookies anymore. There's no one who can ruin Alec's good mood like his own brain.

Judging by the look on Theo's face it's obvious he's still waiting for an answer, so Alec tries to be as honest as he can without exposing everything. "No one ever likes being told what to do, do they?"

"Some people might," Theo says.

"Are you some people?" Alec asks, poking Theo's thigh with his toe. He's infinitely more comfortable having the tables turned on Theo.

"I like knowing what to do," Theo muses, "but I can't say I am particularly fond of being told exactly what to do."

"Imagine being told what you can eat and drink, when you're supposed to work out, when you can rest, and what extracurriculars you are and aren't allowed to do," Alec says before he can think better of it.

Holding his breath, he waits for Theo's probing questions or worse, for him to tell Alec it's the cost of getting what he wants. Rio settles on his stomach, and he focuses on her instead.

"That sounds hard."

Understanding is somehow worse than anything he expected. Leave it to Theo to be the one person who gets it.

"The cost of being talented. We can't all be a superstar," Alec jokes.

"Sure thing, hotshot." Theo pats Alec's ankle, and though it's a fleeting, playful touch, Alec's entire body burns, and he shoves his feet under Theo's thighs in the shameless hopes of more contact. Theo lifts one eyebrow but doesn't say anything. He doesn't touch Alec's ankles again, doesn't touch any part of him, but he also doesn't make any move to dislodge Alec's feet.

"So you mentioned the pet store. Does it matter which one?"

"Not really, except that the chain pet stores are shit. There's an independently owned one off Maple Street. They'd have everything we need, and then we're not supporting those corporate fuckers and their hamster breeding rings."

"I have no idea what a hamster breeding ring is, but I'm going to take your word for it."

"Good," Alec says, not in the mood to spiral about the unethical acquisition of rodents.

"You probably have better things to do today than spend it with me. I'm sure I could order whatever I need online."

"No, you can't," Alec protests, lifting himself up on his elbows. It startles Rio, who meows adorably. "Look at this baby. She needs all that stuff now. Well, realistically you could probably get away with just going to get her food right now. A lot of the other stuff she will need eventually, but online shopping is boring. Don't you think it's boring?"

"It's efficient."

"Efficient," Alec snorts. "What the fuck, are you eighty?"

"Twenty-nine, thanks so much," Theo retorts, leaning back. He rests his arms over the back of the couch, causing his sweater to stretch taut over his chest. Theo's a big boy, and that's evident in the swell of his pecs. More than once Alec has wondered how it's possible that Theo has no idea how sexy he is. It makes Alec want to bite something.

Wishing he had another Oreo to chomp on, or a piece of gum, he settles for tapping his fingers on the edge of the couch. "The pet store should be open by now. We could go."

"Together?"

"Unless you wanted to go figure out kitten shit on your own," Alec says, shoving his bony toes into Theo's ass.

"Little shithead," Theo grumbles, though he doesn't shove Alec away. "I definitely do not want to do it alone."

"Great, then it's a date."

"A date," Theo croaks.

Alec laughs, inordinately charmed by Theo's spluttering. "Don't worry, Mr. Allergic-to-commitment, I'm teasing you."

"Hey." The lines of Theo's handsome face draw together, surprise warring with something sharper. "I'm not allergic to commitment."

"Yes, you are," Alec retorts, withdrawing his feet from beneath Theo. Careful not to knock Rio over, he holds her to his chest as he turns, stretching his legs out before rising.

"Some of us don't need a significant other to complete us," Theo counters.

"'Course not. No one has to be in a relationship if they don't want to," Alec agrees, unruffled by Theo's tone. "But it doesn't change the fact that you are in fact allergic to being in a relationship."

Theo gapes. "I'm not allergic to relationships."

It would be funny if it weren't true, and if the truth didn't serve as another reminder of why Alec can never have Theo. Alec might be young, but he knows what he wants: a partner, a family, commitment. It's life's cruel idea of a joke that he wants it with a man who doesn't want those things, especially not with Alec. It should make it easier to get over Theo, but it doesn't. Not when Alec knows exactly why Theo is terrified of commitment.

"When was your last one?" Alec asks, proud of himself for managing to sound casual while inside his heart shatters into a million pieces. It's nothing new. Alec's heart is a puzzle; no matter how many times it's shaken apart and broken, it can be put back together again. Probably.

"Last what?"

"Relationship," Alec clarifies, mentally refitting the pieces back together. He's got to get tougher if he wants to be friends with Theo, and he does, which means it doesn't matter if some of his puzzle pieces get lost or ruined. When he stretches his arms overhead, he can't bite back the wince from his bruised ribs. "Damn, that's going to sting in practice tomorrow. By the way, can I borrow one of your shirts? Mine was ruined, obviously, and while I'm sure almost everyone would love the gift of seeing me half-naked this morning, I'm not really in the mood to get kicked out of the pet store for public indecency."

"That's not the point," Theo mumbles. "I've dated."

"The guy from REI?" Alec says, recalling the incident with painful clarity. He'd only learned about him afterward, but he'd hated him as much then as he does now. Anyone who hurts Theo lives on Alec's permanent bad side.

"Why do you know about Richard?" Theo gapes.

"Richard is a stupid name."

"He was stupid," Theo agrees with the faintest hint of a smile. "But that still doesn't answer my question about why you know about him."

"I know about Richard because Andrew was at Jason's when you came over upset, and then you know how he and Charlie are. I swear those two came out of the womb unable to keep a secret from each other. Once Charlie knew, he told me because, well, it doesn't matter why Charlie told me. The point is that it was two years ago, and you haven't dated anyone since. Just because he was a fucking asshole who didn't deserve you doesn't mean that all love will fail. I think love is always worth it, don't you?"

"I think it's sweet you think so. One day you'll find a nice boy to settle down with, and I hope it works out for you."

The words are probably supposed to be encouraging, but they're anything but.

"Maybe I don't want a nice boy."

"What does that mean?" Theo asks.

Alec's throat tightens. It means he wants a man. It means he wants Theo. "Nothing," Alec shrugs, kicking himself for letting the conversation get turned back around to him. "Can I borrow a shirt or what?"

"You know you can," Theo says. "The bedroom is down the hall and—"

"I know where your bedroom is, Theodore."

"Oh, right."

Without waiting for further permission, Alec lowers Rio to the floor, pleased when both the kitten and Theo trail after him.

Theo's bedroom is dark, the heavy curtains drawn, letting only a sliver of light through them. Alec flips on the light, hovering in the doorway to observe. He's seen Theo's bedroom only once before when he first moved in, and while it looks much the same, there are small touches that make it look more lived in. Obviously Theo wasn't expecting company, from the unmade bed to the stack of books on the nightstand. His dresser has a pile of glasses along with his favorite cologne. If Alec closes his eyes and breathes in deeply, he can almost smell the familiar musky scent. Theo's worn the same cologne since high school. At one point, Alec had even bought a bottle and hid it under his pillow. He'd been such a fucking idiot at sixteen.

Not wanting to be caught staring, he hurries to the closet and flings the door open. "Wow, Theodore, you have even more sweaters than I realized. Maybe you should open, like, a sweater museum."

"I like my sweaters."

"And they like you," Alec says, not waiting to find out if Theo catches the double meaning. "Where the hell are all the t-shirts? I know you must have some somewhere."

"They're in the top dresser drawer. I don't wear them

much," Theo says. He crosses the room and pulls open the drawer. It's wedged full of his college t-shirts and a few random plain v-neck ones. "Take your pick. They're all gonna be way too big."

"Yeah, yeah, rub it in, you giant." Alec laughs.

The novelty of being in Theo's room and being allowed to wear his clothing is not lost on Alec. This is basically every one of his teenage fantasies come true. He could just grab the first shirt he sees off the top of the pile and be done with it, but this is a chance he won't ever get again, and he's going to take it.

Pretending to be very interested in his choices, he rifles through the shirts, not at all surprised to find them messily folded and haphazardly shoved in the drawer. For all Theo likes neatness and orderliness in his work and personal life, he's not actually a very tidy person, something Alec remembers very well from the year Theo spent living with them. He was only nine then, but he definitely remembers Jason and Theo's messy-ass bedrooms. He figured a lot of stuff out about himself that year.

Fingering the worn cotton, he can't help but wonder when Theo wears these. He answered the door in a sweater, but there's no way he slept in it. Does he sleep in them? Or maybe he sleeps shirtless? That's a train of thought Alec needs to shut down quickly. Unfortunately, Alec's got a very vivid imagination, and his brain is immediately full of Theo's masculine body and light chest hair, of wide hips and soft thighs. It's enough to have him ready to throw himself back down into the river bottom. Thankfully, Theo is behind him and can't see Alec's flushed face.

Willing his overactive imagination and dick to calm down, he continues to rummage through the t-shirts, not even sure what he's looking for when his hands settle on a very familiar shirt. This t-shirt had starred in more than one of Alec's nighttime fantasies, which is maybe ridiculous since it's nothing more than a faded college t-shirt, but it's Theo's shirt. He still remembers going to visit Jason and Theo with his parents when they were at college, the way Theo ruffled his hair and pulled him in for a hug wearing this shirt.

The t-shirt definitely used to be black but is more of a dark gray now, the lettering of Theo's alma mater faded and peeling. Unlike Alec, who stuck close to home attending SLU which is in the same city where he was born and raised, Santa Leon—as much for the D1 soccer scholarship as it was being close to his family—Jason and Theo had gone to school four hours away. Together, of course, because those two never did anything alone. Alec had been relieved when they both moved back home after graduating. Even if things never returned to the way they'd been with Theo before, it'd been good to have him and Jason home.

The years they spent away at college had left Alec painfully lonely, and while his *abuela* had moved in with them when Alec was a freshman, she'd died less than two years later, leaving a gaping hole. Time has soothed the harshest edges of hurt, but Alec still feels more settled having all his family in the same city. He's not sure what he'd do if any of his brothers decided to move away again like they all did in college. It's funny to realize most of his friends went to college to find themselves or get away from their family, when Alec knows who he is best when he's around them. They drive him nuts, they worry too much, and they treat him like he's still a kid, but he loves them fiercely.

Pulling Theo's shirt close, he breathes in the familiar scent of him, his cologne wafting through the room along with fabric softener and something inherently just Theo. He might not be Alec's the way he wishes, but he's part of Alec's family, and Alec will do anything to keep it that way.

"Looking for something specific in there?"

Alec startles, realizing exactly how long he's been standing there.

"Yes, actually, I was hoping to uncover your deepest, darkest secrets," Alec retorts, tugging the shirt on. It's at least three sizes too big, the collar stretched out so it hangs half off his shoulder and exposes his collarbone. It's loose around the midsection, reminding Alec of just how much bigger Theo is than him. Fuck, Alec likes big boys. Big *men*. Older men. His jaw aches with the need to bite or suck, and it's all he can do to stay still and act normal.

"I'm afraid you're looking in the wrong drawer. I keep all my secrets locked away in the basement."

Alec's hand clenches in the shirt, and he tucks the front into his waistband near his hip just to give himself something to do.

"You don't have a basement," Alec points out, turning around to face Theo.

"I—" but Theo stops, licking his lips.

"What?"

Unexpectedly, Theo's hand settles at the center of Alec's chest, almost as if trying to feel the rise and fall of his chest or the steady beating of his heart. There, hidden beneath his walls of indifference, is the faintest hint of a smile, but it's there and gone in a flash when Theo drops his hand away.

"This used to be my favorite shirt. It was the first thing I ever bought at college. Made it feel real, that I'd actually done it and gone to college. I was gonna make something of myself, or at least that's what I thought."

Alec knows that already. It's exactly why he picked it out of all the others. He just can't say that out loud. "Guess I have a knack for knowing what's special." *You*, he thinks. *You're special.*

"I stopped wearing it because I was sure I'd wear it out and lose it. Probably sounds dumb to want to keep something and yet be too afraid to wear it."

"I'll wear a different one," Alec offers, already reaching behind his neck to tug it off when Theo stops him with a gentle touch. He gives Alec's wrist a squeeze before yanking his hand back and then promptly shoving both his hands into his pockets.

"You can keep it on."

There's something there, but Alec isn't sure what. He has the feeling he's walking a tightrope: push too hard and he will fall, play it too safe and risk falling anyway.

"It does look good on me," Alec smirks, trying to relieve whatever tension is simmering. "Or maybe you're just afraid of seeing me naked and falling in love with me."

"Is that a regular occurrence?" Theo asks in a way that's impossible to tell if he's being serious or teasing. That's the thing about Theo, he has a good sense of humor, but it's drier than Alec's and sometimes harder to parse. Theo is understated and quiet, even his humor.

"Oh, yeah. Everyone's a little bit in love with me." Alec winks. "I promise not to hold it against you if you do. I am pretty irresistible."

Theo laughs, shaking his head like Alec is ridiculous. The thing is, he *is* ridiculous. He knows he is, but he likes that about himself, even if other people sometimes find it too much. He likes being happy, and more than that he likes making his favorite people happy, too. It's an added bonus that all his positivity and outlandishness earns him all the attention his dopamine-deprived brain craves.

"Just remember I warned you, Theodore."

"I promise I won't fall in love with you, Alec," Theo says with a smile.

Alec offers him a smile in return, wondering how he can be so happy and so heartbroken all at once. "I know, Theo."

"I'm sure you don't have time for romance, anyway. You'll be too busy with your senior year and then, the way your parents tell it, you'll be off in the MLS becoming famous. Or more famous."

"I am not famous," Alec grumbles, fidgeting the hem of the shirt. He really wishes he'd brought a pack of gum on his run. If he doesn't get something in his mouth soon, he's going to crawl out of his skin.

"That's not the way Twitter tells it. I've seen—" Theo snaps his mouth shut.

Alec's gaze fixes on Theo. "Theodore Taylor James, did you look me up on Twitter?"

"Shit, you used my middle name. I feel like I should be going to the principal's office." Theo swallows, his Adam's apple bobbing as he rocks on his heels. "What are the odds I can get out of answering the question?"

"Absolutely fucking zero." Alec cackles, jabbing his finger into Theo's chest. He knows better than to read into it, but the knowledge that Theo had thought about him at all makes his insides feel all warm and mushy and disgusting in the best way possible. "Were you desperate to look at my handsome face? Did you miss me while I was in Mexico? Oh my god, you missed me, didn't you?"

"If I say no, would you believe me?"

"Nope." Alec grins, feeling the same kind of adrenaline high he gets after scoring a goal.

Theo snorts. "And if I say yes, will you let this go?"

Alec throws himself forward, draping himself dramatically over Theo. "Absolutely fucking not."

"I can't win with you." Theo doesn't sound particularly put out, which only spurs Alec on.

"You will never win against me, Theo. Admit that now, and our friendship will be smooth sailing."

"Are we friends?" The question is so unexpected and so earnest Alec can do nothing but gape for a few seconds. That is, until the words register.

"Are we—holy shit," Alec groans, wondering how he can be in love with someone so emotionally stunted. "Of course we're friends."

Theo seems to realize he's hurt Alec, his face deflating. The sight of it has Alec softening, his own hurt feelings paling in comparison to the idea of Theo feeling bad.

"Sorry, I didn't mean—"

"Yes, you did," Alec interjects. "But it's okay."

While they haven't been close in a long time, Alec still thought they were friends. Apparently Theo didn't, and that hurts a fuck ton more than Alec wants to let on. He spent years shoving his feelings down, hiding his hurt, and pretending everything was okay to get his friendship with Theo back.

"Don't look so upset, Theo, it's fine."

Theo's sigh is heavy. "You know a lot changed when, well, you know."

There is no need for Alec to ask for clarification because he knows exactly what Theo means, even if he wishes he didn't. There's a buzzing in his ears; his heart rattles in his chest, and his breakfast is dangerously close to coming back up. Never in Alec's short life has he experienced such a drastic change in moods, his high from a few seconds ago crashing hard and fast. Alec's entire life flashes before his eyes, and it's not pretty. They are absolutely not going to bring this up. Not over Alec's dead body.

"Did you know cats shed a lot?" Alec blurts, righting himself. He fusses with Theo's sweater, needing to do something with his hands. "This is going to be covered in cat hair soon."

"Cat hair." Theo looks perplexed by the change of conversation, but he doesn't try to divert it back. "I feel like you shouldn't tell me that. Aren't you supposed to tell me the sunshine and rainbow version of having a cat so I want to keep her?"

"Fuck that," Alec says. "Look, if you can't handle her, or she's too much, we should know now. It's fine, she's little and we can find her a good home. I'm not gonna lie and pretend it'll be easy because that wouldn't be fair to you or Rio. She's gonna shit on your stuff and pee on it too until she figures out the litter box. She's gonna get cat hair on everything you love, and she's either going to be a cuddly angel or an absolute demon. It's a crapshoot really. You're gonna spend a lot of money on vet bills and food, and you'll need to catify your place, and it might be really hard."

"Wow." Theo blinks.

Realizing he possibly went a little too hard, Alec clears his throat and looks towards Rio in the corner, where she's currently swatting at the curtain like it's her mortal enemy. Theo's eyes follow Alec's, a soft laugh falling from his lips when Rio knocks herself over, looking surprised and confused by the turn of events. She leaps, clinging to the curtain as she climbs halfway up.

"You'll also get a cat, which is pretty great if you ask me."

"She's climbing the wall."

"The curtain, technically."

"You and your 'technically.'" Theo snorts. "I remember when you were a kid, you'd argue with anyone and everyone over 'technically.'"

"Like I told you, I'm a fucking delight." Alec knocks his shoulder into Theo's gently. He can be cool and chill. He can. "Look, I know I was kind of intense, but that's just because I want you to be prepared and make the best decision for both of you. But the truth is pets are the best. They don't care about how your day went or how many goals you score or what your GPA is. You don't have to make small talk or try to win their affection or pretend to be anything but yourself, and they still always love you unconditionally. They're not gonna leave you or change their mind. They're just there, always."

Theo's looking at him like he's said too much and maybe he has. Alec's always running his mouth, and he wishes he could stop, but so far he hasn't figured out a way to shut himself up that doesn't involve running away.

"Are we talking about you or me?"

Warning bells sound in Alec's mind. Yup, he definitely said too much. "You, obviously," Alec answers, unable to explain how it's possible for him to be desperate for Theo's attention and yet want to run away screaming from it when he dares to ask anything that feels like it might be exposing or personal. "If it turns out you don't love having a cat, that's okay, too. This isn't permanent."

"Right, trial run. Fostering."

"Exactly."

"I can do that."

"Good man, Theodore. I knew you could." Alec moves across the room, carefully pulling Rio off the curtains. She flails a bit before she realizes that it's Alec who grabbed her and begins to paw at him instead. It makes his chest ache, and he brings her up to his face, feeling her silky fur against his cheek. It's kind of ridiculous how attached to her he already is, but Alec's never been good at keeping his heart or mouth in check.

"You still want to do this?"

"And waste this sexy outfit staying here? Please."

"We can't have that." Theo laughs. "You ready now then?"

"I'm always ready," Alec answers, anything but.

8 THEO

"THAT REALLY ISN'T SAFE," Theo says.

"But I'm comfortable."

"Comfortable doesn't mean safe. You're gonna get hurt if we get into an accident."

"I didn't know you cared so much about me." Alec stretches his legs out, wiggling his socked toes against the windshield. "How about we make a deal? I'll stay here nice and comfortable, and you don't get into an accident."

"Statistically speaking, ninety-four percent of accidents are caused by driver error, so even if I don't make any, the odds of someone else doing it are still high enough that I would feel better if you took your legs down."

"What if I don't want to?" Alec asks, stroking Rio's back. He really does look comfortable, legs stretched out and all but melted into Theo's seat, wearing Theo's shirt. It's a little disorienting, which is the only explanation for why Theo's pulse feels like it's racing. When he'd picked Alec up from the airport, he'd thought it was dangerous, but he had pushed it aside because Alec was a grown-up who could make his own choices. Suddenly the consequences of those choices feel closer. Something has changed, and the uncomfortable feeling in Theo's chest that demands he makes sure Alec is safe is louder than ever.

"Well, you need to do it anyway, because I said so."

"Oh, that sounded bossy." Alec cackles. "Theodore, are you trying to boss me around? Gonna tell me what to do, big guy?"

"I don't think anyone in the world could tell you what to do."

"Damn right." He turns his head, watching Theo with unmasked mirth, and Theo's heart lodges itself in his throat. Alec looks relaxed and comfortable, and Theo's hands tighten on the steering wheel as he takes their exit.

Theo sighs. "If we did get into an accident—"

"You're too safe of a driver. That won't happen."

"I said *if*, smartass."

"Oh, *if*. Talk dirty to me, Theodore."

"I'm gonna get into an accident if you don't stop that."

"Stop what?" Alec asks in an entirely too innocent voice. "I'm not doing anything."

Theo's cheeks heat. "Has anyone ever told you that you're a handful?"

"In or out of the bedroom?" Alec asks.

If Theo didn't already know Alec was a virgin, he would've been absolutely certain that Alec was serious right now, his tone giving nothing away. It raises the question of how much of Alec's brashness is real and how much is false bravado. Before he can reply, Alec is speaking again.

"To answer your question, yes," Alec says. "I've been informed I'm the perfect size for two hands or a—"

"Want music?" Theo interrupts, pretty sure if Alec finishes that sentence he might actually crash.

"Sure."

Theo grabs the auxiliary cord, passing it to Alec. "You can plug in your phone and put on whatever you like."

"Wow, I didn't know we were at this stage in our relationship. Way to make a boy swoon, Theodore."

Theo keeps his eyes firmly on the road, refusing to look at Alec because he knows if he does, his entire face might burst into flames. If he'd thought teenage Alec was a showoff, it was nothing compared to Alec now. The difference six years makes is everything.

"I don't have any emo sweater playlists, so this will have to do," Alec announces, putting on a loud, fast tempo song Theo's never heard.

"I'm not emo, fuck you."

"Oh, Theo cursed! Say shit next."

"Jesus Christ." Theo laughs.

"That works, too. In fact, maybe double points for taking the Lord's name in vain."

"Does that work if you're an atheist?"

"Good point. I'm more of an agnostic, so I guess you can have half a point."

"I take it back. I want my half a point back."

"Fine, one point for a fuck and two points for a Jesus Christ. Happy?"

"Very," Theo answers, unsure why he wants Alec's imaginary points.

They're going to be there soon, maybe five minutes, and he doesn't want it to end. He flips on his left blinker, merging into the lane with the most traffic. If Alec notices, he says nothing.

"Sing with me," Alec pleads, turning the volume up.

"I can't sing," Theo says.

"Me either. What's your point?" Alec taps his fingers on his thighs, drumming out the same quick beat as the song.

He catches Theo's eye and grins, the only warning before he starts singing along, off-key and full of exuberance. When Theo cracks a smile, Alec whoops, singing even louder. It's ridiculous. Alec is ridiculous.

"Sing with me," Alec requests again.

Alec tips his head towards Theo's, his big eyes trained on him as his curls fall sideways. As a kid and teenager, his hair had been kept incredibly short. Theo hadn't even known Alec had curly hair until he'd started growing it out in high school. Even then, it'd been wild and wavy. It's clear he's been learning to manage it because the curls are soft and thick now, tumbling into his eyes when Alec leans all the way across the center console to rest his cheek on Theo's shoulder.

To his surprise, Alec's hair smells sweet like flowers. Theo's mind conjures up an image of Alec running through the grass, the scent of summer and sun surrounding him.

"Please, Theo. For me."

He's using those damn puppy eyes on Theo, and it sends all the blood rushing south. There was a time when Theo was the only person who could resist that look, but things changed. When Alec bats his thick eyelashes at him, Theo knows he's a goner. Alec is the embodiment of everything warm and bright, his entire personality written in goddamn sunshine, and there's not a chance in hell Theo can tell him no.

"Fine, I'll sing."

Normally he doesn't sing in front of people. In fact, he can count on one hand the number of times he's sung in front of Jason, and each of those were only because he was drunk.

"Yes," Alec crows. "That's my boy."

For some reason, those words have Theo's knuckles

turning white on the steering wheel. "You have to put on a song I know though," Theo says. "Unless you want me to just sing the alphabet or something."

"As charming as I'm sure that would be, I'll have to pass. Let me see what else I have."

Theo focuses on the movement of traffic around them, eyes flickering from his rear view to side mirrors to Alec, whose tongue is protruding from his lips as he scrolls through his phone looking for a song. In his lap, Rio appears to have fallen asleep, apparently as enamored with Alec as Theo is becoming. It's a problem. A big problem, and one he doesn't want to solve.

"Ah-ha. Perfect."

The second the song starts playing, Theo's lips curl up in a smile.

"Livingston. Is that just for me?"

Alec neither confirms nor denies his song choice, and instead rolls the window down to let the summer air whip through his hair. This side of town is always cooler because of its proximity to the sea, close enough Theo can smell the salt on the air as it enters the car. Despite the fresh air, Theo finds himself warmer than ever, wishing he'd put a shirt on under his sweater so he could take it off. He settles for shoving the sleeves up to his elbows, exposing his forearms and offering him a modicum of skin to cool off.

The familiar cadence of a violin hits, and Theo takes a steadying breath. Ignoring the prickle of anxiety that comes with drawing any kind of attention to himself, he opens his mouth and sings. He starts quietly at first, his voice barely above a whisper. Then he hears Alec belt out the chorus. He's absolutely horrible and doesn't seem to care, and somehow it makes Theo feel braver.

When the last chorus begins, he sings louder. Not quite

as loud as Alec, but then again, no one is ever as loud as Alec. As soon as the song ends, Alec puts on another one. Whether by coincidence or choice, he's put on Theo's current favorite song. Without overthinking it, he sings along with Alec again, his voice loud enough to be heard over the radio this time.

Outside the car, traffic whizzes by, but inside the car, there's nothing but Alec and Theo singing as the breeze whips through their hair. It occurs to Theo he hasn't felt so happy or free in a long damn time. Something about this moment feels like a photograph come to life: Alec's head tipped back and his curls everywhere, the scent of summer in the air, and the freedom of the open road. With every word he sings, the smile on Theo's face grows, and he allows himself to get caught up in the melody while he turns into the shopping center. His own voice drops to barely above a whisper, unable to stomach the idea of the people walking to and from their cars around them being able to hear them. Alec suffers no such self-consciousness, continuing to belt out the last of the chorus at a frankly impressive and deafening volume while Theo parks.

He chooses a spot halfway back, the shade from the tree beside them offering a refuge from the sun as he rolls the windows up and shuts off the engine. Theo takes a few slow, deep breaths, unused to singing out loud. When he reaches for the door handle, he realizes how quiet it's gotten and turns to find Alec staring at him like he's grown a second head.

"What?"

"You can sing. You said you couldn't sing."

"I mean, technically anyone can sing. You just talk out loud but with a different pitch and cadence."

"Fuck you." Alec laughs. "You know what I mean. You're good. Really good."

The compliment has Theo flushing. He's never been good with accepting praise. "Just singing along to the radio."

"Well, whatever you call it, I could listen to you all day," Alec says. "You're singing to me when we drive home."

"No, I'm not."

"Yes, you are."

"No, I'm not," Theo objects, unsure why he's fighting it. He liked singing with Alec. It wasn't a hardship, it was fun, so he isn't sure why he's being so stubborn.

A little voice in the back of his mind whispers, *yes, you do. You don't let yourself want things. You don't let yourself enjoy them.* Thinking that makes Theo's entire body flush with a buzz of anxiety. He enjoys things. He likes things. He's happy.

Rio meows, climbing up towards Alec's shoulder.

"I know your Daddy is so stubborn, but he's gonna give in, baby. Just you watch."

The words do nothing to calm the waves of anxiety crashing in Theo's mind. When he was a kid, the Kings used to take him with them on beach days. Theo was never a very strong swimmer. The twins and Jason had all taken swimming lessons at the Y, but Theo had learned to swim awkwardly from summers at the high school pool, or times when the waves weren't too strong at the beach. Sometimes, though, the currents were strong, too big, and the twins and Jason used to take their boogie boards out and ride them. They'd always looked so excited to face something dangerous, while Theo would stand close to the shore, letting the waves crash around his ankles.

When he got older, he used to let Jason drag him out. He never got to be a better swimmer, but he got stronger and taller, which made the sea seem less scary. At least as long as he didn't go out as far as Charlie or Andrew, who used to goad each other into trying to see who could swim out the furthest. It'd backfired when Andrew had almost drowned when he was fifteen.

Theo had been there. Thirteen years old, watching lifeguards drag Andrew out unconscious. He'd gotten caught in the undertow that day. Andrew had been the best swimmer of all of them, and yet he'd almost drowned. Theo had stood there watching while Charlie screamed and Jason tried to keep a tiny, wailing Alec away from his big brother who was immobile on the sand because their parents had gone to the little food cart down the street to get everyone snow cones. The chaos had been terrifying. Theo still remembers the way the cherry red snow cone stained the sand when Mr. King dropped it and ran to his son.

Theo had looked down at the water lapping around his ankles and wondered if Andrew was going to die. He knew that no matter how safe things looked, the smallest thing could pull you under.

"You're daydreaming about saying yes to me, aren't you?" Alec asks, dragging Theo back to the present.

He startles, looking around at their surroundings. "Not exactly," he whispers.

Alec makes a humming sound as he swings open his door, turning so his long legs are halfway out then pauses, tipping his head back to look at Theo. Alec smirks, his curls tumbling back. He's got freckles all along his jaw, and the shirt he's wearing—Theo's shirt—hangs loose around his throat, exposing the line of his sharp collarbones.

"You're going to sing to me again, Theodore."

"How are you so sure?" Theo croaks.

"I just know." Alec smirks, shooting Theo a wink before

hopping out of the car with Rio, leaving him no other choice but to trail after them both. He shoves his keys and wallet into his pocket and hurries after Alec. For someone so much smaller, he's quick on his feet, and he's halfway across the parking lot by the time Theo catches up with him.

"What is it, a race?" Theo asks.

"If it was, you would've lost."

Theo isn't sure if he's turned on by Alec's cocky attitude or if he wants to laugh. Possibly a little bit of both, which is unexpected to say the least. There are people Theo enjoys, mostly only Jason, and then there are people he gets turned on by. There is usually no overlap, which is possibly why Theo's few attempts at dating over the years have failed so miserably. He doesn't find it hard to find people attractive, but he'd gone out of his way to pick people he wouldn't have picked as friends to keep things easy.

Nothing about Alec is easy, and while he should prob-ably hate it, he doesn't, not even a little bit.

"Considering I'm standing right next to you, obviously not."

"Not for long," Alec replies, taking off. It's hard to tell if Alec is trying to take it easy on him or if he's sore from his fall, because even though he's running, there's some-thing stilted about his movements. What Theo lacks in speed he makes up for in having really long legs, and he catches up to Alec just in time to catch sight of his profile and the pain on his face. The expression is there and gone, replaced with an easy smile by the time Theo's stop-ping beside Alec in front of the large double doors. Before he can get a chance to ask Alec about it, he's holding Rio out, much the same as he had when Theo had first opened the front door this morning and found them standing there.

"Look at her, Theo. Isn't she the cutest thing you've ever seen?"

As if to prove his point, he presses his face into her side and rubs his cheek into her fur, prompting the kitten to turn and attack Alec's curls.

"She's cute," Theo laughs, grateful Alec is too distracted to notice his flush.

It's painfully embarrassing at how equally taken he is with the man holding the kitten. Alec's cheeks are flushed pink and his smile so earnest and uninhibited that it robs some of the air from Theo's lungs. He can't imagine living life with your feelings just out there all the time for anyone to see. How can Alec stand to be perceived so often? To have people just know how he feels? It makes him vulnerable. And brave.

Thinking about that bravery sparks a train of thought Theo isn't sure he likes. What if he's not attracted to Alec? What if instead he's jealous of him? It would make more sense than anything else. Somehow the thought isn't very comforting. Alec is a great guy who has worked his ass off to get where he is, and despite his easy-going demeanor, he's endured some stuff that would've made other people lose their spark. Being jealous of his happiness and light, of how easy he makes life look, kind of makes Theo feel like a dick.

"Let's go, Theodore. Little Miss needs food."

"Just for the record, I have no idea what we need. You're going to have to be in charge, sorry."

"Oh, no," Alec sighs dramatically. "Me be the boss? Whatever will I do? How on earth will I cope? This is a lot of responsibility and work. I'm not sure if I can handle the pressure. I might crumble. I might—"

"Alright, alright." Theo snorts. "Point made."

"Is it, though?" Alec grins, disentangling one of the

kitten's claws from his hair and pulling her back towards his chest. "If not, I can keep going."

"I have no doubt you could."

The thought makes Theo strangely happy. His life is quiet, at least when Jason isn't around, and he's always liked it that way. Or so he thought. He likes this time with Alec too, noisy and unplanned as it is.

"As long as we're both in agreement, I win and I'm the boss. By the way, did you know cats have thirty-two muscles in each ear?" Alec announces, hip checking Theo. He leaves Theo no time to actually reply before he's moving into the store. "Come on, Theo, we don't have all day."

Theo scurries after him for the second time that day, doing as he's told and withdrawing a shopping cart from the row of them that line the front door. Theo's eyes trail all over the store, the bright lights and sparkling white linoleum floor at odds with the shelves, overflowing with animal supplies. There's an entire aisle dedicated to birds, another for reptiles and even one for small rodents. Theo's senses are overwhelmed by the scent of hay for the horse feed area on the right, and something else that Alec assures him is merely pet food smell. Whatever it is, he's not a fan and he wrinkles his nose, sticking close to Alec, who meanders through the store like it's a second home.

Forty minutes later, the cart is full of more things than seems possible for something as small as Rio. There are the basics like the pet bed, though, why Alec insisted on getting one that looks like a banana is beyond Theo. There's also food of various kinds, including wet food and formula, both of which Alec insists are necessary, along with a litter pan, a pooper-scooper because this is apparently going to be Theo's life now, and finally, food dishes. All of those things had been easy enough, but then they'd come for the collar last, which is where they'd been stuck for the last twenty minutes.

"Do you like the blue or the green?" Alec asks, holding up two options.

Five minutes ago, he'd been debating between a pink one with a bell, and a red one with soccer balls. The soccer one had nearly made it into the cart, but then Alec appeared to have some kind of internal argument with himself and put them both back, leaving them at square one again.

"Blue seems fitting."

"That might be too on the nose though," Alec sighs, as if the color choice of the collar is life or death.

"You know you can just get both? Or buy one and change it later."

"No, I can't. It's your kitten. I'm not gonna just change her collar because I want to."

"And yet, you're the one picking it out now," Theo points out. "You picked out the food bowls and the bed too."

"Shit," Alec curses. "You're right. You pick."

Theo frowns. He hadn't meant to earn himself this responsibility. Rio might technically be his, but he still has no idea what to do with her and feels a lot safer with Alec holding her while making all the decisions.

"You can pick," he tries.

"No, you're right, she's yours. You should pick."

Alec takes a step away from the row of collars, not at all subtly nudging Theo forward. When Theo doesn't move, he presses his hand into the center of Theo's lower back and gives a shove, surprisingly strong for his size.

"No pressure, but you're basically choosing her future."

"It's just a collar."

"Nope, it's her entire future." He says it so seriously

Theo isn't sure if he's being hyperbolic or not. "This could determine her future vibes forever. When I was born, my baby blanket was covered with soccer balls and look where that got me."

"To be fair, that blanket also had tennis balls and footballs," Theo grins, reminded of a much smaller version of Alec who used to drag that blanket all over the house, including into Jason's room to try and play with them.

"See, ball obsessed. It's like the universe took one look at me when I was born and they knew I'd be gay. I fucking love balls. Why are you blushing? You're a sexually active bisexual man, don't you like balls?"

All the blood in Theo's body rushes directly to his cheeks. "I really don't think you're supposed to ask me that in the middle of a pet store."

"Does that mean there's somewhere I can ask you that?" Alec is the least bashful virgin Theo's ever met.

"I genuinely can't tell if you're joking or serious."

"I'm always serious," Alec deadpans. "Unless I'm not."

"That isn't helping in the least," Theo sighs, pulling his sweater down over his hands. He toys with the wrist, the feeling of knotted yarn beneath his fingers familiar enough to ground him. "Do you actually want to know what I like?"

The question sits heavy in his gut as he waits, unsure why he cares what the answer is. He doesn't want to like Alec like that. He can't like Alec like that, so why does he want Alec to like him? He's spent years making sure Alec got over his crush. Is that what this is? Is he being a selfish prick wanting attention he isn't willing to give back?

"Wouldn't you like to know." Alec grins in a way that has Theo's insides twisting up. It's hot, sudden and burns, and Theo is a teenager again, trying to subtly check out guys in the locker room, worrying he's going to get punched in the face or lose his best friend. Probably not jealousy, then, Theo thinks as he tries to tamper down the flare of arousal. *Try* being the operative word. Alec really is devastatingly pretty, with his full lips, golden skin, dark eyes and freckles. He's got so many freckles, and Theo wants to brush the collar of the too-big shirt Alec is wearing aside and trace the ones near his collarbone with his fingers and– oh no.

Oh no.

"Like I was saying," Alec continues, blissfully unaware of Theo's life threatening to fall apart all around him. This could determine her entire future."

"No pressure." Theo groans.

"I believe in you. Also, I gotta piss." Rio is unexpectedly pressed against his chest, Alec's fingers skimming his sweater. The contact is brief, leaving him with his hands full of kitten and on unsteady feet as the realization sits heavy and loud in his mind.

He likes Alec. He *likes* him. He can't even recall the last time he had an honest to god crush on someone. High school probably, and even then he was smart enough not to do anything about it.

"Pick a collar," Alec reminds him without bothering to turn around.

Unfortunately, the world does not steady as Alec gets further away, likely because Theo can't take his eyes off Alec's backside and the movement of his hips and thighs. It's only when Alec has rounded the end of the aisle and disappeared from sight that Theo's gaze snaps down to the kitten in his arms. She appears equally confused by the turn of events, clearly not as comfortable with Theo as she is with Alec, judging by the way she half-meows and half-hisses while she tries to crawl away.

"I know how you feel," Theo mutters.

Desperate for a distraction, he turns to the little wall of collars. When it'd been Alec choosing, he hadn't really paid too much attention, but now that it's all on him he does, gaze roaming over the selection. It should be simple, but nothing in Theo's life has been simple since Alec came back into it.

As if to echo his thoughts, his phone rings, Theo doesn't even need to pull it out of his pocket to know who is calling him on a Saturday morning. The phone rings several more times, and Theo debates not answering, because he isn't in the right frame of mind to make small talk or explain what the hell he's doing when he barely knows himself. On the fifth ring he pulls it out, knowing it's Jason and also knowing there's nothing his best friend hates more than being ignored.

Swiping open the call, he holds it to his ear, wishing Rio would stop attacking his sweater and praying she doesn't loudly meow while he's on the phone.

"Thought you were gonna make me go to voicemail, dude."

"Nah, I just couldn't find my phone." This is a blatant lie, but better than the alternative, which is admitting he wasn't sure he wanted to talk to his best friend. He already knows he's an asshole for catching feelings for Jason's brother. He doesn't need to add on to the pile of misdeeds. "What's up?"

"Do I need a reason to call my favorite person in the entire world?" Jason asks.

The ease with which he says it somehow lessens and worsens the invisible rope around Theo's heart. He can't act on this crush with Alec. He can't risk his friendship with Jason. Nothing in the world is worth that.

"Let me guess, you just woke up and realized you forgot to grocery shop last night, and you have no food but didn't want to eat breakfast alone."

"Fuck off," Jason laughs.

"I'm right and we both know it."

"Fuck you." There's some more cursing and strange background noise as if Jason dropped the phone. Probably did, knowing him. "So are you coming?"

"Coming where?"

"To breakfast, asshole."

"I already ate."

"Then have a coffee."

Rio's tiny claws unravel one of the threads of Theo's sweater. It's fitting, since Theo feels like his entire life is on the precipice of unraveling with one small revelation.

"I, uh," Theo pauses, staring down at Rio and wishing she would stop staring back. "I'm just running some errands."

"I could come run them with you," Jason offers. "I need to get out of the house and get groceries today anyway. There's jack shit in my house to eat."

The offer isn't exactly unexpected. Though they don't always make an actual plan, inevitably he and Jason see each other most weekends. Even though Jason has a lot of other friends from work, he always makes time for Theo. That, and Jason hates being alone, which means he'll often follow Theo around on his errands, or watch tv at Theo's house if he has a report to work on and is too busy to go anywhere. Theo's never minded, but he's never been with Alec before. Jason would probably be delighted to come buy kitten supplies and meet Rio, and the fact that Theo doesn't want Jason to be part of this yet has guilt churning in his gut.

For the first time in Theo's entire life, he's got a secret he doesn't want to share with Jason, and he has no idea what that means. He wants to tell himself he's protecting his friendship with Alec while it strengthens, but it's yet another lie. The truth is the one it protects is Theo.

"I can't, Jason."

The line goes quiet, making Theo's ear rush. "You've got someone at your house, don't you?"

"No," Theo answers too quickly.

Jason cackles. "Dude, if you're with a hookup, you just need to tell me. You know I'm not gonna judge."

"I'm not with a hookup," Theo hisses, looking around the aisle. He's still alone, with no sign of Alec. "I'm alone."

He doesn't feel too guilty about that one since it's not entirely untrue. Alec is in the bathroom so he is alone, sort of. If you don't count the kitten in his arms, which he really doesn't want to.

"Uh-huh." Jason's tone makes it clear he doesn't believe him.

"I'm not with anyone, I swear."

"Oh, so you just don't want my company then." Jason laughs, but the joke is too close to home for Theo, who recalls being eight years old and having Jason hold his hand. He thinks of being twelve and Jason letting him sleep in his bed because that's what brothers do, even though they weren't really. It might not be a romantic love, but he loves Jason, and he doesn't want to hurt him.

"I was thinking we could go hit a club tonight," Theo blurts.

"A club?" Jason perks up like a dog being given a bone. "We haven't gone out to one of those in months."

"I know. We should go, get some drinks and relax."

"Is 'relax' code for wild sex? Do you need a wingman?

I'll be your wingman. What are you feeling? Straight club or gay club? The guys love me at a gay club. Please say gay club, please say gay club."

"Are you sure you're straight?" Theo laughs.

"No attention-shaming, asshole. A guy can wanna have someone buy him a drink and tell him he's a snack without it meaning anything," Jason protests. "Besides, I'm not in the mood to hook up."

It's on the tip of his tongue to ask if Jason is still upset about his ex, although calling her that might be giving her too much credit. She'd let Jason date her for a few months, take her out and buy her things, and then dumped him when she found someone new. Jason deserves better, but every time Theo tries to bring it up, Jason changes the subject. If he wants to go to a club, then that's exactly where Theo will take him.

"Well, I definitely want to hook up."

He's already lied to Jason once today, one more won't hurt. Maybe if he says it out loud, it'll become true. Besides, maybe getting out and finding someone to scratch an itch will rid him of this ridiculous crush on Alec.

9 ALEC

"WELL, I definitely want to hook up."

Alec's feet stop moving, the lightness in his chest dissipating. When he was a kid, Charlie bought him a balloon at the fair. He told him it might pop, but Alec hadn't cared; he'd loved that balloon. It had been blue. Alec's favorite color is blue. Blue like the sky on a warm summer day. Blue like the endless sea. Blue like Theo's eyes.

That balloon didn't pop. It stayed in Alec's room until the helium was gone, and it shriveled up and collapsed on itself. Alec had tried to hide it under his pillow, but someone threw it away. He wishes someone would throw away his heart.

"Yeah, I'm sure," Theo continues, pitching his voice lower. Alec doesn't want to hear anymore, yet his feet drag him towards the end of the aisle anyway. Maybe this is what he needs—to have his heart popped in a way his balloon hadn't.

Part of him wonders who Theo is talking to, but the other part already knows. It's Jason. It has to be. Theo is too introverted and antisocial to have more than one friend, and there's no way he'd go clubbing with anyone else.

"Yeah, sure. You can pick me up at eight. We can hit The Cherry."

Alec's frown deepens. The Cherry is the only queer club in Santa Leon and a well-known hookup spot for Theo, which makes sense given what Theo just told Jason, yet it still makes bile rise up Alec's throat. This is why you can't be friends with people you're in love with. Because they go and do things they have every right to do, and it makes you want to lay down and cry.

"I told you I'm not with anyone, idiot."

Theo laughs, and Alec's heart shrivels up and dies the way it should have a long time ago.

Giving himself an extra moment, Alec wills his breathing to calm down and schools his features into nonchalance while he waits for Theo to get off the phone. It's only once he's heard Theo say goodbye that Alec smooths his hands down his belly, fingering Theo's shirt once before forcing his feet to move. He is under no illusions about whose fault this is—his own. If Theo had any inkling of the kind of pain he was causing, he would probably do everything to stop it like last time. The problem is, the only way to end this pain is to not be around Theo, and years of that did nothing to dull his crush. Sure, there were months where Alec let himself try to move aside and forget, but all it would take was Jason talking about Theo or Theo coming over for a family dinner, and it all came rushing back.

At this point, Alec has accepted he's probably going to spend his entire life in love with someone who doesn't return those feelings, and he's fine with it. Mostly. Except for times when he's reminded Theo's out there hooking up.

The idea of him fucking other people makes Alec feel like puking, but he knows it's not his business. He has no right to be this upset, which is why he puts a lid on those feelings.

The only way to make sure Theo doesn't run away from him again is to never let on how big his own feelings are. The one upside is Alec is great at faking shit, and has an entire six years under his belt pretending he's no longer in love with Theo. He can totally do this.

Resolved to hide his feelings until he dies, he turns the corner and halts at the end of the aisle when he catches sight of Theo talking to Rio.

"We've got to pick one. Alec is gonna be back soon. Which one do you like?"

Theo holds her out as if she might pick a collar off the display and the fucking balloon in Alec's chest inflates. He loves this stupid idiot so fucking much.

"I know I took a while in the bathroom, but I didn't realize it was long enough for you to learn to speak cat."

Theo startles, pulling Rio back against his chest. "You scared the shit out of me."

"I have that effect on people." Alec smirks, hating the way his own smile grows when Theo laughs. "Did you miss me?"

"Yes, Alec, I missed you terribly while you were gone for an entire five minutes. How did you know?"

"Aw, you timed my absence. How sweet. I get it, life is very boring without me, isn't it?"

"It's quieter."

"Like I said, boring." He waits to see if Theo will say anything else, but when he doesn't, Alec moves to his side, letting his arm brush up against Theo's. "How about we change tactics? You're overthinking this."

"One, how do you know I'm overthinking it? And two, you literally told me it was important."

"One, I've met you, Theodore. Two, I was giving you shit."

"Oh." Theo's shoulders slump forward while Rio tries to force her way out of Theo's arms to get to Alec. "I think she likes you better."

"She has impeccable taste."

The laugh he hopes for never comes, and it's clear Theo's doing his anxiety spiral thing. Alec pulls his bottom lip between his teeth while he thinks, unconsciously leaning his side against Theo. He holds his breath when he notices that Theo doesn't pull away, so neither does he.

"Remember that summer we went to Yosemite?"

"I do," Theo agrees. "That was what, ten years ago?"

"Eleven," Alec supplies. "We stopped at the gift shop on the way out after two weeks of camping, and we were looking at souvenirs. Charlie and Andrew and Jason were all loading up on shirts and hats and shit. But do you remember what you bought?"

"Uh, not really," Theo says, rubbing a hand over the back of his neck.

"A postcard. Mom came and asked you if there was anything else you wanted, and you told her it was all you needed, but there was this hat you kept looking at. It was brown with a mountain range on it, and you tried it on when no one was looking. I saw you smile and then put it back. You never pick things for yourself."

Theo's cheeks have the faintest pink to them, the rise and fall of his chest slow. "Why the hell do you remember that, Alec?"

Because I've always seen you, even when you tried to hide. Because I know you. Because I love you.

"Pick which one you like. Don't worry about what I said or what I was looking at. Just choose the one that you like the best, okay?"

"Alec."

Alec's heart beats hard in his chest. Theo's arm is warm against his own. Rio licks his hand, and Alec wordlessly counts to five before he speaks. "I know your favorite color is brown. They don't have brown, but they have tan."

"It is brown," Theo agrees, reaching out for one of the collars on the bottom row, a darkish tan one. It's simple, plain, and exactly what Alec would've expected him to pick. "This one is good."

"Good choice, Theodore. Now let's finish shopping."

ALEC TRUDGES up the front stairs to his apartment, pausing outside the front door. Someone put a welcome mat out while he was gone that says 'Go Away'. It makes him laugh, some of his tension dissipating. Of course, that same tension returns tenfold while he digs out his keys and thinks about the missed messages from their group chat and from Riley this morning about his disappearing act. He half expects the third degree the moment he steps inside, which he probably deserves for vanishing for ten hours without a note or a reply, but that doesn't mean he's looking forward to it.

Steeling himself for a telling off, he pushes open the front door. He's surprised by the relative quiet, aside from the blasting coming from the television. Hunter is sitting on their couch playing some video game where you shoot things. Alec can't remember the name despite Hunter telling him at least twice already. Alec's never been a fan of video games. Way too much sitting for someone with as much energy as him. Hunter, Logan and Riley all play them a lot though, so he might want to learn to at least understand what's happening just so he isn't lost.

He's barely got his key hung on the little key hook and his shoes on the shoe rack before Hunter looks up, eyes snapping from the tv to Alec's face.

"I know I'm gorgeous, but it's rude to stare."

To his surprise, Hunter doesn't flip him off or laugh. Instead, he blushes, a reaction Alec has absolutely no bandwidth to try and examine.

"What the hell happened to your face?"

"Nothing," Alec says, crossing the room and flopping down onto the edge of the couch opposite Hunter. Now that he's far away from Theo, the fatigue of the day is catching up with him. He's sore in places he doesn't want to be, his lip is throbbing, and most of all, his chest aches. Glad as he is to not face a lecture, he kind of wishes Antonio or Riley were here.

Hunter lifts an eyebrow. "Doesn't look like nothing."

Were it anyone else he might be honest, but Alec still doesn't know Hunter that well, and while he's definitely warming up to the guy, the last thing he wants to do is feel even more exposed than he already does. "Nah," Alec shrugs, closing his eyes and tipping his back on the couch, trying to come up with a distraction. "Where is everyone?"

"Riley came by to see why you were ignoring him, and then he and Antonio went to the store to get cereal and milk."

A fresh wave of guilt rolls in. He shouldn't be ghosting his closest friends. He debates texting them but decides to wait until they get home. This isn't a conversation he wants to have over text, and knowing his friends it's not a conversation they're going to let him avoid.

"Is Logan still at practice?"

"I think so," Hunter answers, unpausing the game. Despite the sound of things exploding, Alec doesn't bother opening his eyes. "Sports sound exhausting. You guys are nuts. You can't do jack shit because you've got practice or training, or you're tired from one of those. I don't know how you do it."

Alec hums, not sure either. It's only been a week since he moved back onto campus, and he already feels like he's gonna crumble. He can't imagine adding a full schedule on top of all the practice, not to mention the games. There was a time where nothing made Alec feel more alive than being on the field, but those days are fewer and farther between. He'd felt an inkling of it playing in Mexico, chasing the ball for fun and not because scouts or a coach was watching him. This semester isn't for fun. This semester has to be perfect. He needs to maintain his scholarship, keep his grades up and—

"You're sighing a lot for someone who has nothing going on."

Alec exhales again, louder this time, grinning when Hunter slams a couch pillow into his head. "So what exactly are you playing again? Donkey Kong?"

"Are you fucking shitting me?" Hunter levels him with a look that could kill. "It's Call of Duty."

"My mistake." Alec laughs, already in a better mood. "Let me try."

"You'll tank my K/D ratio." Hunter scoots sideways, trying to keep the controller out of reach, but Alec launches himself forward and ends up half in Hunter's lap as he attempts to take the controller from him.

"Come on, let me try your little make believe thing."

"Call of Duty," Hunter corrects, using his stupidly long arms to lift the controller out of reach. It occurs to Alec that Hunter is actually really handsome with his blond hair and blue eyes. "Besides, I thought you didn't play video games."

I don't, Alec thinks, desperate as fuck for any distraction from his brain. "Teach me."

Hunter pauses, looking at Alec with a fairly intense level of eye contact. Alec can't imagine what he looks like with his bruised cheek and split lip, trying to steal his new roommate's controller. He doesn't play video games. He still barely knows Hunter. Maybe he's losing his mind.

"Is this about that guy that was here last week?"

"Why would you ask that? Did someone say something?"

"Is there something to say?" Hunter says. If the questions weren't being directed at Alec, he'd be far more impressed at Hunter's perception. As it is, he feels squirmy, like he wants to run until his legs burn or to bite something. He settles for tapping out a pattern on his leg.

"Who blabbed? Was it Riley? He's got a big fucking mouth. Or Antonio? He never shuts up."

"You never shut up," Hunter says.

Alec flips him off, and Hunter laughs before retrieving the second controller and setting up player two.

"To answer your question, no one told me anything." He passes a controller. "I do have eyes, though."

"Don't say that," Alec groans, tipping himself sideways so he's half off the couch. "I'm subtle, and no one knows anything."

"You're about as subtle as a stoplight."

"Fuck you," Alec grumbles, shoving his socked feet at

Hunter, who merely laughs again. "I can be subtle. I am the king of subtle. I am—fuck, I'm not subtle."

"If it helps, I don't think he has any idea. He's pretty old, maybe it was past his bedtime."

"He's twenty-nine." Alec snorts, wondering what's happening to his life. He wasn't even gonna confess this to Riley and Antonio, and here he is all but spilling his guts to Hunter. "He's—"

"Oblivious as fuck?"

Alec collapses, his hand hanging off the couch. "Yes, that."

Hunter nods. "Sounds brutal." Alec holds his breath, waiting for the sympathy Riley or Antonio might offer or twenty questions. To his surprise, he gets neither. "Wanna shoot some shit?"

"Yes, I do," Alec says, twisting until he's back on the couch. He ends up far too close to Hunter, his side entirely smashed against him. "Sorry, I can move. Hang on."

"You're good," Hunter says, eyes on the tv as he leans against Alec.

The pressure is a relief, and Alec tries not to overthink it. Were it one of his close friends, they'd know without being told how much Alec likes physical contact. They'd know what it means and everything it doesn't. Part of Alec wants to explain, but the rest of him is raw and exhausted, relieved that Hunter isn't prying. Alec's not even sure if Hunter is straight or queer, but he doesn't seem remotely bothered about another guy all up in his personal space, so Alec figures he's safe.

"You'll never be as good as me, but if you try really hard maybe you won't totally suck, King."

"Wow, you're such an inspirational teacher."

"You wanna learn or not?" Hunter grins.

"Alright, boss man, let's do this."

"AM I HALLUCINATING?"

Alec squeezes his eyes shut tighter, willing the loud voice to go away.

"Did you drug him?" a second voice adds. Riley.

"Why the fuck would I do that?" Hunter asks, clearly unfamiliar with Riley's joking tone.

"He's sleeping. In the day," Antonio continues. Alec can't blame his incredulity. Alec barely sleeps at night, and he never naps. "What happened? Why is his face all jacked up?"

"No one did anything to me, you loud fuckers," Alec grumbles, stretching out his legs. He opens his eyes, blinking when he finds himself in Hunter's lap. "Hey."

"Hey," Hunter grins.

"Is anyone going to tell us what's going on?" Riley asks.

Alec turns to see Riley and Antonio staring at him, and Alec rolls himself off the couch and onto all fours. He tries to make his way from the room, but Riley throws himself down and grabs his ankles. The asshole is strong, and despite Alec's attempts to wiggle free, he can't.

"What the fuck, Alec?"

Alec can't blame Antonio. He's being kind of intense even for him, but Alec isn't prepared to face reality. "I was just gonna, uh—"

"Run away," Antonio finishes.

Alec sighs, collapsing on the floor. The carpet smells stale, and it's rough against his sore cheek. When Riley lets go of his legs, Alec doesn't move, remaining on the ground with his arms and legs spread out like a starfish.

"We need to talk."

"No, thank you," Alec mumbles into the carpet.

"I'm going to head out," Hunter says, though whether he's trying to escape from the awkwardness or give them space, it's impossible to tell.

Antonio and Riley wait until Hunter leaves before they join him on the floor. Alec closes his eyes tighter, unable to look at them. Of all the people in the world, they're the two he can't lie to.

"We were worried this morning. It's not like you to disappear for so long, and then you ghosted us both, which you never do."

The guilt is more than Alec can bear, and he lifts his face, resting his chin on his folded arms. Leave it to Antonio to go there. He never minces words, which is probably why he and Alec are so close. It's just that he's not in the mood to have that directed at him.

"M'sorry."

"What the fuck happened?" Riley asks. "Where were you?"

"Who says something happened?" Alec says.

"Your face." Antonio reaches out, his hands warm on Alec's cheek as he turns it. "Did someone hurt you?"

"Say the word and I'll fuck them up." Riley tells him.

Alec laughs, wishing he hadn't when it makes his lip hurt. "You're like a fucking golden retriever Riley, you wouldn't hurt a fly."

Riley clutches his hands to his chest. "I don't know if I should say thank you or fuck you."

"He's not wrong," Antonio tells Riley, laughing. The sight of them getting along is a balm to Alec, who'd toed the line of mixing friendship when he'd gotten closer to Riley. He'd been afraid Antonio would feel like he was being replaced, which he had, but things seem to have improved. Alec kind of wants to tease them, but also doesn't want to risk it.

"How's Elsa?"

Antonio's smile fades. "Don't change the subject, asshole."

"He called her while we were at the store. I don't speak Spanish, but there were a lot of disgustingly-in-love tones happening."

Antonio flips Riley off. "At least I have a girlfriend. Wait, fianceé. Damn, that sounds good."

"I don't think I want to get married," Riley admits, stretching his long legs out. Alec takes that as an opportunity to flop over them, using Riley's thigh as a pillow. It's a lot more comfortable than his arms.

"Ever?" Alec asks.

"Nah, too much work. My parents put me off it."

"Aren't your parents still married?" Antonio asks.

"Exactly," Riley groans. "All that bitching and moaning and they're never happy. Don't get me wrong, they're wonderful parents, mostly. But they're fucking miserable together and wouldn't get divorced for the kids. Like we wanna hear all that fighting. It just sounds like too much work. Sorry, that's depressing, you're getting married soon. Marriage is, uh, fantastic."

Antonio shrugs, unbothered.

"I wanna get married," Alec admits. "One day. Not like right now, but in a few years. It seems nice to share that with someone."

"Of course you do, you big romantic." Antonio ruffles his hair. "I bet you'll sob like a baby walking down the aisle."

"Maybe my husband will sob when he looks at me being all sexy and shit."

Riley laughs. "Cocky fucker."

Alec grins, rolling onto his back to look up at Riley. "I have a mirror. I know what I look like."

"How the fuck does your ego fit in this room?" Antonio says.

Alec's smile fades. "I think I fucked up."

"When you say fucked up, do you mean like need a lawyer fucked up, or in trouble with Coach fucked up, or—"

"I spent all day with Theo fucked up," Alec says, staring at a stain on the ceiling. A familiar weight settles on his stomach as Antonio uses him like a pillow while Riley's big hand rests at his head. Neither of them are as tactile as Alec, but they know him well, maybe even better than he ever realized, and offer the kind of comfort he isn't brave enough to ask for right now. "I don't wanna be in love anymore."

"So are you gonna stop seeing him?" Riley asks.

There's a tightness in his chest. He knows what he should do, and yet he can't. "No."

"Fuck." Antonio whistles.

"Fuck," Riley echoes.

"Big fuck," Alec agrees. He counts the beats of his own heart, glad Theo has no idea each of them beat for him. "Maybe I can get some distance. I won't stop seeing him, but I'll be cool and aloof. I'll make him come to me."

"Now we're talking," Riley says. "Make him beg."

"That's not—"

"Make him see how great you are," Antonio agrees. "Not that we're gonna share you. You've already got two best friends."

"I think that's the first time you've admitted we're all

besties." Alec grins. "I feel like I should make us friendship bracelets."

"No, you're fucking not." Antonio laughs.

"Bradley makes friendship bracelets. He handed them out on pledge night. Had everyone's names and shit, too."

"Is Bradley the guy who always wears those pink polo shirts and the shell necklace?"

"That's him. Strange dude, but cool. Dudes can totally wear friendship bracelets."

"Now I kind of want one," Antonio admits, holding his arm up and twisting his wrist. "But I want red. Do they make lion beads? I want a lion bead."

"I want hot pink," Riley says. "Oh, and maybe some flowers. My little sisters would love that."

"Bossy besties." Alec snorts, fully determined to give them exactly what they want. "I want blue."

"Of course you do," Riley says. "Predictable fucker. Blue, blue, blue. Always blue."

He isn't wrong. Alec's favorite color has been blue since he was seven. What no one knows is that it's because of Theo. At the time, Alec didn't fully understand what it meant to be gay, but when he looked at Theo's eyes, so bright and kind and as deep blue as the sea, he began to prefer it to all others.

"Are we gonna have a sleepover now too? Do each other's hair?"

"If you're angling to stay the night here and avoid your siblings, the answer is yes," Alec tells Riley, earning him a whoop.

Riley and Antonio set off on a tangent about needing to go back to Target to get candy for their sleepover, and Alec breathes a little easier. He loves his friends and he loves Theo. It's not the same, but he can totally do this. He can have another friend and not make it weird. He knows he can. He just needs to give himself a little buffer to get his head on straight.

———

ALEC MAKES it four days before he ends up on Theo's front porch unannounced. He could've called or texted first, but that would've involved planning, and Alec is more of a 'just run into things without thinking' kind of guy. Especially since any prior notice would have also involved the opportunity for Theo to say no, and Alec's tolerance for rejection is at zero.

Their coach has been running them ragged for preseason training, Hunter and Logan are up half the night playing video games since classes don't officially start until Monday, and his insomnia is at an all-time high. Maybe, probably, he should talk to someone about it, but just because he has problems sleeping doesn't mean he needs to tell anyone. He's showing up for practice, pulling his weight, and yeah, he's probably gonna snap once a full class schedule is added on top of that along with their games, but Alec's good under pressure.

Or he used to be. This year is different, or maybe Alec is different. Ever since he got back from Mexico, it's like something in his brain won't switch back. He used to be able to hyperfocus on soccer and not give a shit when his teammates talked about hooking up. He could focus on the game and not care that it took every ounce of energy he possessed to play at his level, leaving him with nothing for himself. He used to be able to pretend this life was everything he wanted.

Pretending is getting harder and harder.

"Alec?"

Theo's standing in the doorway, looking confused and cozy. He's got another sweater on, but this is clearly a house-only sweater, misshapen and worn thin. There's a hole at his collar and at the elbow, but the yarn looks as soft and comfortable as the brown pajama pants he's got on.

"Why are you in pajamas?"

"Uh, because it's eight-thirty."

"Eight isn't late," Alec says.

"I'm an old man, Alec." Theo pushes his hair out of his eyes, the corners of his eyes crinkling in amusement. He's so stupidly handsome when he's happy. Well, he's always handsome, but there's something about the way his strong, masculine features soften when he's relaxed and happy that does things to Alec.

"I forgot. You got your AARP membership and *telenovelas* on standby? Should I get you a hot water bottle?"

"I don't watch *telenovelas*. That's you." Theo arches an eyebrow knowingly, and yeah, maybe he'd walked in on Alec crying over them once when he was eleven, the year Theo lived with them. In Alec's defense, he'd had a really long day at school only to come home and find out his favorite character had died. Granted she came back a few weeks later with amnesia, but baby Alec hadn't known how it would turn out. Whereas his brothers would've teased him mercilessly, Theo had brought him a folded napkin with two Oreos and ruffled his hair before closing the door.

"Look, *Abuela* turned me on to them, and there's nothing better after a long day like someone else's drama." Alec moves under Theo's arm, halfway inside when he asks, "Mind if I come in?"

"You know you're always welcome here."

It's clear Theo wasn't expecting company. There's

Chinese takeaway containers on his coffee table, the lights are dimmed, and the coffee table is littered with cups—a coffee mug, a Hydroflask with fading National Parks stickers and a mostly empty boba. The television is paused on a nature documentary, and there's a blanket draped over the couch, tousled haphazardly like he threw it off his lap. All of it screams "Theo" in the most familiar way possible.

"Do you mean that?" Alec asks. "Sometimes you say shit just to be nice. You can hurt my feelings if it's not true."

"I don't wanna hurt your feelings, Alec."

Alec shrugs. "I'd rather have hurt feelings than be lied to."

"I'm not lying, I—"

Rio chooses this exact moment to make herself known, meowing loudly for attention.

"She was sleeping. She must have Alec radar."

"To be fair, my presence is pretty exciting. Isn't it, baby girl?" He squats down, picking her up. Impossibly, she seems bigger than a few days ago, and Alec vows to come over more. For Rio. That's all. No other reason. "Look at you, little angel. Did you miss me?"

"Angel." Theo snorts. "A menace is what she is. She's hyperactive, cries for attention constantly, acts like I starve her to death if I go one minute past mealtime, and is clingy as all get out. She even tries to sit in my pants when I'm in the bathroom. She's a total pain in the ass."

The words make Alec's chest tighten unexpectedly. He'd meant everything he said about the placement being temporary. Cats weren't for everyone. He'd really hoped Theo would warm up to her, though. So far no one else he knew was looking for a kitten, and he hated the idea of dropping her at an already overcrowded shelter.

"I'll look harder for a new placement."

"Slow your roll, whipper snapper." Theo's smile is playful, and while Alec has seen this side of him, it's been a long time since it was directed at him. "I didn't say anything about that. I like her."

"You said she's a pain in the ass."

"She is," Theo agrees, reaching out to give her a scratch between the ears. She lets out a contented purr, the faintest hint of pink coloring Theo's cheekbones. "Maybe I like feisty pains in the ass."

"Are you referring to the kitten or me?" Alec asks, fighting off the biggest smile. His lip has mostly healed, giving only the faintest twinge of pain as his lips spread wide.

"The kitten, you, Jason...take your pick. I'm a magnet for needy people."

"Must be your delightful personality." Alec flips him off just to be sure he knows Alec is being sarcastic, in case his tone wasn't a dead giveaway.

Theo's laugh is full-bellied and amused, and Alec can't be bothered with anything as insignificant as being offended when the teasing has made Theo so obviously happy.

"Not that you're not welcome here, because we've now established you are. But what are you doing here, and more importantly, how did you get here? I didn't hear a car. Did you run?"

"It's not that far." Alec shrugs.

"You and I have different definitions of not far. Nine miles, Alec. I don't run nine miles in a week."

"You don't run at all," Alec points out.

"I don't," Theo agrees, patting his tummy. "I don't look like I did in high school anymore."

Football had made Jason and Theo both all muscle, but age has both softened him out and bulked him up. His waist is still trim, but he's no longer in pursuit of a six-pack. He's both strong and soft, and Alec loves the way Theo's body looks lived-in.

Alec knows people like his body. Fuck knows they tell him enough, as if all that matters about him are the sharp lines of his Adonis belt or his muscular thighs. Alec might have an athletic physique, but to him there is nothing more attractive than Theo's body—big and strong and a little soft in all the right places.

"No need to fish for compliments, Theodore."

Theo balks. "I wasn't."

"Lies," Alec says with an exaggerated sigh. He knows Theo wasn't, because Theo is the least conceited person Alec has ever met with absolutely no concept of how gorgeous he is, and unlike Alec, he is borderline allergic to too much attention. Alec can't relate in the least. He's pretty sure if he goes more than twenty-four hours without someone complimenting him, he starts to wither like a plant deprived of the sun.

"I'm not lying," Theo continues with the kind of earnestness only he can manage.

"You just want to hear how handsome you are, which is fair. You *are* handsome. Theo, you are the most handsome sweater-wearing man I've ever seen. Happy?"

He waits for Theo to splutter or laugh, but he does neither. "You think I'm handsome?"

Alec gapes. "Is that a serious question?"

"Uh, yes?"

Alec has tried very hard to keep his flirtatious personality in check with Theo, to not make him uncomfortable by toeing too close to the line of attraction he still holds, but this is too much. He knows Theo isn't exactly insecure, he's just oblivious about himself and the effect he has on people.

Alec still remembers Theo in high school, having no idea the way people would trip over themselves when he was around. He's pretty sure Theo thought they were clamoring for Jason's attention, and while some of them were, people wanted Theo's, too. But Theo never sees these things. It's like he's got on blinders and can't see when people like him.

Apparently, it's going to be up to Alec to let him know he's the sexiest goddamn man to ever walk this earth. Lowering Rio to the floor, he stalks closer to Theo, grabbing his face between both hands while trying not to laugh at the look in Theo's eyes. It's clear he has no idea what to make of Alec, which is great. Maybe then he'll be too confused and surprised to comprehend how painfully true Alec's next words are.

"Theodore James, you are like a sexy librarian fantasy come to life. Your quiet confidence oozes sex appeal, and everywhere we go, people look at your ass because it's as thick as the rest of you." Theo's entire face is red as a tomato, but Alec can't stop. He squeezes Theo's cheeks for good measure. "You are one sexy fuck of a man. You should own it."

When he's done, he gives Theo's stomach a playful pat and then turns around. "Do you have any Coke? I'm fucking thirsty." With that he walks out of the room, not waiting to see if Theo will follow.

Alec is totally nailing this friendship thing.

10 THEO

SEXY LIBRARIAN FANTASY *come to life.*

Theo pushes his glasses up his nose and looks down at his threadbare sweater. He's never thought of himself as anyone's fantasy. Sure, in high school a lot of girls, and a fair few guys who didn't wanna admit it, were into him, but that had more to do with the jersey and the letterman jacket, and the popularity that came with being a varsity football player. He'd been their fantasy because of a role he played, not who he was.

Once the football thing ended, so did most of the attention, which suited Theo fine. In high school, he'd hidden behind his image or Jason, and after he hadn't needed to hide at all. He'd quickly realized that despite his bulk, something about his appearance—the plain tortoise shell frames, neutral sweaters and just this side of overgrown hair—lent itself to hiding in plain sight.

When Theo needs to hook up he changes things, dresses in a way to attract people with jeans and tight shirts, club clothes that are as much of a uniform as his football jersey had been. There's a safety in knowing that what he gives to people is a version of his choosing. The idea that someone finds Theo handsome in his most authentic state is unexpected.

"Why do you have so much LaCroix?" Alec yells from the kitchen. "Six kinds, Theodore. There are six kinds."

"I like it," Theo yells back, following him in.

There in front of the open fridge is Alec, hands on his trim waist as he eyes the contents of Theo's refrigerator. "What the fuck is 'pamplemousse' anyway?"

"Grapefruit."

"Disgusting," Alec grumbles, picking up another can. "Limoncello? Really? Fancy-ass water. Why don't you have Coke?"

"I don't drink Coke. Besides, didn't you say your nutritionist told you to cut back?"

Alec makes a derisive noise, ending up grabbing one of the tangerine LaCroix before shutting the fridge door with his hip. "She did, and she can pry my Coke addiction from my cold, dead hands. I've already had to restrict my carbs and drink fourteen protein shakes a week. I am not giving up my Coke."

He cracks the top on the LaCroix, gulping it down with a frown before moaning pitifully. "This taste like Alka-Seltzer, fuck that. Take me to get a Coke."

"I'm in my pajamas."

"Then we'll go through a drive-thru. Take me to Sonic. I want some of that good pebble ice."

"You're going to crack your teeth eating ice."

"I'm sorry, I missed the part where you went to dentistry school." Alec snorts. "Besides, I need to cut back on chewing gum. It's giving me jaw problems. I tried switching to sunflower seeds, but the team nutritionist complained about my sodium intake. Watch your sodium, watch your sugar, your body is a temple. Blah, blah, blah."

As a kid, Alec had forever been eating lollipops or blowing bubbles with his gum. Apparently he never did outgrow it.

"You seem kind of stressed out, Alec. Are you okay?"

Alec's expression flickers, but before he can reply, Rio loudly makes her presence known again. Alec bends down to pick up a very irritated and noisy Rio, who is clearly displeased at not being the center of Alec's attention.

With Rio held close to his chest, Alec fixes his honey brown eyes on Theo. "Come on, old man, we want Coke."

It doesn't escape Theo's notice that Alec didn't answer his actual question, but if he's not comfortable telling Theo what's going on, he won't push. He's too afraid of messing up this tenuous thing between them. He hasn't earned that part of Alec. Not yet.

"'*We*,' huh?"

"Can't you hear Rio whining?" She's not. The second Alec picked her up, she quieted down. Theo's spent the last three days with her meowing her tiny head off night and day. Turns out all she needs is Alec around, and she's happy as a clam. Theo's not sure if that makes him want to laugh or cry. Poetic justice indeed, since he's also been moping about wishing Alec would come over, too chicken-shit to go visit him first. "She clearly understands my duress and thinks I deserve one."

"Has anyone ever told you that you're ridiculous?"

"Not in the last six hours," Alec replies, moving past Theo towards the front door. "Are you coming?"

"Apparently," Theo says with a shake of his head. "Are you sure I shouldn't change?"

"It's a drive-thru. No one gives a fuck what you're wearing." Alec stops at the door, turning to wait for him. "If you do need to get out of the car, I give you permission to tell people you were kidnapped."

"Why is every scenario with you the most extreme possible?"

"Because I have a gifted imagination." Alec purses his lips. "Fuck, I forgot my wallet."

"Pretty sure I can manage treating you to a Coke. You're a cheap date."

The tip of Alec's button nose turns pink, his big eyes wide and focused on Theo. For a second, Theo forgets how to breathe, frozen in place under Alec's watchful gaze. Embarrassed by his own reaction, he tries to recover and ends up fumbling. "Not that it's a date. Because we would never."

Something dark passes over Alec's face, and Theo wants to get that light back. He had to go and make it weird because he's awkward and stupid and unsure how to navigate this. He knows Alec is over him. He didn't need to go insulting him.

"Alec, I—"

"Less talking, more walking," Alec interrupts, clearly intending to pretend whatever just transpired never actually happened.

With a bitten-off sigh, Theo follows. Maybe one day he can figure out how to stop accidentally hurting Alec's feelings. Or maybe this is exactly why he's better off not having feelings of his own. His attempts to hide his own crush made him say the wrong thing entirely, and there's really no way to fix it without admitting what he actually meant.

Apparently, Theo will choose letting Alec have hurt feelings over the alternative, which makes him feel like an asshole. He sighs again, scrubbing a hand over his face. He doesn't just feel like an asshole, he is one. Maybe if he's lucky, Alec won't take it too personally.

The first ten minutes or so in the car are awkward, or Theo is, opening and shutting his mouth so much he might as well be a fish. Alec either doesn't notice or is polite enough not to call him on his impression of a Moray eel. Instead, Alec chatters away to Rio about where they're going, acting as if she'll be able to get a kitten combo meal.

Sonic is located closer to the shore, along with a string of other fast food restaurants meant to entice the summer travelers who can't afford to eat on the pier or broke college students. This time of the year, there's just enough students moving back to town combined with the end of season tourists to make it completely packed, and Theo has to circle the parking lot half a dozen times before a slot opens up for them to pull in.

"I haven't been here in forever," Theo says, glad to have something else to focus on. The menu is massive, the blinking screen advertises current specials and makes his dinner seem like it was days ago and not hours. "I kinda want fries."

"Fair warning, if you get fries, I'm stealing some."

"Pretty sure I can buy you your own fries, Alec."

"I can't have my own," Alec says, the lines of his face flat. "Not with the Coke, too, and I need that carbonation STAT or I might die."

"You can't have fries?" Theo frowns, thinking about the detailed nutrition plan and training schedule that had been taped up on the King's fridge. He hadn't realized it was that strict.

"Not on the meal plan," Alec answers, leaning his seat all the way down to give Rio free rein to crawl across his belly. She swats at his fingers, the tension on Alec's face fading as he focuses on her. "I'll be too sluggish to run in the morning if I eat that. That's what the coach says. Between you and me, I can run nine miles in my sleep, but it's not worth the risk with the season kicking off this weekend."

"You have a game this weekend?"

"Yeah," Alec confirms. "Classes start back up Friday and we've got our first game against Cal Poly. It's just an exhibition game, but there's really no 'just' at a D1 school. Every game matters. There's no room to have an off minute or an off game. One of those and you've fucked your entire season."

"I'm sure one game isn't that important."

The look Alec gives him makes it clear he's wrong. "At this level there is no room for error. Sure, the team as a whole can recover from a loss, but an individual player? You could lose your starting spot, fuck over your chance to play in a club tournament in front of scouts, you could jeopardize your scholarship. Every second of every game you have to be perfect."

On some level, Theo knew the intensity, but his own experience with sports was so different. Plus he'd turned down his own chance at collegiate sports, so he'd never had to worry about logistics. The idea that Alec lives under that level of constraint sounds exhausting.

"That sounds like a lot of pressure."

"I guess," Alec shrugs, right hand tapping on the door rapid-fire. "Can you get me a large Coke but with extra ice?"

"Sure," Theo says, rolling his window down to push the order button. It takes a few seconds before a voice crackles through the speakers. Once he's ordered Alec's Coke, a large fry, and a milkshake for himself he sits back, trying and failing not to stare at Alec.

"I'm sure your parents are excited for the game."

"They're not coming."

"They're not coming?" Theo echoes, utterly surprised. As a teenager, some of his strongest memories had been hanging out with Jason during one of Alec's games. Jason's parents always gave them cash to use at the snack bar, so they'd load up their pockets on Red Vines, gum and bags of chips, walking around like they owned the place. Hell, most of the time they didn't even watch Alec play, too busy with their own teenage bullshit. What he does remember clearly is that one of Alec's parents was always there, no matter what. He'd never imagined they would stop going.

"Nah, I mean, this is my fourth year playing. They've been to a lot of games. The novelty wears off after a while, and they've been pretty busy."

"What about your brothers?"

Alec shakes his head. "They all have adult lives. I mean, they came to a lot of games my freshman year, but you know, it gets boring after that, I'm sure."

"I find it hard to believe anyone could be bored watching you."

"I am fun to watch." Alec grins. It's honestly staggering for Theo to realize how much he likes being the one who made him smile like that. "Not that you'd know. You've never been to one of my games."

"I've been to lots of your games."

"Not for the Lions. You saw me play as a kid, and even a few high school games, but you've never been to one of my college games."

"That can't be possible."

"It's not a big deal. You were busy and it's just, whatever."

Except it doesn't feel like whatever. It feels like the

exact opposite. Theo opens his mouth, maybe to apologize or get Alec to keep talking, but he's interrupted by the arrival of their food. As the tray passes through the window, Alec snatches his Coke like a goblin, lips curling around the straw as he chugs.

"Fuck, that's good," he mutters after a moment, turning his eyes on Theo with a playful smirk. "Pass over a fry and no one gets hurt."

"Who's gonna hurt me?" Theo asks, pretending to think it over. "You're the size of Rio."

"Fucking excuse you?" Alec lowers his soda into the cupholder. "I'll show you small, you fucker."

Above them the neon lights from the restaurant flicker, the sounds of people around them talking dim to background noise, and the only thing Theo has eyes for is Alec and the way he's trying to crawl over the center console. Alec looks happy, relaxed even, and Theo knows he's completely screwed, because he wants to do anything and everything to make sure Alexander King never stops smiling.

"OPEN THE DOOR," someone bellows. A very loud, familiar someone.

Theo wastes no time hurrying to the front door before Jason bangs the damn thing down. Swinging the front door open, he's met with the sight of a smiling Jason, a six pack of beer under one arm and a pizza in the other.

"Well, hello there, stranger. Long time no see."

"It hasn't been that long," Theo protests even as he knows it has, at least for them.

"Not that long," Jason mimics. "You skipped Friday

night pizza two weeks in a row and were busy all weekend. That makes it thirteen days since we hung out. Thirteen, dude."

"You counted?"

"Shut up and let me in," Jason grumbles good-naturedly. "A man notices when his best friend disappears."

"I didn't disappear. I replied to your text messages."

"Yeah, in one word replies, with punctuation. I let you have some time to figure it out, and now it's time for the big guns. I'm bringing out the contract."

"You can't be serious."

"I'm so serious," Jason says, moving past Theo to head inside the house and deposit the pizza and beer on the coffee table before pulling his wallet from his back pocket. He flips open the worn brown leather of his trifold wallet, thumbing through pieces of paper and money. He's the only person Theo knows who always has cash. He's pretty sure it's because he's addicted to the vending machines at the high school, but it's endearing just the same.

Shoved beneath his driver's license is a folded up piece of paper that Theo hasn't seen in over a decade.

"You did not keep that."

"I did." Jason grins, looking satisfied as hell with himself. He unfolds the paper, clearing his throat before reading it, "I, Theodore James, promise not to be a giant dickface—"

"I didn't write dickface," Theo interrupts.

"It's a dramatic reading. I'm giving it flair." Jason smirks. He clears his throat again, starting from the beginning. "If you insist on historical accuracy, I'll read it as you wrote it. Okay, here goes. 'I, Theo, promise not to shut out my best friend, even when I'm scared. Signed, Theo and Jason.'"

There's something burning in Theo's gut, but whether

it's love or guilt, he can't be sure. Jason had made him write
and sign that when he'd found out Theo had been scared to
come out as bisexual. He'd thought it was just Jason being
dramatic as always, and the idea that he kept it and has been
holding onto it for thirteen years is more than Theo can
bear.

"I wrote that when I was sixteen, Jason."

"Yeah, well, apparently it's a good thing I kept it, isn't it?
Now pop open a beer, eat some pizza, and tell me what's
going on."

"You could've just called me," Theo says.

"And given you a chance to pretend to be busy? Not a
chance. You can't avoid me for two weeks and not face the
consequences."

"I wasn't avoiding you," Theo lies like a goddamn liar.

"Uh-huh," Jason hums, dropping down onto the couch.
He kicks off his sneakers and stretches his feet out onto the
coffee table, making himself very comfortable. Relief and
apprehension hit Theo all at once. He's missed Jason.
"You've been weird and distant and—what the ever loving
fuck is that?"

It happens to be Rio, who appears from beneath the sofa
and proceeds to attack the laces on Jason's sneakers.

"Ah, yeah. About that."

"There's a kitten in your house, Theo." Jason's expression would be hilarious if Theo weren't on the hook for the
explanation.

"There is."

"A kitten," Jason repeats, as if Theo doesn't know. "You
don't have pets. Why do you have a pet?"

"So the thing is," Theo starts, filling his lungs with air
and then holding it. He has no idea how to explain this
without lies upon lies. And now that he's staring at Jason

after he pulled out that damn contract, he doesn't have the heart. Then again, Theo doesn't have the heart to be honest when he barely knows what the truth is himself. "Uh, well—"

"Alec got to you, didn't he?"

"Alec," Theo croaks, ears ringing.

"Damn kid and his bleeding heart. Me and Charlie have been placing bets on who he'd rope into taking the next stray. I figured that Riley kid, and Charlie was sure it'd be me, but I guess he came to you. Did he do it when you helped him move?" Jason doesn't give him time to answer, leaning forward to look at the kitten. "What's her name?"

"Rio," Theo answers, dropping onto the opposite end of the couch. He grabs a beer, cracking the can open and chugging it.

"She's so small. Is she healthy?" Jason asks, petting her. She looks ridiculously small in his massive hands, and she lets out a tiny hiss. "Damn, she's feisty."

"Pretty sure she only looks that small because you're huge."

"I know, right?" Jason grins. "I've been training with the boys."

"Aren't you kind of old to be training with high schoolers?"

"I'm the same age as you are, asshole. I'm also their coach. I'm setting a good example. Plus it makes me bigger."

"If you get any bigger, your clothes are gonna pop," Theo points out, nodding to Jason's sweats, which might as well be painted on.

"Thank you." Jason grins, lowering Rio to the couch. "Now back to you."

"Do we have to go back to me?" Theo groans. He flops back against the couch cushions, nursing his beer.

"We do," Jason affirms, grabbing his own beer before flipping the pizza box open. The scent of garlic and cheese assaults Theo's nose. Jason grabs a slice, folding it half before fitting most of it in his mouth in an obscenely large bite. He lifts one eyebrow in a silent invitation for Theo to speak.

He knows Jason. He knows there is going to be no getting out of this when he's being so direct. The best he can do is deflect with the smallest bit of honesty possible and absolve himself of the guilt through the assertion he's protecting their friendship.

"I, uh, there's a person."

"Dude, if you've been in a hookup mood, you just needed to tell me. I'm not gonna judge if you've been getting freaky more often than normal."

"I haven't been getting freaky." Theo snorts. "It's not like that."

Jason swallows his second bite, taking a huge gulp of beer before fixing Theo with a piercing gaze. "What do you mean it's not like that?"

"I mean, it's not like that."

"It's always like that. If there's a person, you fuck and move on."

Theo stares at his beer. This was a bad idea, a horrible idea, and yet he knows he can't backtrack. As wrong as it feels to deceive Jason, the truth is he needs his best friend, now more than ever.

"I haven't fucked them."

He's careful to use gender-neutral language and offer as few details as possible. Lucky for him, Jason isn't nearly as nosy as Alec. The thought catches him off-guard. Since when does he compare Alec and Jason?

"So there's someone, and you haven't fucked them."

"Yup."

"And you haven't fucked them because?"

Because they're hung up on someone else. Because I missed my chance. Because they're your baby brother.

"Lots of reasons," Theo sighs, tracing the rim of his beer. "They deserve more than a one and done fuck." The words are too close to the truth, but they slip out before Theo can censor them.

"You like them." Jason slaps his thigh. "Holy shit, Theo! You've got feelings. I never thought I'd see the day."

"I don't know if I'd go that far," Theo hedges, trying to walk things back. It's no use, though. Jason knows him too well.

"There's no shame in having feelings, dude. Own it."

"I don't want feelings," Theo whispers, voice tinged with the painful edge of truth.

Jason is quiet for long seconds, sipping at his beer. "You know it's okay to let people in, right?"

"I let people in," Theo mumbles.

"You let me in. You don't let other people in, you never have. If you were happy with that, if it was all you wanted, I wouldn't say a damn thing. But—"

"But?"

"But I wonder sometimes if you're happy."

"I'm happy," Theo insists. He likes his house and his job, mostly. He likes Jason and his routines. He's happy. He is. But if that were the truth, then why does it feel so much like a lie?

"I can't believe my baby boy has feelings." Jason's tone is playful, his smile wide as he reaches for a second slice of pizza. That's the thing about Jason, he's always there, always steady, but he never pushes too far. Not like Alec, who calls Theo on his shit, who makes space for himself without letting Theo make excuses.

"Shut up," Theo grumbles, knocking against Jason.

Jason is undeterred, throwing his right arm around Theo's shoulder and clanking their beers together. "To Theo's first crush. When can I meet them?"

Meet them.

Theo's gonna puke. He didn't think this through, didn't plan ahead.

"She doesn't live here."

The lie is out before he even thinks about it and he hates himself, but not as much as he would hate himself if Jason knew the truth. His sole consolation is the knowledge that the lies are to protect their friendship.

"Alright, alright. I'll give you some time to see what happens, but if things get serious, you've got to promise me I can meet her first. Make sure she's good enough for you."

"I promise," Theo whispers. This is an easy promise, because things won't get serious.

Jason grabs another slice of pizza, passing it to Theo. He's just taken a huge bite when Jason speaks, causing him to nearly choke.

"I'll talk to Alec."

"Why?" Theo asks around a mouthful.

"About that cat. I'm sure you didn't want it. I mean it's cute, I'll give you that but—" Jason watches Rio, who is rolling around on the ground on the other side of the room playing with one of the little cat toys Alec picked out. "He's persistent, and you're not very good at telling people no. I'm sure you didn't want to upset him, but he can't just foist a kitten on you."

"He didn't," Theo says.

"I know Alec. He's a persistent shit."

You don't know him the way you think, Theo wants to say. He wants to explain the way Alec had shown up on his doorstep hurt and uncharacteristically quiet, how he hadn't even asked Theo to take her. Theo wants to say a lot of things, but all of them would lead down a path of admitting things he isn't ready to admit, even to himself, so he takes the coward's way out.

"It's fine, really. Alec's looking for a permanent place, anyway."

Just saying the words makes his throat tight. They're true, but it's the first time he's said them out loud since Alec offered. At the time it had felt like a failsafe, but he's growing attached hard and fast. Possibly to more than just the kitten.

"Alright, but if you need me to step in, just let me know."

The last thing Theo wants is Jason talking to Alec for him, so he stays quiet and eats his pizza. He's halfway through his next slice when his mouth runs without permission.

"When's the last time you watched Alec play?"

"Shit, I don't know," Jason answers, leaning back against the couch. "Probably last year. Or was it his sophomore year? I don't even know for sure. You know how busy I was coaching. We made the playoffs the last two years and I just couldn't make time. He told me it was fine, that he didn't care if we came to watch him play. You know how he is."

Theo hums, not trusting himself to speak. He thought he knew Alec, but he's not so sure anymore. He's starting to wonder how many people really know Alec, and how many only know the easy-going guy he lets them see.

"What makes you ask?" Jason's question is easy, but the answer is anything but.

"I was just thinking, it's his last year with the Lions, and I realized I've never seen him play. No big deal."

"Huh." Jason hums, rubbing a hand over his jaw. "You're right, it is his last year at school. I wonder when his next game is."

"Tomorrow," Theo blurts, fumbling for a recovery. "I saw it online. Some exhibition game against Cal Poly."

Jason hums again, staring at the ceiling. "We should go."

"We?" Theo counters, trying to keep his cool. This is exactly what he was angling for, wasn't it? Hoping if he brought it up, Jason's brotherly guilt would kick in, and he'd go to the game so that Theo could have an excuse to go.

"Obviously I'm not going alone." Jason sits up grinning. "I wonder if I have time to buy face paint?"

"Why the hell do you need face paint?"

"School spirit, obviously."

"You're such an idiot." Theo laughs.

"That says more about you than me if you're my best friend."

Theo laughs again, his tension bleeding away. This is fine. He can do this. He can figure out how to be friends with Alec without losing Jason and everything will be fine.

EVERYTHING IS NOT FINE.

"Dude, why didn't you bring a hat?" Jason asks. "Your face is so red. You look like a fucking tomato."

The sun has nothing to do with Theo's face being red. Rather, it has everything to do with Alec who is currently sprinting across the field like a badass motherfucker with the soccer ball, his footwork as impressive as the rest of him. He looks damn good in his soccer uniform, his bright blue jersey tight across his shoulders and tiny waist, and the movement of his strong thighs as he runs is enough to have Theo nearly panting.

"It's the sweater. Take off that damn sweater," Jason grumbles, shoving his water at Theo who takes it without a word, gulping down huge mouthfuls of ice water. It does nothing to quench his other thirst, but at least his mouth no longer feels like sandpaper.

The coastal breeze means it rarely gets sweltering in Santa Leon, but with the sun beating down on their heads, sweat rolls down Theo's neck. Even his light sweater vest feels too heavy, and he concedes to Jason's advice, shrugging it off, leaving him in nothing but his thin white undershirt. He feels under-dressed and still hot, rubbing both hands over his face.

His attention returns to the game when the crowd screams, drawing Theo's eyes to the field where Alec just scored his second goal. He kisses his two fingertips, lifting them towards the stands where his classmates go wild. Seconds later, Antonio slams into him, followed by several other players Theo doesn't know.

"King, King, King," the crowd chants.

Beside him, Jason whoops loudly, thumb and forefinger sneaking between his lips as he lets out the world's loudest whistle. Alec's eyes are drawn towards the stands and rise to Jason, who is making an absolute fool of himself waving his arms around and yelling. It's only a few seconds before Alec's gaze drifts sideways and lands on Theo. Even at a distance, his surprise is evident. Hundreds of people are screaming Alec's name, and yet the only person he looks at is Theo, who is acutely aware of every bead of sweat that rolls down his face, of the air that fills his lungs and the blood that pumps through his veins.

The coach is throwing his arms up, and Antonio leans in to whisper something in his ear while pulling on Alec's arm, but the entire time his gaze stays locked on Theo, the smile that spreads across his face enough to knock Theo sideways. His face lights up like the Fourth of July, and Theo feels the curl of Alec's lips in his guts, the weight of Alec's pleasure tangible.

"That's my baby brother," Jason screams loud enough for everyone, including the players, to hear. It earns him two middle fingers from Alec before he takes off across the field.

Though Alec doesn't turn to look at Theo again, the ghost of his smile lingers on Theo's skin.

Soccer was never Theo's favorite sport, but he understands just enough to follow the game and to appreciate that Alec is an absolute beast on the field. The rest of his team is good, as is the opposing team, but there's something magic about the way Alec handles a pass and his footwork when he has the ball. He's not just fast, he's coordinated and smooth, running laps around the other team.

When Alec scores a third time, the cheers are nearly deafening, or maybe that's Jason, who seems determined to be the most embarrassing, proud big brother on the face of the earth. Alec flips him off again when Jason manages to get everyone doing the wave, but he never stops smiling.

It's clear Alec is a crowd favorite from the way the stands erupt in cheers when he's in possession of the ball, as well as from the numerous students wearing his jersey. The sight of "King" plastered on so many people's backs has an unfamiliar feeling clawing its way up Theo's spine. There's a level of pride at seeing so many recognize Alec's skill, but there's something else, too. The bitter tang of jealousy darkens his mood as he thinks about the social media comments and the way people talked about him like they knew him, like they were entitled to a piece of him because of his popularity or skill.

He can't help but wonder if Alec knows, and if he does, if he likes it. He likes attention enough; he probably revels in it. Is that all Theo is? One more pathetic fan in the crowd, angling for a piece of Alec?

The thoughts nag at the edges of his joy. Though Theo tries to keep his head in the game, it's difficult to focus on anything except Alec and the longing that makes his heart race. Coming here was probably one of the stupidest things he could do, yet when the game ends and Alec seeks him out in the stands and waves—that smile of his enough to power the sun—Theo can't regret his choice.

Maybe what he wants from Alec is more than he can have, more than he should want, but that doesn't mean he can't be here for Alec and support him.

11 ALEC

THE SECOND HALF of the game passes in blur. It's as if Alec can do no wrong. Every pass is perfect, and their opponents are unable to stop him. It doesn't hurt that his team matches the energy. For all Alec's been questioning his future lately, one thing remains true—Alec loves soccer. Today he remembers that with every interception, pass, and goal. He remembers what it means to be part of a team and love it, and most of all, he remembers to play his heart out. Of course, this is made all the easier when his heart is sitting in the stands cheering him on.

Fuck, he can't believe Theo is here.

It's possible that Theo mentioned his late night ramblings to Jason, and they came out of pity, but it's also possible that maybe, just maybe, Theo came because he wanted to. That maybe fuels Alec on to play like it's a championship game and not some nothing exhibition. Much as Alec would love to say he dominates the game solely because of hard work, he knows the truth is that he's showing off. He might have come to dread the life that comes with playing D1 soccer, but not even that can dull his love of the sport. The games are what he lives for, the sacrifices and anxiety and loneliness falling away. For ninety minutes, Alec is just a boy who loves to play again.

It's been years since Theo came to see him play, and having him out there, knowing he's watching Alec, makes him feel invincible.

When the game ends, Alec's jersey clings to his stomach while sweat drips down the most inconvenient places. He's exhausted in the best way possible, and his legs ache with fatigue, but he won, they won, and it feels good. After a big loss Alec often retreats, replaying the game in his mind while damn near chewing his own nails off as he replays every mistake he made. Today isn't going to be one of those days. Today is a day for victory, for pride.

"We did good," Alec says, slapping McMillan and Chaucer on the backs before moving closer to Antonio. He leans into him, relieved when he slings an arm around Alec's shoulder and pulls him closer.

Some of the other guys had been standoffish when Alec joined the team, and while most of them have come around, Alec still holds himself back with a lot of them. Not Antonio, though. He never cared that Alec is gay. They'd bonded immediately during their freshman year and never looked back. Not once, in all that time, has Antonio ever made Alec feel uncomfortable about his sexuality or how tactile he is. Antonio gave the middle finger, figuratively and literally, to the guys who'd made Alec hold himself back that first year.

"You were on fire, King." Antonio's breathless and happy, as high on their win as Alec is.

"Don't act so surprised. I told you I'm amazing."

"And so modest," Antonio snorts, ruffling Alec's hair.

"Don't mess up my curls," he grumbles, not at all put out. Alec's a fucking goner for having his hair touched.

"Sorry to be the bearer of bad news, but your curls are a sweaty mess."

"You're sweaty."

"Doesn't stop you from laying on me."

"You're the one suffocating me with your abnormally long arms."

Antonio laughs. "They're not abnormally long, you're just—"

"If you say short, I will end you."

"Aw, is my short king touchy?"

"I'm only two inches shorter than you." Alec pouts. "I need to make shorter friends. Why is everyone I like so tall? What the fuck did you all eat growing up?"

"Tortillas," Antonio answers with a laugh, ruffling Alec's hair again before tugging on him to guide him towards the locker room with the rest of the team. "Speaking of Theo—"

"How in the hell did you get from tortillas to Theo?"

"They're both white, and both things you'd like to stuff your mouth wi—"

"I hate you, and I'm never telling you anything again," Alec snaps, slapping his hand over Antonio's mouth. It silences him long enough for the coach to start his post-game speech, where he congratulates them on their win, then reminds them it means nothing unless they keep it up.

"That's not true and you know it." Antonio smirks.

"Quiet down," the coach yells, saving Alec from responding.

The euphoria of winning quickly dwindles as the coach reminds them what is at stake. His eyes find Antonio and Alec, reminding them that the players hoping to make it to the MLS need a game like today every game. No pressure, they just need to be perfect for every game, every three days, for the next four months straight. It's not that Alec needs to study or relax or anything. He can totally afford to spend every waking moment following the meal plan and training.

The worst part is the way Antonio beams. If anyone was made for the big leagues, it's him. He thrives under pressure, he lives and breathes soccer in a different way. He lives for it all, wants nothing more than to make it to the MLS and make his family proud. While Alec loves the game, everything that comes along with their level chips away at his passion. Sometimes he wonders what will happen when there's nothing left.

Times like this remind Alec why he's never told anyone about the anxiety that claws its way into his chest when he stops moving. He's worked his entire life for this, it's the game he loves, and he's playing with one of his best friends. He should be happy. So why is it the second he steps off that field he feels like he's suffocating?

ALEC TAKES the fastest shower of his life, not even bothering with his normal hair care routine. His curls are going to look stupid and tangled, but he can't be bothered spending twenty extra minutes doing his normal post-shower ritual when Theo is out there waiting for him. At least, he hopes he's out there. When he'd checked his phone after returning to the locker room, he found a text from Jason congratulating him on the win and telling him to meet him outside. Since Jason and Theo are basically a matched set, if Jason is waiting for him, then so is Theo. Probably.

On second thought, maybe he does have time for his hair, which is giving drowned rat at the moment. He towel dries it as much as he can, spending a few minutes adding in his leave-in conditioner and curl shaper before giving it a few scrunches. Ultimately, he decides this will have to be good enough. If he spends too long they might get bored and leave, and while Alec wouldn't blame them he would definitely, privately, get his feelings hurt.

Affording himself one final look in the mirror, he decides he can handle this damp, haphazard thing his hair has going on. He might be a little, or a lot, vain about his hair, but he also is confident enough to rock whatever the fuck he's got going on right now with confidence. Deciding to go for broke, he chooses his tightest, thinnest pair of sweats and then throws his team hoodie on last.

Despite his intentions to be quick, by the time he's leaving the locker room Antonio has taken off to FaceTime his fianceé, and the majority of the team is long gone. Even the stadium is mostly empty, except for a few jersey chasers. He fights back a frown, trying not to think too hard about the way some of them sneak photos of him in the dining hall or during training. He pulls his hood up and slinks along the fence, hoping they won't see him.

With his head down and his gaze on the ground, he doesn't see the wall he walks into, one with a stupidly familiar face.

"Why does it feel like you keep growing?" Alec grumbles, unsure why all his brothers are so big while he stopped in ninth grade.

"What can I say? I'm perfect." Jason grins, throwing his arms around Alec in a bone-crushing hug.

"Fuck you." Alec returns the hug with equal force. Jason might be a pain in the ass, but Alec loves him, and he's currently far more emotional than he wants to be about having someone finally come see him play again. It's his own fault for telling everyone he didn't need them to watch, but he'd always hoped someone might realize he was giving them a way out, that he was lying to make things easier on them.

"You guys were on fire! Cal Poly never stood a chance." Jason claps him on the back. The praise makes Alec stand taller. Growing up, his older brothers were his heroes, and even now, hearing them be proud of him scratches an itch he tries really hard to ignore.

"Of course we were, I was there." Alec smirks, taking a step back.

Part of him doesn't want to look around to see if Theo is here, but he can't stop himself from letting his eyes wander, heart lodging itself in his throat when he finds Theo hovering a step behind Jason with a soft smile on his face.

"You played really well, Alec."

That praise scratches an entirely different itch. "Thanks," he mumbles.

"Oh, no cockiness for him, huh? I see how it is." Jason laughs.

He doesn't, he really doesn't, but that's probably a good thing.

Alec plays with a loose curl at his temple. "Thanks for coming, Theodore."

"I am literally standing right here," Jason says. "Aren't you glad I came?"

"I have to look at your ugly mug all the time." Alec shrugs, unsure why the prospect of simply admitting how much he misses any of his brothers is worse than pulling teeth.

"What about this ugly mug?" Jason asks, wrapping an arm around Theo's shoulders and squeezing his jaw. Theo slaps at him, laughing at Jason's antics. Sometimes the two of them act more like teenagers than two men about to turn thirty. Idiots, both of them. The one upside to them being fools is that it gives Alec a moment to fully take Theo in, from the fit of his pale, worn jeans to his obscenely thin white t-shirt that hugs every inch of his masculine body, showing off light chest hair and the faintest swell of his tummy and pecs. It's been years since Alec saw Theo's body without a sweater covering it up, and the reminder of all of Theo's strong, thick features makes Alec wish he'd chosen looser sweatpants.

"Theo's definitely not ugly," Alec mumbles.

"Fine, fine. I see how it is. Theo is the favorite. Why am I surprised after all these years?"

Alec's entire body flushes, but before he can deflect the conversation Theo is speaking.

"What does that mean?"

"Come on, don't you remember how he used to follow you around like a puppy when he was a kid? 'Can I sit next to Theo? Can I come if Theo is coming?'" Jason pitches his voice high, and while Alec knows he's teasing, the reality hits too close to home. "Remember that time—"

"Shut the fuck up," Alec snaps, afraid his heart might damn well explode in his chest. Jason smirks, but Theo's gaze does the most unexpected thing and softens, as if he feels sorry for Alec. That is one thousand percent worse than the embarrassment. Alec would rather die a thousand deaths than have Theo pity him for being a pathetic lovesick fool. Which, incidentally, is exactly why he can't ever let on that he definitely never got over his crush.

Jason looks delighted, always happy for a chance to embarrass Alec. Theo looks, well, Alec's not sure. Confused, maybe, or surprised. It's not like it's a secret Alec had a crush on him. If Jason actually knew Alec never got over it, knew how much it hurt, he probably wouldn't tease. But he doesn't know, and Alec would rather keep it that way. Jason might be his brother, but he's Theo's best friend, and Alec never wanted to test where his loyalty lies if given a choice.

The last thing he needs is Jason or Theo realizing that Theo was responsible for Alec's sexual awakening. He would never live it down, and it's not like his brothers need any more ammunition to tease him. Besides, he's pretty sure that would make Theo run for the hills. Again.

"So what are you two doing after this?" Alec says a bit too loudly, trying to keep the conversation in safer territory.

"Not sure. You wanna hit the club again?" Jason asks Theo. "Last weekend was pretty fun."

"You say that because you got three numbers."

"To be fair, one of the guys wanted help with his plumbing. Though why he thought I could help him is—oh wait."

Alec can't help but laugh, hard enough that his stomach hurts. The harder he laughs, the more impossible it seems to stop, and then Theo joins in, and Jason grumbles while trying not to smile.

"Not all of us are all stocked up on queer pickup lines, you assholes. I can't believe you guys are ganging up on me like this. My best friend and my brother, laughing at my innocence."

"You're not innocent. You're just oblivious as fuck," Alec says.

Jason turns to Theo. "Am I oblivious?"

"We love you," is all Theo says, patting Jason's back.

"Yeah, yeah, nice way of showing it." Jason crosses his arms but doesn't look remotely put out, his even-tempered personality almost impossible to ruffle. "So, club tonight?"

Alec's right hand sneaks into his pocket, withdrawing a piece of gum. Maybe he's supposed to quit, but there's nothing else to bite right now, and he can feel that unease crawling up his skin as he waits for the answer.

"Yeah, sure."

Sad. It makes Alec sad.

"You should come with us," Jason says. "Celebrate your big win."

"You're inviting me clubbing with you two?" Alec asks.

"Well, you're finally legal. Unless you've got other plans."

Theo rocks on his feet. "I'm sure Alec has other plans. He's a popular guy. He's got to have better things to do than hang around with us boring old guys."

"Speak for yourself." Jason frowns. "I'm not boring or old."

Alec chews his gum with such force his jaw aches, his gaze resting on Theo. He can't tell if Theo was offering him a way out or trying to get him not to come. The smart thing to do would be head back to his apartment and catch up on sleep before classes start Monday or maybe play some video games with his friends. He's getting better at blowing things up. Hell, there are half a dozen things he could do that would be a better choice than going to a club with his big brother and his crush while suffering through watching people flirt with Theo.

Unfortunately, Alec's brain is amped up on endorphins and jealousy, and he makes the stupid fucking choice.

"I could come."

"See." Jason grins at Theo. "Alec wants to hang with us. We're still cool."

"Fair warning, no one will pull anyone while I'm around. I'm too handsome. You two won't stand a chance."

"Aw, baby Alec is all grown up," Jason says, throwing an arm around Alec's shoulders. "Make sure you bring your ID. They're gonna take one look at that baby face and wonder if it's fake."

"Not all of us are hairy as a lumberjack," Alec shoots back.

"Alec's just jealous because he can't grow a beard," Jason tells Theo, pushing Alec's hood off before messing up his curls. "This beautiful head of hair is all he's got. Do you remember how he was almost bald until he was two?"

Alec ducks out of Jason's hold, shaking his hair out. "Fuck off, you overgrown jackass. Touch my hair again and I'll end you."

"Aw, such a feisty baby."

Alec scoffs. "Not a baby, a man." He waits for the ribbing, but Theo and Jason just stare at him like he's grown a second head. He fidgets with the sleeves of his hoodie, pulling them over his hands while chewing his gum so hard his jaw throbs.

"I guess you did grow up, didn't you?" Jason replies, the sincerity somehow more difficult to handle than the teasing. At least from Jason. Their entire relationship is built on pissing contests and competitiveness.

"Took you long enough to notice," Alec says, avoiding Theo's gaze. He can't look at him right now, not when a single sentence has him feeling exposed.

"Alec."

"Don't," Alec mumbles, staring at the grass.

"I'm sorry."

"Nope, no pity," Alec says, shaking his head at his brother. He yanks his hood back on, hunching his shoulders. His body might be exhausted, but his mind is anything but. "I'm gonna head back to my place. I'll meet you guys at the club."

"I can pick you up on the way," Theo offers.

Alec's head snaps up. Theo's face is unreadable, but his gaze is unwavering, and Alec isn't sure he's ever seen Theo look at him like this.

"Good man, Theo. I've gotta swing by Andrew's place and help him move a piece of furniture, but I can meet you guys there at nine."

"Sounds good," Theo replies, his eyes never leaving Alec. It's unfamiliar and heady. Alec has no idea what it means. The offer was the kind of thing friends do, and Alec wants to be friends. But friends don't usually stare at each other like they're trying to figure something out. Then again, it's Theo, and he's not exactly like other people. He's quieter, more intense, better in every way.

Letting himself read into every word and look from Theo is a recipe for a broken heart, but Alec's has been broken so many times that at this point it's held together with duct tape and stubbornness. It can handle a little more pain.

———

"WHY DO you look like you're sneaking out?" Hunter asks. He pushes his cordless headphones back so they hang around his neck, his video game continuing to blow up in the background.

With Logan spending the night at his girlfriend's place, Antonio on one of his marathon FaceTime calls with Elsa, and Riley helping his frat brothers move in, Alec had thought he'd escape judgment. Then he'd realized Hunter was home and he maybe, possibly, spent an extra ten minutes waiting until Hunter was absorbed in his game before trying to casually sneak out the front door. Apparently, he did a shitty-ass job.

"You're losing," Alec says, pointing at the tv.

"You deflect a lot, you know that?" Hunter pauses the game, smiling. "There, better. Now, why do you look like you're sneaking out?"

Alec curses under his breath. Hunter is direct in a way Alec's not used to from his other friends, and while Alec has come to appreciate his no-nonsense ways, it still catches him off guard sometimes.

"Just heading out."

Hunter hums.

"What?" Alec snaps.

"Just wondering where. You sneak out a lot, but usually you take your AirPods and wear running clothes. You don't look like you're going running."

"How do you know where I go in the morning? Aren't you asleep?"

Hunter shakes his head. "I'm an only child. We don't sleep through anything like you weirdos with siblings have to learn to do."

"Shit, sorry. If I'd known I was waking you up, I wouldn't have—"

"You don't need to apologize," Hunter says. "There a party on campus already?"

"Not exactly."

"You got a date?" Alec's face must answer that question before his mouth can, and Hunter laughs. "That's a no, then."

"It's just—ugh." Alec stalks over to the couch, throwing himself down. "You know Theo."

"The guy you're in love with," Hunter finishes.

"I never said I was in love with him."

"No, but the way you answered me right now does. Continue."

"You only children are bossy," Alec grumbles. He leans forward, resting his elbows on his knees and dropping his head into his hands. "He and my brother are taking me out to a gay club to celebrate."

"That sounds complicated."

"Right," Alec groans, pulling his own hair so hard it hurts. "I couldn't say no because, well, I didn't wanna say no, but I shouldn't have said yes because Theo is gonna be there looking gorgeous, and he's always gorgeous so that's not new, but he's gonna pick someone up. I mean, he usually does. And it's one thing to know he only likes casual sex, but it's another to have to see it. But maybe I should go, because then it'll be like ripping a bandaid off. Maybe if I see him dance, or kiss someone, or take them home, maybe I can finally get over him." Alec's breathing faster by the time he finishes. He drops his hands, rubbing them on his jeans. "I know what you're going to say," Alec sighs.

"Do you?"

"You're going to tell me he's too old for me or that it's pathetic to be in love with the same guy for over six years when he doesn't like you back. You're going to tell me that I'm just being an idiot by refusing to stay away and that tonight is just going to break my heart, and I should stay home."

"Damn, I was gonna say all that?" Hunter laughs.

"Weren't you?"

At his silence Alec turns, expecting to see the kind of pity he's used to from Antonio or Riley. He knows they mean well and that they support him, but he also knows as his best friends they're mad at Theo, even if Theo has never actually done anything wrong. It's not Theo's fault Alec loves him. Which is maybe, probably, why he didn't want them to know he was going tonight. Because all those things he just told Hunter he was going to say, those are all the things he knows Antonio or Riley would tell him.

"I was going to ask where there's a gay club in Santa Leon?" Hunter's smile widens, and Alec almost wishes he could develop a crush on someone like him. He's so easy to like and funny in his own deadpan way, but he's not Alec's type. All he feels is a growing appreciation for their friendship.

"It's down near the pier off Seaward. The only one in town."

"Interesting," Hunter remarks. For someone as high strung and dramatic as Alec, it's a welcome change to be around someone so chill. "I've never been to one."

"A club or a queer club?"

"Either. Both," Hunter answers. "All we had was a Dollar General and a few shitty fast food places. I grew up in a pretty small town. Nothing but agriculture and cows. I think sometimes there were parties at the river bottom, but that's not really my scene."

"Would you have gone if there was one?" Alec asks, careful to leave it open to interpretation about what kind of club he means.

The nice thing about being openly gay is that people usually feel pretty open coming out to him. It's part of why he's so out and proud. It feels good to be himself, but also to imagine that maybe sometimes that makes it easier for someone else to be themselves around him. That being said, he doesn't judge anyone who doesn't come out, to him or anyone else. The world can be shitty, and labels are confusing, and nobody owes anyone anything. For as much as he and Hunter have become close since moving in a couple weeks ago, they don't know each other well yet and Alec has no idea how to tread this conversation.

"Probably," Hunter nods. "I'm not sure what label I'd be, but it's there somewhere under that giant rainbow umbrella. Probably."

"It's okay to not be sure."

"How did you know?" Hunter asks. He drops back on the couch, sitting side by side with Alec, both of them staring at the paused video game.

"Honestly?"

"Yeah."

"Theo."

Hunter whistles long and low. "That's a whole other level. Does he know?"

"Are you kidding me? He literally ran away when he found out I was in love with him as a teenager. I'm never telling him that. I've actually never told anyone."

"Not even Antonio and Riley? I thought you guys were inseparable."

"We are, but there are some things they can't understand." Things like what it means to never be able to let go of the guy who helped you realize you were gay. To grow up and realize your hero was also your crush. To become a man and find out that crush wasn't as perfect as you once thought and love him even more for all his flawed, imperfect edges.

"And I can?"

"I dunno, maybe." Alec tugs on his necklace, pulling the chain between his teeth. The metallic taste distracts him from his burgeoning anxiety.

"Is this like queer solidarity?"

"Maybe," Alec mumbles around the chain in his mouth.

"Dude, you know they make special jewelry to chew on, right?"

"I like the taste," Alec admits, letting the chain fall from his mouth. "Don't judge me."

"Older men and sucking on necklaces. Anything else I should know about you?"

"Yeah, I can't hold my liquor for shit."

"Why do I need to know that?" Hunter asks.

"Because you're coming with me," Alec says, snatching the remote from Hunter's lap and switching off the game before grabbing his hand.

If Hunter minds being manhandled he says nothing, allowing Alec to drag him towards the door. Alec's already reaching for the handle when he turns, fixing his gaze on Hunter. "I didn't even ask if you wanna change."

"Am I supposed to change?" Hunter looks down at his jeans and wrinkled shirt, plucking at his Santa Leon University t-shirt. In the two weeks since moving in, Alec's only ever seen him in different variations of that outfit. "I don't think I can pull off what you're wearing."

"First, all bodies are crop top bodies."

"Your body is definitely a crop top body," Hunter interjects, and though the words seem flirty, the tone is the same one he uses to explain to Alec why he's losing at video games or complain about who drank all the orange juice. Hunter's a tough egg to crack, and Alec decides not to read too much into it.

"Second," he continues, not addressing Hunter's comment, "you wear whatever you're comfortable in. I, for one am, uh—" Alec pauses, looking down at himself. He basically lives in athletic wear. His closet is full of team hoodies and shirts. He rarely wears anything besides sweats or running shorts. The loose jeans and crop top he's wearing

tonight are casual, but a far cry from his normal attire. Truth
be told, it's the first time he's ever worn the damn top.
Antonio and Elsa had taken him on a day trip to Mexico
City to play tourist, and he'd inevitably been dragged shopping. He'd found the top in the women's section while
following Elsa around and trying to get to know the person
his best friend loved. He could see why Antonio loved her.
She was beautiful, funny and incredibly perceptive, grabbing the shirt off the hanger and passing it to Alec, who had
bought it without a word.

Tonight seemed like as good a night as any to break it
out. He feels different in the shirt, hyper aware of his own
body but not in a bad way. It shows off his well-earned
stomach muscles, and maybe Theo won't ever see him the
way Alec wishes he would, but it doesn't mean Alec can't
look sexy in front of him.

"I get it," Hunter says.

Alec nods, grateful he won't have to try and say any of
that out loud.

"So since neither of us have a car, how exactly are we
getting across town? Did you call a ride already or—"

"Theo's picking us up."

"Theo," Hunter echoes in that damn casual tone
of his.

"Jason is busy helping one of my older brothers. He's
gonna meet us there," Alec explains. "Theo's house isn't too
far from campus, and since he would pass this way anyway,
he offered to pick me up. No big deal or anything. That's
what friends do and we're friends."

"And he won't mind you bringing me along?"

"Why would he mind?"

"No reason." Hunter hums. "Alright, let's do this.
Although fair warning, I've never had sex with a guy."

"Pretty sure you can go to a club without fucking," Alec points out.

"And if someone...wanted to?"

"Wanted to fuck?"

"Uh-huh."

"I wouldn't know," Alec shrugs, wondering why his own virginity keeps popping up lately. He went years keeping it off the radar. "Casual sex isn't really my thing."

"Fair," Hunter nods, slipping his hands into his pockets. "Do you—"

Alec's phone rings, interrupting Hunter's question and making Alec jump. No one ever calls him besides his parents and that's not usually on Friday night. He pulls it out of his back pocket, a smile forming on his face when he reads the name.

"Aw, Theodore. You missed me already."

"I appreciate that you assume that's the only reason someone would call you."

"When texting is an option and someone chooses to call, the only logical assumption is their fondness for my voice. Admit it, you like listening to me talk."

There's the briefest pause where Alec worries he's gone too far before Theo laughs. "Maybe."

Maybe.

No word has ever sounded so beautiful. Honest to god butterflies erupt in his chest. Alec has lost track of how many times people have gotten tired of him talking. Told him he talks too loud or too fast, telling him to water himself down to be easier to handle. The idea that maybe Theo doesn't mind Alec at full strength is possibly the most affirming thing he's ever heard.

"You weren't outside when I got here, so I thought I'd call and see if you needed help with anything."

"What, are you gonna help me get dressed?" Alec teases, blaming his sudden confidence from Theo's words spurring on his flirty side. If he doesn't mind Alec being unabashedly himself, then maybe he can stop holding back. They're friends, and Alec flirts and teases his friends. Maybe when he does it to Theo it's secretly true, but Theo doesn't need to know that. "I'm just teasing. Calm down, Theodore. Old people have delicate hearts, so I've been told."

"You're such a shit." Theo laughs, and the sound is warm through the phone. Alec can picture the shape of Theo's smile and the exact place where the lines form near his eyes when he's happy. "Get your sarcastic ass downstairs."

"Yes, sir." Alec grins, his smile faltering when he hangs up and finds Hunter staring at him with a curious expression. He shifts, tugging on the hem of his shirt self-consciously. "What?"

"Nothing," Hunter says, though it seems anything but. "You still wanna do this?"

"Hell yeah," Alec answers, a renewed sense of energy thrumming through his body.

He taps his fingers against his hip, unable to fight off his own growing smile. His team kicked ass today, Theo is his friend again, and Hunter came out to him tonight. While his body might ache from the game today and his entire future is overwhelming, none of that matters tonight. Tonight he's just a guy hanging out with his friends. He's gonna have a drink, dance, and relax. Tonight is going to be amazing. He can feel it.

Hunter curses behind him. "I forgot my phone."

"I can wait for you," Alec tells him, pausing in the open doorway.

"Nah, that's fine, I'll be out in a minute. Don't wanna keep Theo waiting." He winks at Alec, and the act has him blushing more than he has any right to. It occurs to him that as painful and ill-advised as his feelings for Theo have always been, no one has ever let him have them. Charlie has been overprotective and judgmental, as have Antonio and Riley, and while he knows that it always came from a place of love, those reactions made him feel more defensive than he ever realized.

He knows nothing will ever happen with Theo and that dressing up to go out to a gay club with him is silly, but Hunter isn't telling him that or reminding him not to be an idiot. He's teasing Alec, letting him have his crush, and it feels surprisingly nice. That feeling lasts all of thirty seconds until he steps outside to find Theo leaning against his car waiting for Alec.

Theo's usual sweater is nowhere to be found. Instead he's wearing a dark blue, long-sleeved button up that fits him like a second skin. The dark color highlights his tan skin, even in the dark glow of the apartment lights. His long legs are splayed wide, the dark wash denim hugging his thighs and waist in all the right places.

Theo looks like sex on legs, and Alec is so fucking screwed.

12 THEO

IT'S a good thing Theo is already leaning against the car, because watching Alec walk towards him with a wide smile and unmistakable confidence is enough to have Theo's knees trembling.

He's seen Alec spend a year wearing a superhero cape to soccer practice when he was in elementary school and has seen him in various stages of teenage awkwardness. More recently, he's seen Alec in nothing but athleisure, a style that suits him. But Theo's never seen Alec like this. Gone are his sweats, barely-there tanks, and his oversized hoodies paired with tiny running shorts. Tonight, Alec is dressed in a pair of loose fitting jeans that hang so low on his waist Theo has no idea what's even keeping them up. The thick waistband of his stretchy boxer briefs are visible along with the Adidas logo. The band is crisp white, like they're brand new, and the mental image is enough to have Theo glad his pants are way too tight to show off his own reaction.

As good as Alec's pants and boxers look, the shirt is the star of the show, or perhaps lack thereof. Theo doesn't know much about fashion, but what he does know is that Alec looks sexy as hell in his crop top. The shirt has a low scoop at the neckline, showing off the hollow of his throat and collarbones, both of which have a glorious amount of freckles. The boxy fit of the shirt flutters when he moves, hanging free around his chest and showing off his impressive physique.

The fact that Alec is a D1 athlete is all too obvious in the expanse of muscles on display, his belly taut with a defined six pack. Even the jut of his hips are sharp enough to cut diamonds. The most tantalizing of all are the freckles splattered across his belly and around his hips. Theo got glimpses of them when Alec showed up on his doorstep with Rio, but he'd been a lot more worried about tending to Alec's wounds than mapping his freckles. He's interested in tracing them now, his tongue too big for his mouth as his eyes hone in on a dark cluster near Alec's treasure trail, both of which disappear beneath his waistband.

Appreciating Alec's beauty before had felt almost objective, like looking at a piece of art and recognizing it was stunning. Whatever he's doing now is anything but objective.

"You clean up nice, Theodore. You trying to get someone's attention?"

"You never know. I might see someone at the club worth picking up," Theo lies, knowing there won't be a goddamn person there who can compare to the man in front of him.

"Of course," Alec says. His smile slips for half a second, gone and back so quickly Theo isn't sure if he imagined it. "I'm sure you're very popular. You could have your pick of anyone."

"Maybe—"

"Here I am," Hunter announces, skidding to stop next to Alec.

"Hunter is coming," Alec says, swinging an arm around Hunter's waist. "Isn't that great?"

It's only years of practice schooling his facial expressions in front of his boss that stops Theo from frowning. He met Hunter the day Theo helped Alec move in. He was kind of quiet, blunt, and overall not very memorable. He was also, to Theo's knowledge, straight. Then again, Antonio and Riley are straight and always touch Alec, but this is different. Hunter's looking at Alec like, well, like he also knows how good Alec looks tonight. Not that Alec seems to notice.

"It's going to be great," Alec insists, turning his attention away from Theo and onto Hunter. "You want the front or the back?"

"I get carsick in the back. You mind if I take the front?"

"Not at all. Right, Theo?"

"Of course I don't mind," Theo smiles, lying through his teeth. He minds very much. He was looking forward to a few minutes of alone time with Alec before they met up with Jason. He also wanted to find a way to tell Alec how much he enjoyed watching him play, to see if he might casually suggest Theo come again, so he'd have an excuse to do just that. Now instead of fifteen minutes alone with Alec, he's got some kid he doesn't know climbing into his front seat.

To make matters worse, by the time he's walked around the car to the driver's side, Alec has situated himself behind Theo so he can more easily talk to Hunter, who he is instructing to put on whatever music he wants. When Theo starts the engine, something very loud and very country blares through the speaker.

"This okay?" Hunter asks, and Theo forces on a smile.

Theo doesn't like country music. Theo doesn't like that Hunter is sitting where Alec should be sitting. Theo especially doesn't like that he's so put out by the entire thing when he has no reason to care, and certainly has no right to have an opinion on where Alec sits, or whether he wants to bring a friend clubbing with them.

"It's fine," Theo insists, pulling away from the curb with a heavy foot and the sound of tires screeching on asphalt.

"Try not to crash! You have precious cargo in the backseat," Alec yells.

Hunter laughs, and something unfamiliar and unwanted twists in Theo's gut, the same feeling he'd had watching Alec dance with Riley at his birthday party.

"You laugh, but you know it's true," Alec says loudly enough to be heard over the blaring music. "I am irreplaceable."

Theo's hands grip the steering wheel so hard his knuckles go white. Where he would normally smile at Alec's cockiness, this time it's Hunter who smiles, and that makes something heavy settle in his chest. He tries to ignore the feeling, focusing on the traffic and the annoying beat of the music as he drives them across town. Alec never stops talking, but the majority of it is directed to Hunter, which saves Theo from having to make small talk but also increases the uncomfortable weight in his ribcage.

It's a good twenty minutes with traffic before Theo is pulling into the city lot across from the club, by which point he's developed a headache and aching fingers from gripping the wheel too tightly. It doesn't take them long to park and exit the car, and Jason flags them down the second all three of them hit the sidewalk.

"Over here," Jason yells, like they can't see his massive

frame towering above the people around him. "Dude, I was starting to think you guys ditched me."

"Never," Theo tells him. As sure as he is that Jason is joking, Theo affirms him anyway.

Sure enough, Jason's face breaks into a massive smile. The sight reminds Theo of what this night is supposed to be: a few friends heading out to celebrate Alec's win and take him to his first club.

It's only a few seconds before Theo's gaze drifts sideways to Alec, who looks like a kid in a candy shop, his hips already swaying to the beat of the music that spills through the open door. He's so uninhibited, oblivious to stares as he lifts his arms up and dances, his pretty eyes fluttering shut.

"Someone is excited." Jason laughs. His voice drags Theo back from the edge. If he wants any hope of surviving tonight, he needs to get himself in check and remember what's at stake—his friendship with Jason.

"We should probably get in line." Theo eyes the crowd of people around them. Aside from the groups milling around street corners and sidewalks, the line itself is already wrapped around the side of the building. With all of the students back on campus it makes sense, but Theo hadn't really stopped to consider how much more crowded the club might be tonight. Apparently neither did Jason, judging by the silent conversation he tries to have with Theo with his raised eyebrows.

"We'll be lucky to get in before eleven at this rate," Jason says with a shake of his head.

Theo falls into step beside him, realizing Alec isn't following suit. Before he can say anything, Hunter leans in to whisper something that has Alec's eyes snapping open and a smile blossoming on his face as he nods.

The tightness in Theo's chest is sharp and uncomfortable, and he wishes the line weren't so long, desperately needing a drink to dull the edges of bitterness taking hold.

"Hey asshole!" Jason yells when he notices Hunter and Alec walking towards the front door. "The end of the line is over here."

Alec and Hunter exchange embarrassed looks before bursting into laughter. Before they can follow Jason and Theo, the bouncer is lowering the rope.

"He can come in," the bouncer says, pointing at Alec.

There's a flicker of surprise on Alec's face before he grins, blowing the bouncer a kiss. The bouncer appears unaffected, but Theo can't help marveling at the way Alec takes the attention in stride.

"Dance for us, sweetheart!" someone yells from the line, followed by a few catcalls and whistles.

"Hey, that's my baby brother!" Jason yells, but no one pays him any attention.

Alec turns, standing in the open doorway, the pulsing lights flickering behind him as he turns to Jason and offers him two middle fingers. "Cock blocker."

Jason is saying something, but Theo's ears are filled with white noise as he stares at the curve of Alec's spine, remembering the freckles that hug his lower back.

"Dude, I said move it, or they'll get in without us," Jason repeats, grabbing Theo's arm.

Theo curses under his breath, hurrying to follow, but the bouncer shakes his head, pointing to the end of the line. It's impossible to tell who is more upset, Theo who gets a sick feeling at the idea of Alec in there without him or Jason who looks like someone stole his piece of birthday cake.

"He's my brother," Jason says, lifting his chin.

The bouncer shrugs. "Hottest ones first."

"I'm hot." Jason frowns.

"Of course you are, big guy," Theo tells him, clapping him on the back.

"We're hot," Jason repeats, clearly put out. Theo can't even be offended because one of his main goals in life is to be invisible, so he can't be annoyed that the bouncer agrees. Besides, he and Jason always wait in line, and it's never been a problem. Then again, they've never brought Alec before.

"This is bullshit," Jason grumbles. "What if someone in there makes a move on Alec? At least Hunter is there, I guess. What's his deal, is he—"

"Are you guys coming?" Alec yells, popping his head back out of the door.

Theo doesn't want to think too hard about the fact that Alec noticed that they weren't with him. His heart skips a beat.

"We would, but he won't let us in," Jason says, frowning at the bouncer like he's responsible for every wrong Jason has ever suffered in his life. It occurs to Theo that Jason and Alec are equally dramatic, though Jason tends to be a bit quieter about it. Apparently, this time he's too offended to keep his mouth shut.

"I'm sure he would for me, wouldn't you?" Alec grins, leaning against the doorway. He arches his back, crossing his arms in a way that pulls his top up even further and exposes most of his stomach and ribs as he stares at the bouncer sweetly. When that doesn't immediately work, Alec leans forward, whispering something in the bouncer's ear that has him nodding solemnly before lowering the rope.

Theo holds his breath watching the exchange, eyes darting between Alec and the bouncer when the man's stoic countenance breaks. Jason and Theo don't wait for further permission, hurrying inside after Alec.

"What did you tell him?" Jason asks, yelling to be heard over the music.

"None of your business," Alec retorts. "You're welcome for saving your asses, by the way."

"I could've gotten in on my looks if I tried," Jason grumbles.

Theo wonders if maybe they're both getting too old for this kind of thing. More than once, Theo's left the club physically and emotionally unsatisfied. Jason, the serial monogamist, never picks up at clubs and only goes for the vibes.

Until right now, Theo never stopped to think about the source of his growing dissatisfaction. He never let himself consider that maybe he's tired of blow jobs in the back of a club or nameless bathroom sex. He never let himself think about the fact that he's growing tired of cheap hookups, that maybe he's tired of them altogether. Probably because admitting that means admitting he might want something else. But does that mean he wants a relationship? He sure as hell hasn't before. He's not a relationship guy. He promised himself a long time ago he wouldn't fall in love or deal with that level of heartache.

Unfortunately, looking at Alec standing there so carefree and sexy, he can feel his heart wanting things his brain has no intention of letting it have.

Jason scoffs. "I'm still in my prime."

"Sure you are," Theo agrees.

At the exact same time, Alec yells, "You're old!"

"Fuck you!" Jason fires back.

Alec laughs before turning towards the dance floor. He

watches for a few seconds before turning to Jason and Theo. "I'm going to dance. You guys coming?"

Theo shakes his head. "I'm gonna get a drink first.".

"I'll dance," Hunter says, almost making Theo wish he'd said yes. He has no reason to dislike Hunter, yet every time he looks at him, he likes the guy less. Theo watches them weave through the crowd, his heart lodged in his throat at the sight of Alec's delicate fingers curled around Hunter's forearm. He's holding on to him so they don't get lost in the crowd. Probably.

"I need a drink, pronto. How about—" but Jason cuts himself off, pulling his buzzing phone out of back pocket from a frown. "God dammit."

"What?"

"It's an alert from my doggy cam."

"Stella again?" Theo guesses.

"Yes," Jason sighs, pinching his nose. "How the hell did she get in the yard? She's just stupid enough to try and dig her way out or use the patio furniture to get over the fence. I swear to god that dog is Houdini."

"You going to come back after you get her inside?"

"I dunno, man, it's gonna take me twenty minutes to get home, and even if I can get her in quickly, she's gonna cry once she sees me and—"

"You won't be able to leave them again without feeling guilty," Theo finishes. "Also the line. You'd probably never get back inside even if you did come back."

"You're not mad, are you? I know you don't usually come here alone."

"I'm not alone, Alec's here. Somewhere. Besides, you know I would never be mad at you for anything."

"You should. Maybe not this because it kind of sucks

and isn't my fault this time, but you don't feel your feelings enough."

Theo groans. "I thought we were having club time, not therapy time."

"Bro code says it's always therapy time when feelings need to be felt."

Despite the uncomfortable mix of emotions churning in his gut, Theo can't help but smile as he shoves Jason. "Get the hell out of here."

"Fine, but make sure and watch out for Alec."

"Alec's a big boy," Theo says, unsure if he's trying to convince himself or Jason.

"Dude, you remember that conversation in the kitchen." Jason's words might be vague, but the meaning is clear. "I'd feel better if I knew you were watching out for him. Make sure no assholes try anything."

The *'anything'* is underlined even if Jason doesn't say it. Theo knows exactly what Jason is worried about. He's been here enough. While plenty of people come here just to dance and have fun, a town like Santa Leon doesn't have a huge queer scene, and while there are tons of inclusive spaces, this is the only one like this.

"I'll watch out for him," Theo promises.

"Thanks." Jason claps him on the back before disappearing into the crowd.

Once Jason is out of sight, Theo heads to the bar, wasting no time in ordering himself a drink before sitting in the corner. His position gives him the benefit of a perfect view of the entire club. His eyes track the booths along the far wall filled with college kids enjoying their last weekend of freedom before the semester kicks off, strangers looking for a connection, or people nursing a drink after a long week.

There's no sign of Alec there, so Theo sips his beer slowly while scanning the crowded club for any sight of wild curls and freckles. Fifteen minutes pass before Theo gets frustrated by his inability to locate Alec. When Theo comes with Jason, they usually get a booth and hunker down, waiting for someone else to approach. Of course, Jason isn't here, and Theo's not looking for a hookup tonight, which means his propensity to chill in one spot isn't going to work if he wants to keep his promise to Jason and watch out for Alec.

Grabbing his beer, he inches closer to the dance floor. Unfortunately, the club is more crowded than Theo has ever seen, and a single loop around the edge provides no sight of Alec, especially since Alec doesn't exactly tower above the people around him.

Changing tactics, Theo decides to look for Hunter and his boring, plain face instead. Sure enough, a few minutes later he spots Hunter's head of dirty blonde hair near the center of the dance floor. The best Theo can do for now is keep an eye on Hunter and wait, hoping Alec is still with him.

Standing there staring at Hunter makes Theo's anxiety rise. Usually he can distract himself with Jason's endless conversation or playing the '*who looks like they might be good to hook up with*' game. Neither of those distractions are available to Theo tonight, leaving him far too much time in his own brain.

Hyper-aware of his surroundings, he notices the way the heavy bass of the music vibrates in his chest. The flickering neon lights above the dance floor seem brighter than usual, the music louder and the crowds more oppressive. His natural instinct is to find a corner and hide there, but that would mean losing sight of Hunter and therefore any chance of keeping an eye on Alec. Instead he remains in place, even when someone stumbles into Theo so hard it sends his beer sloshing all over on his hand.

"Sorry," Theo apologizes automatically, even though he's the one who got knocked into.

"Fucking move," the person grumbles.

They're clearly drunk, so Theo doesn't bother replying, shaking beer off his hand before wiping it dry on his pants. When he returns his gaze to the dance floor, he's dismayed to realize Hunter is no longer there. Theo moves forward with a frown, fully prepared to get on the dance floor to find them when Alec comes stumbling out of the crowd, hand clasped in Hunter's.

Theo's tongue is like sandpaper in his mouth, and he gulps the last of his beer as he watches Alec drop Hunter's hand in favor of pushing sweaty curls off his forehead. Hunter is saying something to Alec, but it's too loud to hear what. All Theo can make out is Alec's nod before Hunter turns and makes his way towards the bar, leaving Alec alone.

Somehow, Theo expects him to head off the dance floor entirely now that he's alone. Instead, he closes his eyes and raises his arms overhead, moving his body to the beat of the music. That's the thing about Alec, he can have fun anywhere, even a crowded dance floor without a partner.

It's clear Alec's an athlete and not just from the impressive cut of his Adonis belt above his boxers or the miles of abs on display. The real evidence is in his muscle control and the way he knows every inch of his own body, at complete ease in his skin. It's a wonder to watch, and Theo's eyes are honed in on the sway of Alec's hips.

Without warning or permission, an unfamiliar hand curls around Alec's hip. His eyes fly open as he tips his head back to seek out the source of the contact. There's a flicker of surprise when he sees it's not Hunter. Theo fully expects Alec to push the man away, but then the guy's fingers spread wide on Alec's hip, far more familiar than they have any right to be. He leans down to whisper something in Alec's ear that has Alec laughing. To Theo's complete and utter disappointment, Alec doesn't step away or tell the guy to fuck off, letting his arms encircle the man's neck as he tips his back against his chest and rocks his hips.

The guy is easily twice Alec's size, from the breadth of his chest and thighs to the massive hands that encircle Alec's much smaller waist. He's older too, maybe even older than Theo, with dark scruff on his face and the hint of lines at his eyes. Theo holds his bottle so hard he's surprised the glass doesn't shatter.

That's not some youthful college guy. That's a man. If Alec had danced with someone who looked like Riley or Hunter, would he be having this same reaction? Or is it the sight of someone so similar to Theo in age and build that has his pulse racing and his feet moving?

Unsure what he's doing but equally unable to stop, Theo stalks toward Alec and the stranger, planting himself directly in front of them. The man lifts his eyes to meet Theo's gaze, unblinking as the guy looks Theo up and down before spreading his hands wide over the center of Alec's belly.

White hot anger pulses in Theo's veins. It's just being protective, he tells himself, refusing to think about why he wants to punch the guy touching Alec when he's never been in a fight in his entire life.

Alec laughs, eyes flying open. "That tick—oh, Theo." His expression changes rapidly, his amusement shifting into something impossible to read.

"You know him?" the man grumbles, the fingers curled around Alec's hip tightening.

A flare of jealousy rages inside of Theo, consuming and demanding and so unlike anything he's ever felt before. There's no pretending he's only being protective now, even if he wishes he could. Theo never cared about the people he hooked up with being with anyone else. Hell, his ex had all but admitted to cheating, and the most Theo could do was be glad he was going to disappear so Theo didn't have to break up with him. He's seen men and women he hooked up with leave the back room of the club and immediately seek someone else out and not give a damn. Yet some guy has his hand on Alec's waist and Theo's heart thunders in his chest so hard he can barely breathe.

"Theo, are you alright?"

The man leans down to whisper something in Alec's ear, but he doesn't laugh this time, shaking his head and trying to taking a step forward. It's clear the man isn't eager to let Alec go, his grip unwavering. Theo is ready to throw his first punch, but it's unnecessary because Alec pries the hands off his waist with a frown, stepping closer to Theo.

"Fucking tease," the man snarks. "You're not worth it."

Alec's shoulders tense and despite being positive that guy could probably lay Theo on his ass, he's never been closer to punching someone.

"Alec."

"Don't," Alec mutters.

"Don't what?"

"Just...don't," Alec says, averting his gaze. With those two simple words, some of his light dims. It makes Theo want to punch that man even more. Alec should be allowed to have fun, to dance and enjoy himself, without assholes assuming they're entitled to things from him.

"Drink time," Hunter announces as he slides in between Theo and Alec, unaware of what he just missed. He passes Alec something colorful with a cherry in it before his eyes land on Theo, and he frowns. "Why do I feel like I'm interrupting something?"

"You're not," Alec answers, taking his drink. Rather than sip it, he chugs it down quickly. Some of the sticky sweet drink runs down the side of his mouth and drips down his chin. He licks the last of it off his lips, leaving them stained a pretty pink.

"Alec," Theo tries, hardly sure what he wants to say.

"What?"

"Be careful."

Alec visibly bristles. "I'm a big boy, I can handle myself. In fact, I need another drink."

"Don't you think you should—" but before he can finish that thought, Alec makes a beeline for the bar. "God dammit." Theo sighs, running a hand through his hair and wondering how the hell he always manages to fuck things up with Alec despite his best intentions. It's a good thirty seconds before he realizes Hunter is still standing next him staring. "Uh, that was...that is to say that—"

"That was awkward," Hunter says, taking a leisurely sip of his own beer.

"Yes." Theo sighs.

"You know he can handle himself pretty well, right?"

"I know." Theo groans, because he does know. Alec is strong, and Theo's a fucking neanderthal who got jealous and possessive and made things uncomfortable for Alec, who was just trying to have fun.

"Wow."

"What?" Theo asks.

"Just wow," Hunter answers, taking another slow sip of his drink. "You're not what I expected."

"I have no idea if that's a good thing or a bad thing," Theo replies, utterly confused by this kid.

"Me either," he shrugs, so utterly honest Theo can't even be offended. "This beer is shit, by the way."

"People don't really come here for the quality of drinks," Theo admits.

"So why do they come here?"

"To meet someone, usually."

"And you brought Alec?"

"Well, me and Jason."

"So you and Alec's big brother brought Alec to a queer club to meet someone."

"That's...no," Theo shakes his head.

"So you don't want him to meet someone?" Hunter asks, his level of eye contact slightly jarring.

Somehow that feels like a trick question, and Theo's anxiety spikes, his limit for small talk reached. He takes a step backward, mentally rehearsing his sentence before he blurts out, "I'm gonna go look for Alec and get a drink."

"Can you tell Alec I bailed?" Hunter yells.

Theo pauses, turning around with a frown. "Won't he miss you?"

"I don't think I'm the one he came for," Hunter says, closing the distance between them and passing Theo his beer.

"Do you need a ride?"

"I can call an Uber. Don't worry about it. Just be careful with him." The warning is reminiscent of Jason's, but there's something softer there. Where Jason's warning was loud, Hunter's is quiet, the implications far more subtle.

"I thought you said he could protect himself."

"Just because he can, doesn't mean he will. See you later, Theo."

With that, Theo is left alone for the second time tonight, confused, out of sorts and still eager to reassure himself of Alec's well-being. As Hunter's words echo in his head, he heads to the bar, but it's more crowded than before. The reason for that becomes clear when Theo pushes himself closer and sees half a dozen men watching Alec. What they're watching, he isn't sure, until the bartender slides over a shot glass, a lemon wedge, and salt shaker.

"Alec." Theo snaps his mouth shut, wondering why he seems to have no control over his words or feelings around Alec anymore.

Alec's head swivels towards Theo, and he grins, that playful smirk back in place. He mouths a hello before lifting his hand. There's a half a second where Theo forgets how to breathe, watching Alec's pretty pink tongue dart out to lick to spot between his thumb and forefinger, moistening it with his own saliva before he sprinkles salt. A few of the guys whistle and cheer, making Alec laugh.

"Hurry up," someone yells, which earns the guy a middle finger from Alec and a chorus of laughter and barks from the people around him.

Undeterred by the positive and negative attention he's gathering, Alec grabs the shot but pauses to lift his face to Theo. He holds his gaze for exactly three seconds before he winks, his smile hidden behind his hand as he licks off the salt he just put there. The people gathered make more lewd sounds and cheers when Alec takes the shot, then sucks the lemon wedge dry before he slams the empty shot glass on the counter.

Not even ten seconds pass before one of the guys from the crowd leans in far too close to Alec. His body is angled into Alec's space, his hands overly friendly as he curls one of them loosely around Alec's wrist and moves his mouth to Alec's ear. It's too loud to hear what he says, but Alec slides off his barstool, taking the fruity drink the bartender slides him and holding it above his head to avoid spilling while he lets this new guy pull him to the dance floor.

Once Alec is gone, the group of people disperse quickly, half of them finding various positions at the bar while the rest slink off to the dance floor, leaving Theo alone again. He plops himself on one of the barstools at the end with a grunt, eyes boring holes on the throngs of people dancing. He sips at the beer Hunter gave him and sighs heavily. It is shit, bitter and weak, just like Theo's rapidly souring mood.

Unlike before, Alec isn't hidden away in the middle of the dance floor. This time he's on the edge, sipping at his drink and laughing while the guy who brought him out there eye fucks Alec without an ounce of shame. His gaze is hungry, roaming over the lines of Alec's pretty face and down to his stomach, most of it exposed with his arms over-head and his crop top lifted. There's so much tanned skin, so many freckles and muscles. Though the guy's eyes wander, his hands remain firmly on Alec's hips, swaying them side to side before pulling him closer between the spread of his long legs.

Much like the guy before, this one is older, maybe twenty-five if Theo had to guess. His face is clean-shaven, his hair perfect, and his clothing all but painted on. He's big, too, and Theo's brain short circuits at the idea that Alec must have a type. Bigger. Older. Confident. Or maybe it's a coincidence. Maybe those men have a type? Maybe they like them smaller and pretty like Alec, his body a juxaposi-tion of hard lines and muscles meeting delicate lips and hands.

When the man's thumbs hook under the waistband of Alec's boxers, Theo chokes on his beer. When Alec doesn't pull away, he chokes on something else, the bile in his throat sour. Every part of Theo is screaming at him to turn away, to find something, *anything*, to distract himself. He doesn't. He doesn't look away. He can't.

Whatever flip was switched in his brain can't be turned off. He can't pretend Alexander King isn't the most beautiful man he's ever seen. Attractive without a doubt, but more than that, his confidence and personality shine brighter than every strobing light. Theo isn't the only one who notices, the eyes of Alec's dance partner and more than a few others nearby unmistakably on Alec as he moves his body freely.

Eyes still shut, Alec gulps down the remainder of his drink in one go. Once it's gone and the cup deposited on an empty table nearby thanks to his dance partner, Alec's movements grow wilder. The man he's dancing with gets handsier, pulling Alec's hips closer until Alec's writhing against his leg, damn near humping it. Not once does Alec open his eyes, lost in his own world as he rolls his hips and throws his head back.

Without warning the man leans down, drawing his tongue along the hollow of Alec's throat while he digs his hands into Alec's ass, trying to shove his finger in places he definitely didn't get permission for.

Theo's up and moving before Alec's eyes have even opened. When they do, a frown mars his face and he attempts to step back, but he's once again prevented from doing so by the hands on Alec's ass.

"Where do you think you're going, baby?" the man says in a disturbingly saccharine tone.

"Who the fuck said you could call me baby or lick me?"

Alec asks, giving him a hard shove and spinning on his heels, crashing directly into Theo's chest. "Fuck you, I—oh, it's you."

"It's me," Theo says, unsure what to do with Alec now that he's got him.

"Where's Hunter?"

"Oh, he told me to tell you he left. I don't think the club is his scene."

Alec nods, accepting the news easily. Maybe he's not as surprised as Theo assumed he'd be. "S'hot," Alec grumbles, blowing his hair out of his eyes. His curls are hanging heavy, clinging to his forehead while rivulets of sweat drip down his neck. The neck another man just had his mouth on. "I'm thirsty. I need a drink."

"I feel like maybe you've had enough."

"What are you, the alcohol monitor?" Alec asks, blinking up at Theo with those big eyes of his. They're brown, the color so deep and warm Theo could get lost in them. He knows over the years people have commented on his own blue eyes being special, but as far as Theo is concerned, Alec's eyes aren't just his favorite color, they're the color of everything grounding and safe and beautiful. They're the very color of the earth itself if Theo dug his hands into the soil and let it cling to his fingertips.

"Just worried about you," Theo admits.

"I knew you cared about me." Alec grins, swaying into Theo's personal space. He lays his palms on Theo's chest, patting him. "Big, big softie. So big."

Theo inhales sharply, watching as Alec toys with the button at the center of his chest. "Theo, will you dance with me?"

More than anything, Theo wants to say yes. He wants to let his hands wander, for his own hands to be the ones wrapped around Alec's waist. He wants to be the guy standing so close he can feel the thrum of excitement when Alec sways his hips, feel the thud of his heartbeat if they were to be pressed chest to chest. He wants to trail his own mouth down the curve of Alec's throat and taste the sweat and leftover fruity drink that clings there. He wants to devour Alec the way those other men had, and it makes him just as bad as they are.

"I, uh—"

"It's okay," Alec says, smiling despite the flicker of hurt in his eyes. He pats Theo's chest. "I'll find someone else to dance with."

Theo's hand flies out, his fingers curling around Alec's wrist. He's never held Alec's wrist before, and he didn't realize exactly how delicate it might look in his much larger hand.

"What are you doing?"

"You need to be careful."

"I can handle myself, Theodore." Alec grins, his eyes crinkling in the corners as he tries to step away, but Theo doesn't let go. He can't.

"They only want one thing, Alec."

Alec's body goes rigid and when he turns to face him, the smile is long gone. "So?"

"So, that's not what you want."

"How would you know what I want?"

"I was there in the kitchen," Theo reminds him. "I know—"

"You—" Alec pokes Theo in the chest. "Don't." He pokes him harder. "Know anything."

"You don't want to fuck some random guy in a club," Theo says, shocked at his own boldness. "I know that much."

Alec's inhale shudders. "Well, the person I want doesn't want me, so what the fuck does it matter what I want?"

"Alec, they're gonna take advantage of you." *I want to take advantage of you*, he thinks, knowing exactly why he can't dance with him. Theo's not built for relationships, and even if he was, it's clear Alec is in love with someone else, which is yet one more reason Theo needs to be careful. "Just don't dance with them."

"Then you dance with me," Alec challenges. There's a fire blazing in his eyes, the rise and fall of his chest rapid. For all the delicateness in his features, it's easy to forget how strong Alec is. Strong in ways that have nothing to do with muscles. Strong in ways Theo only dreams of.

Alec isn't afraid of Theo, isn't afraid of anything, but maybe he should be.

"Alec," he whispers. It's not a yes or no, but it's the only answer he can give, and it's the wrong one.

"Fuck you," Alec grits out, yanking his arm from Theo's grasp. "So what, you won't dance with me, but no one else should either?"

Theo doesn't say anything. There's nothing he can say. He's too much of a coward to let Alec know how much he wants him and just enough of an asshole to ensure no one else can have him.

Casual hookups and one-offs in a club are fine for people like Theo, but not for Alec. Something like that would ruin him. Theo might not know Alec like he used to, but he knows how much he wants romance and love and all the things his parents have. Despite his loud bravado, Alec has a gentle heart, and it deserves protecting. Even from Theo. Especially from Theo.

The silence stretches on too long, and Theo's inability to reply only makes Alec more upset.

"I can't believe you," Alec groans. "I'm going to get a drink."

"I'm coming."

"Now you talk," Alec snaps. He pulls the coin that dangles from his necklace between thumb and forefinger, tapping at it rapidly, agitation oozing from every pore. "Don't follow me, Theodore. Don't you dare."

With that he stalks off, leaving Theo alone for the third time that night.

13 ALEC

LIGHTS FLICKER in his peripheral vision as he all but runs to the bar, slamming himself against the wooden edge as he struggles to catch his breath. He's such an idiot. Part of Alec wants to cry, and the rest of him wants the ground to swallow him whole or get drunk enough that he won't remember tonight.

Turns out, not even when Theo wants to protect Alec is he desperate enough to dance with him. He'd danced at Alec's party, but that was different. Alec knows how he looks tonight, how he's been dancing, and Theo doesn't want any part of that. Which should be fine. It's not Theo's fault he's not interested in Alec, not his fault that while Alec tries to forget him on the dance floor, the touch of every other man repulses Alec because they're not Theo.

None of those men are the man with blue eyes and quiet smile that Alec has been in love with since he was fifteen, and it hurts so goddamn much he can barely breathe. He thought he could do this, thought he could just be friends, but every single day it hurts more. Sometimes,

Alec isn't sure if there's a point to even having a heart when it hurts this much.

He turns around, half-hoping Theo ignored his petulant warning and followed anyway, but he didn't, and the relief at his boundaries being respected is diminished by the cold ache of loss. For the briefest of moments, Alec thought maybe Theo didn't like those other men touching him because he wanted to dance with Alec. Clearly, those were foolish thoughts from a foolish boy who let a few drinks get to his head.

Theo doesn't like Alec, not like that, and he never will. Jason probably told him to watch out for him. He probably came over out of some stupid misplaced sense of obligation, which makes Alec want to puke.

"You look like you need this," someone says, sliding a drink in front of Alec.

Alec stares at the mystery drink before turning his gaze on the guy who passed it to him.

"I'd prefer not to be drugged, thanks." Alec slides it back across the bar.

The man laughs as if what Alec said is funny. It's not funny. Not even a little bit. Alec is tempted to flip him off, but he then has the bartender give Alec a fresh drink, definitely not tampered with, and Alec accepts it because he might be pissed off, but he's not going to turn down a free drink.

"Wanna dance, sweetheart?"

The guy can't be much older than Alec, and with his ridiculous aviators tucked into the front of his t-shirt like it's fucking sunny or something in here, he looks like an idiot. He's got dark hair and a pretty face, and he's got maybe two inches on Alec. Nothing about him makes Alec's heart race. Not his pompous laugh or his baby-faced looks.

"Alright," Alec answers, because despite all the reasons he doesn't want to dance with the guy, the one person he does want to dance with said no, and Alec is so tired of not being wanted. Just for one night he wants to let himself see what it's like to be the object of someone else's attention—to be desired. And there is no mistaking the desire in this guy's eyes as he drags his gaze up and down Alec's body.

This isn't what Alec wants. It isn't *who* he wants, but maybe if he gets drunk enough that won't matter. Besides, he isn't going to have sex with any of the guys here, regardless of what Theo thinks. He just wants to dance, have fun, and pretend that he's someone else's fantasy.

"You coming, pretty boy?"

"Coming," Alec replies, grabbing his drink before moving closer to the guy. "Show me your moves."

Together, they make their way to the dance floor. The guy is an objectively terrible dancer, but he plies Alec with drinks and compliments. It's not so bad, really. The music thunders in his ears as he closes his eyes and gets lost in the sound. He loses track of how long they're out there, the songs keep changing, the drinks keep coming, and Alec lets himself forget the blue eyes that he knows aren't watching him.

More than once, the guy whose name Alec never bothered to ask lets his hands wander, but Alec always shifts them higher. Inevitably, they move lower again, and after the fifth time, Alec gets annoyed. He tries to step away, but he's prevented by someone holding onto the loops of his jeans.

"What the fuck is with everyone grabbing me tonight?" Alec grumbles, turning around and glaring.

"Damn, you're pretty even when you're mad." The guy laughs again, like this is funny and suddenly, Alec doesn't want to dance with him anymore. He doesn't even want to look at him. "I bet you're pretty on your knees. You wanna come back to my place, baby?"

"No."

"Don't be a tease," the guy sneers, tugging on Alec's belt loop hard.

Alec slaps his hand, annoyed when he doesn't remove it. "I said no, asshole."

"Yet your mouth kept saying yes to drinks." He smirks, pressing himself against Alec as if buying Alec drinks is somehow permission to ignore his firm no. The guy rocks his hips, and he's hard, because of Alec, for Alec, and bile rises in Alec's throat because this is not what he wants. The fuzzy haze in his brain is not so fun anymore. "You like that, don't you? You like pretending you don't want this."

"Fuck you," Alec grits out, yanking himself back so hard he falls to the floor with a painful thud.

Someone yells, and the people around them move as someone very large and strong shoves them out of the way. That someone drops to his knees, moving in front of Alec and, *oh*, Alec knows this very large someone.

"Alec," Theo whispers. "Are you in trouble?"

"I'm not in trouble. I am the trouble, Theodore."

It's such a lie. Alec is in trouble. He's in so much goddamn trouble. He's so tired of having to hold back and pretend he doesn't want to be touched or have attention, because guys think it means more. Even worse is that he's desperately, *painfully*, still in love with Theo. The lights are too bright, and the ground is spinning, and he's never felt more out of control, but he can't say that. He can't say any of that.

"I think it's time for you to go home," Theo says.

"I can take him home," the handsy asshole offers.

"Over my dead fucking body," Alec slurs, flipping him off. "I wouldn't go home with you if you were the last man on earth."

"Cocktease."

Alec jumps up, fully intending to yell at the dickface some more, but the ground spins, and he stumbles sideways, ending up on the floor again. He squints, watching Theo lean in close. He can't hear what Theo tells him, but the guy looks pissed.

"Keep him. He's more trouble than he's worth," the guy says before turning to walk away.

"I'll fucking fight you," Alec yells from the ground. He's not sure how he thinks he can fight if he can't stand up, but that's beside the point. He's offended, god damn it. He's also got major ick from being groped against his will. And he's kind of sad, but he's not entirely sure why, and the corners of his eyes are leaking just a little bit.

"Calm down," Theo tries, a hand on Alec's shoulder.

The tears go from sad to angry as Alec swats his hand away, unsure why he's so mad. "No one in the history of fucking anything has ever calmed down after being told to calm down."

"Okay."

"I don't want to calm down!" Alec yells, grabbing onto Theo and using his body as leverage to stand up.

"Alright."

"You can't make me," Alec huffs, shoving his bony finger into one of Theo's soft, squishy pecs. He doesn't argue, and that just makes Alec madder, although why he isn't sure. He feels a bit like a deregulated toddler. There are so many emotions, and he can't figure out which one he's actually feeling. "You can't make me," Alec yells again. "Do you hear me, Theodore?"

"Yes, Alec."

"Why aren't you arguing?"

"Because you're drunk and emotional."

"I am not emotional. Fuck you," Alec snaps, climbing to his feet. He turns, intending to run away, but stumbles.

"Careful."

"I'm fine," Alec says to no one in particular, pushing past the crowds of people staring to get to the door. Suddenly, the club is too crowded, hot and loud, and if Alec doesn't get outside, he might suffocate.

Every step takes more effort than it should with his head spinning. He only makes it about halfway before someone asks him to dance, and Alec is either going to throw up on him or punch him in the face. Alec isn't even sure what he says, but the guy walks away with a shake of his head. Alec thinks he's in the clear, but then someone grabs his arm. Alec flinches, curling in on himself. It's not fair that just because he's a tactile person, people think they can grab him without permission, that they think his enjoyment of dancing meant more. He just wanted to have fun.

The hand holding his squeezes, and Alec nearly pukes. He doesn't want to be touched by strange men anymore.

"Don't touch me," Alec yells, standing still in the hope that the room might stop moving. "I'll punch you if you do."

"You look more like you might throw up on me," Theo says.

The fight goes out of Alec. It's just Theo touching him. Theo is safe. He came back, even after Alec yelled at him and tried to start a fight—albeit a justified one—then ran away again. He came for Alec, and Alec is reminded exactly why he doesn't drink. Not only can he not hold his liquor, he's a fucking messy drunk. He's emotional and whiny, his stomach hurts, his head is spinning, and he might cry. He really doesn't want to cry. "I don't feel so good," Alec admits, voice very small.

"Let me take you home."

Alec's jaw trembles. He doesn't want to go home. He doesn't want to go back to his own cold, tiny bed. He doesn't want to explain to Antonio where he was or why he's drunk.

"I'll stay here."

"What the hell, Alec. No."

"M'fine," Alec says, dropping to the floor and kicking his legs out. Someone steps over him to get by, but Alec doesn't care. Not even when they spill beer on his leg.

"Alec, stand up."

"Ground is good," Alec says, pretty sure fighting with Theo is the only thing keeping him from flat-out sobbing right now. He feels so fucking out of control. He's never been this drunk before, and that floaty, relaxed feeling from earlier is long gone, replaced by a wave of nausea and unease.

"Why are you so stubborn?" Theo sighs, squatting down. He pushes some of the hair from Alec's eyes, his hand cool and soft. Alec shouldn't, but he leans into the touch, closing his eyes and pressing his forehead into Theo's palm. "You're hot."

"You're just noticing?" Alec mumbles. "M'very sexy."

"Yes, sitting on the floor of a club drunk as an elephant is so sexy."

It's a joke. Probably. Except it floods Alec with embarrassment and shame, and then the tears are coming fast and hot.

"Oh, shit." Theo tries to wipe away the tears, but Alec flinches, flinging himself back so hard his head slams into the floor. He cries harder, throwing his arms over his face. "Alec, I was teasing."

"Leave me here to die," Alec wails.

"You are not going to die."

"Yes, I am."

"No, you're not. We just need to get you up and take you home. You can sleep it off at my place, alright? It's closer."

Theo's place. Theo is taking Alec back to his house? "Can I see Rio?"

"Of course you can see Rio. She lives there. Just stop crying and come with me, please," Theo begs, unable to stomach Alec crying.

"I'm not crying," Alec lies, scrubbing his hands at his face before opening his eyes to stare at the ceiling. The lights are flashing so bright he feels like he might have a seizure. He's never had one before, but his brain feels like it's screaming. "Theo, I think someone poisoned me."

"Is he okay?" someone asks. It's a girl with long brown hair on one side and shaved on the other. She looks nice, and Alec doesn't want her to worry.

"Yes," Alec answers at the same time Theo says no.

"I am fine, Theodore." The fact that his words slur probably lessens their impact.

"Stand up and prove it."

"Fine, give me space," Alec grumbles, rolling onto his belly. He gets onto his hands and knees, and then stops when the world spins. "Nevermind." Before he can collapse on the ground, strong arms are wrapping around his middle and lifting him to his feet.

"I could've done that," Alec insists, swaying on his feet. "You just beat me to it."

"Uh-huh." Theo hums, slipping Alec's arm around his waist.

"Did you get bigger?" Alec grumbles, patting Theo's side.

"Maybe you shrunk?"

"I don't have room to shrink," Alec moans pitifully. "I don't wanna shrink."

"You're not shrinking," Theo assures him, slipping his arm around Alec's waist so his bare fingers rest on Alec's belly, just under his crop top. "Just hold on to me and let's get you to the car."

They make it two steps before Alec nearly falls on his face. "Stop tripping me," Alec grumbles.

"I'm not," Theo says, sounding like he's trying not to laugh. "I think you forgot how to walk."

"I'll have you know I'm very...very...what the fuck is that word?"

"Coordinated?"

"Yes, that." He pats Theo's tummy. "Good man."

Theo doesn't argue with Alec, not even when he proceeds to trip over his own feet four more times before they make it out of the club. It's only when they're standing in the middle of the street that Alec stops to appreciate how good the cool night air feels on his flushed skin.

"Stop walking," Alec says, pushing Theo away.

"What's wrong?"

"M'hot," Alec answers, struggling with his shirt. He yanks on it, but it gets stuck around his neck, his necklace tangled as he tugs pathetically. A moment later, big hands are smoothing the cotton down, untangling his necklace so he can yank his shirt off. He sighs in relief, throwing out his arms and taking a deep breath.

"Happy now?" Theo asks.

"I'd be happier with a Coke."

"You had enough to drink."

"Coke isn't beer. I want a Coke."

"I'm taking you home."

"But I want a Coke." Alec is pretty sure he's whining, but he doesn't care. He really wants a Coke now that he's thought about it. Maybe the carbonation will help him feel less like someone ran over his emotions with a lawn mower. "Take me through a drive-thru."

"I have Coke at home."

Alec stumbles, staring at Theo through squinted eyes. "You don't drink Coke."

"No, I don't," Theo agrees, his touch gentle as he spurs Alec to keep moving. His feet go forward, one after the other. Theo's body is slotted against his own once more, his big steady hands the only thing keeping Alec from crumbling.

"Why do you have Coke, Theo?"

The answer seems obvious, but the idea that he bought it for Alec, that he thought about what Alec liked and then went and got some just in case Alec came over, is more than Alec's alcohol-addled brain can handle. Had he thought about Alec when he bought it? Does that mean he wanted Alec to come over again?

"For you," Theo answers.

It's only two words, but they break something in Alec. For the longest time, he thought his heart was held together by duct tape and glue, but he knows better now. It was fused together with the lies he told himself. *I can be casual. I can just be his friend. I can get over him.* Those lies shatter into a million and one pieces, because of a goddamn can of Coke.

Unable to move, Alec stops walking. He pulls himself out of Theo's hold and sits down in the middle of the road, lying on the macadam. He looks up at the sky and stares at the moon, so big and bright, and he knows without a shadow of a doubt that there is no getting over Theodore James. He can spend the rest of his life lying and running and fighting against his heart, and none of it will make a goddamn difference because he is in love with Theo. Somewhere along the line, while Alec was growing up and learning how to be a person, Theo's presence solidified itself so that Alec's heart grew around a Theo-shaped hole that no one else will ever fit into.

"What are you doing, Alec?"

"I'm going to live here now," Alec answers, throwing out his arms and legs so he's spread eagle in the middle of the street.

Someone honks but Alec doesn't move. He can't move. How can you move when you realize the kind of love you have for someone is steady as the roots of a tree? You can cut the top of the tree off, but those roots will always be there. There will be no getting over Theo. Not now, not ever.

Perhaps Alec should want to sob or scream, but all he feels is a floaty kind of peace. Well, that and a lot of nausea and dizziness, but the peace is nice. He's tired of fighting, tired of hiding. He loves Theo, and it's alright if Theo never loves him back. He'll take all the friendship and scraps of love and cans of Coke Theo will give him, and it will be enough because Theo is enough. Theo has always been enough.

"You're stopping traffic."

"I am amazing." Alec smiles. "Look at the moon, Theo. It's beautiful."

"Oh my god, you're so drunk." Theo snorts seconds before his arms are slipping beneath Alec's back and under his legs, lifting him from the ground like he weighs nothing.

"If you wanted to hold me, you just had to ask," Alec

laughs, following that up with a groan when Theo starts to walk, making Alec's stomach churn. "I don't feel so good."

"What were you even drinking?" Theo asks, hitching Alec up against his chest in a bridal carry. Alec might be smaller than him, but he's got a lot of muscle and weighs more than he looks, and yet Theo holds him with ease. A pitiful sound falls from Alec's lips as he buries his face in Theo's neck and breathes in the achingly familiar scent of his cologne.

"It's gonna be okay, Alec."

Alec doesn't reply. There's nothing to say. He's drunk off his ass and in love with the man holding him. Nothing about this situation is remotely okay.

"Think you can stand if I put you down?" Theo asks.

"No, thank you," Alec mumbles against Theo's neck.

The reverberations of Theo's soft laughter jostles Alec, making him hold on all the tighter. "It's my fault for making it a question." He attempts to lower Alec's legs, but Alec tries to curl himself around Theo, not wanting to be put down. "Alec."

Alec ignores his words while shoving his nose into Theo's neck further. He's not gonna get another chance to be this close, and he's going to take full advantage of their proximity. Theo's body is strong and warm, his scent intoxicating, and if Alec didn't feel close to puking or passing out, it would be perfect.

"I have to put you down so I can drive."

In response Alec tightens his arms around Theo's neck, refusing to return to reality.

"Alexander."

Alec sucks in a sharp breath, head spinning as he loosens his koala death grip on Theo. Carefully, he's lowered to the ground, his feet unsteady and his head spinning as he opens his eyes to find pretty blue ones staring back at him.

"What?"

"Nothing," Theo whispers, pushing a loose curl behind Alec's ear. "Alec—"

Bile rises in Alec's throat. Suddenly, a gut wrenching sound comes from his own mouth as he shoves Theo away just in time to prevent spewing his guts on him. He falls to his knees, losing everything in his stomach. His muscles spasm, his throat closes as he gags, and tears prickle at his eyes. Alec hates puking, and he hates crying, and he never, ever wants to drink again.

"You're crying," Theo whispers.

"I'm not," Alec insists, even as the tears fall. "I'm never drinking again."

"If you say so."

"I do say so," Alec insists, rising to stand but falling into the side of the car. "Fucking door hit me."

"Let me help," Theo offers. If it were anyone else Alec might push them away, but since it's Theo, he lets himself be guided into the car. Wasting no time in kicking off his shoes and leaning his seat all the way back, he stretches his legs out on the dash and closes his eyes, finally comfortable. At least until the engine roars to life and the car moves, and then Alec's holding on to the door for dear life.

"Why are you driving so crazy?"

"I'm just pulling out."

"Nuh-uh," Alec says, slamming his mouth shut and shaking his head. He's pretty sure the odds of him being sick again are high.

"Alec."

"I need something to chew on."

"Like what?"

"Anything," Alec snaps, afraid he might cry again. He's so nauseous, and the ground is moving, literally, while Theo continues to drive. He needs to bite or chew on something. Right now.

He feels the brush of Theo's cotton shirt on his belly as Theo leans over him, digging around in the glove compartment until he finds a silicone reusable straw neatly folded in a little stainless carrying case. He passes it to Alec, who breathes deeply through his nose before biting the straw between his teeth.

Theo drives, Alec chews, and no one talks. By the time they make it to Theo's house, there are teeth marks embedded in the silicone, and Alec isn't sure he ever wants to get in a car again. Driving is the worst. Or maybe drinking is the worst. Or both.

As soon as Theo turns off the engine, Alec throws the door open, rolling out of the car with a painful thud and dragging himself to the grass where he flops belly down. Theo's sprinklers must've been on recently because the grass is wet, cold against his flushed skin and soaking his jeans.

"Are you ok?"

"Fucking great," Alec mumbles.

"Why are you in the grass?"

That seems like a stupid question to Alec, so he doesn't bother dignifying it with an answer, instead lifting himself onto his hands and knees, making it about a foot before collapsing back down again. He gets grass in his mouth, which is a great companion to the taste of puke still lingering. Alec's a real fucking catch tonight.

"Do you need me to carry you inside?"

"No," Alec snaps automatically, rolling onto his back.

He's met with Theo's kind eyes and something in him shatters beyond repair. "Maybe."

"Come on, then," Theo says, squatting down beside Alec. His pants are so tight it looks like his thighs might split them, the smallest hint of a belly hanging over his jeans. His strong arms move under Alec to pick him up and cradle him close for the second time tonight.

"Why is this happening to me?" Alec wails, flinging his head back pitifully.

"You drank enough for someone twice your size," Theo answers, far too honest for Alec's current state of inebriation.

With a grunt, Alec lets his head fall onto Theo's shoulder. The top two buttons of Theo's shirt are undone, and if Alec moved his mouth a bit he might be able to taste him, might feel some of Theo's pale skin beneath his own, or the brush of chest hair against his lips.

"You're not going to puke on me, are you?"

Shame and embarrassment well up in Alec like a fucking dam, and he shakes his head, pressing his face into Theo's neck and trying not to break down. This is why he doesn't drink. He can get wild and have fun sober. Drunk Alec isn't just messy, he's pathetic, needy and emotional. Every single desire he's ever had has been unearthed and laid on display. He feels exposed, raw, and so close to falling apart.

"We need to get you lying down."

"Shower," Alec grunts.

"Can you handle a shower?"

"M'not a fucking baby."

"Alright, alright," Theo says, his tone making it clear he's worried Alec might snap. Newsflash, he might. "Let's just get you inside. I can help you shower and—"

"I don't need help," Alec interjects, not sure why he's being so stubborn. For some reason it seems like a good idea, but so does kissing Theo. He's at least coherent enough to know that would ruin everything, but not enough to stop himself from refusing help he desperately wants.

There is no relief when Theo doesn't argue, only the foreboding sense that maybe this time Alec has found Theo's limit. Everyone always tells him he's a lot to handle. Too fidgety, too loud, too talkative, too cocky, too competitive, too honest. You name it, and Alec does it to the extreme. Drinking only magnifies that, which is why Alec's only ever had a few drinks. He's never even been drunk before, never wanted to get that out of control or find out who can't handle him.

Somehow, Theo manages to get the front door unlocked without dropping Alec. Once the door swings open, Theo carries him into the living room and lowers Alec down to a standing position beside the couch.

"Thanks," Alec mumbles, too out of it to try and check if Theo watches him stumble his way through the darkened living room. Somehow, his legs feel even shakier than before, and he just barely makes it across the living room. It's only sheer stubbornness and muscle memory that get him down the long hallway to the bathroom. More than once he nearly falls, but Theo hasn't followed Alec, letting him make his own way. Theo did exactly what Alec asked, so why does that make Alec so miserable? With a choked off sob, Alec scrubs at his face and falls against the bathroom wall with a loud crash.

"Alec?" Theo yells.

"M'fine," Alec lies, his hands shaking as he slams the door behind him and collapses against it. His hands continue to shake as flicks on the light, immediately wishing he hadn't. The illumination hurts his eyes, like a knife to his throbbing head. He slaps the light off before fumbling his way towards the shower in the dark. He tugs the shower curtain open and then tries to undo his jeans, nearly screaming when the button won't go through the hole. He tries three more times, but his vision is blurry, and his hands won't stop trembling.

"Fuck," Alec grunts, wishing he could rip the jeans off.

In hindsight, what he should've done was take Theo up on his offer, even if it would've robbed Alec of all of his self respect. At least then Theo would be here with him to stop the rising tide of melancholy. Yet another reason Alec shouldn't drink; it makes him sad. Other people like Alec because he's happy. Right now he is not happy, and he can't imagine anyone else would want to be around him like this when he doesn't even want to be around himself.

Alec wills away another round of tears. Unbidden, the mental image of Theo here undoing Alec's pants for him before pushing them down his hips appears. He wishes Theo was in the darkened room, brushing his hair off his face and asking if he's alright. He's not. Not even a little bit. Maybe if Theo were here, he might even tell him that.

At this point, it's become automatic to tell people he's fine when they ask, regardless of the real answer. He spent so long trying to escape his brothers' shadows and prove he could handle things himself that he sometimes forgets it's okay to ask for help, to need people. Right now, Alec needs Theo. Or maybe he just wants him. It's hard for Alec to be sure which one it is.

Alec wishes Theo was here with his steady hands to help Alec rinse away the memory of tonight: liquor, puke and the hands he didn't want on his body. He wants to wash it away, wash *them* away.

Between the frustration of being unable to get his stupid fucking jeans off and the throbbing in his head, he wants to collapse to the floor and stay there, but he knows that would only make everything worse. He holds out hope that getting into the shower might help, but getting those few feet into the shower feels nearly insurmountable. It's only the feeling of dried throw up on his stomach that propels Alec forward, his knees hitting the tile floor as he falls into the tub and lets out a choked sob. He doesn't bother standing up, doesn't care that he's still half-dressed. He reaches for the knob and turns the water on high, too disoriented to figure out the temperature. Freezing cold water pounds down on his head as he tries to wash away the sadness that clings to his skin like a stain.

Every part of his body, from his ankles to his head hurts. He's not sure if it's from falling into the damn tub or what's sore from the game earlier, all he knows is that every inch of him aches. His muscles hurt, his head hurts, his eyes hurt. His stupid fucking heart hurts.

"I got some Gatorade for when you're done," Theo calls from the other side of the door. He's so damn close. If Alec called for him, he would come. "It's green apple, I hope that's okay. That's all I had."

Green apple Gatorade. Jason's favorite flavor. Of course that's what Theo has.

"Alec?"

Intending to offer some kind of reply, Alec opens his mouth, but nothing comes out. Water splashes into his mouth, and Alec opens it wider, tipping his face so the spray stings his eyes and fills his mouth, taking in so much water he chokes on it.

Peripherally he's aware of Theo speaking again and the door opening, but none of that makes sense. The only thing that registers is Theo falling to his knees beside the tub, soaking the sleeves of his shirt as he reaches for Alec.

"Why didn't you let me help?" Theo asks, his tone gentle as he pulls Alec into a standing position with him. Then he's doing exactly what Alec wished he would earlier and removing his jeans, shoving them down so they fall in a heavy wet pile in the shower. "Can I?"

Alec nods, floating above himself while Theo's nimble fingers peel off his wet boxers. The entire time Theo keeps his eyes on the shower wall. It's just one more reminder that Theo's kindness now has nothing to do with wanting to see Alec naked and everything to do with Alec being a pathetic, hot mess. Theo is careful as he washes Alec's belly, rinsing soap from his body and scrubbing away the reminders of the club.

"Let's get you dry," Theo says, shutting the water off before wrapping a towel around Alec.

Though Alec tries to dry himself off, something in his brain has stopped working. He's fuzzy, confused, and exhausted. The towel nearly falls to the floor, but then Theo catches it, pulling it back around Alec's shoulders and whispering softly while he towel-dries Alec's curls. Theo's hands are everywhere, running the towel across his back and down his spine, curling it around his hips and the insides of his thighs, even wiping away the water collecting on his toes. He's so gentle and kind that whatever is left of Alec falls apart.

It's impossible for Alec to know if Theo senses this or is just equally tired, but he keeps the questions to a bare minimum as he guides Alec out of the bathroom and into his bedroom. With breathtaking care, Theo lowers Alec onto the edge of the mattress before searching for some clothes for him. He returns with a pair of sweats that are several sizes too big and a t-shirt, frowning when he catches sight of Alec shivering. Theo uncaps the Gatorade before passing it to Alec along with a couple of Advil, making sure he chugs as much as he can.

"Why'd you have the water so cold, Alec?"

A shrug is all he can manage. Theo's eyebrows knit together, and he mutters to himself before turning around and heading back to his closet where he rummages through his sweater collection, returning with something thick and soft. He pulls it over Alec's head, helping him get his arms in the sleeves, and politely ignores the way Alec's eyes water. Unable to believe what's happening, Alec breathes in Theo's familiar scent, fingering the sleeves of the sweater where they hang over his hands. He's pretty sure he's had more than a few fantasies about Theo and his sweaters, but they usually involve things a lot sexier than being pulled out of the shower too stupid and drunk to wash himself.

Regardless of the reason, the comfort of Theo's sweater unlocks something in Alec, and he gives up fighting and pretending he doesn't desperately want to be taken care of. He's so exhausted from always smiling, always pretending, that the smallest bit of comfort from Theo has him shattering into a million pieces. The alcohol seems determined to pluck out every insecurity, worry and burden from the recesses where Alec keeps them locked away, making them feel bigger and stronger than they do in the light of day.

"Let me change, and I'll help you to the living room," Theo explains, turning his back on Alec while he undresses. "I already made up the couch and got you extra pillows and blankets."

Alec knows he's truly wrecked because he doesn't even check out Theo while he undresses, too exhausted and achy to do more than collapse on Theo's bed. The temptation to crawl up and use Theo's pillow, to wrap himself in the same blankets Theo sleeps in, is nearly overwhelming. He tries to resist temptation, at least until Rio's quiet meow comes from the floor. A second later, she's leaping onto the pillow as if by invitation.

"Hi," Alec whispers, scooting the rest of the way up the bed to bury his face in Theo's pillow while Rio curls herself into Alec's throat. When Alec's fingers smooth over her soft fur, his hands tremble. He's so tired.

"Alec."

Theo's talking again, the sound of his feet padding across the floor a warning for his approach. Alec squeezes his eyes shut, waits for Theo to pick him up and physically move him to the living room so he can have his space back. Instead, a blanket is draped over his bare legs, pulled up to his chest and tucked around him and Rio as if they are welcome in Theo's most personal space.

"I'll take the couch," Theo whispers.

Without thinking it through, Alec's eyes open while his hand flies out, seeking Theo's gaze in the dark. He curls his fingers around Theo's wrist, nails digging into the delicate underside. Beneath his fingertips, he feels the beat of Theo's pulse, slow and steady in sharp contrast to Alec's heart, which is speeding like a freight train in his chest.

"What is it?"

"Stay," Alec whispers, that one word costing him everything he has. "Please." Unable to look at Theo's face if he rejects him, Alec squeezes his eyes shut again and loosens his grip. He's asked, damn near begged, and if Theo says no, he won't ask again.

At the sound of Theo's feet moving, Alec's heart falls. He waits for the sound of the door shutting, surprised when the bed dips with Theo's weight. Ever so slowly, Theo slips beneath the sheets, a barrier between their bodies as he scoots closer. Even with the blankets separating them, his proximity soothes, and Alec inches as close as possible, snaking an arm out to slip it across Theo's middle.

Over the years, Alec's shared a bed with Antonio or Riley on more than one occasion. They'd always indulged his need for touch without much commentary, but this isn't one of his best friends. This is Theo, and though blankets keep their flesh from touching, he's never been so close to him before. He's never been nearly naked in his bed, wrapped in one of Theo's favorite sweaters, breathing in the scent of Theo's soap and cologne on the pillow.

Theo's presence is everywhere, from the firm side wedged against him to the sound of his breathing. It's so much and not enough, and Alec wants the kinds of things he only ever dared to imagine when he was alone. Maybe it's the alcohol, or maybe it's the way Theo's hand rests over Alec's wrist, which could just as easily be an accident as much as something more. Whatever the reason, Alec's mouth has no more filter.

"What's it like?" Alec whispers.

"Hmm?"

"Sex."

"Shit, Alec."

"S'just a question," Alec mumbles, fighting against his own exhaustion. He wants to talk to Theo.

"I'm not sure I'm the right person to answer that. Don't you want to ask one of your brothers or friends?"

"I'd rather walk into oncoming traffic than ask my brothers about sex," Alec huffs. "And all my friends sleep with women."

"I sleep with women."

"You're so annoying," Alec grumbles, swatting his chest.

Rio readjusts herself immediately, resettling under Alec's chin. "You sleep with men, too. I know you do."

"Do you actually want to know how I sleep with men?"

No. It will break him into a million pieces so small no one will ever put them back together.

No.

No.

No.

"Yes," he whispers because he is drunk and weak. "I'm tired of being a virgin."

"There's nothing wrong with being a virgin, Alexander."

"You only say that because you're a sex god. Maybe I should've told one of those guys yes. They all asked." He yawns, eyelids drooping.

Theo makes a choking noise, long fingers wrapping around Alec's forearm. If Alec weren't so drunk and damn near passing out, he'd almost think Theo was holding onto him on purpose. His touch is grounding, steadying, and Alec wiggles closer, throwing his leg over Theo and shoving his own face into the crook of Theo's neck so the two of them and Rio are all smashed together in the center of the bed.

"I just wanna know what it's like," Alec slurs, everything getting so damn heavy. "I wanna—" but Alec can't finish the thought, because Theo's big hand ends up on the back of his head, long fingers smoothing down the back of Alec's skull, and his body collapses. Surrounded by Theo, he gives up trying to stay awake and lets go.

14 THEO

THE THING about being an only child is that you're allowed a fair bit of control. There's no one else to compete with for attention, assuming there's any to get in the first place. There's no one else to move your things or hog the bathroom or leave things lying around. No one to eat all your favorite snacks or change the channel because they want to watch something different. There's no one to steal your stuff or outshine you. There's no one for teachers to look at and compare you to, and no one will ever meet you and say, "oh, you're so-and-so's sibling."

Everyone always told him he was fortunate to be an only child. "Oh Theo, you're so lucky not to have to share your bedroom, your bathroom, or your dad with anyone." Except going home to a quiet house didn't feel so lucky when the silence was oppressive. When his dad was either working or blowing off steam from working so much, Theo was always home alone. Shared dinners or someone stealing your food didn't sound so bad to the little boy who ate peanut butter and jelly on a tv tray alone because he didn't know how to cook, and there wasn't much food to cook in the first place. Having someone steal the remote didn't sound so bad when you didn't care what you watched because all you wanted was for the silence to stop.

Theo was so lucky, they said, but he never felt that way at home. He felt the luckiest when he was with the King family, when they'd invite Theo over for a sleepover or a family picnic. When Charlie would steal his cookie and Jason would take off after him, nearly knocking the house down because his brother had dared to pilfer from his best friend. Theo never told Jason he liked it. He never told anyone that having his cookie stolen made it feel like he was one of them.

Sometimes, when he closed his eyes and listened to Jason and the twins fighting, while Alec tried to join in with no idea what was going on, Theo would pretend he was one of them. At least until he went home to an empty house with darkened rooms, and then he remembered he wasn't one of them. Sure, he was important to Jason. He was his best friend and that meant something to Theo, but it changed nothing at home. As much as Theo loved Jason and his family, at the end of the day, Theo wasn't a King.

No matter how many family dinners and sleepovers he got invited to, he was still the only child of a single parent who wasn't there when Theo needed him. As a kid, Theo hated his dad as much as he loved him. Alone in his room, he would close his eyes and think that maybe if he could be the smartest or the strongest kid, maybe his dad would have more attention and love for him. By the time he was a teenager, he'd stopped crying. He'd grown up, and while his childhood stung, he kind of understood, in the shittiest way possible, why his dad was the way he was. Theo's mom and dad were so young when they had him, and then his mom had taken off with the rent money when Theo was six weeks old and never came back. Theo had no idea what her face looked like or the sound of her voice, but he understood what the shape of the hole she'd left in his dad felt like.

His dad was sixteen from a broken home of his own when Theo came into the world. He hadn't been good at emotions or bedtime stories, but he didn't leave. He did the best he could, even when his best wasn't really good enough. He put food on the table and worked dead-end jobs without a high school diploma to make sure the rent was paid and Theo had what he needed for school and football. Growing up, Theo saw firsthand that love could break people, that wanting to do the right thing wasn't always good enough, and it absolutely terrified him. There's a very specific kind of trauma that comes from knowing that one of the people meant to love you forever walked away from you. A kind of trauma that makes it hard to imagine anyone else might love you, might decide to stay.

As far as Theo is concerned, love isn't beautiful—it's terrifying.

His dad had loved his mom and she'd broken his heart. His dad had loved him, and Theo still had a difficult childhood. The only reason Theo knows he loves Jason is because Jason told him first when they were seventeen and drunk. Theo had started to cry because he'd been scared to lose his best friend after realizing his own bisexuality. It wasn't something he'd needed to worry about, though, because Jason had pulled him into a bear hug and told him he loved him, and that was that. Jason hasn't said it again, probably because he knows Theo would run away if he tried, but he doesn't need to say it for it to be true. Jason is as solid and steady as an oak tree and the closest thing to a brother that Theo will ever have. In every way that matters, he is Theo's family, and nothing in the world can change that. At least he didn't think so, before tonight.

Tonight, Theo has Alec in his bed, naked aside from Theo's sweater. He has Alec wrapped around his body while he holds him close. He has Alec asking to know what sex is like, giving Theo thoughts about what it might be like to teach him, and Theo has never been so terrified of his own feelings in his entire life.

Every laugh Alec pulls from him, every longing look and hopeful smile, makes Theo want things he has never wanted before. Equally as scary, is the growing suspicion he might want them with Alec. Heart in his throat, Theo squeezes Alec so tight he's afraid he might wake him. Thankfully he doesn't stir, leaving Theo free to hold him close. Theo lets his hand smooth over Alec's hair, willing his own body to relax.

Theo has no idea what's happening between them or what tomorrow will bring. The only thing he knows for sure, is that under no circumstances can he fall in love with Alexander King.

ALEC HAS freckles on his ass.

On some level, Theo knew he had freckles everywhere. They cascade across his face and down his neck. There are smatterings of them on his ribs, down his hips, and a dark cluster at the base of his spine. There are even some on his calves and the insides of his ankles. Yet none of the freckles affect Theo as much as the ones on his ass. Or maybe it's just that Alec's ass is out at all.

At some point in the night Alec shifted, kicking off the blankets and curling into a ball so that Theo's sweater is rucked up his back, leaving his entire naked ass turned toward Theo. It's a testament to the hours of training he does; his ass is muscular, pert and very, very round. It is also covered in freckles. Not one or two, but too many to count, a constellation of freckles on one perfect ass.

If he reaches out, Theo could lay one of his hands on each cheek and freckles would still show where ass meets thigh, twisting up between his cheeks. Theo has always been an ass man. That first day he accidentally checked Alec out, it'd been over his perfect ass. Weeks of trying to forget that moment have apparently led him here: Alec nearly naked in his bed, that beautifully plush, firm ass on full display.

Not even a racing mind or the fear of being caught can diminish Theo's morning wood, so he rolls away from Alec and out of bed, sneaking into the bathroom. This is his own damn house but he feels like a stranger, a stranger in his own body. Theo can't even remember the last time he woke up hard. Apparently, having Alec in his bed is enough motivation for his cock to pay attention.

Refusing to jerk off to his best friend's baby brother who is currently wearing nothing but his favorite sweater while passed out in his bed, Theo undresses and takes the world's fastest, coldest shower. He considers it his due punishment for lusting after Alec. When he gets out, he wastes no time towel drying his hair roughly before doing the same to the rest of the body. He wraps the towel around his waist, retrieving his glasses off the counter before heading back into the bedroom. He spends an embarrassingly long time looking at Alec, who, in Theo's absence, has starfished on his belly, managing to take up nearly the entire king size bed. The sweater is still tangled up at his chest, his entire bottom half on display.

Rio meows from her position beside Alec's head, as if demanding to know why Theo is daring to stare at her human. Because really, that's what Alec is. While Rio doesn't seem to mind Theo, she clearly adores Alec, and for that reason alone, he knows he can't ever get rid of her. There is nothing temporary about Rio, even if there has to be about his feelings for Alec.

"I'm not doing anything," Theo tells her.

Talking to his cat might be the first sign he could be losing his mind. Or maybe that happened when he developed a crush on Alec.

Sexually unsatisfied, exhausted, and riddled with guilt, Theo dresses. It doesn't seem like Alec is going to move any time soon, but he still tries to be as quiet as he can, pulling out boxers and pants from his drawers before choosing his second favorite sweater from the closet. He breathes a sigh of relief when the familiar weight settles over his body. Alec's wearing Theo's favorite sweater in the entire world, and he absolutely does not want to think about what made him pick that one last night. He has a closet full of sweaters, many he never wears. There was no reason for him to go directly for his favorite and pull it over Alec's naked body.

Thinking about Alec being naked beneath his sweater makes Theo's cock chub up again. He sighs heavily, refusing to touch himself like this.

Hoping a little distance might clear his head, he sneaks out of the bedroom and makes his way to the kitchen. He's pleased when Rio follows suit a minute later, heading directly to her food bowl and acting like she hasn't been fed in a year. Theo makes sure to refill her food and water before he sets about making coffee, brewing it strong enough to wake the dead, which is about how he feels.

All night Alec slumbered beside him, alternating

between clinging to Theo like an octopus or stealing all the blankets and cocooning himself up like some kind of hibernating bear. Unused to sleeping with anyone and acutely aware of Alec's near nakedness, Theo had spent the majority of the night awake and staring at the ceiling.

When the coffee pot beeps, he nearly jumps out of his skin, pouring himself a huge cup without even bothering with cream or sugar today. It's kind of disgusting, but the part of Theo's brain that feels like he's done something wrong, that feels like he doesn't deserve something sweet or comforting, is too loud to ignore. He spends the next twenty minutes leaning against the kitchen counter, forcing down the bitter coffee.

He doesn't bother with a second cup, leaving his mug next to the half-full pot before puttering around the kitchen. There's not much to clean up since Theo is pretty tidy, but a sparkling kitchen always makes Theo feel more in control. He discards the few pieces of old mail left on the kitchen island, loads the dishwasher and wipes down the counters, frowning when the clock has only moved twelve minutes. He remembers being a kid, puttering around the house while his dad slept the day away after overnight shifts at the liquor store. He'd always needed to be so quiet then, picking up the house so his dad wouldn't have to when he woke up later.

It's strange how easily the comfort of a quiet home can become oppressive, how sometimes the stillness reminds Theo of his own loneliness. Perhaps that's why he loved the King house so much. It was never still, never quiet. With two parents and four boys—and at one point their *abuela*—the house had been as full of people as it was love.

Theo doesn't want to be alone right now, but he can't call Jason. Not now. What would he say? *"Hey, I miss you, but don't come over. Your brother is passed out in my bed, and no, I didn't fuck him, but I'm thinking about offering, which has me torn up inside and feeling like I'm on the edge of a cliff.*" Or maybe, "*Hey, you wanna talk me down from this mental spiral I've got myself into, knowing the thing I'm going to do could jeopardize my friendship with you, but for some reason I can't stop myself?*" Neither of those things would go over well.

What's a man supposed to do when he needs his best friend to help him through one of the most confusing moments of his life, but that best friend is the one person in the world who can't ever know what's going on in Theo's messed-up head. Unable to pull himself together, Theo ends up in the living room rewatching a documentary about the tundra he's seen half a dozen times when Alec walks by with his head down and his hands over his face.

"Why are you awake?"

"You don't see me," Alec mumbles.

"I definitely see you." Theo laughs, rolling over to watch as Alec's bare feet pad across his living room. The sweater hits just at the top of his thighs, material hanging loose as he walks past Theo and towards the kitchen. "Where are you going?"

"Where the coffee is," Alec answers.

Theo jumps off the couch and follows Alec into the kitchen. "I can make a fresh pot. This one has been sitting for a while."

Alec scrunches his nose, breathing deeply before shaking his head from side to side, which Theo can only assume means don't bother. A second later, he reaches for Theo's mug from earlier and fills it to the brim, apparently not caring that it wasn't clean. Not that Theo can blame him, he looks like death warmed over.

"Can I have—"

"Sugar," Theo finishes, leaning over him to pull the sugar out of the pantry. If his chest happens to press against Alec's back for a few seconds longer than necessary, no one needs to know.

"And—"

"Creamer," Theo says, grabbing it from the fridge and passing it to Alec. He forces himself to take a few steps backward as he keeps his eyes on Alec, noticing he uses less of both than last time. Alec lifts the coffee, muttering under his breath before he sips it. He stands like that, shoulders hunched while he gulps down the entire mug of coffee, immediately making a second. Only then does he turn around, a smile in place.

"Morning, Theodore."

"Why are you smiling?"

"Would you prefer I flip you off?" Alec asks, moving to the kitchen island and half-slumping over it. The act brings the hem of the sweater up so the bottom of Alec's ass peeks out, a few freckles making a rather cheeky appearance. Theo nearly bites off the end of his tongue before hurrying around to the other side of the kitchen island, pretty sure he can't be trusted with that in his line of sight.

"Uh, no, I like your smile. It's just that you know, you had a lot to drink last night."

"Wow, did I?" Alec hums, his words not at all matching up with his body language.

"Do you remember last night?"

Alec clears his throat. "Coffee is fantastic."

"The coffee has been sitting for an hour," Theo points out, refusing to be sidetracked.

"I was being a polite house guest, Theodore. Here, let's

practice. I'm going to tell you that your bed was exceptionally comfortable, and you'll thank me."

"Alec."

"Your bed was comfortable, Theo," he repeats.

It would be so easy to pretend nothing happened. Too easy. Theo can't, even if he should, even if Alec clearly wants to. He can't explain why when it's not the smart, safe choice. But something tells him it's the right one, and he's determined to do right by Alec. "I think we should talk about last night."

"I think I should walk into the ocean."

"Glad to see that not even a hangover can dull your dramatics."

Alec flips him off, the faintest hint of a smile playing at his lips as he slumps the rest of the way over the kitchen island so his forehead hits the counter. When he speaks the words are garbled, but Theo manages to understand them all the same. "I'm dying ,Theodore. Take pity on me. It's a lot of work to be agreeable all the time."

The confession takes Theo by surprise. He'd never considered that Alec being Alec didn't come naturally. "Alec."

"If this is about your sweater, I promise to return it. In fact, you can have it right now if you want." He stands up straight, immediately starting to pull off the sweater, leaving Theo with the mental image of a completely naked Alec standing in the middle of his kitchen, bathed in the soft light of morning.

"Keep it on," Theo croaks, moving close enough to tug on the bottom of the sweater before Alec can get undressed.

"If you insist." Alec grins, head popping back through the hole. "Glad we had that talk."

"About last night—"

"Look, I was a drunk idiot, I puked everywhere, stole your bed, and cried in the shower. That cover all of it?"

"You're not an idiot, Alec, and that's not—"

"Please, we don't need to talk about the rest." Alec's fingers clench around his coffee mug. "If this is about the guys at the club, don't give it a second thought. Sure, the guys were dicks, but it's nothing new. I'm used to it."

Theo's thought's take a detour, slamming into a wall of absolute fury. "What does that mean?"

"Nothing." Alec clacks his teeth together while his fingers tap on the edge of his coffee mug.

"Bullshit." Theo closes the distance, lifting Alec's chin so his eyes meet Theo's.

"Look, I like being touched, it's not the first time someone's accused me of being a tease because of it, alright? It's fine. Can we please not talk about it?"

Theo hates the idea that anyone has ever made Alec feel bad about his desire for tactile affection. He wants to erase the memory of anyone who ever made Alec feel uncomfortable or ashamed for what he wanted or didn't want. "There's nothing wrong with you, Alec. Don't ever let anyone make you think otherwise."

The sound Alec makes is hard to read. Eager to reassure him, Theo lets his fingers skim lightly over the side of Alec's cheek. When Alec doesn't move away, he continues the exploration, letting thumb skim over Alec's jaw. While it's only the most fleeting of touches, Alec's entire body trembles. "This okay?"

Alec's eyes are locked on the floor, but he nods. It's only when Theo lowers his hand that Alec lifts his eyes to meet Theo's, the confusion in them plain as day. He can't blame him for not knowing what Theo is doing when Theo isn't even sure. All he knows is he doesn't want to ignore this pull to Alec. He just needs to find a way to safely get him out of his system, to make sure he doesn't hurt Alec while trying to get over his crush.

"There was something you said last night."

"Was it about your taste in beer?" Alec tries to laugh, but it's forced. "Or why you refused to dance with me? I'm a really good dancer, you know."

"I know," Theo whispers. "It's not about that."

"You're being weird, Theodore."

"I know."

"Stop saying I know, you're freaking me out." Alec crosses his arms over his chest. Where Alec is normally brash and confident, now he only looks unsure. It makes him look so much younger, so much more vulnerable.

"How is your head?"

"My head?" Alec scoffs. "My head feels like I drank too much last night, so it wants to split open. My head feels like you're being weird, which is confusing and making it hurt more. That's what my head feels like."

Despite the outburst, Theo smiles. He shouldn't but he can't stop. He likes the way Alec pushes buttons and speaks up when things are weird. He likes that Alec is always more than everyone else. He likes it too damn much.

"Why are you smiling at me?" Alec asks, narrowing his eyes. "Did you drink too much last night?"

"You're cute."

"I'm—of course I'm cute," Alec huffs. "I've always been cute. You're just blind as a bat, not just because of your glasses, but because—"

"I want to help you with your virginity."

Alec's mouth falls open, his arms wrapping tighter around himself while he stares at Theo like he's lost his mind. Theo can't blame him. Being this blunt isn't like him, and neither is offering to fuck Alec. Or maybe it is like Theo, and he's just never had the guts to say what he wanted. "You said last night you were tired of being a virgin," Theo reminds him, his need to over-explain making him run his mouth. "And you didn't mind when I touched you right now, and I thought maybe...maybe I could help."

Theo's never seen Alec so still, and it unnerves him. There's something that looks dangerously close to panic in his eyes, and Theo feels an echo of it clawing up his spine. He knows he can't have Alec for real, knows this can't ever be a relationship because Alec is over his little teenage crush, not to mention Theo doesn't do relationships, but he didn't expect Alec to react like this. He thought Alec would either happily agree or flip him off and assume it was a joke.

"Say something, please."

"I don't think anyone has ever asked me to talk. Usually they're telling me to shut up or talk quieter."

The words are like ripping off a bandaid, painful and swift, as Theo recalls a younger Alec always running and laughing. How often had someone told him to be less? How often had he smiled in the face of those kinds of requests in order to make everyone think it didn't bother him? Theo is beginning to understand how much he doesn't know about Alec. The scary thing is that doesn't put Theo off or make him want to walk away. Instead, it makes him want Alec more.

"I'll never tell you to be quiet, Alexander."

Alec doesn't say anything, but his knuckles are turning white where they're digging into his forearms and the clench of his jaw is visible. Theo turns and yanks open the snack drawer under his coffee pot, shoving aside protein bars and honey sticks until he finds what he's looking for.

He curls his fingers around it before turning to pass it to Alec.

"Thanks," Alec whispers, taking the gum and unwrapping it slowly. He twists the paper wrapper in his fingers while he starts to chew, some of the tension in his shoulders dropping. "So you're not like...pranking me are you?"

"I would never do that."

He starts to rip the gum wrapper, his jaw moving a mile a minute as his gaze finally lifts from the floor to Theo. He looks so damn unsure, and yet he meets Theo's gaze head-on. Theo is awed by Alec's bravery. For his own part, Theo feels mildly nauseous; his heart is racing so fast it's hard to breathe. He's pretty sure this is a horrible idea, but he can't stop it now even if he wanted to.

He doesn't want to stop it.

"It doesn't have to mean anything serious," Theo offers, knowing all the reasons this can't be more. This is just a way to get over his crush and make sure when Alec does lose his virginity, it's to someone who will treat him right, not a one-off in a seedy bathroom.

"Nothing serious," Alec echoes, his tone unreadable.

"Exactly," Theo agrees. "You said you were tired of being a virgin, but those guys at the club won't treat you right. You deserve more."

"I deserve more," Alec says, chewing the gum so fast his jaw pops.

"You know you do," Theo whispers. "You deserve more than someone who won't remember your name in the morning. More than someone looking for a way to get off, someone who won't care about you or your feelings or whether it's good. Or whether it hurts."

"Are you speaking from experience?" Alec asks carefully.

Theo breathes deeply. This isn't supposed to be about him. He doesn't want it to be. He's made his peace with his own bad choices.

"It doesn't matter."

"Why?" Alec challenges, taking a step closer. "Why does it matter how I fuck and not you?"

"Because," Theo answers quietly.

Alec jabs a finger at Theo's chest, pushing. Always pushing. "Because why, Theodore?"

"Because you deserve to have the kind of relationship you want."

"How do you know what I want?" Alec asks, the finger turning into his entire hand. It doesn't poke this time, just rests over Theo's fragile heart.

Because you're beautiful and good, and you deserve love. "Isn't that what you want?" Theo counters, unable to answer the way he knows Alec wants him to. "You want love."

"Yeah," Alec whispers. "I want...I want that."

Something in Theo cracks at the confirmation. Alec wants a forever kind of love. He wants the kind of love Theo could never give anyone. Even if Alec weren't in love with someone else, Theo couldn't be Alec's forever. He wasn't made to be anyone's forever. Not even his own parents had wanted him forever. How could anyone else?

"I'm not...I'm not the guy who can give you those things." All Theo wants is to give Alec the kind of memory that lasts, a first time that's special. A first time where someone treats him right so that whoever comes along later, Alec will know never to accept less than he deserves. Theo can't be Alec's future, but he can be his right now.

"I know, Theo."

There's something sad in Alec's eyes, and Theo wishes

he knew what it meant. Maybe he's thinking of the guy he likes, the guy he wishes were his first.

"You can tell me no. You can tell me to fuck off, Alec."

"You know I wouldn't," Alec mutters, twisting his fingers in the front of Theo's sweater.

Theo doesn't know that, doesn't understand why he would be the one person Alec wouldn't say no to. A braver man might ask, but Theo's already used his allotment of bravery for the day, especially since he isn't sure he could handle the answer. He's hurt Alec so many times, and maybe none of them were on purpose, but that doesn't change the hurt that probably still lingers.

"I know you don't have feelings for me anymore, but that makes this easy, right? Just two friends. No expectations. No one gets hurt."

"Just two friends," Alec whispers.

The fingers in his sweater tighten, and for one dizzying second, Theo swears Alec is gonna punch him. He doesn't, instead rising up onto tiptoes to crash their lips together. The kiss is as unexpected as it is demanding. Theo finds himself backed up to the kitchen island, the wood digging into the base of his spine as Alec kisses him like he dances—with confidence.

15 ALEC

KISSING THEO. Alec is kissing Theo.

No matter how many times he reminds himself it's actually happening, it doesn't feel any less like a dream. For all the years of fantasies, the real thing is still infinitely better than he ever imagined. Theo's lips are soft and gentle, and he tastes like coffee. It's a goddamn miracle Alec hasn't simply passed out from pleasure. This might be the only time Alec ever gets to kiss Theo, to touch him, and he isn't going to waste a single moment.

Deepening the kiss, he hitches his right leg up, all but trying to climb Theo like a goddamn tree. It has the desired effect, because Theo's massive left hand skims down Alec's back and over his ass. Technically the sweater is blocking most of the skin-on-skin contact, but it's still Theo's hand on Alec's ass while his tongue teases along Alec's mouth. It might just be the single greatest moment of his life. Alec is nearly delirious with the sensory overload of Theo's fucking huge chest and big hands.

"Alec," Theo whispers.

There's a choked-off moan that Alec is pretty sure came

from himself, but considering the circumstances, he feels like it's justified. Kissing Theo is a revelation, and every time Theo tries to gentle the kiss, Alec demands more, plunging his tongue into Theo's mouth and kissing him for all he's worth, until Theo spins them around and lifts Alec up in a single movement so his legs hang off the kitchen island, bringing him eye-to-eye with Theo.

"Hi," Alec grins.

"Hi," Theo replies, almost bashfully. There's a flush to his cheeks, and the fact that Alec was the one to put it there is going to ruin him forever.

"So, uh, was that a yes?"

"Oh sorry, was the tongue down your throat not obvious enough? I'd be happy to stick my tongue somewhere else, just so we're entirely clear."

The tips of Theo's ears go bright red, and Alec can't help but cackle. He might be a virgin, but he isn't a blushing one. He swings both of his legs out, hooking them around Theo's waist to get him as close as possible.

"Wait." Theo's face scrunches in confusion. "Weren't you chewing gum?"

"Uh-huh." Alec's smirk widens. "I swallow."

"Jesus Christ, Alec."

"*Yo no soy Jesús,*" Alec deadpans.

"I know you're teasing me, but you sound really sexy when you speak Spanish."

"Oh, Theodore, I always sound sexy." Alec tightens his legs around Theo so his erection

comes into contact with Theo's belly, leaving Theo with no question about how Alec currently feels. There are so many things Alec can't say, but maybe just this once he can let his body do the talking. "*¿Cómo te gusta coger?*"

"That's about sex right?" Theo grunts, his eyes firmly on Alec's lap. "My Spanish is not nearly as good as yours."

"Sí." Alec leans forward, delighting in having Theo's mouth at the same level as his own. "I said I want you to show me how you fuck—more or less. It definitely sounds sexier in Spanish."

The blush on Theo's cheeks darkens. "Are you always in such a hurry?"

"Hurry?" Alec barks. "I'm twenty-one. There is no hurry about it. Chop-chop, mister. I expect the fucking of my life or else I'll demand a do-over."

"Will you?" Theo laughs, a pretty flush spreading down his neck.

Maybe Alec should be overthinking things now. Maybe he should be more upset about the fact that Theo thinks Alec doesn't have feelings for him, and made sure Alec knew this is a friends with benefits arrangement, which is definitely not Alec's thing. Or maybe a one time fuck arrangement. He probably should've clarified since neither of those are Alec's things. What is Alec's thing, is Theo.

Sure, when this is done, his heart will be broken beyond repair, but that's Alec's choice to make.

You deserve a special first time. That's what Theo said. Who better to make that special than the love of Alec's entire goddamn life? Even if he has no idea. Even if he won't return the feelings. Even if all he wants from Alec is the same thing everyone else has always wanted from him—sex. The love in his heart has hurt for so long, maybe for once he can let it out. Maybe then it won't hurt so badly.

"Any hard nos?" Theo asks, settling his hands on the side of Alec's hips.

Alec shakes his head.

"I guess if you haven't done a lot you might not know,

but if there is anything you think you might be uncomfortable with or you realize partly through that you are, you can tell me. I know how much you like to run that mouth of yours."

"You like my mouth," Alec smirks, letting his legs swing on either side of Theo.

"Don't tell Jason, but yes."

Alec's smile threatens to split his face in two, and he's surprised Theo isn't calling bullshit on his pathetic lie. He has no idea how Theo doesn't look at him and immediately know he's in love with him. It's a blessing and a curse that Theo's got the world's biggest blinders on when it comes to Alec.

"I'm serious though, if you're uncomfortable with anything or—"

"You can do anything to me."

"Don't tell men that," Theo hisses. "Men are the worst."

"Well, yes, they are. But I'm not telling random men, I'm telling you."

"Well, don't tell me that. What if I take advantage of you?"

"I would say please and thank you." Alec leans back on the kitchen island, lifting his leg so his heel presses into Theo's ass. He still can't believe he's doing this, that he's actually talking about sex with Theo.

"What the hell am I going to do with you?" Theo groans.

"Ideally fuck me, unless you changed your mind. Do you need a nap?"

"Cheeky asshole." Theo runs one of his big hands from Alec's knee up his thigh so his bare fingers sit on Alec's bare hip. His fingers curl around flesh, holding on tight as Alec might leave, as if anything in the world could drag him away from this moment.

"So, fucking? You said sex, and honestly all I'm hearing is a lot of talking."

"That's because you never stop talking." Theo half-laughs, saying it in a way that has Alec's insides filling with butterflies. "I was trying to ask you something, but you keep distracting me."

"My bad." Alec tries to make his expression neutral while he drops his leg from Theo's ass and sits up very straight. "Alright then, Theodore. Out with this important question."

Theo's smile falters. "How much have you done?"

"Is this like a job interview? Because I gotta be honest, I wasn't prepared to list all of my past partners to lose my virginity."

"Alec, I'm serious."

"Me too. Who fucking cares?" Alec grumbles, unsure why he's suddenly self-conscious. He's the first one to point out that virginity is a social construct, but it's also one he's been forced to live under, especially playing college sports at his level. The endless expectations are exhausting, and the few times he braved trying to go on a date, it always ended up in disaster. Well, it'd probably also gone horribly because Alec mentally compared every man he met to Theo, but the way his dates assumed Alec would want to fuck on the first date also ruined things.

"I care."

"Why? If I was slutting around, would you change your mind?"

Theo's head tips forward, and he groans loudly. "You can be so difficult, you know that?"

"Yes, I get told that often, thank you." Alec crosses his

arms, unsure how things turned so quickly. This is his fault. This is why he's a virgin. His standards are too high, and his mouth is too big, and he fucks things up. People are fucking weird about sex, and Alec's exhausted by it.

Taking two deep breaths, Theo lifts his gaze to meet Alec's. "I'm not going to judge you."

"Everyone says that and no one means it."

"I mean it, Alexander."

Alec worries his bottom lip between his teeth before tugging his necklace out from beneath the collar of Theo's sweater. He twists the pendant in his fingers, the light catching on it. For the first time Theo realizes what it is—a *peso*.

"I've never seen you wear that before. Before last night, I mean."

"*Abuela* gave it to me before she died. It was one of the only things she brought with her when she came here. Me, Jason, Andrew and Charlie all got one. She said you could go anywhere with a *peso* and a dream." Alec smiles, and Theo is reminded of how close Alec was with her. "I took it with me when I went to Mexico with Antonio, and it felt like bringing a piece of her back home, you know? She never got to go back after she married. Anyway, there was this jeweler down there, and he made it into this. Last night was the first time I wore it."

"Taking that *peso* and a dream for a test run," Theo teases, giving Alec's hip a gentle squeeze.

"If you're implying I used my dead *abuela*'s good luck charm to lose my virginity you would be wrong." Alec snorts, unwilling to admit the real reason he'd worn it last night, or the dream he hadn't been willing to let go of just yet.

"Can I kiss you, Alec?"

The question takes Alec by surprise. "I already told you that you can stick your dick in me, so I'm pretty sure that makes me a sure thing for kisses."

"There's no such thing as a sure thing," Theo says softly, leaning forward. His hair is longer than it's been in recent memory, dark blond locks hanging over his eyes and his glasses a little crooked from their kiss.

"There is with me," Alec assures him, straightening Theo's glasses.

"I'm not going to assume," Theo says, the corner of his mouth turning up when Alec tucks some of the hair behind his ear. For this being nothing more than sex, it feels more intimate than anything Alec's ever experienced. Or maybe sex is always like this. How would Alec know? "I don't want to hurt you."

It hurts right now, Alec wants to whisper. He wouldn't cry. He'd be so much quieter than he's ever been before, but Theo would still hear him, which is why he doesn't say it. Why he can't ever say it. The last time he let Theo know how he really felt, he'd lost him, and he can't risk that happening again.

"You can kiss me," Alec says, realizing Theo isn't going to until he says something.

"Thank you." Theo leans forward, his hair tickling Alec's forehead and his glasses pressing into Alec's nose before he seals their lips together. Where Alec's kiss was demanding and needy, Theo's is as steady as Alec expected. He deepens the kiss, tongue sliding into Alec's mouth while his hand slips around the back of his head.

"Yes," Alec whimpers.

"I didn't ask you anything," Theo murmurs against his lips.

"Preemptively, yes," Alec groans, wrapping his legs around Theo's back in a wordless request for more.

Never one to be rushed, Theo scratches his nails down the back of Alec's head before letting his palm rest at the back of Alec's neck in a soothing touch, almost as if he can sense Alec ready to jump out of his own skin.

Any hopes he had of playing it off are long gone. There is nothing cool or collected about Alec. He's a bundle of nerves and desires all honed in on Theo and his gloriously large hands and sweet mouth. When Theo's other hand skims down Alec's back to rest at the base of his spine, Alec damn near scoots all the way off the counter while tightening his legs around Theo's waist.

"I think—" Theo tries.

"Less thinking, more kissing," Alec demands, slamming his lips against Theo's. Every atom of his body and brain is screaming to touch Theo, to take as much as he's allowed. He wants to memorize every inch of Theo, because soon this is going to be taken away. All he's going to be left with is the phantom of Theo's touch and the memory of how he tastes.

"Come on." Alec wraps his arms around Theo's neck and shimmies himself off the kitchen island. Alec has never been a man with much patience, but he doesn't have an ounce of it right now. Thankfully, Alec doesn't have to beg too much. Theo's hands move down to Alec's ass to hold him steady, his thick fingers warm on his bare skin.

Being drunk might've been one of the stupidest things Alec ever did, but deciding to sleep pantless was one of his best because it means when Theo adjusts his grip, two of his fingers slip in between Alec's ass cheeks and no one, *no one*, has ever touched him there.

"Please."

Theo's grip tightens. "Please what, Alexander?"

"You're really gonna make me say it?" Alec whines.

"I want to hear you tell me what you want, what you're ready for. This isn't going to be an accident or something that happened because you got swept away. I don't want it to be something you'll regret later. If this is going to happen, then it's going to be your choice."

There isn't a single thing Alec could regret with Theo, and he tangles his right hand in Theo's hair to remind himself this is real. This isn't a dream, and Theo isn't going anywhere. Even knowing that, his next words come out sharp, revealing the edge of defensiveness he's had to build around himself to survive hyper-masculine sports culture as a gay guy who doesn't like casual sex.

"You want me to tell you I've never done anything even close to this? That the most I've ever done is some making out and a few one-sided blow jobs in high school, because a guy blowing half the varsity team was only gay to them if they reciprocated? That I stopped doing anything at all because I got tired of being used? That I gave up wanting anything because wanting to be kissed and touched meant guys called me a tease every time, and I had boundaries? You want to know that I got tired of guys saying they were cool with me not wanting sex, only to get mad at me when they got hard from kissing, and I wasn't comfortable with more? You want to know that I got tired of being too much and not enough for everyone, so I stopped doing anything?"

"Alec."

Now that he's started he can't stop.

"You wanna know how the only people in my life I trust to touch me besides my family, are my two best friends because I know they're not gonna call me names for how much I like to be held? They would never...they wouldn't push me." It's clear Theo wants to interrupt, wants to ask who has tried to push, but Alec is grateful he doesn't, because that's not a story he wants to relive. Not right now.

"I never wanted sex with some random guy or with someone I didn't trust." Alec loosens his grip on Theo's hair to smooth it back as his voice drops, the fight gone. Theo is still here. He hasn't pushed him away. Maybe it's okay to be honest. Or as honest as Alec can be right now. "Do you wanna know that no one else has ever had their hand where yours is right now? That I've had a few shitty hand-jobs and that's it. No one else has ever had their mouth on me, has ever been inside of me. But you...you could. I'd let you."

"What do you want?" Theo asks, nudging his nose against Alec's cheek before kissing the corner of his mouth.

Alec groans. "I just told you."

"You told me a lot, and I appreciate you trusting me. You told me what you haven't done, but I still don't know what you're ready for right now."

"Sex," Alec blurts, pretty sure that was obvious.

"I did pick up on that." Theo grins, the sweet timbre of his voice going straight to Alec's cock. There's something different about Theo right now. He's a little more confident than Alec is used to and boy, does he like it. Not that blushing, awkward Theo isn't great, because he is, but steady and calm Theo is amazing. Especially since Alec kind of feels like crawling out of his skin.

"Oh good, I was ready to spell it out for you otherwise. Take a Sharpie and just write those three letters on my forehead."

"That would be one way to get attention."

Alec shifts, unwilling to point out the only person he's ever wanted that kind of attention from is Theo.

"Someone's hard," Theo whispers, dropping his gaze to Alec's dick, which is currently pressed into Theo's stomach.

"Did you just notice?" Alec quips. "Maybe you need a picture of my cock on my forehead too? Or a diagram. I can make you a chart."

"You're such a little shit." Theo laughs, silencing Alec with a kiss that has him trying to mold himself around Theo's body, his cock so hard he's pretty sure he's going to come the second Theo touches him.

"Mmm, talk dirty to me."

"Smartass." Theo kisses Alec again. This time is deeper, the promise of more making Alec's toes curl with pleasure.

"Speaking of my ass," Alec says a bit breathlessly when Theo breaks the kiss, "you're welcome to it."

"You have a mouth on you."

Alec smirks. "You know how to shut it up."

Theo crushes their mouths together, this kiss messier and more demanding than the ones before. Alec isn't under any delusions that it's because he's something special. He knows Theo enjoys sex and has had a lot of it. Yet Alec lets himself pretend that Theo deepens the kiss because it's Alec, lets himself pretend this means something it doesn't. Closing his eyes, Alec gives in to the feelings, rolling his hips and imagining that the way Theo's fingers dig into his ass is because he's desperate for Alec and Alec alone.

"Tell me," Theo demands between kisses. The ground shifts as Theo takes one step towards the bedroom, then another. The hand at the back of Alec's neck lowers to his ass, a change Alec isn't mad about at all, his entire body aching with anticipation. "You want my mouth, my hands, my cock?"

"Yes," Alec whimpers. "Yes, yes, yes."

"Which one, Alexander?"

"You're seriously going to test my powers of executive functioning now?" Alec exhales. "Get me to the bedroom and make me come, Theodore. I don't fucking care how."

"Bossy." Before Alec can question if that was too much, Theo's smile turns a little dirty. "I like it."

Heat pools in Alec's gut, arousal making him ache. If Theo wants bossy, he can give him bossy. "Come on, Theodore. Are you gonna take me to your bed and show me how it's done? You promised." He rocks his hips in a way that makes his cock drag against Theo's sweater, causing Theo to tighten his grip on Alec's ass. Feeling Theo's control waver is heady, and it raises Alec's confidence despite his inexperience. "No one has ever tasted me, Theo. No one has ever gotten their mouth on my cock or my ass. It's all for you. You'll be the first one. Anyone else I ever fuck will always be compared to you."

These words are risky. There's a line he has to toe to make sure he doesn't accidentally let on exactly how true his words are. Alec's always been a boundary pusher, and this is no different. He wants Theo, needs him. He wants to see Theo want him back.

It doesn't matter if Alec can't imagine ever wanting anyone else to share this intimacy with him, or if that last bit was a lie meant to goad Theo into action. Wrapped in dirty talk, he can almost say the truth. "Are you gonna teach me how to fuck, Theodore? You going to show me how good it can feel to have a cock in me?"

"That mouth is gonna get you in trouble one day, Alec."

"Mm, trouble. One of my favorite words. You got some trouble for me, Theo?"

"I've got something for you," Theo says, massaging Alec's ass as he walks them down the hallway.

Afraid of saying too much, Alec settles on kissing

Theo again, relishing in the way Theo lets him take what he wants. Desperate as Alec is for the fucking part, he can't deny how much he likes this, too. Alec has always loved kissing, always loved the slide of lips and shared breath. Most of all, he loves being so close to someone else you can literally taste them, swallow their gasps and moans or dip into their mouth with his tongue. Kissing is good in all forms, but his favorite is like it is now, a little desperate and needy, a little wet as Alec all but devours Theo.

Anything like this is top tier for Alec, whose brain quiets whenever his mouth is full. It settles something in him to be nipping, licking and sucking at the man of his dreams.

"Breathe, Alec."

The reminder is pointless. Alec can't breathe, can't stop, because this thing between them has an expiration date, and he isn't ready to face that.

"Look at me," Theo instructs, the simple demand bypassing Alec's defenses. He complies, pulling out of the kiss and struggling to catch his breath. "You don't have to rush this. I'm not going anywhere."

Yes, you are, Alec thinks pathetically.

"We can take this slow."

"Fuck slow."

Theo smiles sweetly, kissing the tip of Alec's nose before lowering him to the bed. If he thinks Alec is going to let go, he's got another thing coming because Alec holds on for dear life until Theo topples over him, crushing Alec into the mattress with his bulk.

"Shit, sorry."

"I'm not." Alec laughs, damn near delirious with arousal and endorphins. He knew Theo was huge, but he had no idea how good it would feel to have all of him on top of Alec. "You can crush me any time. Ten out of ten."

"Good to know." Theo chuckles. "Except I can't exactly get naked if you don't let go."

"Naked, you say?" Alec releases his koala hold on Theo, sprawling out on the bed instead. "Have at it. Let's see the goods, big boy."

Theo braces his hands on either side of Alec's head, staring down at where Theo's sweater has ridden up so most of his body is now on display. He pauses, skimming his fingertips over Alec's stomach to trace down along the sharp cut of muscle where hip meets thigh. His tongue darts out, something darkening in his eyes.

"I don't look like you. Fair warning."

An ache pierces Alec's chest. The idea that Theo would compare himself to Alec is ridiculous. Only apparently it's not, because he is.

"If I wanted to have sex with myself, I'd use my two hands and a mirror, Theodore."

"That's a nice mental image," Theo huffs out, the ghost of a smile on his lips. Alec would do anything to make this man smile.

"You're welcome for that. Full permission to jerk off to me any time you want." Alec grins, his heart racing. "You gonna give me a pretty mental image, too?"

"Is that what you want?"

What Alec wants is to brand himself with Theo's release. He wants Theo so deep inside of him he can feel it long after Theo walks away. He wants to memorize every inch of Theo and lock it away so when this is over, he can close his eyes and remember it wasn't a dream.

"You know what I want," Alec answers.

Theo's chest visibly shudders with the force of his

exhale before he rises onto his knees, sitting over Alec's thighs. Slowly he tugs the sweater off, revealing miles of pale skin. Theo's body is nothing like Alec's. Where Alec is compact and lithe, muscled from sports but small in build, everything about Theo is big, from his strong arms to his jiggling pecs and his soft tummy. He wasn't wrong when he said his body isn't like Alec's, but what Theo fails to realize —what he never realizes—is that Alec loves everything about him. He loves the thickness of Theo's body, loves the quiet strength with the hint of softness in all the best places.

Everything about Theo is sturdy and safe. Alec gives into temptation and plants his hands on Theo's pecs, giving them a squeeze.

"What are you doing?" Theo asks.

"Appreciating the goods." Alec's smile turns playful, his apprehension receding. Whatever darker thoughts and worries that hover at the edge of his mind are something for future Alec to deal with. It doesn't matter that this is only going to be once, that it's going to break him beyond repair. All that matters is the here and now. Just this once, Alec wants to live in this moment. He's going to appreciate every second that Theo is giving him.

"Are you now?" Theo says. "I thought this was me teaching you?"

"You might be teaching me how to fuck, but I know how to appreciate a good-looking man."

"You said that once before, and I wasn't sure if you were serious or—"

"I don't say things I don't mean, Theodore." Alec rubs his thumbs over Theo's nipples, watching as the nubs harden. He wants to suck on them so badly.

Some of that longing must show on his face because

Theo pushes the hair off Alec's head before asking, "What do you want?"

Telling Theo he wants his cock was easier than this, and Alec has no idea why. Maybe because the one time he'd let on to another guy how much he liked to kiss and suck, he'd taken that as an assumption that the boundaries they'd agreed on no longer applied. Maybe because in some ways, this seems more intimate to Alec than taking a cock up his ass. He's not sure if that makes any sense, and he isn't about to say it out loud, but it's true regardless.

"You told me I could do whatever I wanted to you before, but I didn't tell you the same." Alec starts to yank his hands back, but Theo grabs his wrists, pulling them back. "I should have. I asked you to be clear and I wasn't, so here's me being clear. You can touch whatever you want, do whatever you want. If you're not sure, you can ask, but I don't have any hard limits, at least not that I've found out yet, so I doubt think you're gonna find something I'd say no to and—"

"I want to suck on you," Alec blurts, squeezing his eyes shut.

When Theo doesn't immediately reply, Alec hears his heart pounding loudly in his ears.

"Hey, look at me, Alexander." His knuckles graze over the back of Alec's hand. "Please."

The *please* breaks through the walls Alec is trying to put up to protect himself, and though everything in him is screaming to burrow inside of Theo's sweater and hide, he resists, forcing his eyes open and locking his gaze on Theo. Alec waits for the annoyance or pity or whatever else he expects, but the only thing he sees on Theo's face is the same kind of gentle understanding he's always had. It's so easy to remember why Alec always trusted Theo, why he was the one Alec wanted when something was wrong when he was younger. Theo never judges or yells. He's patient and calm even in the face of Alec's intensity, and it soothes the part of Alec that has always, always been too much for most people.

"You can," Theo whispers. "If you want. You don't have to tell me what's going on in that head of yours, but you can do that, too."

"Fuck you, Theodore." Theo blinks, looking blindsided before Alec continues. "How the fuck do you do this to me?"

"Do what?"

Alec can't answer that question, but he can answer the other one.

"There was a guy...last year." Alec grabs the pillow from behind him, pulling it over his face so only his mouth is visible, because if he actually looks at Theo while having to say this out loud, he's not going to get it out. "We had a few classes together so I knew him. Or I thought I did. Anyway, there was a party, and we were dancing, and I just wanted to have fun and...and be touched. Not like sex, just, I like physical contact."

Memories rush in, flooding Alec with white-hot shame. It doesn't matter how many times he's told himself it wasn't his fault; it still feels like it was. He should probably get therapy for that, or for the way school is making him feel like the walls are closing in around him, but who the fuck has time for therapy? He's got grades to keep up and practice and—

"Alec."

"Sorry," Alec mumbles, embarrassed again at his own spiraling. This is why he keeps himself so busy. That way he doesn't have time to be alone with his thoughts.

Here he is with his dream man, about to lose his virginity, and he's ruining it. This is what happens when Alec goes off his meds. Every summer, he gets a little glimpse of what life might be like if he stayed medicated, then he goes off them to compete, and he falls apart.

"You don't need to apologize. Not to me, not ever."

Inhaling deeply, Alec throws his arms over the pillow to pull it down, white spots springing up behind his closed eyes.

"It's stupid. I was lonely or something, and so we danced a lot, and he asked if I wanted to go upstairs to one of the empty rooms. I told him I didn't do one night stands, that I didn't want...*that*." The memory of the guy's smile still makes Alec's stomach curl. He'd seemed so fucking nice. "It'd been a long few months, and I was stressed, and it seemed like it would be okay to say yes, that he meant it when he said only kissing was fine. Only the more we kissed, the more this buzzing filled my brain, and you know how I am—my mouth thing."

"There's nothing wrong with an oral fixation. There's nothing wrong with you, period."

Alec huffs but doesn't reply. Theo knows more about Alec's behavioral struggles than he would like, both because he was living with them when Alec finally got officially diagnosed in fifth grade and also because Jason has a big mouth.

Whatever Theo thinks he knows about Alec, it's one thing for him to say those things and another for Alec to live in his own body and brain. Theo isn't the one who got called a beaver by his friends in middle school for chewing off the ends of all his pencils when he had to sit still for too long. He wasn't the one who constantly got yelled at by teachers for being too fidgety and unable to stop talking, constantly singled out like he was choosing to misbehave and not deeply unregulated. Theo wasn't the one who sucked his thumb until he was nine, who has to carry lollipops and gum everywhere he goes, and who needs his mouth full for his brain to be quiet. His medication helps, but it's banned under NCAA rules, and while he could get a medical exemption for his diagnosis, he never wanted to. Instead he goes off them every season and just white-knuckles it, dealing with a world built for neurotypicals.

"You don't have to keep going," Theo reminds him.

The offer is appreciated, but Alec knows if he doesn't tell this to Theo now, he won't ever tell him, or anyone else ever again.

"He said he was okay with kissing, just wanted to do it without an audience to give me his full attention. I agreed because kissing is the fucking best, you know, and—" Alec's voice trails off realizing what comes next. "You probably don't wanna know the rest."

"I want to know anything you want to tell me."

Were it anyone else, Alec would assume they were just being polite, but Theo has never lied to Alec before. Even when it hurt, even when he broke Alec's heart. Theo doesn't lie to him, and so Alec is going to do one of the hardest things he's ever done, he's going to believe him.

"I started, you know, sucking. On his neck and chest and his stomach, it just...felt good. I didn't even really care about the guy, but he seemed safe, which in hindsight was fucking stupid."

"You're not stupid."

Alec makes a derisive noise, realizing he's maybe not as over it as he wants to be. Probably because he's refused to think about it at all.

"He, uh, he got turned on by what we were doing,

which is obviously fine. It was an ego boost, and I was turned on too, but it didn't mean I'd changed my mind. He started touching my hair, which I like, but then it got too tight and—" Alec pauses. He's never said any of this out loud. Only one person knows, because he walked in on it, but even then they didn't talk about it. "I tried to pull away, but he started saying I was a cocktease. He said if I wanted to suck, I should be doing it right. I tried to pull away, but he was a lot bigger, and he shoved his pants down and—you know."

Memories meld together. That night. Last night when the guy at the club had shouted the same thing at Alec.

"Nothing that happened was your fault, Alexander."

"You pick up mind-reading at some point?"

"Maybe I just know you," Theo replies, giving Alec's hip a squeeze. He must know him, because the contact is exactly what Alec needs. Theo isn't moving away, isn't taking his offer back or calling Alec a mess. He's touching Alec, offering the kind of physical reassurance Alec has trained himself out of needing. "I'm so sorry you had that happen. Did you report it?"

"Fuck, no," Alec says, pressing the pillow over his eyes so tightly it borders on uncomfortable. "It would've messed everything up. The team didn't need that. Anyway, it's fine. It's not a big deal. Riley, that's how we met. It was Riley's frat, and he'd gone upstairs to get something for one of his frat brothers, and he walked in on that whole thing. He kind of punched the guy in the face, and the asshole never talked to me again, so, it's fine. Besides, I got Riley as a friend out of the deal so—"

"You don't have to try and make light of sexual assault."

"It wasn't sexual assault," Alec hisses. "It was just... some guy being handsy."

"It was assault."

"Well, this is fucking fun. Any wonder I'm still a virgin? I sure know how to ruin a moment."

"You didn't ruin anything. We don't have to do this."

Alec flings the pillow aside, blinking at the spots that dance in front of Theo's pretty face. It takes a second for Alec's vision to clear, and he doesn't like what he sees. It looks too close to pity, and bile rises in Alec's throat.

"This is why I don't tell people. Why I didn't want to tell you." He jabs his finger in Theo's chest. "Don't you dare look at me with those sad eyes, Theo. Or else."

"Or else what?"

"I don't fucking know."

"Alright," Theo whispers, reaching for Alec's hands. "Maybe we shouldn't have sex."

Alec yanks his hands away, scrambling backwards until his back hits the wall. Theo's still talking, but Alec can't focus on the words as his stupid brain hones in on the rejection. If it were just Theo changing his mind about sex, Alec would be fine. People can stop whenever they want. Consent can always be revoked, but this is different. Alec told Theo something he's never told anyone; now Theo doesn't want to have sex with him anymore, and his brain is freaking the fuck out.

He'd known he was going to lose Theo again; he just didn't realize it was going to be before he even got to have him.

16 THEO

ALEC IS SPIRALING. Theo's never seen it firsthand like this. He's heard stories from Jason, knows enough about trauma and rejection sensitivity dysphoria to know it's likely some messy mix of both, but he doesn't know how to fix it.

He's pretty sure Alec thinks he was being rejected, which wasn't Theo's intention. All he was trying to do was avoid being one of the many assholes who'd made Alec uncomfortable or taken advantage of him. The idea of doing that to Alec turns his stomach. He never wanted to hurt him, only he apparently had, yet again.

"Alexander, look at me."

Alec's body goes still, unnaturally so for him, and he lifts his gaze to meet Theo's. There's so much confusion and pain there, but the trust is what undoes Theo. For all the times Theo's inadvertently hurt him, he must've done something right too, because Alec still trusts him. He can't begin to imagine what he's done to deserve that faith, but he wants to be the kind of man that Alec seems to think he is.

"I'm not rejecting you, Alec."

"That's not what it feels like," Alec mumbles, scrubbing at his watery eyes with his sweater-covered fists. He pulls his knees inside the sweater, everything but his head hidden beneath the fabric like it's some kind of protective shell.

"I know, but brains can be kind of mean sometimes." Theo inches closer, not sure if he should touch him or not. "Also you might've noticed, but I'm not the best at saying what I mean. I'm kind of bad at communicating."

Alec settles his chin on knees, staring at Theo. "You are horrible at it."

"Wow, don't spare my feelings," Theo teases, relieved at the way Alec cracks a smile. "We can't all be as perfect as you."

"I am pretty perfect," Alec sniffles, his bravado making Theo's heart clench. Even if all the reasons make sense, it's hard for Theo to reconcile how many years he's spent missing out on how great Alec is because of his own shit. "Took you long enough to notice."

"What can I say, sometimes I'm a little slow."

"That's all right, you have your other strengths," Alec says, some of his smile returning. It renders Theo speechless, the air in his very lungs hard to access. Alec should always be smiling, should always be happy, and it's a little terrifying for Theo to realize he wants to be one of the reasons that his smile stays on his beautiful face.

Some of that smile flickers as he twists Theo's sleeves between his fingers. "I'm sorry. For ruining things."

"You didn't ruin anything. Please don't apologize. Unless you do something really stupid or reckless, like getting drunk or picking a fight with someone twice your size again."

"I don't ever want to drink again," Alec groans. "Though I can't make any promises about the other part. "

He's pretty sure Alec is joking, but the idea of him getting hurt without Theo there to step in has Theo's chest roaring with defensive instincts. He's felt protective of Jason before, but not like this. He wants to wrap Alec up in his sweaters, in his bed, wants to make him laugh and smile and never let anyone else hurt him ever again. He wants to keep Alec safe and happy, but he has no idea how to do that when he's positioned himself to be someone who could break him.

Virginity might be a stupid convention, but the trust Alec has placed in Theo isn't. He trusts Theo to keep him safe, to make him feel good, and to not demand things from him he isn't willing to give. Alec might be offering Theo his body, but Theo is under no delusions about his heart. That is entirely off limits, not that Theo would have a clue what to do with it if it weren't. It's for the best that Alec won't get attached to Theo. What's happening now might be toeing the line of friendship, but it's still a line, and it's one Theo isn't going to cross.

Theo can absolutely fuck Alec—beautiful, feisty, fierce as hell Alexander King—and not get feelings. He knows he can. He's never gotten them for anyone else, and this won't be different. Some mutual sexual gratification, a little harmless flirting because honestly anyone with two brain cells wouldn't be able to resist Alec's charm, and then they can each move on.

"You look like you're about to take a test and forgot to study."

"That is not what I look like right now," Theo says.

"It totally is." Alec laughs, moving onto his knees. Theo tries to keep a straight face, but Alec's inching closer, his face screwed up in the world's most over-exaggerated expression. Theo can only assume he's making fun, but seeing stern frown lines on Alec's face are as out of place as they are ridiculous.

Theo laughs. "You are such a pain in the ass."

"And yet my ass is still empty," Alec says, flopping down on the bed dramatically. There's something heady about how comfortable he is in his own skin, how much he doesn't seem to give a fuck that he's naked beneath Theo's sweater and his cock is exposed. It's softened from their talk earlier, only half-hard now.

Most of Alec's body is smooth, from his toned chest to his thighs that only have the lightest dusting of hair. Even his treasure trail is sparse, the faintest bit of hair leading from his belly button to his cock, which is nestled in a sparse patch of curls.

"You're staring," Alec says, hitching a knee up then tipping it sideways and exposing himself further.

It's clear he likes the weight of Theo's gaze, widening his legs until he's on full display. Where Theo would recoil under the attention, Alec basks under it, dragging his hand to the hem of the sweater and pushing it until it's tucked under his chin, his gorgeous body right there, just for Theo.

"You like me staring."

It's not a question, but Alec answers anyway. "Yes."

"You always did love attention," Theo murmurs, skimming his palm over Alec's thigh and delighting in the goosebumps that spring up. Alec's thighs are a beautiful thing, the thickest part of him with muscles hardened from years of dedication to his sport.

Every touch from Theo seems to turn him on more until his cock begins to harden again, the foreskin stretching as it lengthens. He's a grower then, still noticeably smaller than Theo, even when erect but still perfect like the rest of him. Alec has a pretty cock, flushed and pearling at the tip.

Theo is under no delusions that it's him specifically making Alec widen his knees and arch his back. He's young, aroused and has never experienced this before, so of course he's going to be needy, but it's an ego boost for Theo to pretend it's solely for him. He's always enjoyed sex, enjoyed the play of bodies and the exchange of power. He likes the feeling of skin on skin and the release of finding climax, all things Alec has never done with another man. Things he's going to do with Theo.

"You look like you're waiting for something."

"You know damn well I am," Alec retorts, blinking at Theo with those big brown eyes of his. He waits only a second before locking their gaze and then pulling the sweater up further, until some of the material is bunched up between his teeth. Then he lets out a groan, mouthing at the sweater. There's not an ounce of shame in him as he does it, and the sight of Alec uninhibited and clearly feeling safe enough to do what he needs to regulate has Theo's world tipping off-kilter.

He says something, but with the sweater between his teeth it's impossible to make out what.

"What's that?"

Alec huffs, letting the material fall from his mouth. "I said, are you gonna stare all day, or are you going to touch me?"

The words send a scorching bolt of arousal to his gut. It should figure that the most inexperienced person Theo's ever fucked is also turning out to be the most brazen. It's so very Alec.

"I'm gonna touch," Theo says softly, "but only if you promise to tell me to stop if you need me to."

"I already told you I'm not going to tell you stop so—"

Theo lets his body fall forward, the mattress bouncing

as Theo's hands fall down on either side of Alec's head. It earns him all of Alec's attention and an unexpected look of surprise that Theo knows is going to haunt his dreams.

"Yeah, you did, and I'm telling you right now I'm not letting this go any further unless you promise to tell me if you need me to stop. I'm not small, and it might hurt, and there's nothing wrong with not being ready or changing your mind. I don't care if I'm balls deep inside of you, Alec. If you're done, you tell me."

Alec blinks, his mouth falling open.

"I don't want to hurt you. Jason would kill me."

Alec's face screws up in displeasure. "That. I don't like that. Don't talk about my brother while I'm naked. Ew."

"Right, no talking about Ja—"

Alec's hand flies out to cover Theo's mouth. The look Alec gives him is probably supposed to be a menacing glare, but is just kind of adorable. Not that Theo is thinking about how adorable Alec is. Naked and sexy, sure. Adorable is verging way too close to feelings.

"*CanItalkyet?*" Theo mumbles around Alec's hand.

"Depends on what you're gonna say," Alec replies, slowly lowering his hand.

"I want to see you moan around my sweater while I fuck you."

The prettiest shade of pink blossoms on Alec's cheeks.

"You wanna choke on it, Alec? Want your mouth stuffed full while I fuck you?"

The blush deepens, spreading down his neck and drawing Theo's eyes to the hollow of his throat where his gold chain is pooled. With a delicate touch, Theo tugs on the chain, smoothing it out around Alec's throat.

"Did I finally find a way to shut you up, Alexander?"

"I'll show you shut up," Alec huffs, throwing himself at

Theo. He could easily push him back, but he doesn't, letting Alec shove him back onto the bed and straddle his thighs. "You—you—"

"I what?" Theo asks, resting his hands on Alec's bare thighs. He can't seem to get enough of them, giving the meaty flesh a squeeze.

"You're teasing me," Alec grumbles, his cheeks deep red now. Between his curls in disarray and the collar of the sweater stretched out and wet from Alec's spit, he looks wrecked already, and Theo hasn't even fucked him yet.

"What are you going to do if I am?" Theo asks, unsure what's happening. He never talks during sex, doesn't tease and flirt once he's naked with someone, but this isn't some random hookup. This is *Alec*. He's not just Jason's baby brother, he's also Theo's friend. Maybe that last bit is what is messing with Theo's brain. He's never fucked someone he actually knew first or someone he liked. Maybe that's all it is. Except watching Alec above him, he's not so sure. There's a spark in Alec's eyes, something playful and free, and it makes Theo forget to overthink and close off like he normally does.

Looking at Alec makes it difficult to remember all the reasons he's supposed to hold back when Alec clearly isn't. There's no one else quite like Alec, so it makes sense sex with him might be different. Theo just needs to mentally prepare. He needs to regain control. He needs—

"You have way too many clothes, Theodore." Alec moves his hands to Theo's pants, fingers toying with the button. "Can I take them off, pretty please with a cherry on top? I'll be a good boy."

The laugh bubbles out before Theo knows what's happening, and when Alec gapes at him in surprise, he laughs harder.

"Theodore James, how dare you laugh at me during sex?"

"I can't help it." Theo continues to laugh. "You're never a good boy."

"Oh, fuck you." Alec swats Theo's chest with the sleeve of the sweater that's hanging over his hands and despite his words, the smile on his face is wide. "You know what I'm realizing? I think I'm a bad influence on you."

"Little too late to realize that." Theo grins.

Alec shrugs. "Might as well corrupt you completely. Come on then, dick in ass and more kissing, Mr. James. I don't have all day. Unless you think I should go back to that club later and—"

Theo doesn't let him finish, fingers digging into Alec's hips as he flips them so Alec is under him. Alec might be young and fit, but Theo's got nearly six inches and eighty pounds on him, so he can put Alec anywhere he wants him, which right now happens to be beneath him. "No club."

"No?" Alec says with mock innocence.

"No," Theo repeats, shocked at the gravelly tone of his voice. He needs to get a goddamn hold of himself. He sounds like a possessive boyfriend. He's going to freak Alec out.

"Damn, Theodore." Alec's fingers curl around the back of his neck. "That's hot as fuck."

Any reply Theo might have is lost when Alec pulls him down in a filthy kiss, reminding Theo that while Alec might be inexperienced, he isn't bashful. Deepening the kiss, he lets his own tongue slip into Alec's mouth, delighting at the guttural moan it earns him.

"Fuck."

"Yes," Theo whispers, breaking the kiss to focus on getting his pants off. He pops open the button, tugging the zipper down so he can shove them over his ass along with his boxers. He has to get off Alec to remove them the rest of the way, but the momentary loss of physical contact is worth it when he catches sight of Alec's flushed face and dilated pupils. Any lingering insecurity Theo might have held about his body flees under Alec's appreciative stare.

This moment is a perfect reminder of what Theo likes so much about sex, it has such a clear, defined start and stop. Sex has always been easy to separate from feelings because all he had to focus on was the other person's arousal. When he turns his focus on someone else, making them feel as good as possible, then they don't stop to focus on Theo too deeply.

Sex has always been about physical gratification. Nothing more and nothing less. The one time he dated someone, there'd only been a few dates, and Theo had done everything in his power to keep his emotional distance. So he hadn't been surprised when it blew up because he hadn't even really tried. He'd gone on dates more to get Jason off his back, because his best friend was a stupid romantic and had been worried Theo was lonely.

Thankfully after that epic crash and burn, Jason stopped suggesting Theo might want a relationship. Theo happily went back to his fuck-and-done mentality, which has been serving him just fine. *Or has it?* a little voice screams in the back of his head, reminding him of the last two times he went to the club and came home alone.

Theo tries to ignore the voice, focusing on the rise and fall of Alec's chest and the weighted way he's looking at Theo. This is still just sex. He's scratching an itch, making sure he gets over his little crush on Alec, while also making sure Alec's first time is with someone who won't hurt him.

"How do you feel?" Theo asks.

Alec snorts. "Is that a serious question?"

"Obviously."

"Horny."

A smile plays at the corner of Theo's mouth while he lets his gaze travel up Alec's body, taking in every muscle and curve. He's beautiful.

"You wanna take that sweater off?" Theo asks, already reaching for it when Alec shakes his head before averting his gaze.

"You want me to fuck you in my sweater, Alexander?"

Alec exhales slowly. "Fuck, yes."

There's something else in his tone, but Theo doesn't want to push. It isn't his place. Besides, the idea of fucking Alec while he wears Theo's sweater is incredibly arousing. He's never fucked anyone who was wearing his clothes. Maybe he has a kink for that. His cock certainly likes the idea, judging by the way it's rock hard and leaking.

Theo must stare for too long because Alec groans loudly. "You can get on with the fucking now."

"It's not a race," Theo tells him, smoothing his hands down Alec's thighs to rest at his knees.

Alec's entire body trembles, and his eyes stay focused on the ceiling. "That's good, because if it was a race I'd win, you know."

"I'm sure you would," Theo replies, letting his fingers ghost down to brush over the backs of Alec's knees as he spreads his legs to make room for himself.

"I—good," Alec croaks.

"Alec."

"Just do it," Alec grunts, squeezing his eyes shut.

The shift in his demeanor is unexpected and flips a switch in Theo's brain. Alec is nervous.

It occurs to Theo that he's known Alec his entire life,

and he's never once seen him nervous. Hyped up on adrenaline, exhausted, confused, worried, but never nervous. The realization triggers that protective instinct urge deep in Theo. It makes him want to curl around Alec and hide him away from the world. It's not something he's used to feeling, and he doesn't at all want to examine what it means. It probably just has to do with the trust Alec is placing in him. It's not every day someone chooses you to be their first.

Part of Theo feels a little guilty. Alec deserves his first time to be with someone he loves, but he also deserves for it to be on his terms. Alec told him he wants this, and Theo needs to trust Alec.

"Breathe."

"I'm not dead yet so—" Alec gives a thumbs up, which might be funny if Theo's need to shield Alec from discomfort wasn't so strong.

Unfortunately, he doesn't think asking Alec if he's nervous would go over very well right now, when Alec isn't in a conversational mood. It's obvious Alec wants this to happen, but it's equally clear he's anxious, even if Alec doesn't want to admit it. Which means it's Theo's job to get him relaxed and out of that pretty head of his. What he needs to do is give Alec's brain something else to focus on. Watching Alec's jaw open and close, he gets an idea.

"Alec."

"If you ask me if I'm okay, I'll kick you out of this bed."

"Wasn't going to." Theo snorts, oddly amused and turned on by Alec's sass. Even while he's out of sorts and nervous, he's still full of fire, and Theo likes it a whole lot more than he was prepared for. "I was going to ask if you wanted to suck my dick."

"I thought you were gonna fuck me?" Alec blurts,

raising himself onto his elbows to peer at Theo with wide eyes.

"You saying you don't want your mouth full of my cock?"

At that, Alec actually moans, letting Theo know he's on the right track. It also makes Theo bolder. "I thought maybe you could fill that mouth of yours while I get you ready. Think you can do that, Alec? Think you can have a mouth full of cock while I prep you to be fucked?"

"Yes," Alec groans.

"Good," Theo says, crawling off Alec and moving to the bedside table. He opens it, pulling out a condom and the bottle of lube he keeps there. When he turns back, it's to see Alec biting on his bottom lip so hard it looks like it might bleed. He drops the lube and condom onto the mattress then reaches out to gently pry the lip out from between Alec's teeth. Alec's jaw trembles, and while Theo isn't entirely sure what he's doing, it's obviously the right thing because as soon as his fingers press down on Alec's lips, he sucks them into his mouth.

It's Theo's turn to moan as Alec sucks hard on two of his fingers, swallowing them down like he would a cock, his tongue lapping at the underside of Theo's fingers and hollowing his cheeks.

Saliva runs down the side of Alec's lips while Theo pulls his fingers slightly out, unprepared for the whimper it earns him. It makes him curious to see what would happen if he slipped them back in. Experimentally, he presses his two fingers to Alec's bottom lip, shuddering when Alec opens his mouth wide to accept them again. He knew Alec liked things in his mouth, but he still wasn't prepared to see Alec eager to deep-throat his fingers.

"You want them?" Theo asks.

Big brown eyes blink at him, offering more of an answer than words ever could. Slowly Theo presses them inside, barely able to fight off his own groan of pleasure when Alec sucks them in harder and deeper than before, until Theo's fingertips reach the back of his throat. Instinctively, he tries to pull them back, but Alec grabs his wrist to hold him in place, moaning around the fingers as he sucks.

There's no spluttering or choking, and this unexpected new knowledge that Alec doesn't have a gag reflex has Theo yanking his fingers out of Alec's mouth and replacing them with his tongue. He pulls Alec to him with demanding hands, shivering at the way Alec lets Theo take control. It's been a long time since Theo was this turned on, this desperate to fuck someone. He wants to crowd Alec into the mattress, cover his smaller body with his own and bury himself so deep in Alec he can't tell where each of them begin and end.

With every touch of lips, Alec moans louder, and Theo's patience snaps. He pulls back, desperate to be inside of Alec, but the loss of contact has Alec whining while he tries to pull Theo back down to him.

"Shh," Theo soothes, kissing Alec's forehead. "I'm gonna make you feel so good."

"Fuck."

"Soon," Theo promises, thumbing at Alec's spit-soaked lips. They're so full and pretty, delicate on his otherwise masculine face. They're going to look so good wrapped around his cock, and Theo wishes he could watch and enjoy it, but this isn't about him. It's all about Alec, and Theo is more than prepared to make him the star of this show.

"Pinch me."

The request takes Theo by surprise. "Wait, are you into painplay?"

"What? Hell no, I just wanna check if I'm hallucinating," Alec says, somehow managing to make a joke even while clearly on unsteady ground. It sends another wave of protectiveness through Theo. Alec is so damn special.

"Well?" Alec arches one eyebrow.

"I'm not going to pinch you."

"So you'll stick your fingers and dick in my ass but pinching is too—ow, fuck," Alec yelps, rubbing his ass. "I meant like a baby pinch, asshole! I can't believe you actually pinched me."

"Sorry!" Theo laughs, not entirely sure what's happening. One second he wants to swaddle Alec in bubble wrap to protect him from the world, the next he wants to fuck him into the mattress until he's a writhing mess. Now he's laughing because Alec is ridiculous, even in a situation that could be awkward. All of it should be weird, yet somehow, it's not.

"You don't sound sorry," Alec says seriously, but it's clear he's trying not to laugh.

"I—" but Theo can't get another word out because Alec is trying to tickle him.

"What the hell are you doing?"

"Whatever I want." Alec smirks, his delicate fingers finding purchase on Theo's belly. He gives it a little squish before tickling until Theo's laughing so hard that he can hardly breathe. He grabs both of Alec's hands and pulls them away, enclosing them in his grasp to keep Alec's hands where he can see them.

"You win," Theo gasps, breathless, horny, and most unexpectedly of all, happy.

"Even when something isn't a competition, I win." Alec grins. "You know, I haven't heard you laugh that hard in a long time. You sound good."

"I laugh," Theo protests.

"Not with me," Alec whispers, lowering his gaze to where Theo has both Alec's wrist trapped in one of his hands. Alec's wrists are small and delicate, reminding Theo that beneath the bravado and muscles is just a boy who could easily be broken.

"Alec."

"Don't," Alec whispers, leaning forward to press a kiss to Theo's lips. "You promised."

He loosens his grip on Alec's wrists, reaching up to brush a stray curl from Alec's face, unsure how the mood shifted so quickly. He doesn't know what to say, what to do, but Alec doesn't share his hesitation and presses Theo down on the mattress with a hand to his chest. Theo offers one last kiss that feels almost the end of something that hasn't even started yet.

"Just...be gentle, okay?"

"I'd never hurt you, Alexander."

Alec's expression shifts, something unreadable in his eyes as he opens his mouth and then closes it just as quickly. Theo wants to ask, wants to push, but once again, he holds back. This is already veering into dangerous territory.

"How do you want me?"

Such a loaded question. How doesn't Theo want him would be an easier thing to answer.

"Straddle my chest with your ass by my face and—" but Theo doesn't even finish before Alec is swinging a knee over Theo's chest, having to spread his legs to fit over Theo's much wider body. The position brings his hard cock to rest in the center of Theo's chest, his perfectly full ass right in front of Theo's face while he wastes absolutely no time moving his mouth to Theo's dick. There's no teasing licks,

only the warm, wet heat of Alec's mouth as he swallows
Theo down as far as he can.

For a few seconds, Theo forgets himself, lost in the pleasure of Alec's willing mouth. Theo isn't small by any means,
and while Alec definitely can't deep-throat him, it's clear
he's trying, damn near choking on Theo's girth. It's not until
he whines, rutting into Theo's chest that Theo remembers
himself. He's supposed to be distracting Alec so he can prep
him, not be the one distracted.

"Take it easy on me, or I might come before I can fuck
you," Theo admits, not wanting to ruin Alec's experience.

Alec stills, the line of his back taught. Theo almost
worries he's ruined the moment, but then Alec's body
relaxes as he sags, no longer sucking but still keeping Theo's
cock situated in his mouth. It's a little unexpected to have
someone's mouth on him without them doing anything, but
not at all unwelcome.

Exhaling a shuddering breath, Theo retrieves the lube
from where he dropped it, uncapping the lid and squeezing
some on his fingers. He rubs it between thumb and forefinger to try and warm it up before moving his hand to
Alec's ass. Spreading him wide, he takes a moment to appreciate Alec's ass, the freckles that hide in the crease, and the
hole no one but Theo has ever touched before. He's
gorgeous, and Theo isn't sure he's deserving of this moment,
but he's going to take it, because for once in his life he
doesn't want to do the smart and safe thing. He wants this,
wants Alec, and judging by the way Alec leaks on his chest,
Alec wants him too.

"I'm going to—"

"Please," Alec begs, pulling off Theo's dick. His voice is
rough, desperate, and Theo's never heard him like this

before. It's a beautiful sound and one he's not likely to ever forget.

Dragging his lubed-up thumb over the puckered hole with one hand, Theo uses his other to rub circles on Alec's lower back. He keens, arching his ass back so the tip of Theo's thumb presses inside, which makes Alec squirm even more. He thrusts back and makes a desperate, needy sound that will fuel all of Theo's jerk-off fantasies for the next decade.

Continuing to rub circles on his lower back, he presses his thumb in deeper, and it earns him another one of those delicious sounds from Alec.

"You want another?"

"You fucking know I do," Alec groans.

Theo pulls his thumb out, adding more lube to his fingers and then switches to his pointer finger so he can get in deeper. He thrusts it in and out, mesmerized by the sight of his own thick finger pressing into Alec's hole. The resistance is there, but it's not what Theo expected so he adds a second, unprepared for Alec to damn near choke himself on Theo's cock.

"I've got you, you're okay," Theo soothes, letting his palm roam over as much of Alec's back as he can reach while Alec's mouth remains suctioned around him. He's still not sucking, just holding it in his mouth as deep as he can go, as if having a mouthful of Theo's dick is the only thing keeping him from falling apart.

A flashback to Theo's first time flitters at the edges of his consciousness, recalling awkward kisses and hands, not enough lube ,and the sharp sting of a door handle in his back. He'd been seventeen and stupid and very horny, none of which were a good combo. The sex had been pretty horrible given they were both virgins, and while neither of them had done it on purpose, Theo had it on good authority he hadn't made it great for his partner. Inexperience, impatience and a lack of sex-ed could do that. Thankfully, Theo isn't a bumbling teenager anymore. He understands what it takes to make sex good, what it takes to make another person feel physical bliss, and if he can spare Alec painful awkward memories, he will.

"You've got to breathe," Theo reminds him, adding a third finger.

There's a rumble from Alec, the vibrations making Theo's cock twitch and his hands plunge in deeper. At the push of fingers, Alec makes the sound again, humming loud and deep around Theo until Theo crooks his fingers to brush over Alec's prostate and then he's damn near howling. He takes Theo's cock so deep, the tip breaches the back of Alec's throat, while Alec comes in heavy spurts between them, completely untouched.

Before Theo can react, Alec is pulling off, rolling onto his back and trying to suffocate himself with one of Theo's pillows for the second time.

"Alec."

"Alec isn't here," Alec mumbles from beneath the pillow.

"Oh, so there's a different naked man in my bed?"

A few seconds pass before one of Alec's hands unclenches itself from the pillow so that he can lift it to flip Theo off. A good sign, if Theo ever saw one.

Careful not to spook him, he inches closer very slowly. When Alec doesn't recoil at the dip of the bed beside him, Theo tentatively reaches a hand out to touch Alec's thigh. When he doesn't flinch at that, Theo adds another hand, sliding them up until he's got two hands on Alec's hips, his grip firm and unyielding as if telling Alec all the things he can't with words.

"Alec, I—" His words are cut short by someone banging on the front door. Three solid, firm knocks. Theo knows that knock pattern. "Fuck."

The cursing is apparently enough to get Alec's attention because he lifts the pillow off his face, eyes red and wet. Theo wants to kill himself for what is happening right now. After what they just did, he should be reassuring Alec—who is clearly not okay—but he can't because if he doesn't answer the door in the next two minutes, Jason is going to use his spare key. If Jason walks in, if Jason finds Theo in bed, naked and covered in his baby brother's come, Theo will lose everything.

Suddenly, the world is closing in around Theo, the reality of what they just did damn near suffocating. How did he let this happen? How did he think he could fuck Alec and nothing would change? How is he supposed to look Jason in the eyes?

Struggling to find any scenario where things will be okay, Theo rolls out of bed, determined to at least try. He grabs a handful of tissues and wipes the evidence of Alec's release off his belly. His own erection is already wilting, done in by the prospect of losing his best friend. Fuck. He is so stupid.

"Theo?"

Alec's sitting up now, the pillow in his lap and his big, brown eyes looking at Theo with confusion. This is exactly what Theo was supposed to be avoiding. He'd promised Alec a good first time so that no one would hurt him, and now Theo is doing just that.

He's not cut out for this, especially not with Alec.

"You have to go."

The look on Alec's face is one of the worst things Theo has ever seen.

"Oh," Alec whispers.

Three more solid, firm knocks. A reminder their time is running out.

"I forgot I was supposed to meet Jason for breakfast at ten." Theo glances at the clock and wants to scream. It's nearly eleven thirty. He's usually so good with time. He never stands Jason up, which means Jason's probably out there worried and ready to come barreling in. "You need to leave, right now. He can't know you were here."

"Theo."

"You can keep the sweater and shit, your clothes from last night are in the wash. I forgot to put them in the dryer."

Theo hurries to the dresser, digging around until he finds a pair of sweats with a drawstring. They're going to be huge on Alec, but they're the best he's got. He hands them over along with a clean pair of socks. Theo is a coward, keeping his eyes on the ground. He cannot look at Alec's face again, cannot see the proof of how much he's hurting him.

"Thanks," Alec mumbles.

The silence that follows is louder than any words could be. Part of Theo wishes Alec would yell at him, remind him what a horrible person he is, but Alec doesn't say anything as he dresses quietly, and somehow, that hurts more.

Every beat of Theo's heart thunders in his ears as he pulls his jeans and sweater back on. When he dares to look up at Alec, he almost wishes he hadn't. Standing there in Theo's clothes, he looks so young and vulnerable. The sweater cuffs hang over his hands, and the sweats pool over his bare feet. He's beautiful.

"I'm sorry," Theo whispers. "I made you a promise and—"

"It's okay, Theodore." Alec offers him a smile he doesn't deserve, offers him the kind of reassurance that Theo should be giving to Alec. It twists a knot inside of Theo, a harsh and painful reminder of how horrible he is at feelings. "I can sneak out the side gate. I won't tell Jason. You don't have to worry."

Much as Theo wishes he could tell Alec it doesn't matter, they both know that's not true. Even though the thought of Jason finding out makes Theo want to fall apart, watching Alec walk away hurts just as much. Alec doesn't yell or protest, even though he has every right given that he's all but being kicked out. He's mature, understanding, and doesn't hesitate to walk away from Theo. It's exactly what needs to happen, yet the knot around Theo's chest doesn't loosen.

"You need a ride home and—"

"It's fine," Alec interrupts, eyes focused on the ground. Rio streaks past Theo, moving to paw at Alec's legs, but he doesn't pick her up despite her noisy mewls for attention. "I can't, baby. I gotta go."

She doesn't understand, letting out a pitifully unhappy sound as Alec ignores her. "I'll just sneak out the back door and down the side gate and—"

The rest of his words are cut off by the familiar sound of a key in the lock. Theo freezes. There is no explaining this away. He was supposed to watch out for Alec, not let him get drunk then try and fuck him. Alec probably hates him and now Jason will, too.

When the door flies open, there's a moment of confusion as Jason hovers in the doorway, eyes wide as he stares. Theo's standing by the couch with his attention on Jason, while Alec stands there with an unhappy kitten desperate for attention. He's also wearing Theo's clothing, which is going to complicate everything and—

"Oh, damn you caught us," Alec says.

Theo's lungs stop working as he glances between Alec, who is smiling, and Jason who looks like he's not sure what the hell is happening, which is exactly how Theo feels.

"I caught you," Jason echoes, stepping into the house.

"Yeah." Alec blows out a breath, leaning against the couch. "Theo was being a good guy and trying to help me avoid my hangover embarrassment. I made a fool of myself."

Jason looks at Theo, whose expression must confirm Alec's lie because Jason shakes his head. "I knew you'd be trouble, Alec. That's why I asked Theo to keep an eye on you."

"That's me, trouble." Alec laughs, but the sound is hollow, and Theo can't find it in himself to laugh along with them. He knows exactly what Alec is doing, and he's sick to his stomach that he's letting him.

"I got pretty wasted and well, just be glad you weren't there. Ruined my clothes, too, but Theo was nice enough to let me sleep it off here and borrow some of his things. It's my fault he missed breakfast. You know how I am."

Alec shrugs as if any of this is his fault, as if he was some kind of trouble. As if Theo didn't willingly take him home and take care of him. As if all of this isn't entirely Theo's fault. He was the older one last night, the sober one. He made these choices, not Alec.

"It's all right," Jason says with an easy smile. He crosses the room to ruffle Alec's hair. "We were all young and stupid once. I'm just glad everything is okay."

Alec slaps Jason's hand away, flipping him off before he

finds his shoes and slips them on. "I'll, uh, get out of your hair, Theo. Thanks again."

"Don't mention it," Theo mumbles.

"You need a ride home?" Jason asks Alec.

"I'm good," Alec shoves his hands into his pockets, grabbing his sneakers and moving towards the front door. "See you guys later."

Jason waits until the door is closed behind Alec to blow out a breath and shake his head. "I'm sorry you had to deal with him alone. I didn't actually think he'd get that drunk."

"It was no big deal," Theo says softly.

"You're a good friend, man." Jason claps him on the shoulder, grinning. "You got anything to eat? I'm starving. By the way, did I tell you Mr. Hanover, the science teacher, quit? I've gotta tell you all the *chisme*."

Hearing Spanish immediately has Theo thinking of Alec. He does his best to push those thoughts aside. While Jason shares every bit of gossip he's managed to hear about Mr. Hanover's breakdown, involving an exploded beaker and a missing frog, Theo's mind wanders through an unsettling maze of relief and confusion. Despite what Jason says, he doesn't feel like a good friend. He doesn't feel like a good anything. He betrayed Jason, and he let Alec down, and the worst part of it all is that the entire thing did nothing to rid Theo of his desire for Alec.

"You coming?" Jason asks, already halfway to the kitchen.

"Coming," Theo confirms, following Jason. All it takes is one look at the kitchen counter where he held Alec just that morning for Theo to want to puke.

What the fuck has he done?

17 ALEC

ALEC RUNS FASTER than he ever has before. His lungs burn and his legs ache as he pushes himself past his limit, unable to quiet the noise in his brain and the itch under his skin.

When the familiar sight of his campus apartment building comes into view, he runs faster, desperate to get back home and shower, desperate to change out of Theo's clothes which went from from feeling like a safe embrace to a dirty reminder of all the ways he fucked up. He knew it was stupid to say yes, knew nothing would come of it, yet he'd pathetically taken anything Theo offered. The worst part is that he can't even regret it, even as his heart breaks, because he would do it all over again. That alone makes him feel like an idiot.

He takes the stairs two at a time, not thinking about anything except escaping to his room, when he arrives at the door and realizes his key was in his jeans.

"Fuck." He knocks on the door, hoping Hunter is the one to answer.

He's not.

"There you are." Antonio drags his gaze from Alec's head to his toes in a way that makes Alec feel uncomfortably exposed. "You didn't come home last night and—"

There's no way Alec can do this. Pushing past Antonio, he walks into the apartment only to be met with the wide-eyed stares of Logan and Hunter, who pause their video game to gape at Alec. To make things more complicated, Riley is here leaning against the wall with his arms crossed, his entire face falling when he catches sight of Alec. He can't even imagine what he looks like. His fucking clothes—Theo's clothes—are way too big, he ran all the way here, and he's so tired. And his hangover, which had seemed like nothing while Theo touched him, has returned tenfold, making his head pound and his stomach churn.

"Alec?" Antonio's voice is low, gentle somehow, and that makes it so much worse.

"I know I'm sexy, but can everyone please stop staring at me?" Alec says, trying for funny and missing by a mile, judging by the way Riley looks at him with undisguised worry while Hunter elbows Logan, whispering something.

"We're gonna go get something we forgot," Hunter declares, shutting off the television before grabbing Logan's arm and all but pulling him off the couch. "We'll see you guys later."

Logan spares an extra glance at Alec, clearly unsure, but follows Hunter towards the front door without protest, leaving him alone with Riley and Antonio.

"Alec."

Before Riley can get started, something in Alec finally snaps.

"It's—" Except he can't say it. After years of longing and wanting, it finally happened, and he's not sure how the best thing that's ever happened to him can also feel like the worst.

"Did he hurt you?" Riley asks, voice like venom. He crosses the room to put his hands on Alec's face, tipping his chin up.

Riley might be younger than Alec, but he's got that big brother energy that reminds Alec of his own brothers, which is unexpectedly reassuring considering Alec can't tell his siblings what happened, not even Charlie. It's too risky, and he won't do that to Theo, but the secret is like lead in his gut. Not telling his brothers about his virginity had been a choice. This was something else, and those kinds of secrets twist Alec up inside. He hates secrets.

"I'll kill him if he did," Riley grits out at Alec's silence.

"Calm down, Rambo." Alec tries to smile, but it's more than he can handle.

"I'm serious," Riley tells him, and Alec knows he is. He knows Riley would do anything to protect him, just like he did that night they met. He'd given the other guy a black eye and scared him off ever coming near Alec again. While nine times out of ten it's unnecessary, it's always felt good to know he had Riley in his corner, to know he had someone who didn't judge him, who he didn't have to hide things from.

"Am I missing something?" Antonio asks.

Alec scrubs a hand over his face, trying to figure out what to say next. After that night, he hadn't been ready to tell anyone, not even his best friend, and somehow as time passed he'd still never felt ready.

"You don't have to tell anyone," Riley says, pulling him into a hug. His arms are strong and safe, and even though it would be so easy to stay there and hide, Alec knows he can't.

"Tell anyone what?" Antonio's eyes dart between Riley and Alec.

"I think I want to," Alec whispers, so goddamn tired of keeping secrets he feels like what's left of him might shatter if he has to hold one more in.

It's obvious Riley isn't sure what to make of Alec's change of heart, which is fair considering Alec's made sure to change the subject any time Riley even got close to ever mentioning it. Pulling out of the hug, Alec turns, offering Antonio a shaky smile.

"So, uh, fun fact about how me and Riley met. You've asked, and I always refused to tell you because he found someone trying to...trying to—" Theo's earlier words come back to Alec. *Sexual assault*. Something Alec had refused to admit, even to himself. He'd convinced himself at least part of it was his own fault, while refusing to admit how much it had twisted him up inside. That stupid night had been haunting Alec for too long, tainting his every interaction and making him afraid to even let a guy kiss him in case he got accused of leading him on. He'd downplayed it, ignored it, until it all came spilling out to Theo last night. Now it's like an open wound that he wants to cover, but also one that he knows he needs to finally let breathe.

"Alec."

"Riley stopped someone from sexually assaulting me," Alec blurts.

Devastation is written in Antonio's expression. Alec drops his gaze to the floor, knowing he won't be able to finish if he keeps looking at him. "That's why Riley and I got close so fast, I know you were jealous and confused. I should've told you instead of letting you think I was replacing you, but I couldn't say it out loud, and I'm so fucking sorry." He barely pauses for a breath before he's going again, unable to stop now that he's started. "Also, I got shit-faced at a club last night, which for the record I'm never doing again, and Theo took me home. We slept in the same bed, and then he was going to fuck me, but I came before we could. Then Jason suddenly knocked on the door, so I had to sneak out and I lost my phone, which is why I didn't call you guys and—"

Before he can get the rest of his word vomit out, Antonio slams into him with such force he stumbles into Riley, Alec ending up crushed between his best friends.

"I love you, you fucking idiot." Antonio squeezes him tighter, holding on like he might never let go.

"I'm sorry," Alec chokes.

"You don't need to apologize to me," Antonio says. "Not for anything, you hear me? Except maybe for the going MIA thing. Try not to do that again. I was worried as fuck, and Riley was ready to organize his frat brothers in a search party."

"Only half of them," Riley says, officially joining in the group hug. "Also, I can still kill Theo if you want."

"I don't want you to kill him," Alec grumbles, the deep pressure of being wedged between his best friends soothing the fight or flight part of his brain that's screaming at him to do something stupid or reckless to try and regulate. They know, he realizes. They know him, and they know his quirks, and they're supporting him the only way they know how. He's so fucking grateful for them.

Neither of them let go of Alec for a long time, but when they do finally break from the hug, neither of them mentions Alec's tears as he scrubs them away with the palms of his hands.

"So the sweater," Antonio prompts, tugging on the front of it with a shit-eating grin. "This like a virginity souvenir?"

"Fuck you."

Riley snorts. "Pretty sure you did the fucking last night."

"Fuck you, too," Alec laughs, grinning. "And I'm still a virgin. I think? I dunno."

"What do you mean you don't know? Come on, tell us the details. I can't believe after all this time Theo actually returns your feelings. I know I told you he didn't, and you needed to let it go, but even I can admit when I'm wrong," Antonio says, and he looks so happy for Alec that it's suddenly hard to breathe.

The mood crash is swift and painful. Turns out not only can he not hold his liquor, but he can't hold his emotions in either as he blinks away tears he refuses to shed. Not again. Fucking hangover tears.

"He doesn't."

"I'm sorry, what?" Antonio's head tilts like a confused spaniel.

Riley frowns. "Alec."

"It's fine," Alec says, instinctively taking a step away from them both and wrapping his arms around his middle. "He's a good guy. You guys don't know him like I do. He doesn't...he doesn't know I have feelings still, or he would've never offered."

"Offered what, exactly?" Even as Antonio asks the question his face falls. For all Alec tries to keep his own expression neutral, he must not do a very good job. "Oh, Alec, *no*."

"It's fine," Alec insists, even though it's so clearly not. "I can do no strings attached sex."

Riley shakes his head. "No, you can't."

"Fuck you," Alec croaks, embarrassed at how pathetic and small his voice sounds.

"So what, he was drunk too, and you guys fooled around?" The accusation in Antonio's tone is too much. He knows they're gonna hate Theo after this, and he can't stand that.

"Theo wasn't drunk. I wasn't drunk anymore this morning either." Alec frowns. "He was just...helping me out."

"Helping you out with what, breaking your own heart?" Riley's tone is sharp, and Alec can't even blame the judgment or concern. They've both borne witness to the pain that Alec's inability to get over Theo has caused.

"It was my choice. I knew going into it that he didn't have feelings for me, but I still went ahead with it because —" *Because he knew it was as close as he would ever get to having Theo.* Something he is not going to say out loud. "Look, I can handle this just fine."

Alec stands up taller, the line of his back painfully straight as he waits for their reaction. They're going to be angry, probably not at Alec but at Theo. They're going to judge, which Alec would do if he were them, but he's not sure he can handle their disapproval right now. The worst part of all is that they're going to demand answers Alec can't offer, because he doesn't understand why he can't get over Theo any more than they can. He doesn't know why he keeps putting himself directly in positions where he gets hurt, over and over like an idiot.

Holding his breath he waits, unsure what kind of silent conversation Riley and Antonio are trying to have.

"Did you eat?" Riley asks after an extended silence.

"What?" Alec blinks, sure he's misheard.

"Eat," Riley repeats. "Did you have anything yet? I'm starving. You hungry, Tony?"

"Call me Tony again, and you can eat my fist," Antonio snarks.

Riley cackles. "So spicy."

The panic in Alec slowly fades as he watches Antonio and Riley continue to bicker over food and nicknames. Realistically, he knows this isn't over, that they're probably going to end up finishing this conversation at some point, but for now his friends are going to let it end, just like his thing with Theo ended.

Peripherally, Alec is aware he should be happy, but all he can muster is a gnawing sense of emptiness. He got the one thing he always dreamed of—a chance with the man he loves—so why does the Theo-shaped hole in his heart feel bigger than ever?

"REMIND me why we majored in business again?" Alec groans, collapsing facedown on his bed. His backpack was tossed to the floor seconds before, his microeconomics and financial planning textbooks heavy enough to knock down a goddamn brick wall. Two back-to-back seminar classes, followed by a brutal three hour practice means Alec doesn't even want to look at his syllabus, let alone to start the reading.

"Because it's what everyone else on the team is majoring in," Antonio reminds him. Which is true. Business is the number one major for at least half the college athletes he knows. "Besides, once we get scouted we won't need the degree anyway, so what we majored in won't really matter."

Alec shoves his face into the mattress, biting his tongue. He hasn't told anyone he doesn't think he wants to get scouted. Hell, he doesn't even have the heart to tell Antonio how much he hates his major. More fucking secrets.

Turning his face from the mattress to take in a ragged breath, he tries to smile at Antonio, but it feels like more of a grimace.

"We can study together, Alec. It'll be fine. I promise."

"Fine," he says, because Antonio is actually competent at this stupid business shit and also doesn't have ADHD. Unlike Alec, he also doesn't want to run into the sun every time someone mentions stats or accounting. Everything to do with his major makes Alec want to curl into a ball and scream because he hates it so much. He thought taking all introductory classes his first few years would make the adjustment easier, and it had for a time. Only now Alec's stuck with the hardest classes for his last year in a major he loathes, while facing a future he doesn't want.

He's not sure he's going to survive his senior year.

"Earth to Alec." Antonio snaps his fingers. "You look like you saw *La Llorona*. What's up?"

What's up is that it's only been one day, and Alec already misses Theo. What's up is that he's one day into the semester, and his classes are already filling him with dread. What's up is that the new season has barely started, and his body is already exhausted. What's up is everything feels out of Alec's control.

"Probably just hungry," Alec tries, relieved when Antonio easily accepts the lie.

"I had lunch in the cafeteria, but it wasn't that good. You wanna make us *chilaquiles*?"

Alec is so tired he doesn't want to move, but his brain didn't get that memo, going a mile a minute with worst-case scenarios and intrusive thoughts. He isn't sure he has the energy for cooking, but at least it's better than studying.

"Fine," Alec says, dragging himself onto his hands and knees. "But you're doing the cleaning if I cook."

Antonio whistles happily. "Don't tell my mom or she'll disown me, but I think your *chilaquiles* are better than hers."

"Of course they are. My *abuela* taught me." Alec swings his legs over the bed, his eyes drawn to the corner where Theo's sweater is draped over the back of his desk chair.

"Have you talked to him?" Antonio asks.

It's the first time he's mentioned it since Alec stumbled home yesterday morning wearing Theo's clothes, and he's honestly surprised Antonio lasted so long.

"No. My phone was in the mailbox this morning, along with my clothes." Alec swallows, thinking of the note that had been tucked inside. *I'm sorry, Alexander.*

The note is folded up, hidden in his sock drawer. He's not sure why he's hiding it. *Yes, you are*, a little voice whispers. He's hiding it because he knows he's being stupid and reading too much into it. He doesn't need his friends to be the voice of reason or judge him for getting naked with someone who doesn't share his feelings. He already knows he's pathetic, and while neither Riley nor Antonio would say that to his face, it would be written in their pitying eyes, and he can't handle that.

"We could order in," Antonio offers, clearly not sure what to make of Alec's prolonged silence, always looking for an excuse to break his own nutritionist derived meal plan. "You know, if you're not up to cooking. My treat."

"No," Alec says with a firm shake of his head. "I can cook."

Thoughts of Theo plague Alec's mind as they both head to the kitchen, the sounds of the guys playing video games and joking fading into the background. He's made this meal often enough that he can do it without thinking, which is exactly the problem. With his mind free to dwell on Theo, cooking offers none of the mindless distraction he'd hoped.

The kitchen fills with the savory scent of simmering *guajillo* chiles and roma tomatoes, followed by fried tortillas, but there is no comfort in the familiar smells. Not only because Alec can't even eat this on his stupid fucking nutrition plan, but because it conjures memories of Theo's smile as they'd shared tacos on his birthday. The thought of one smile, just for him, makes Alec think of another, and now there are far too many moments twisted up with memories of Theo in knots too tangled to unwind.

If anyone should be mad, it's Alec, except he's not. He can't be. He knows exactly why Theo did what he did. Alec knows he won't ever be more important than Jason, and he's made his peace with that. Mostly. It would be unfair to be angry at Theo, because he's unable to give something Alec never admitted he wanted. So no, Alec isn't mad at Theo. Hurt, yes. Achingly, desperately and painfully so. It's the kind of hurt that makes sitting through lectures or running practice drills feel like torture, because it seems so unfair that life goes on as normal while Alec's heart is in a million pieces.

Inevitably, his thoughts drift to the text message he sent Theo this morning as soon as he got his phone back. It was nothing more than a stupid text teasing him about a gross new flavor of LaCroix he saw in the dining hall last night, a feeble attempt to pretend things could go back to the way they'd been before. He knew he couldn't have Theo as a lover, but he'd at least wanted him back as a friend. Only it's been nine hours, and Theo hasn't replied, and a part of Alec suspects that maybe he isn't going to. Jason showing up made things too real for Theo, and painful as it is, he's not at all surprised by the sharp sting of Theo's actions.

What hurts the most is how Alec walked into this thing with Theo with eyes wide open. Everything that happened feels like his own fault because he knew exactly what Theo was willing to offer.

Fingering the coin that hangs from the chain around his neck, he closes his eyes and tries to calm his nerves. The metal is cool to the touch as he zones out, rubbing it between thumb and forefinger. He hasn't taken it off since yesterday, and he has no plans to take it off anytime soon. All day, the weight of the chain around his neck, the tang of metal on his tongue when he'd put it into his mouth, has been a sharp reminder of the two people he loved most. The two people he lost.

If he thought the distance Theo put there at fifteen was bad, it's nothing compared to the way it hurts now. At fifteen, Alec had been in love with Theo the way you love something beautiful from afar, like looking at a painting in a museum and knowing you can never have it. Loving him up close is so much fucking worse. Now he knows the feeling of Theo's bare skin beneath his hands, knows the feeling of Theo's lips against his own, and the memory is there every single time he closes his eyes. Alec had laughed and touched, and he was never going to get over this man.

Alec knows all of Theo's flaws and shortcomings now, he knows the shape of his smile and the shadows of fear that haunt him, and somehow he adores him all the more for it. Theo is far from perfect, but Alec loves him. Always has and probably always will.

Love is a painful, beautiful, terrible thing, and Alec is pretty sure that loving Theodore James will be the thing that breaks him.

WHEN THERE'S no reply from Theo after a day it stings, but Alec tries not to read into it too deeply. Theo might just need some time. He's a thinker, a worrier, and he might still come around. Except one day becomes two, and two becomes three, and after a week, Alec knows there is no message coming. The finality of the lack of reply is like a physical wound. As the days pass, the hurt doesn't lessen but grows like a weed, wild and unwanted, digging roots into Alec's heart and lungs until he's suffocating.

Desperate to numb the pain, Alec throws himself into school and the team, convinced if he works hard enough that somehow he can be good enough to forget. His goal is keep himself too busy to think about Theo or being rejected, which isn't very difficult considering his course load combined with their five practice days and two to three games a week. It all barely leaves him enough time to piss.

If he's not in class, he's at practice or a game, and if he's not busy with either of those, he's trying to force himself to study to keep his grades up so he can continue to play. In the past, maintaining his GPA was never a problem. Despite his disinterest in his major, passing classes hadn't been too difficult because his motivation to stay on the team surpassed his boredom with the subjects. This year, that's not enough, and every class, every assignment, is like dragging his brain through the mud.

Days turn into weeks, and as more time passes, Theo never reaches out. It's clear at this point that Theo is ignoring him. His disregard is so deeply triggering to Alec that it makes him want to scream, but doing so would shatter the image he's upholding where he pretends he's perfectly fine. Every day that passes without a word from

Theo makes it harder and harder for Alec not to be angry, despite how badly he doesn't want to be.

Desperate to forget, he pushes himself harder until he's nearly collapsing at practice or close to puking after a game. He plays like it's the only thing he has left, and maybe it is. At least on the field Alec knows exactly who he is supposed to be.

All in all, Alec thinks he's coping pretty damn well, considering his body is exhausted and his mind won't shut the fuck up. When his body screams at him to slow down and rest, Alec pushes himself harder. When the coach finds him in the gym long after practice ends, he jokingly tells Alec to cool down, but in the same breath also praises his work ethic. It reaffirms Alec's need to hide his real feelings. When Alec's jaw aches from chewing too much gum and his knuckles have calluses from biting them, he continues to push because he doesn't know how to do anything else.

Weeks of sleepless nights and a gnawing sense of deregulation lead Alec to making an impulse purchase in the middle of the night, where he uses his emergency credit card to buy a fancy pebble ice machine. The serotonin is short-lived, but the euphoria of having unlimited access to crunchy ice has its benefits. Alec eats so much ice he might as well become a goddamn penguin. His roommates threaten to hide the ice machine if Alec doesn't stop crunching all the time, but what he doesn't tell them, any of them, is that he can't stop. He can't bring himself to admit that every second he's not biting or chewing on something or fidgeting, he feels like he's going to crawl out of his skin.

Everyone has always looked at his inability to stay still or his oral fixation as a quirk, not something he has to do to feel sane. If he told them, he knows they'd stop teasing him or getting annoyed, but telling them feels too close to admitting he's not okay, so Alec bottles up the feelings and packs away the ice machine.

All the while, his classes continue to get harder, and the workload increases to the point he can't keep up with the reading and homework. As pressure from the team and the relentless practices mount, every day Alec is reminded of who he's supposed to be and all the ways he couldn't be what Theo wanted.

He bites the ends off all his pencils, develops fresh calluses on his knuckles from chewing on them, and pushes himself so hard in the gym he nearly passes out. No one notices. The worst of all is that none of it quiets the storm raging inside of Alec, because the harder he tries to pretend everything is okay, the worse everything feels.

The biggest problem comes when he can't run himself to the bone anymore, when classes and practices and games pile up so high, Alec feels like he's drowning. Suddenly, he's too tired to keep using the weight room in the gym to avoid studying. Only when he tries to study, Alec's dread grows, as does the hatred for his classes. He hates his major, hates every second of his business classes, and his damn brain has decided that his lack of interest means he is no longer capable of mustering the will to study.

For the first time in Alec's entire college career, he fails a test. It's only a practice quiz that barely counts for any of his grade, but panic takes hold anyway. After class, his professor holds Alec back to discuss his progress, reassuring him that this won't affect his ability to play as long as he studies hard for the next test. What Alec doesn't say to his professor is that he had studied, but the words went in his brain and right back out, like waves succumbing to the changing tides.

Walking out of the classroom and back to the quad,

something inside of Alec crumbles. It's not a crack or a break, not something that can be fixed with some strong will and stubbornness. It's as if something inside of him disintegrates into a thousand pieces, shattering like a windshield.

The rest of the day passes in a blur, and Alec hardly pays attention to his classes, only peripherally aware of his teammates' worried looks as he runs himself ragged at practice, all but bolting when practice ends so he won't have to face Antonio. He knows if he has to look at his best friend, he's going to let it all out. Scrambling to maintain control, he realizes he has none, and in a moment of utter weakness a thought calls out to him, unwanted and suffocating but true nonetheless: *he's angry at Theo.*

Anger is Alec's least favorite emotion. He's gotten mad at bullies or bad ref calls, but those were fleeting feelings about injustice, not about him personally. Getting mad at someone when all Alec's wanted his entire life is to be liked by people is kind of counterproductive. Hell, he can't even really get mad at his brothers for more than an hour without guilt churning in his stomach. He hates being mad at people, so he tries to let the growing fury fade away, and tries to remind himself that Theo didn't make him any promises.

Except that, well—he had made Alec a promise. Theo promised Alec he wouldn't hurt him, but that's exactly what he did. He *hurt* Alec. He hurt him so much he can hardly breathe. The hurt twists inside, offering his brain something to focus on besides his practice and his classes, and how painfully out of control everything feels. Thoughts spinning, Alec starts to walk and doesn't stop with no idea where he's going. Eventually the sun sets, and after a long trek around the city, instead of ending up back home, he arrives in front of Theo's house.

The lights are off, and a glance at his phone tells him why. It's after ten on a weeknight. Fuck, how long did he wander around town? Hours. Hours of mindless movement that did nothing to dull his pain. Of course Theo is asleep, because he's a man with a life and a job and a routine. A routine in which there was apparently no room for Alec.

Before he can think through what he's doing, he's on the porch and knocking so hard his fist hurts, banging over and over until the door swings open, bringing him face to face with a sleepy, confused Theo. He stares at Alec like he's never seen him before, and the last bit of Alec's heart is swept away with the tide.

"You sent me away." His voice cracks, dropping to barely above a whisper, but the broken look in Theo's eyes lets him know he's loud enough. "You sent me away."

"Alexander."

Alec chokes, unable to stomach the way Theo says his full name like it's important. Like *he* is important. "How could you?"

"You know I'm not good at this." Theo sags, scrubbing a hand over his face. "I told you, I wasn't going to ever be the guy who could give you what you need. Maybe this was better. You can go find someone better for you."

"Bullshit," Alec cries, refusing to let him get away with excuses.

"Alec."

Theo steps closer, and something in Alec's expression shutters.

"No." Alec gives Theo's chest a shove. He's solid, unmovable, and Alec's fist presses against Theo's chest as he tries not to cry. He fucking hates crying. "I didn't ask you for anything, Theo. I knew what I was getting into, but you weren't supposed to pull away from me again. You've been ignoring me, and I fucking hate being ignored. You know me, you know how much I hate it, and you did it anyway. Why? Why are you ignoring me?"

Even in the face of Alec's desperation, Theo is quiet, and it makes the storm raging in Alec so loud he can hardly hear his own messy thoughts, can barely breathe through the pain and fury he's been ignoring.

"No clubs, you said." Alec's other hand comes up to Theo's chest. He's not even sure what he's doing, both his hands balled up against Theo's chest. He wants to shove him again, wants to do anything to show Theo how much he's hurting, but he can't do more than fist his hands in Theo's sweater and remember what it felt like to be held. "You said someone might hurt me. *You hurt me.*"

18 THEO

YOU HURT ME.

Three little words that cut Theo to the core. Three words to ruin the shell of what's left of him after weeks of self-loathing, not about what he'd done with Alec, but about what he still wants to do.

When Jason showed up, Theo shut down. The panic and the guilt had been all-encompassing. He's been pushing it all away, ignoring the remorse and longing while convincing himself it was for the best. Then Alec had texted him like everything was normal, and Theo had no idea how to go back to what they'd been before when his dreams were filled with warm brown eyes and galaxies of freckles. He didn't know how to go back to a time before his heart was full of a man he couldn't have.

One day turned into two, and by the end of the first week, Theo was so ashamed of himself for not replying, and for the desires he couldn't avoid, that he continued to ignore Alec even knowing how much he hated it. As a child, when his big brothers had been annoyed at him for breaking something or tattling, they'd sometimes pretended he didn't exist, and Alec would wail. There was nothing he hated more than being ignored, something that, according to Jason, was even more true when he got older.

Thinking back to the way Theo had shut Alec out after his teenage love confession, even knowing he did it to protect Alec, sometimes made his stomach ache. He hated hurting Alec, hated it now more than ever.

The more time that passed, the more he deluded himself into thinking this was for the best. Every day that went by without a new text from Alec, confirmed his illogical and selfish belief that this must be what Alec wanted. Without having to look him in the face, Theo could pretend he hadn't betrayed his best friend and Alec both. He'd been a paragon of self-control, refusing to continue to engage with Alec and thus hurt him. Turns out he'd done it anyway.

"I'm sorry."

"Fuck you," Alec chokes, pulling on Theo's sweater. Theo almost wishes he'd do it harder, wishes he'd hit him like he deserves.

Alec's chest heaves as he stares at Theo with those soulful eyes of his. Even with the tears glistening in them, he doesn't flinch or turn away from Theo. The bravery in that one look is Theo's undoing. It's a reminder of everything Theo adores about Alec—his tenacity, his strength. It's amazing to realize he'd gone years without being close to him when the last few weeks without his presence have been woefully lacking. In such a short time, Alec wedged himself into Theo's life and his heart without asking permission first, and Theo's been reeling ever since.

He missed Alec hogging the couch, and taking up a shocking amount of space for someone so much smaller. He missed Alec's nonstop chatter and teasing, and the way he never lets Theo get away with anything. He missed Alec's laugh and his smile, and he especially missed the sight of him and Rio curled together. Even Rio has been upset, hiding under furniture and only eating when Theo leaves the room, as if she is holding Theo personally responsible for the loss of her favorite human.

"I'm sorry," Theo whispers, knowing those two words aren't close to enough.

"For which part?"

"All of it," Theo says, shame making his insides burn. How did he think one time with Alec would be enough to get him out of his system? How did he think anyone could ever get over Alexander King? It was foolish and selfish, and he's ruined everything.

"All of it." Alec's grip on the sweater loosens, and he takes a step back. "Fuck you."

"Alec."

"So what, you just realized you didn't want to fuck me and that meant we couldn't even be friends?" He sounds even more hurt than before, and Theo wonders why people want to fall in love when it's so goddamn hard. All he wants to do is protect Alec, but he keeps fucking up. His good intentions don't mean everything when he's breaking Alec's heart.

Are you protecting him, or you? a little voice whispers. The answer is clear and sends shame burning like a wildfire. That lie wasn't protecting anyone but Theo. He's a coward.

"You could've just told me," Alec yells, his hands shaking now. "You could've just said you didn't want to do it again."

"No, I couldn't."

"Was being with me so terrible it made you not want to even look at me?" Alec's voice drops to barely above a whisper. It was easier to handle when he yelled. Alec being this quiet feels like someone has dimmed his light. Like Theo dimmed it.

"That...that wasn't it," Theo stammers.

"Fuck." Alec pulls at his hair, his normally perfect curls in disarray. Even in the dark, lit up only by the soft glow of his porch light, he's beautiful. He also looks exhausted, his eyes rimmed in red. The knowledge that Alec's distress is Theo's doing is more painful than he could have imagined. "Stop it."

"Stop what?" Theo asks.

"Stop being so fucking calm." Alec's lips quiver as his chest heaves. Theo wants so much to crush him a hug and promise everything will be okay, but he doesn't know how much he can keep lying to Alec. Everything isn't going to be okay. He finally wants someone, and it's someone he can't have. Not just his best friend's little brother, but a man in love with someone else. It's like fate's sick twist. *Here*, the universe taunts, *here's someone who isn't afraid of all your walls and edges, someone who could be your perfect match, someone who loved you once but doesn't anymore.* Because relationships are horrible, Theo is horrible, and he made Alec walk away before he could choose to do it. Because he would, eventually. Theo knows it.

"What do you want from me, Alec?"

"What do I want? Fuck you, Theo! I want you to fucking feel something without pushing me away!" Alec shouts. "I want you to tell me something and not just what I want to hear. Tell me what is so fucking awful about me you just keep pushing me away!"

"Nothing about you is awful," Theo croaks, grabbing Alec's wrists. They're delicate, his own hands easily wrapping around them to pull them against his chest, bringing

Alec's body close enough to feel the weight of his shuddering exhale. "How could I look at you and say no, Alexander?"

The confusion on Alec's face is clear, not that Theo can blame him. He's not exactly been forthcoming about his desires, and he still can't now. Even as he tries to be honest with Alec, he knows he has to hold some of it back

"What?"

"I couldn't talk to you, Alec. How could I when I promised you not to hurt you, and it was the first thing I did? I'm sorry. I'm so goddamn sorry." He rubs his thumbs over the inside of Alec's wrists, the thrum of Alec's pulse beating in time with Theo's racing heart. He's done nothing but think about this moment for weeks, imagining what he might say and rehearsing possible conversations. He's imagined all the ways to make sure Alec knew it wasn't his fault, it was Theo's. He's imagined all the right ways to put distance between them to ensure it didn't happen again. With Alec in touching distance, all of that means nothing. Nothing means anything in the face of Alec hurting.

"I couldn't bring myself to face you after doing exactly what I promised not to do. Especially not when...when—"

"When what?" Alec pushes. He always pushes.

"When I want to touch you again. So much more than I'm supposed to."

"I—*oh*." Alec's entire body sags.

Holding his breath, Theo waits for Alec's reaction. He says nothing, and somehow that's harder to take than any yelling would have been. He wants Alec to be loud and rail, not to stare at Theo like he's one word away from breaking.

"Did I finally find a way to shut you up?" Theo realizes he's still clutching Alec's hands against his chest. He can't let go, even though he should. He can't do a lot of things he should when he's around Alec. "You know I never made good on my promise."

"Please don't tease me," Alec whispers.

"I wasn't teasing about that," Theo assures him.

"You don't make sense." Alec sounds confused and fragile, shattering Theo's resolve. He knows he's supposed to stay away, but he can't. "You said you wanted me, and then —then you chose Jason. I get it, of course you're going to choose him, but you sent me away, and you ignored me, and now what? Fuck, I don't even know what you're saying."

Theo's not sure he knows either. It's not like he can tell Alec how messed up his thoughts are, not when he knows Alec has feelings for another man, and this whole thing started because Theo promised him no strings attached. Alec doesn't need Theo's baggage, but he also doesn't deserve to be tossed aside. He deserves everything, even if Theo isn't the man who can give him that.

"Say something," Alec demands, shoving his fists into Theo's chest. "Something real."

Real. Theo hardly knows real. His parents' relationship crumbling apart and breaking his dad's heart beyond repair was real. His dad doing the best he could and it not being anywhere close to good enough is real. Loving someone else being the most dangerous thing you can do is real. His mom abandoning him is real. Knowing he can't live without his best friend if he fucks this all up is real. Knowing he can't have Alec for more than one night is real.

Alec is real. Alec with his megawatt smile and goddamn bravery. Alec with his heart-on-his-sleeve personality, always demanding authenticity from the people he cares about. Alec with his big mouth and his bigger heart. Alec is the most real person Theo has ever known, and it's absolutely terrifying.

"I'm sorry."

"Theo."

"Let me make it up to you," Theo whispers, brushing the hair out of Alec's eyes. He loosens his grip on Alec's wrists to let them go, resting them between his pecs. "Unless you changed your mind...if you don't want—"

"Goddamn you," Alec hisses, and Theo's sure he's said the wrong thing, but then Alec is surging onto tiptoes and grabbing Theo's face. "Like I could ever not want you."

The words are as loaded as the way Alec kisses him, desperate and demanding and Theo knows he should put a stop to this. He knows they should talk first, but he's never been good at that kind of thing. Sex is easy, talking is complicated and messy. Sex with Alec is going to be both, but he can't stop now, even if it's going to be the stupidest thing he's ever done. Or the second stupidest, or maybe the third if he's counting messing around with Alec in the first place and ignoring him.

God, Alec should run far away from Theo and his commitment and communication issues. He has no idea why he isn't, doesn't understand why Alec still wants him when Theo keeps fucking up.

"Don't break your promise again," Alec demands, and Theo isn't brave enough to ask which one.

"I'll be gentle."

"I don't need gentle."

"What do you need, Alexander?"

Alec opens his mouth and then shuts it, crashing his lips against Theo's again. It occurs to him that they're still standing in the open doorway where anyone could see, so he grabs onto Alec's hips to guide him inside, shutting and locking the door behind them before taking Alec's hand and leading him towards the bedroom.

He takes a look around his room, gaze drifting from his unmade bed to the sweater thrown over the chair, to the book folded open on the nightstand where he abandoned it yesterday. Some of Rio's cat toys are scattered across the floor from where he'd thrown them in his attempt to lure her from under the bed earlier. She's asleep in the spare room, and he's surprised she hasn't run in here and found Alec already. He's grateful for the moment, however, not sure he could fuck Alec with Rio around demanding attention, too.

A moment of hesitation is all it takes for Theo's anxiety to rise. There are so many things Theo could say to Alec right now. So many things he should say. There are lines he should be drawing to protect them both from the inevitable crash and burn. There is no future for them, but there's also no coming back from fucking your best friend's baby brother.

This is going to change everything, and if there is one thing Theo hates, it's change. Part of him wants to run away again. This suddenly feels too real. He never fucks people he cares about, ever. But this is Alec, staring at Theo while he pulls his hoodie off over his head. He's not running away, he's not hiding, and he's not going to let Theo either. It turns his heart inside out. What is Alec doing to him?

"I know it's past your bedtime, old man. Did you need help getting undressed?" There's an attractive smirk on his face. Only Alec would have the balls to be so cocky in a situation like this. "I'm sure it's difficult at your advanced age. I can offer my assistance if you're in need."

"You little shit." Theo's heart twists itself into knots at the reminder that Alec is still someone who can get Theo out of his head, who can make him laugh and smile when that feels impossible.

Alec laughs, throwing his hoodie onto the floor while stalking towards Theo. He doesn't have a shirt on underneath, but he's got that necklace on again, and the gold chain hangs heavy at his throat. Even in the dim light, Theo sees familiar dips and angles of muscles, clusters of freckles, and tanned skin.

"I don't think I've ever wanted to touch anyone as badly as I want to touch you right now," Theo admits.

"What a coincidence, because I really want you to touch me." Alec moves closer, situating himself directly in Theo's personal space. Not even Jason does this. He knows better than to push Theo, knows when to let Theo retreat. Theo always thought he liked it, but with Alec standing before him not giving him an inch to overthink or freak out, he realizes how freeing it feels to have someone who won't let him run.

"You really want me to fuck you?"

"Is asking questions you already know the answer to a sign of aging?"

"I'm not that much older than you."

"You're almost thirty, old man." He drags his hand over Theo's belly, the look on his face full of heat. Theo's not sure anyone has ever looked at him quite like that.

"Maybe you should find someone closer to your age," Theo says, flinching at his knee-jerk reaction.

As soon as the words are out he regrets them, but Alec doesn't shrink. Instead, he shoves Theo's sweater up, watching as Theo takes the hint and pulls it off, leaving him bare-chested. Alec places his palms on Theo's ribcage, drawing his fingers through his fair chest hair.

"I like that you're older," he whispers.

It's on the tip of Theo's tongue to ask about Alec's party boy, but he manages to keep that ill-timed question to himself, not at all wanting the answer. Besides, it would be unfair to Alec to bring that up right now. He has no right to be jealous. It's clear that Alec finds him physically attractive, which is all Theo's ever cared about before when it came to sexual partners. Wondering who Alec is in love with, feeling jealous about who he might want after this, is not something he's used to feeling.

Sex with Alec needs to be a one-time, no strings attached encounter. That's what they agreed on before, and it has to be enough.

"Do you need help with these?"

Without waiting for the answer, Alec moves his fingers to Theo's sleep pants, hooking his thumbs under the waistband and dragging them down until Theo's cock is freed. It hangs hard and heavy between his legs, his excitement visible in the shimmer of precum at the tip.

"Can I suck it?"

"You can do anything you want, Alexander."

This appears to be all the permission Alec needs, because he falls to his knees and grabs Theo's hips. Despite his relative inexperience, there's no hesitation when he swallows Theo down. He grabs at Theo's waistband again, tugging it down the rest of the way and helping Theo step out of his pants, all without pulling off his dick.

If he weren't so determined to fuck Alec tonight he knows he could easily come like this, his arousal flaring at the sight of Alec's pretty lips wrapped around him. He looks sexy bobbing his head, sexier still when his eyes flutter open and his gaze lifts to meet Theo's. It catches Theo off-guard to see him looking unsure. Alec's usual confidence is gone, replaced by something quieter and infinitely more vulnerable. It brings up the same protective urge he keeps getting where Alec is concerned.

"You look so pretty on your knees," he tells him, dragging his fingers over Alec's head.

The curls are too tight for his fingers to run through, so he settles for brushing them off his face and letting his palm settle at the back of Alec's head. He can't stop himself from wanting to reassure Alec, from *needing* to make sure he's okay. Alec moans, trembling at the touch. He presses his head back into Theo's palm so that only the tip of his cock rests between Alec's lips.

Giving in to his own desires, he massages the back of Alec's scalp, unprepared for the way Alec whimpers. He looks blissed out down there, like being allowed to suck Theo is the best thing that's ever happened to him. Or maybe he just likes Theo's hands on his head. Or both. Probably both, judging from the way he widens his mouth while also leaning into Theo's hand. It's heady to feel so wanted, and even though the logical part of Theo's brain knows that this is physical, that he's offering Alec a safe place to finally get what he needs sexually, it's impossible for Theo to not let himself get carried away thinking it's him.

Slowly, Theo leans forward, and Alec's entire body shudders. Theo's never been embarrassed about how much sex he's had, knows he's had enough partners that he can't even remember them all. He also knows none of them have ever looked as good as Alec does now. No one has ever whimpered for Theo's cock like this. Alec is so hard his joggers are tented, a wet patch forming on the front, but he doesn't even touch himself. Instead, his fingers are digging into his own thighs as he tips his head back and moans so loud and deep Theo nearly comes. The only thought running through Theo's mind is that Alec deserves to know how good he is, how perfect, and the words are falling from his lips before he can keep them in.

"You love being full of me, don't you? You like choking on my cock?" Alec blinks, the answer clear as day in the way he takes him deeper, until the tip slides down the back of Alec's throat, and he really is choking on Theo, eyes watering. Theo swipes the moisture away with his thumb. "You're gorgeous."

The praise has Alec shuddering and widening the spread of his legs while hands dig into his knees so hard his knuckles turn white. The urge to fuck into his mouth until Theo's either filling him with come or painting his pretty face in it is staggering. Theo's never felt so possessive of someone he fucked, never wanted to claim anyone else the way he does Alec, and it's more than a little unnerving.

Forcing himself to pull away, physically and emotionally, he takes one step back, his cock falling from Alec's mouth.

"What's wrong?" Alec croaks, his voice hoarse, and his expression so damn unsure.

This is so wrong. Theo is going to hurt him or himself, but he can't stop. Theo's never been selfish, but he is now. He wants Alec so much he can't care about what comes later.

"Nothing," Theo promises, holding out a hand. "You're too good at that. Didn't wanna come before I got a chance to fuck you."

Pretty pink splotches bloom on Alec's cheeks, the expected cocky retort nowhere to be found. He looks almost shy, and it's a side of him Theo's never seen before. He can't help but wonder if this is just because it's Alec's first time, or if he would be like this again in the future. Maybe Alec likes a little dirty talk, likes letting all that bravado fall away in the bedroom. Theo knows he won't be allowed to find out, but thinking about mouthy, brash Alec turning blushy and needy in the bedroom does something to Theo.

"You should take off your pants, Alexander."

Again he waits for the sass, but all that comes is a bitten-off whimper before Alec's standing then shoving his joggers and boxers off. His chest heaves, hands opening and closing at his side as he stares at Theo and waits.

What he should do is get Alec on the bed and prepped. It's not that he wants this to be over, but the longer he drags it out, the more messy his insides get, but he can't seem to make himself do the responsible thing. All he wants to do is gather Alec in his arms, feel his smaller body against his own and make sure he's okay.

"Look at you," Theo whispers, unable to stop his mouth from running. It's like the roles have been reversed, and in Alec's silence, Theo's found his own voice. "You're so beautiful."

Alec doesn't reply, but he lifts his head up to lock eyes with Theo, and while his mouth might not be saying anything, those goddamn pretty eyes of his sure are. There's so much longing, so much trust, that Theo can't breathe.

Slamming his mouth to Alec's, he damn near devours him. He should be slow and gentle, but he's demanding and desperate, swallowing down every sigh and whimper from Alec like he's an addict. Alec might not be talking but he's not quiet, little noises of pleasure falling from his lips.

"I want to fuck you," Theo says between kisses, embarrassed by his own desperation.

He's wanted to fuck plenty of times. He's no stranger to being so horny he paws at the other person. He's come too early and too fast when it was really good. He's been desperate before, but not like *this*. That desperation was for something physical, for a release. This is for Alec, and with every kiss, Theo's heart trembles.

This is so dangerous, so stupid, and yet it's also maybe the best thing he's ever done. Because Alec gives as good as he gets, letting his hands roam all over Theo's chest and stomach, groping and squeezing and writhing like he wants this just as badly.

It's his first time, of course he wants this, Theo tries to remind himself, but it's no use. His hind-brain is taking over, the most primal part of him screaming *I'm the one doing this, he wants me.*

"Bed," Theo grunts, grabbing onto Alec's hips and lifting him.

"Holy fuck!" Alec's legs fly up to wrap around Theo's waist. The bed is only a handful of steps, Alec could've walked it, but Theo's brain has apparently decided he can't let go of him. His fingers dig into Alec's ass, one of them teasing along his crack as he walks them to the bed. In punishment or thanks, he's not sure, but Alec bites on Theo's bottom lip, sucking into his mouth greedily.

With far less grace than Alec deserves, Theo drops him onto the bed, loving the sight of Alec's lust-blown eyes and the sound of his huffed out laugh as he falls into Theo's bed. It's unmade, the spot in the middle where he usually sleeps now taken up by Alec's naked form. For all the sex Theo's had, he never brings anyone home. He fucks in the club, in a hotel room, at their place, but not here. This is Theo's home, his safe place, and he's never let a one night stand into it. Alec isn't not a one night stand. He's not anything, yet somehow he's everything. It doesn't make any sense, but Theo's long past trying to make sense of his feelings and desires where Alec is concerned. Alexander King is everything he shouldn't want and can't have.

Realistically, Theo knows this is the way it has to be. Theo doesn't even understand what exactly they're doing, and he's not sure he's brave enough to explore his own feelings, even if something more were a possibility with Alec. He's not a relationship guy and then there's Jason and—

"Thought you were gonna fuck me," Alec says, interrupting Theo's mental spiral.

Every logical, responsible thought flies from Theo's mind when he re-centers his sights on the gorgeous man in his bed. Not just any man but *Alec*, the boy who used to follow him around, the boy who lives out loud while Theo's been living in the shadows, the boy who is not a boy anymore. Alexander King is all grown up, and Theo has no idea what he did right in life to have the privilege of fucking this beautiful man, but he's not going to question it.

"I am," Theo assures him, knees on the edge of the bed. It dips under his weight, and he drops his hands there, never breaking eye contact with Alec as he crawls up his body, memorizing the way his blush travels down his throat and over his chest.

He's easily the sexiest, most beautiful man Theo's ever seen. Every inch of him is perfect, and Theo wants more, wants it all. "I'm going to prep you now. You know the drill. If it's too much, you tell me to stop."

"Theo," he mumbles.

"I'm serious. You stop me, Alec. If you change your mind or—"

"If you don't fuck me right now, I might die," Alec whines, lips turning down in what can only be described as a pout. "I'm not fucking joking, Theodore."

Theo has to fight the urge to laugh at Alec's petulance. "We definitely don't want you to die."

"Good. Then fuck me. Right now. I need...I—" but he stops, mouth opening and shutting like he's lost for words.

"What?" Theo asks, unsure why he needs to hear Alec verbalize it. He's obviously incredibly turned on, and wants Theo to fuck him. But Theo wants Alec to say it, wants Alec to tell him exactly what he wants from Theo—what he needs.

His hands clench and release in the sheets, eyes fixed on the ceiling when he finally snaps. "I need to be full," Alec groans. "My mouth is empty, and my ass is empty, and it's too fucking much. I feel like I'm going to crawl out of my skin if you don't put something in me right fucking now."

The raw honesty catches Theo off guard and has him crawling over Alec and kissing him. Alec whimpers into the kiss, hands flying up to squeeze at Theo's pecs while he sucks Theo's tongue into his mouth. He wasn't kidding about needing his mouth full, kissing Theo like he might literally combust if he stops. Unwilling to let him suffer, Theo lets Alec set the pace, never breaking the kiss, not even when he uncaps the lube and manages to get a finger at Alec's entrance.

Alec damn near howls, the sound guttural and loud as he sucks on Theo's bottom lip. The time for teasing and going slow is long gone. It only takes a few strokes before he's adding a second finger, surprised at how easily Alec takes him. He's so tight yet the resistance is minimal, and when Theo twists his fingers, brushing over Alec's prostate, he moans.

"Now, now, now," he begs, fingers digging into Theo's sides hard enough to leave a mark.

"Soon," Theo promises. "I'm a little bigger than two fingers."

"A little?" Alec huffs. "You're fucking huge."

"If it's too big—"

"That was not a goddamn complaint, Theodore." Alec's voice trembles, his gaze locked on Theo's face. "Stop teasing me."

"I'm not teasing, sweetheart."

The air in the room seems to leave, Theo's own breathing labored as the implications of what he's just said slam into him. He doesn't use terms of endearment. Then again, he doesn't let sexual partners into his bed, or talk this much during sex, either. He might be the one taking Alec's virginity, but Alec sure as hell is proving to be a first for Theo in more ways than Theo is prepared for.

"Alec."

Alec's hand curls around the back of Theo's neck, pulling him down in a kiss that is far more gentle than Theo expects. Their breaths mingle, mouths gliding together as Alec's tongue slips inside his mouth.

Theo pauses the kiss only long enough to retrieve a condom and roll it on before he's back, sealing his mouth over Alec's mouth, finally positioning himself against Alec's hole. The tip nudges against the ring of muscle. There's the slightest moment of resistance, but then Alec's legs wrap around Theo's back, his heels dig into Theo's spine as he pulls Theo closer. His cockhead slips inside which welcomes him into Alec's tight, hot warmth and then Alec's back arches off the bed as his heels dig in harder.

"More," Alec demands. The lines of his neck cord, every muscle in his perfect body held taut. He's not breathing, not moving, just looking at Theo like he can't believe this is happening.

Theo's never been anyone's first like this, and he's not expecting the rush of affection as he watches Alec take him.

He looks so good, spread out, moaning and gasping like he's made to take Theo.

"Beautiful," Theo praises.

A tiny but noticeable shudder wracks Alec as if he isn't expecting it, which is unimaginable to Theo given that he's one of the sexiest men Theo's ever seen.

"Breathe," Theo reminds him, peppering kisses across his nose, cheeks and down the side of his jaw.

He starts to pull out but Alec whines, trying to drag him back in. "Don't stop."

"I'm not," Theo promises. "Gonna fuck you so good, Alexander. I'll take real good care of you."

Alec's eyes glisten with unshed tears, but whether from pain or pleasure, Theo can't be sure. He hopes it's the latter, but first times aren't as perfect as movies or porn might make you want to believe. For all Theo prepared him and tried to be gentle, it's still new.

"Promise?" Alec whispers.

"I promise."

19 ALEC

THEO'S PROMISE washes over Alec, dragging away the worry and unease like the tide pulling back to the sea. It's still there, swirling and churning beneath the surface, but settled, too.

Showing up to Theo's house in the middle of the night wasn't the smartest choice he's ever made, not that he really chose to do so. He'd sort of lost his mind and come without thinking. He almost wishes he could blame being drunk or horny, but the truth it's just Theo and his goddamn beautiful blue eyes and honey-sweet voice that Alec can't get enough of.

A few words of apology from Theo and all of his previous anger dissipated. The hurt remains, but then again, that's nothing new. At this point, Alec's heart is filled with enough scars it resembles the rings inside a tree, every layer of hurt growing around the last. Each scar is just part of him now. This is just one more layer of injury that makes up Alec's heart, which is maybe a little sad and fucked up, but also not something he cares to change. He's more afraid of never loving again than loving and being hurt.

He knows that Theo would rather wall himself away from caring about people so they can't hurt him. He might not be Theo's best friend, and he might've suffered being pushed away and sidelined for years, but that doesn't mean he didn't pay attention. He understands Theo, which is probably why it's so easy to forgive him. He's difficult and hyper-independent, but no matter how many times he breaks Alec's heart, the one thing Alec knows is that it's not on purpose.

Loving Theo hurts so much he can hardly breathe, but Alec can't stop. With Theo above him, whispering praise and touching Alec like he's something precious, he knows he wouldn't stop even if he could. He doesn't have a damn clue what's happening, aside from the part where Theo's massive cock is in his ass. Emotionally, though, he might as well be a boat lost at sea. Theo ignoring him made sense because Theo's M.O. is to shut down and pull back when he's scared. This is, well, Alec has no idea what's happening now.

While banging on the door, Alec had been absolutely certain he was about to be sent away. Theo wasn't supposed to look apologetic, wasn't supposed to soothe away Alec's hurt and take him to bed as if he could fuck away the pain. That's not how this works, at least not for Alec. Maybe for Theo it does; he certainly views sex differently. For Alec, the only way he wanted sex was with someone he loved, which is exactly how he fell into bed with the one man determined to keep pushing him away.

Only he's not pushing Alec away right now, he's pulling him closer. Theo is so close Alec barely knows where he starts and Theo ends. Everything is bare skin and sweet kisses and the slide of Theo's massive body above his own. It's kind of like having an out of body experience. Alec tries so hard to stay in the moment, but his brain is racing with flashes of the future and memories of the past.

All he wants is to be present, to always remember the way it feels to be held and wanted even after Theo lets go. Because he will, Alec knows. Hopefully not right away. Maybe if Alec is careful and lucky, he can spend more time with Theo.

"You with me, Alec?"

"Mhmm," Alec nods, not trusting himself to speak without word vomiting something awful and embarrassing, like 'I didn't know it could feel so good' or 'I've never felt so close to anyone' or 'my brain won't shut up even though you're literally inside of me' or worst of all, 'it's always been you'.

Good as it feels, it's all so goddamn much but somehow not enough. Alec's body buzzes. The arousal is there, but it's hazy like the gloom that clouds the sky every June. There's goddamn June gloom in Alec's heart.

"Alexander."

Hearing his full name snaps Alec out of his mental storm. Fuck, he likes when Theo says his name. He never lets anyone else get away with it. He's made everyone call him Alec for a long time, but Theo's given graces other people aren't.

"Should I stop?"

Alec clenches his jaw so tightly his teeth grind. He doesn't want Theo to stop, but he doesn't know how to quiet his brain, either. He's supposed to be enjoying sex. The man of his goddamn dreams is fucking him, and it feels so good, but Alec can't shut it off because he needs—*oh*, he knows what he needs.

"Please don't stop," he begs, reaching for Theo's hand.

Something dangerously close to embarrassment swirls

in his gut, but he tries to remember Theo's earlier words. *Nothing about what you like or need is weird, Alexander.* That's what Theo said. He swore it was true, and Alec hopes to god it is, heart in his throat as he pulls Theo's fingers into his mouth and sucks.

"That's what you needed? You wanted to be full everywhere?"

Unable to speak, he settles for humming loudly. It must be the answer Theo wants, because his lips curl up in a private smile that goes straight to Alec's cock. Theo is so beautiful. His blond hair hangs over his forehead, his eyes bright and his cheeks flushed.

"Look at you." Theo croons and fuck, he is looking. His eyes are on Alec, soulful and blue and looking only at him. After a lifetime of wanting, wishing and hoping, Alec finally has all of Theo's attention. It's overwhelming as absolute fuck. He squirms, unable to handle the red-hot, fierce pleasure that coils in his gut. He wants this more than he's ever wanted anything in his entire life.

"I'm going to start moving again. Is that okay?"

Alec gives a small nod, sucking harder so that the tips of Theo's middle and pointer fingers hit the back of his throat at the same time Theo bottoms out and fucks into Alec so deep he damn near sees stars. Pleasure replaces the burn, and every thrust is pure bliss.

Some part of Alec had always wondered if sex would feel this good. Then again, it's not just the sex, it's the man inside of him, the man with his fingers shoved down Alec's throat giving him every single thing he's ever wanted. There is no doubt in Alec's mind, this is ruining him for anyone else. There's not a chance that Alec is ever going to be able to let anyone else see him this vulnerable and exposed.

It was always Theo, and it's always going to be Theo,

and while that hurts, it feels good too. There's a certainty in knowing whatever happens later, Alec got this one moment.

"You look so hot."

Eyes fluttering shut, Alec focuses on the rich timbre of Theo's deep voice and the pretty words he affords Alec.

It's no secret that Alec has always loved compliments, but they hit deeper from Theo. Between the cock in his ass, the fingers in his mouth, and the sweet words from Theo, it's a miracle Alec hasn't shot his load already. Maybe he can thank his ADHD brain for being too scattered to let him come prematurely, but now that his brain finally has what it needs—something filling both of his holes—he's dangerously close to coming. Pleasure makes his legs tingle, and he arches his hips, trying to get Theo in deeper.

Taking the hint, Theo braces his hand beside Alec's head before pulling his hips back and snapping them forward, thrusting so hard and deep Alec swears he feels Theo in his goddamn throat. He's fingered himself before, enough to have been utterly sure he would like being fucked within an inch of his life, but he's never had anything as big as Theo. His cock stretches Alec's rim with every thrust, the pleasure making Alec's eyes water.

Everything about Theo is steady and solid, his voice low as he continues to lavish Alec in the kind of praise that is going to fuel Alec's wet dreams for the next decade. "You look so good under me," Theo murmurs, "like you were born to be full."

Alec moans loudly at the continued praise. Though the urge to keep his eyes closed is there, he forces them open, needing to watch Theo fuck him, wanting to study his face as he murmurs all the words Alec's always dreamed of hearing from him.

"You like that, Alexander? Like knowing how hot it

makes me to see my cock inside of you? You like knowing how hot it makes me to watch you moan around my fingers like you can't get enough of me?"

The whine that falls out of Alec's mouth is loud and needy, and he can't even care, because never in a million years did he dream it would be like this. Not only is Theo fucking him, he's praising him, acting like Alec being wanton and desperate for fucking and sucking turns him on.

Theo's fingers move a little deeper, the weight on Alec's tongue increasing as Theo starts to fuck his fingers into Alec's mouth while his cock fucks Alec's ass and that's it. Alec is fucking done for. His brain quiets as white hot pleasure takes over, and Alec arches off the bed, coming in hot, thick spurts between their bodies.

"Shit, Alec."

Slowly Theo's thrusts stop, hips stilling, but Alec shakes his head, making eye contact with Theo as he gasps around Theo's fingers. Whatever it is Theo's looking for he must find, because he starts to move again in shallow thrusts that have Alec's toes curling. His body is so over-sensitive, the pleasure verges on pain in the best way possible.

"Beautiful," Theo whispers, hips shuddering as he comes with a quiet grunt and eyes squeezed shut.

Alec stills, but his chest heaves while he watches Theo attempt to steady his breathing. His fingers are still in Alec's mouth, and though he's no longer sucking on them, he enjoys the weight of them filling him up. When Theo's eyes open and he pulls his fingers out, it takes all of Alec's self-control not to whimper. That restraint fails when Theo holds the base of his dick to keep the condom on and pulls out, leaving Alec painfully empty everywhere. Alec lets out a pitiful sound.

"Shit, did I hurt you?" Remorse is written on Theo's every feature.

"No," Alec whispers, struggling with the sudden feeling of emptiness.

"Are you sure?"

Unsure how to explain, Alec nods.

"Good. Just...stay here. Let me clean up."

What Alec wants to do is make a joke about being the best lay Theo's ever had, but somehow all that comes out his mouth is a soft, "Okay."

He tries not to think too hard about what Theo might be thinking, but now that his mouth is empty, his brain is back on its bullshit. So much so that it takes him by surprise when a warm cloth presses against his stomach.

"Sorry, I thought you saw me coming."

"Of course I did," Alec lies.

"So I didn't fuck your brains out, then?" Theo teases, wiping up the mess Alec made of himself.

"Think awfully highly of yourself, don't you, Theodore?"

"Kinda hard not to with you looking all fucked out in my bed." The tips of Theo's ears go red as he spends far more time than strictly necessary running the cloth over Alec's belly, which must be clean by now. "Was it, uh, okay?"

A hint of Theo's insecurity is all it takes for Alec's to disappear.

"Are you trying to ask if you were the best fuck of my life? Because listen, there was a lot of competition." Alec lifts his hand, waggling his fingers. "These babies got a lot of practice."

Silent laughter makes Theo's chest shake and goddamn, happiness looks good on him. There's nothing more Alec enjoys than making the people he cares about happy. And Theo, he wishes he could make him happiest of all.

"Alright fine," Alec sighs dramatically. "You've pulled it out of me. You and your demanding ways. If you must know, you were at the top of my list. Ten out of ten fuck. Can't promise you'll stay at the top though. You'll have to work hard to stay there. My expectations are now exceedingly high, you know?"

"You with high expectations? Shocking."

"Fuck off." Alec laughs, rolling onto his side to watch Theo walk towards the bathroom. He tosses the discarded washcloth into a laundry basket and flicks the bathroom light off.

"I think—" but his words are cut off when a tiny ball of black streaks by. "Well, aren't you a sight for sore eyes!" Alec grins, his smile wide when Rio butts her head against Alec's cheek. "I missed you too, pretty girl."

"I'm sorry," Theo whispers, dropping down onto the other side of the bed.

"Nope, no more sorry. That's over now."

"But—"

"No," Alec interrupts. He doesn't want to talk about it again. He knows why Theo did what he did, and he knows Theo means it when he says he's sorry. That's all Alec needs. He'd much rather focus on his blissful post-orgasm haze than feelings that make his insides feel like being stuck on an upside-down roller coaster.

"She missed you," Theo says, moving to sit cross-legged. He's still naked, his cock soft between his thick thighs.

"I'm an easy man to miss."

"You are," Theo whispers.

"Does that mean you missed me?" Alec asks, running his fingers across Rio's back. She's settled herself near his face, her purring soothing away the nerves that are rising in Alec. Asking that question was far too close to what Alec really wants to know.

"I always miss you."

And that right there is far too close to what Alec wants to hear. Losing his virginity didn't even make Alec as nervous as he is now.

"Guess you'll have to keep me around then." Alec tries to tease, but his tone comes out far too unsure for his own liking.

"Alec."

"Alright, you twisted my arm. I'll let you fuck me again, but give me thirty minutes to recoup."

"Alec."

"Fine, fine. Ten minutes, but you got any Coke? I'm really fucking thirsty."

"There's Coke in my fridge, but Alec, we need to talk."

We need to talk. The four worst words in the English language.

"No, thank you."

Theo huffs out a half-laugh, but he doesn't smile, and that twists something painful in Alec.

"If you regret this, don't tell me," Alec blurts.

"I don't regret it, but—"

"But," Alec parrots with a groan. He hates that fucking word.

"I'm sorry, Alexander."

"Don't call me that if you're going to—" but Alec can't finish, can't bring himself to voice his biggest fear. *Don't call me that if you're going to push me away again,* he thinks, biting the inside of his cheek so hard it bleeds.

Theo scrubs a hand over his face and sighs. "Look, I know."

"You know what?" Alec asks sharply. His heart is rattling in his chest, a weird burning in his eyes. Everything was so good, and now it feels like he's losing control. Alec has no goddamn idea what's happening.

"I heard you and Charlie."

The ground beneath Alec seems to sway. If he didn't know better, he'd swear there was an earthquake, but the only thing breaking right now is what remains of Alec's heart.

"No."

"It was that morning after your birthday party," Theo says.

"You were asleep," Alec protests, terrified of what exactly Theo heard.

"I wasn't. I was uh...fuck, I'm sorry. I shouldn't have listened, but I did and I know, alright? I know you're in love with someone else, and that's alright. This was just sex, but I also know you and—"

Theo continues talking, but Alec's ears are ringing, and it's hard to breathe. Theo heard him. Theo thinks he's in love with someone else. His feet are moving without his permission as he crawls off the bed, unsure why he has the urge to back himself into a corner. Rio meows in confusion, following Alec and standing at his feet.

"It wasn't just sex," Alec croaks.

"Hey, it's okay. I'm not upset." Theo's expression is kind, gentle almost, as if he thinks Alec needs handling. "You know me, sex is sex and that's all this was, but—"

"No," Alec grits out, unable to stomach what Theo is saying.

The idea that Alec loves someone else, that he could when Theo exists, is laughable. It's also the out Alec needs to ensure Theo doesn't push him away again. It should be the perfect opportunity, but Alec can't stomach the prospect of living yet another lie.

Everything about his life has become a deception, and the walls are closing in around him. He lies about wanting to play professional soccer. He lies about loving school. He lies about not loving Theo. It's all too much, and Alec can't do it anymore.

He can't do it.

"I love you!" Alec yells.

All the color drains out of Theo's face and suddenly, Alec is fifteen again. He can feel the weight of Theo's gaze back then, the way his kind smile had turned shocked and horrified. He can still feel the sand beneath his toes, smell the way Theo's cologne had mixed with the salt air. One of the best days of Alec's teenage life had turned into the worst, because he'd thought it was imperative he let Theo know how he felt, but that confession had ruined everything. Now he's done it again. The difference is he can't even blame teenage hormones or youthful ignorance on things falling apart now.

"Charlie said you needed to get over some guy."

Alec is quiet, the metallic tang of blood in his mouth the only thing stopping him from running.

"You...you love someone else. I heard you."

"You heard us talking about you," Alec confesses, unsure why his voice sounds so calm when inside he's falling apart. "Charlie is the only one who knows I am still in love with you. He was trying to get me to move on."

"Still? As in, since you were fifteen?" At Alec's silence Theo curses, tugging on his hair. "Alec?"

"Don't look at me like I'm pathetic." Alec's chest heaves as grabs his pants off the floor and tugs them on, unable to handle having this conversation naked. He's not even sure where his underwear went, but at least his dick isn't hanging out. "Yes, I've loved you since I was fifteen. Earlier, probably, if you really want to know. That was just when I told you."

"Fuck, Alec."

"Stop acting like someone loving you is the worst thing in the goddamn world," Alec snarls, scrambling to find his hoodie on the floor. He yanks it over his head, the need to hide damn near overwhelming. "I'm not asking you for anything, okay? I know you don't feel the same, and I don't expect you to, so you don't need to be freaking out about this."

"You should have told me."

Why, so you could stop being friends with me again? Alec thinks bitterly, shoving his hands into his pockets and fighting back the rising nausea. The worst part is that he can't even hate Theo. He knew this would happen, knew Theo would freak out. He doesn't want Alec like that, never has and never will. What did Alec think, a few weeks of rekindling their friendship and a fuck, and magically Theo might suddenly consider dating Alec? He was such a fool.

"Alec."

"It's fine," Alec grits out. Hands hidden inside the front of his hoodie pocket, he twists his fingers. He will not cry in front of Theo. He won't.

"It's not fine." Theo's expression is tight, the hunch of his shoulders making it clear that Alec was delusional thinking that telling Theo the truth might be alright. It was just sex. That's what Theo said. He likes Alec's body and that's all. Alec was a goddamn idiot to think he could survive the way that feels. "I took advantage of you."

"Bull-fucking-shit," Alec snaps. "I knew what I was getting into. I'm grown, and I can make my own choices."

"I shouldn't have fucked you, Alec."

"Shouldn't or wish you hadn't?" The second the question comes out, Alec wishes he could take it back. He doesn't want to know the real answer.

"Alec."

That's as much of an answer as Alec's going to get and a definitive one at that. Theo wouldn't have fucked him if he'd known Alec still loved him. He probably wouldn't have let Alec get close enough to become friends, either.

"You're terrible at keeping promises, you know," Alec whispers.

Theo doesn't say anything to that, instead dropping his head into his hands as if he can't even bear to look at Alec any longer. Everything about his body language is defeated, and Alec has the most ridiculous urge to comfort Theo, but he's pretty sure that's not what Theo would want right now. Not that Alec knows what Theo wants. Hell, maybe he doesn't know him as well as he thought since he dropped that bomb on him for a second time.

A soft meow catches Alec's attention. He looks down to find Rio butting against his leg, clearly agitated and wanting attention, but Alec can't hold her because he can't stay here. He can't stand another moment in this room, the scent of sex still heavy in the air as he stares at Theo naked in the bed, where Theo just took his virginity. He can't stand the sight of Theo upset because of him, because once again Alec's feelings are too much for someone. He's so tired of being too much for people.

"I should go," Alec says so quietly he's not sure if Theo doesn't hear him or ignores him.

Either way, Theo doesn't look up when Alec leaves the room. He doesn't come out while Alec grabs his phone off the couch and slips his shoes back on. The only one to follow him is Rio, who tries to sneak out the door with Alec.

"I'm sorry," he whispers, wishing he could promise to come visit her, but he's unsure if Theo will even want to see him again. He can only hope it won't be another six years.

A very stupid, pathetic part of Alec entertains the possibility that Theo might chase after him. He even imagines that he might tell Alec that even if he doesn't feel the same, they can still be friends.

He doesn't.

Standing at the street corner, Alec accepts that Theo is not going to come after him. He takes off running, the street lamps lighting his way. He's never been out for a run in the middle of the night like this, and it's strange. There's no cars in sight, and the unnatural quiet is eerie. The only sound is the heavy thud of Alec's sneakers as he sprints until his chest aches and his eyes burn.

He stops when the tears blur his vision, making it too hard to keep running. He stops at the intersection, collapsing against the stop sign and pressing his cheek against the cool metal. Struggling to breathe, he squeezes his eyes shut and cries harder than has since he was fifteen. The ache of losing Theo is so much sharper now. He'd been so sure he knew what he was getting himself into, so confident that he could handle the inevitable pain, but he can't. He has no idea how he's supposed to play in the game tomorrow, how he's supposed to go to classes all week and pretend to be okay when he is anything but. It is insurmountable that life is supposed to go on when Alec feels like he's dying inside.

Alec struggles to catch his breath as he cries, lungs burning. It's a long time before he stops weeping, and longer still before he musters the energy to wipe away the tears.

He knows he's got to be pretty close to campus, but he was in too much of a daze to pay attention and ended up in a residential neighborhood he doesn't recognize. On a good day, he could make it back to his apartment if he kept going, but tonight that's more than Alec feels like he can handle. He's so very tired, his body spent from crying. All he wants to do is crawl in his bed and stay there for a week.

Turning so his back is against the metal pole, he digs his phone out of his pocket and unlocks it, swiping through his contacts. He could call Antonio. He'd come if Alec asked. Riley's got a car and would come pick him up too, but neither of them are who Alec needs right now.

Scrolling through his contacts, Alec's finger hovers over the one person he needs.

With shaking fingers he taps the call button, holding it to his ear while it rings. When it goes to voicemail, Alec hangs up and calls again, knowing he's being an asshole by waking him up but needing him anyway. When the call answers, Alec breathes just a little easier.

"Alec?" Charlie's voice is strained, full of sleep, and so familiar a lump forms in Alec's throat.

"Hey."

"Hey?" Charlie echoes. "It's two in the morning. What's going on?"

Alec opens his mouth, but all that comes out is a choked-off sob.

"Ally?" Charlie's voice pitches higher. He sounds so worried.

"I did something stupid," Alec whispers, tears falling freely again.

"Talk to me. What's going on?" Charlie curses under his breath, the sound of him moving around in his room echoing through the phone when he puts Alec on speaker. "Are you at home?"

"No," Alec answers.

There's a pause, followed by more hushed cursing. Knowing Charlie, he probably walked into a wall or kicked his bed frame. He's clumsy when he's tired, and Alec would feel more guilty about waking him up if he didn't desperately need a hug from his big brother right now.

"What happened? Where are you?"

"I lied to you," Alec answers, scrubbing away the tears.

"You're scaring me, Ally. Tell me what's going on. Let me help you."

And that right there is exactly why Alec called him. When he was little, the only one who could calm Alec from a nightmare was Charlie. Andrew tried since they shared a room, but with his sleeping issues, Alec didn't like waking him up if he didn't have to. Besides, Charlie was always a night owl, and often up with the moon sketching or painting. Since he was often already awake, Alec never felt like he was bothering Charlie when he snuck out of bed to find him. A restless sleeper prone to nightmares, Alec spent a lot of time with Charlie while the rest of the family slept. That is, until he went away to college with Andrew. Eventually, he and Anddrew both came back to Santa Leon, but they got jobs and their own places to live, and while Alec knows that's part of growing up, he misses him. He misses all his brothers.

"Don't be mad at me."

"You're being cryptic as fuck." Charlie sighs. "You know that no matter what you did I can never really be mad at you. Just tell me what the hell is going on, please?"

"I don't wanna be in love."

The line goes silent, and for a second Alec thinks the call dropped, but then Charlie's voice rings out clear as day. "Oh, Ally."

Whatever was left of Alec's heart breaks, shattered into a million little pieces that he doesn't even want to try and find anymore.

"I'm sorry."

"You don't need to apologize to me. You know that. Just tell me where you are so I can come get you."

"Downtown somewhere. Dunno the street," Alec sniffles, rubbing his hoodie-covered hand over his nose. "I just started running from—from where I was."

He's not sure why he hesitates to say it was Theo's house. He knows he's going to have to tell Charlie about what happened all too soon, but that seems less daunting to do in person. That way, after the look of knowing disapproval he's sure to get from Charlie, he can at least have a hug.

"That's vague as hell, Alec. You gotta give me an address or a street name so I can come find you."

Alec hears a car approaching, but the light at the intersection is red, and the car is on the opposite side of the road, so he doesn't pay them too much attention. Instead he turns back to the street sign, frowning when he realizes it's partially blocked by an overgrown tree on the sidewalk. He sighs, careful not to move into the street as he leans sideways to try and read the sign.

"Hang on, this tree is overgrown, I think—" but the rest of Alec pauses when the car speeds through the red light. "Fucking asshole drivers at night, I swear."

"Focus, Alec."

I'm trying, Alec wants to say, but he doesn't get a

chance. His phone flies from his hand as the car jumps the curb. For a moment, the sharpest pain Alec's ever felt cracks through him like lightning, and then just as suddenly it's gone, along with everything else.

20 THEO

THEO LOSES track of how long he sits in the dark, staring at the half-closed door and hating himself. Alec's confession had been shocking to say the least, but the most shocking part in the entire situation, had been the tendril of longing that took root in Theo's heart when Alec yelled those three words.

Of course that longing had immediately been dwarfed by regret. Knowing he'd somehow found a way to hurt Alec further was painful, coupled with the sheer and utter panic at how messy and complicated things now were. This thing with Alec was supposed to be no strings attached, something casual to get Theo over his crush and help Alec get rid of his virginity in a safe way. In hindsight, the entire thing had been messy from the start, but Theo refused to see it. Somehow he deluded himself a little into thinking he was the only person who could help Alec, his own desire clouding his judgment. It's why he'd pulled back after that first night they spent together.

He'd realized he was falling for Alec.

Theo doesn't know how to do no strings attached with

Alec, and he'd done what he always did in situations like that—emotionally shut down—at least, until Alec came barging back into his life without invitation, and let Theo know all the ways he'd fucked up. Hearing how much he hurt Alec had been one of the most painful moments of his life. Regret and shame warred within him, demanding he keep the lines drawn. Instead, he crossed the line.

Somehow, Theo convinced himself that because Alec was in love with someone else things couldn't possibly get messier. He stupidly thought he could fuck Alec, and then go back to being friends after. It was reckless and illogical, but Theo had still wanted to fuck Alec. He'd also wanted to do anything to soothe the sharp edges of hurt he'd inflicted.

With a half-cocked plan, he'd given in and fucked Alec, only instead of ridding him of his desire for Alec, it highlighted how much Theo wanted him, and how deeply Alec had wedged himself into Theo's quiet life with one fuck. It scared the absolute shit out of him to have such depth of feeling for the person he was fucking. Having Alec spread out in his bed afterward, fucked out and happy, had reignited Theo's fear, and he'd known then that he needed to make sure they didn't do it again.

Leave it to Alec to turn the tables on him, blurting out a love confession while Theo was trying to end things before they got more complicated. Instead of relief that his feelings weren't one-sided, all encompassing panic had hit Theo like a freight train. He's never been in love before. He's not even sure if that's what he feels for Alec, but the prospect sent him into shutdown mode. If he let himself, he could absolutely fall head over heels in love with Alexander King, but instead of being happy, Theo wanted to sob.

Flashes of his childhood invaded his mind. His mother, abandoning them. His father, broken and alone, unable to ever let anyone else in again. An empty stomach and an even emptier heart. He'd sworn he would never let himself be vulnerable like his parents, never let anyone besides Jason get close enough to him to hurt him. He wasn't supposed to develop feelings for anyone, especially not Alec.

Fear paralyzed him, and by the time he came to his senses and realized he'd let Alec walk out the front door, he knew he'd made a huge mistake. Unwilling to make another one, he tried to call Alec, enough times he started to feel like an idiot with every call that went to voicemail. He debated leaving a message, but he didn't even know what he wanted to say. *I'm so sorry I fucked up and I know I'm an idiot, but I want to be your idiot, but I also don't know how to be in a relationship, and the idea of doing that with you terrifies me because I can't lose Jason, so please forgive me even though I don't know what I want.* Yeah, that would go over really well.

Unable to make a plan about what to say but just as unable to stop calling, Theo redials Alec's number. With every unanswered call, his desperation grows. All he wants is to hear Alec's voice, to at least tell him he's sorry. Unfortunately by the fifth call, it becomes apparent that Alec is ignoring him, not that Theo can blame him. If their positions were reversed, he'd be ignoring him too.

Riddled with guilt and regret, Theo crawls into his bed, tugs the blankets over his face and tries not to cry. His entire life he's been afraid of love, and then someone beautiful and perfect offers it to him on a goddamn silver platter, and he still manages to screw things up.

Eyes blurry with unshed tears, he rolls over and buries his face in the pillow, chasing Alec's scent and wishing he was braver.

THEO'S DREAMS are a mess of anxiety, his sleep broken and unsatisfying, which he figures is what he deserves. By five, he gives up trying to sleep and heads into the kitchen to put on the coffee pot, surprised to find Rio already awake and prowling the room. He bends down and tries to pet her, but she sprints under the couch, setting the tone for Theo's morning. Not even his cat wants to see him.

He's so exhausted he moves on autopilot, scooping coffee grounds into the pot without a filter and cursing. Grabbing the plastic insert, he shakes the grounds off in the trash before fitting it back in the pot, and this time making sure to put a filter in before adding the grounds the second time. His finger is still on the brew button when someone bangs on his front door.

At this time in the morning, there's only one person it might be. A pathetic surge of hope fills Theo's chest. He has no idea what the hell he's actually going to say to Alec, but the relief that he came back after all the shit Theo put him through is staggering. The consolation is short-lived because when he opens the door, it's not Alec standing on his front porch but instead a very different King.

Jason is dressed in his usual uniform of gray sweats and a sweatshirt from the high school where he works, but his eyes are rimmed in red, and Theo knows immediately something is very, very wrong.

"What's going on?" Theo asks. "I didn't know you even knew what this time of day was."

It's probably bad form to make a joke right now, but Theo is shit at feelings and hasn't seen Jason cry in nearly a decade. He waits for Jason to laugh or call him an idiot, but what comes out of his mouth instead is a single word that threatens to ruin everything.

"Alec."

Of all the things Theo expected, this is the last. Alec promised not to tell Jason, and while it was selfish of Theo to want Alec to keep secrets from his own brother, he had been relieved by the offer. Did Alec go straight to Jason? Or maybe he went to Charlie, and then he went to Jason? Either way, Theo's biggest fear is coming true.

"I'm so sorry," Theo says, scrambling to figure out how to save this. "Don't hate me. Please."

"What?" Jason's thick eyebrows pinch together.

"I didn't mean for it to happen." Even as Theo says it, shame burns in his gut. He needs to stop lying to the people he cares about. "This is my fault, all of it. Don't blame Alec."

"What the hell are you talking about?" Jason asks.

"You came over here to yell at me for sleeping with Alec, didn't you?"

Judging by the stunned look on Jason's face, that is clearly not what he came here for. "You had sex with Alec?"

"I, uh—" Theo licks his lips, ignoring the ways his ears ring. "The thing is, uh—yes."

Jason gapes. "I thought you were seeing some girl."

"I wasn't technically seeing anyone. It's...complicated, but it wasn't a girl I was interested in."

"Wait, the feelings you had for someone. That was *Alec?*"

It would be so easy to lie, to pretend the sex had been a one-time mistake and beg forgiveness so things didn't get more complicated. Yet as another lie takes shape on the tip of his tongue, the idea of saying it out loud fills Theo with dread. Even if Alec never speaks to him again, even if it makes Jason hate him, he can't lie about this. Not when Alec was so brave. He might not have much to offer Alec, but the truth is something he does have.

"I didn't mean to," Theo whispers. "We were just hanging out. Friends, you know? He's so easy to like and he's funny. He doesn't take my bullshit, and he pushes me, and he's so beautiful."

"Oh my god, this isn't happening," Jason groans. He scrubs a hand over his stubbled jaw. "What the fuck, Theo? How long?"

"Since Alec's birthday."

"You've been sleeping with my brother for two months?" Jason looks mildly nauseated, but also confused and angry, and Theo hates that he's the cause of it all.

"To be completely transparent, I only fucked him once. Well, and the kitchen thing, but—"

"Wait, that time I came over and he was here? You guys were together? All that shit Alec said was a lie? You made him lie to me? *You* lied to me?"

Theo hangs his head. "Yes."

"The Coke in the fridge," Jason mutters. "I can't believe I didn't see it before."

"What?"

"A few weeks ago when I was looking for a drink, there was Coke in your fridge. I couldn't figure out why it was there. You don't drink that." Jason takes a breath. "You bought it for him."

"He likes Coke."

"I know that." Jason's voice is tinged with unfamiliar sharpness. "He's my baby brother."

"He's not a baby anymore."

"Fuck me." Jason paces back and forth on the front porch. Suddenly he stops, turning his gaze on Theo, and the look on his face is unlike any Theo's ever seen. "Wait, was he here tonight? Is that why he was out at two in the morning?"

"Yes, but how do you know he was out? Did he tell Charlie or—"

"He's in the hospital, Theo."

THE SILENT DRIVE across town to the hospital is tense. It's clear Jason is pissed at him, but whether for fucking his baby brother or lying about it, Theo's not sure. Maybe both. Jason's never been mad at him before like this, and it's a horrible feeling. Along with the guilt at what he's done, there is also fear. The kind that makes his insides feel wrong. Alec is hurt, and every moment without seeing him hurts.

According to Jason, the hospital had trouble figuring out Alec's identity since his phone was broken in the accident, and he had no identification on him, which meant he'd been hurt and alone for who knows how long until someone could find out who to contact. Eventually someone figured it out based on his university hoodie and his player profile on the school website, leading them to call the King brothers since their parents were out of town.

Turns out Jason didn't have any idea what happened, and had stopped at Theo's house on the way to the hospital to get Theo for moral support. Great fucking best friend Theo is.

"Jason," Theo tries when the hospital comes into view at the far end of the road.

"Don't."

Theo rubs his hands over his knees, feeling like he might be sick. "I'm so sorry."

"For fucking my brother, or lying to me? I'm your best friend." Jason slams his hand against the steering wheel, the horn blaring. "We promised no lies. You lied to me."

That answers the question of what he's pissed about, then.

"I didn't mean to. None of this was supposed to happen and—"

"Just stop," Jason sighs, weaving his way through traffic. If he's not careful he's gonna get a speeding ticket, but Theo's not about to point that out. Jason is one of the most even-keeled, mellow people alive, but when he's angry it's bad. Right now he's not just angry, he's scared, which is a dangerous combo. Theo knows him well enough to know from the clench of his jaw and the way he white-knuckles the steering wheel, that he's terrified about his brother.

Much as Theo wants to push the issue right now, he knows Jason needs a minute before he's going to be ready to talk to Theo. Trying to push for a resolution now when he's so upset about Alec would only be for Theo's benefit, and he's been selfish enough already.

This time of day the visitor lot is empty, but it still takes time to get from the parking structure to the main hospital. By the time they manage to get to the main entrance, get visitor passes and find Charlie and Andrew in the second floor waiting room, Theo feels like he's going to pass out.

Spotting the twins is easy, both of them huddled in the corner. Andrew's dressed down in a pair of sweats and a wrinkled t-shirt, which makes him look so much more like Charlie it's unnerving. He didn't even know Andrew owned anything besides perfectly starched polos and dress slacks. Beside him sits Charlie, head in his hands and fingers clenched in his hair. At their approach Andrew looks up, whispering something to Charlie before standing and walking towards them. He's clearly putting some distance between them and Charlie, and Theo doesn't know what to make of that.

"Theo," Andrew greets before being pulled into a fierce hug by Jason.

"Please say he's okay," Jason chokes.

"We don't know," Andrew says, voice tight when he steps out of the embrace. Something about seeing Andrew, the calmest King, looking so disheveled and rattled really hammers home how serious this is. "They think it was a drunk driver. It was a hit and run. Someone driving to work found him bleeding on the curb and called 911. Mom and Dad are in a complete panic trying to get flights home, but everything is booked and—" Andrew stops, swallowing audibly.

"And what, Andrew?"

"He's in surgery right now. His leg is pretty fucked up, Jason."

"How fucked are we talking?"

"Really fucked." Andrew pulls on his hair, looking so much younger than he normally does. "They said something about a compound fracture. They're going to be putting pins in it to stabilize the bone, and he'll need physical therapy after and...they don't know if he's gonna be able to play soccer again. Even if he does play, he's not going to be able to do it this year. He's going to miss the MLS combine in January, which means his chance at being scouted is gone."

"Fuck." Jason looks two seconds from collapsing, which is exactly how Theo feels. This is all his fault. If he hadn't let Alec leave, none of this would have happened.

"It's not just his leg, either. He's got a few sprained ribs and his shoulder was dislocated. I just wish I knew why the hell he was out alone. Charlie said he called him crying right before he got hurt, that he was really upset about something, but wouldn't say what."

Theo didn't think he could feel worse, but bile rises in his throat. The guilt is staggering, and Theo backs himself into a wall, damn near hyperventilating.

"Theo, it's not your fault."

"It is my fault," Theo whispers, unable to stomach Jason comforting him right now.

"Why would it be Theo's fault? Weren't you at home?" Andrew is glancing between Jason and Theo, clearly trying to fill in the puzzle pieces.

"It's nothing," Jason lies, and Theo knows exactly what that must cost him. Jason hates lying as much as Alec. Those damn King boys and their honesty. The fact that Jason would lie to his brother just to protect Theo, is more than Theo deserves.

"Alec was at my house," Theo answers, a sob catching in his throat when Jason leans his shoulder against Theo's. He's still angry, Theo knows he is, but he's not walking away, and Theo can't believe he ever thought he would. Jason is the most loyal guy that Theo's ever met, and he can't believe he doubted him. Fear makes people, makes Theo, do really shitty things. He's not sure he deserves Jason's loyalty, but he's damn sure going to cling to it.

"I'm definitely missing some context here," Andrew says, "I thought—"

"You." Charlie's voice booms out through the almost empty waiting room, his eyes like daggers glaring at Theo. Apparently he heard them, then. Not like it matters. Andrew would've told him the second he sat down anyway.

"Fuck," Jason says under his breath.

Charlie rises from his chair to cross the room. "I should have known it was you. It's always you when Alec's getting his heart broken."

Andrew's eyes widen, but he wisely keeps his mouth shut.

"That's really not fair," Jason says. Theo lets the pressure of Jason's presence at his side keep his tears at bay. He owes Alec's family that much.

"Fuck fair," Charlie hisses. "This is your fault, Theo. I should have known when Alec called me crying."

Theo swallows. "He was crying?"

"Of course he was crying. He was devastated about something he wouldn't tell me." Charlie's tone drips with accusation. "I wondered when he mentioned love, but then I thought no. No way. Theo would never cross the line like that. He doesn't have feelings for Alec. He wouldn't lead him on."

"Easy, Charlie," Andrew interjects, trying to keep the peace as always. "We don't know anything for sure."

"I would never hurt him on purpose," Theo says, voice as small as he feels.

"Yet you did." Charlie moves into Theo's personal space. Theo is the same height as the twins, but right now Charlie seems to tower over him. "What did you do?"

Jason shakes his head. "Stop it, Charlie."

"No!" Charlie shoves Jason when he tries to step between them. "This is Theo's fault. Alec shouldn't have been wandering the streets in the middle of the night. He could've died because of you. He might lose the game he loves forever, lose his entire future, all because of you!"

Every word cuts deeper than the last, because they're all true. If Theo hadn't fucked Alec, they wouldn't be here. If he hadn't been a coward and shut down, letting Alec walk away, none of them would be here. Alec would be safe, not fighting for his life in a hospital bed.

"Charlie, stop this right now before you say something you're going to regret," Jason demands.

"Regret? Why are you taking his side?" Charlie turns his glare on Jason. "Fuck you too, then. Did you know? Did you know he was messing around with Alec? That he was just using him?"

"I wasn't using him," Theo croaks. He can handle the blame and the rage, but not that.

"Yeah, right," Charlie scoffs. "What, did you find out he was still in love with you and think it'd be fun to take what you wanted and leave? I've known you your entire life, Theo. I know you. You might be a decent guy, but you don't date anyone. You don't do relationships or commitment, but he does. Or at least he wants to. All Alec has ever wanted was the kind of relationship our parents have. He's a goddamn romantic who wants flowers and love and promises of forever. You know that, and yet you still took advantage of him."

"I didn't," Theo tries, his protest half-hearted at best. He doesn't want to believe that, but maybe what Charlie says isn't that far off from the truth. Isn't that what he did? He convinced himself that he was helping Alec, because it gave him a chance to be with him with no strings attached.

"Charlie, stop it." Andrew moves in front of him, blocking Jason and Theo from view. He leans his head in close, his forehead nearly touching Charlie's as he whispers something too quiet for them to hear. Then he's wrapping his arms around Charlie, who curls into Andrew like a child and starts to sob, his hands clenching in the back of Andrew's shirt.

Jason grabs Theo's arm and all but drags him toward a set of chairs against the far wall, to give Andrew and Charlie some space. He knows this isn't over, but he's going to take the out Andrew has afforded him.

"Are you still pissed at me?" Theo asks Jason once they're far enough away. With a heavy exhale, he drops down into one of the hard hospital chairs next to Jason.

"Fuck yes, I am," Jason sighs, looking far too big for the chair. "I'm so fucking mad at you, Theo, but I'm not going to walk away. Did you think I would?"

Theo stares at his hands, embarrassed that it's exactly what he thought.

"You're an idiot," Jason grumbles. "I'm not going to ever pick between you or my brothers. You're both my family, and you're not ever going to get rid of me. I can be really pissed off at you and still love you."

All the air leaves Theo's lungs in a rush. "Why?"

"Who knows. You sure as shit don't make it easy to love you, Theo. But you're worth it. I know it and...and it sounds like Alec knows it, too."

Theo hiccups out a sob, shoving his hands over his mouth to try and silence the wounded animal noises he's making. This is too much.

"Shit, you really like him, don't you?"

"Yes," Theo whispers, unable to fight the tears back. "I'm sorry."

"God dammit, I can't be mad at you when you cry." Jason throws an arm around Theo's shoulder, pulling him into an awkward but much needed side hug. "I can't believe you, Mr. I-will-be-single-until-I-die, caught feelings for my annoying baby brother."

"Me neither," Theo admits.

"Aren't you supposed to tell me he's not annoying or some rose-colored glasses bullshit?"

"No." Theo sits up, rubbing his eyes with the back of his hand. "He is annoying and I like it. I don't know if that's weird, but he's just always himself, and I love that about him. I like that he's a mouthy pain in the ass, demanding and never letting me get away with anything. He's such a little shit, and I think I might love it. He makes me laugh and smile and...oh god, I really like him. So much, Jason. What am I going to do?"

"Pretty sure the next step is apologizing and learning how to communicate."

"That sounds fucking hard. I hurt him, Jason. So bad. I might hurt him again. Fuck, he might not even forgive me."

"It's Alec. Of course he's going to forgive you, that stupid kid has a heart of gold. He forgives everyone who hurts him."

"I don't want to hurt him."

"Then don't," Jason says, like it's that easy.

"I can't believe you're encouraging me to ...what? Try and date your brother?"

"I'm encouraging you to be happy. If that involves Alec, then I'll support you, even if it's gonna take a lot of getting used to and be weird as hell." Jason rubs his hands over his face groaning. "So fucking weird."

"That's incredibly mature."

"Don't act so surprised, asshole. Just because I spend all day with teenagers doesn't mean I am one." Jason cracks a smile, and Theo has a glimmer of a future where maybe this is okay, where maybe things with him and Alec work out, and he doesn't lose Jason. He still feels like he's walking on the edge of a cliff, but knowing that no matter what happens, Jason has his back makes it feel like there's something to catch him if he falls. "For the record, I'm still pretty pissed off at you for lying and for hurting Alec, though."

"I get that," Theo sighs, swallowing down his guilt.

"But," Jason continues before Theo can start spiraling, "I'm also smart enough to realize that maybe, just maybe, what happens between you and Alec isn't my business. Not entirely. He's my brother, and I'm always going to worry about him, just like I'm always going to worry about you. Two people I love getting involved makes me want to get in the middle and make sure nothing goes wrong."

"We're not your football team. You can't manage us."

"I know," Jason groans. "I kinda hate that. But even if I could, I don't think I should. Alec's not a child, and he can make his own choices. I'm not exactly going to tell him he's making a bad one. You're the best person I know, Theo. You're smart as hell, you work hard and you care about people, and you always want to do the right thing."

"And yet."

"Stop interrupting my pep talk," Jason says in that teacher tone of his. Theo can imagine that shuts his students up quickly. He might look like an oversized puppy, but he can be firm when he wants. "Good, now back to what I was saying. You're the fucking best. I know you try to hide it behind your ugly-ass sweaters and that ten-foot wall you built around yourself to keep friends and relationships out. But I knew one day someone would get past it, and you deserve that, Theo. You deserve to be loved."

"My sweaters aren't ugly," Theo retorts, because saying anything else is too hard right now. "Alec loves my sweaters."

"Well, we all have flaws."

"It's gonna be like that, is it?" Theo asks, surprised that he's almost smiling.

"Damn right. This is just like double fodder to tease the shit out of Alec. You know, when he's...better."

The mood sobers quickly, whatever relief he'd found at Jason's steadfast acceptance is gone as he takes in the sterile walls and the scent of antiseptic in the air. For a few minutes, it'd been all too easy to get lost in conversation, but reality rears its ugly head to bring back remorse and worry in equal measure. Theo itches to find Alec, to see for himself that he's alright and apologize. Apologize until he dies, do anything to get a second chance.

In a future of unknowns Theo knows one thing, he isn't going to let Alec go without a fight.

———

"HE'S out of surgery and in recovery now," the surgeon says. He's smiling, but Theo can't bring himself to do the same. He isn't going to feel better until he can see Alec for himself. The surgeon continues, "He had a stronger reaction to the anesthesia than expected, so he's taking a bit longer to come out of it."

Beside him, Charlie flinches, and Andrew wraps a hand around his arm, giving it a squeeze. Not for the first time, Theo wonders what it might be like to have a twin who you can read like that.

"The break in his leg was a bit worse than expected once we got in there, which is why the surgery took longer. We won't know the full extent of the damage or his recovery until the cast comes off, but for now we've done everything we can. He'll likely be staying for a few days, but someone will let you know once he's moved into a room and can have visitors."

"Thank you, Doctor," Andrew says. "Can I speak to you privately for a moment?"

"Of course," the surgeon replies, stepping into the hallway and leaving Jason and Theo alone with Charlie.

"Charlie," Theo starts, cut off when Charlie holds up a hand.

"Andrew said I should tell you I'm sorry, but I'm not. I don't think you deserve him. Lucky for you, what I think doesn't matter because Alec's a stubborn fucker and doesn't care what other people think, so you better prove me wrong, Theo. Don't hurt him again."

With that he turns and walks away, throwing himself in one of the chairs in the corner and crossing his arms.

"Huh," Jason hums. "You know Andrew should get a job as a diplomat. He'd do great."

"I don't know if I'd call that great."

"He didn't punch you, so I'd call it a success," Jason says. "And Alec's going to be okay."

"I'll feel better when I see him for myself," Theo says softly, fighting away the moisture in his eyes when Jason squeezes his shoulder.

"Soon," Jason promises.

It is not soon. Alec's reaction to the anesthesia proves to be worse than any of them expect. They let Charlie back into the recovery area to help with soothing his post-anesthesia confusion, but when Charlie comes back out into the waiting room an hour later, his eyes are red, and he proceeds to the bathroom and pukes. The only thing he will tell any of them is that Alec is struggling, then Charlie reverts into his turtle shell and refuses to speak to anyone but Andrew.

The sun has set by the time Alec's moved to a private room, the weight of the day's long wait hanging heavy over all of them. According to the nurses, Alec had been plagued by intense nausea and chills post-anesthesia, which combined with hospital overcrowding, had led to a half-day lag in him being moved. The waiting was plagued by phone calls, and Andrew spent hours on his cell phone handling what no one else wanted to, arranging his parents' return flight and fielding the dozens of phone calls from Alec's friends who had all wanted to come visit once they found out what happened. How any of them got Andrew's cell number was something Theo never got a chance to ask. Thankfully, Andrew was able to keep everyone from visiting, considering he didn't even have a room. Theo strongly suspected Andrew used some of his mediator powers, because he'd had no less than half a dozen calls from Riley and Antonio alone, yet somehow he managed to convince even them not to come see Alec until tomorrow.

The mood is heavy by the time Theo and Alec's brothers finally make their way down the hallway to see Alec. Everyone looks exhausted, and it's clear they're all as apprehensive as they are eager to get their eyes on Alec. The only one who'd been able to go back to see him in recovery had been Charlie, and he'd been kicked out once the worst of side effects kicked in, their only updates coming from sporadic nurse visits.

"He's going to be okay," Andrew says to no one in particular.

"Course he is," Charlie says, the slightest quiver to his voice. "I'll kill him if he's not."

The twins go in first, and Jason's halfway through the door when he turns to face Theo. "Aren't you coming?"

"I think he needs his brothers more than anything right now." Theo shoves his hands into his pockets, his heart aching with how desperately he wants to run into that room and hold Alec. "Just make sure he's okay, yeah? I'll be here when he's ready, and if he doesn't want to see me today, then I'll be here tomorrow and the next day and the one after that. Just...let him know that, will you? Let him know that I'm not going anywhere, unless he asks me to."

Jason nods, reaching out to give Theo's shoulder one final squeeze before he turns back into Alec's room. Theo waits until the door shuts behind him to press his back to the wall, sliding to the floor and pulling his knees to his chest. He hates hospitals, hates the smells and the white everywhere. He hates the lingering threat of loss that haunts the corners. No matter how many times he tells himself that good things happen in hospitals too, all he sees when he looks around is a painful reminder of just how close they all came to losing Alec.

Forcing himself to take a few steadying breaths, he drops his forehead on his knees and waits. After thirty minutes, he starts tracking the seconds on the clock on the wall, wondering if Alec will even want to see him. He wouldn't blame him if he didn't, but he selfishly hopes Alec's track record for forgiving Theo's idiocy will continue. Even if it does, this probably won't be the last time he screws up, but he promises himself that he will try. Theo promises himself that if Alec forgives him that he's going to work on his shit. He's going to get some therapy, and he's going to figure out how to stop being so goddamn afraid of good things happening in his life. For himself, for Alec, and for the future he's never going to have with anyone if he doesn't stop hiding. Most of all, he is going to make sure he's the man Alec seems to think he is.

The minutes tick by as a warning announcement sounds over the PA system, letting them know visiting hours are ending soon. Every moment that ticks by after brings more anxiety. He's not sure what he will do if Jason comes out and says Alec never wants to see him again. He's pretty sure that won't happen, or maybe that's wishful thinking. All he knows is that by the time the door to Alec's room opens, he's thought of every worst case scenario.

Each of them fills his mind as the twins and Jason file out, looking shaky.

"How is he?" Theo asks, rising so fast his head spins.

"He's...struggling," Jason says. "He's in a lot of pain."

"The accident was bad."

"It's not just the accident," Jason says softly. "I think... he's been unhappy for a long time, and none of us could see it."

Charlie makes a choked-off sob, turning to all but run down the hallway. Andrew doesn't even spare them a second look before he chases after him, leaving Theo and Jason alone.

"He said a lot of stuff that I think he's been holding in. It's not my place to tell you, but maybe he will."

"He wants to see me?" Theo asks, chills springing up on his arms.

"Yeah, he does. You've only got about ten minutes until visiting hours are over, but he kicked us out when he realized you were in the hallway. Just be gentle with him. Promise me."

"I promise."

"I'll wait in the car."

"Thank you, Jason."

With that, Jason heads off down the hallway, the slump of his shoulders feeling like a warning for what's to come. Even after trying to steel himself, nothing prepares Theo for stepping into that room and seeing Alec in his hospital bed. His curls are flattened and frizzy, sticking up on one side.

Wires and tubes snake around him, disappearing under his gown and into his skin. His leg is in a cast up to his mid-thigh, and there are bandages wrapped around various parts of his body. The most jarring of all are the bruises that cover his abdomen and shoulders, his lightly tanned skin discolored from the damage, to the point he's barely recognizable. Even his face is bruised, making him look one second away from breaking.

Theo's approach is slow and measured to give Alec time to prepare, but he keeps his eyes shut, his breathing slow and labored. He'd known from the surgeon's report that things were rough, but hearing it and seeing it are wildly different. Looking at Alec in that bed—his vibrancy gone—Theo can understand exactly what made Charlie run from the room and puke earlier. Bile rises in his stomach at the sight of Alec so battered and bruised, knowing how much pain he must be in and what a long road to recovery awaits.

It's only when Theo lowers himself into the chair at Alec's bedside that he turns his head, his eyes cracking open. Theo braces himself for the yelling or anger, ill-prepared for Alec's beautiful, broken face to light up with a smile.

"You came."

21 ALEC

"I'LL ALWAYS COME."

The words are a balm to Alec's aching heart. Everything hurts, from his head to his toes and every inch between. All of his broken bones and bruises have splintered him into some kind of mosaic of a man, leaving him unsure what scraps got left behind.

Nothing about his life is going to be the same ever again. He can't go back to school, not yet, and fuck knows if he will ever play soccer again. He sure as shit won't be playing for his team, which means his scholarship will be gone. All the pieces that make him who he is have been shattered, and he doesn't know which pieces to pick back up.

Through all the pain and uncertainty, the one thing that had hurt the most was how he'd left things with Theo. Maybe the broken ribs and shattered knee should've been his focus, but Alec grew up playing sports at a level most people never reached. He was no stranger to his body aching, and maybe this was different—okay, a lot different— but physical pain he could handle. His broken heart was something else, and all the sharp edges and hollow pieces that had been jumbling inside his chest since last night slotted back together with Theo at his bedside.

"I'm sorry," Alec whispers, licking his lips. His mouth is so dry, but every time he sips water he feels like throwing up.

"You have nothing to apologize for," Theo says, voice hushed. "I'm the one who needs to apologize. I freaked out, and I shut down, and that's no excuse, but you need to know it wasn't because I didn't want you. Even when I pushed you away, you came back. I promised not to hurt you, but I did. Again. I let you leave because I was a coward, and I'm sorry."

Hearing him apologize is almost more than Alec can handle. When he left last night, he'd been terrified he might not be able to have any more moments with Theo, and now he's saying the kinds of things that have Alec's heart lighting up with hope. It's the kind of hope that fills his chest and makes it hard to breathe. Or maybe that's the broken ribs, it's impossible to tell. His meds are definitely wearing off, the sharp edge of pain damn near nauseating, but he doesn't want to buzz the nurse for more because they make him feel dopey and drugged out. He wants to be present for this moment. He wants to remember every second of Theo coming for him, of choosing him, even if it hurts.

"I'm so sorry," Theo repeats, as if he means to keep saying it. As if Alec needs to hear it again when Theo being here means more than those three words ever could.

"Theo."

"I don't know how you could ever forgive me, but I want to try to make this right."

"Theo," Alec tries again, exhausted by the effort of speaking after confessing his secrets to his brothers. All it'd taken was Charlie whispering *how are you, Ally?* and he'd spilled his guts. Much as he wishes he could blame his heavy meds for the breakdown, the truth is it was a long time coming, and though it'd been difficult, physically and emotionally to get the words out, he'd managed. He'd stared at the ceiling, whispering about hating school and not being sure if he even wanted to play soccer anymore, and being in love with Theo. He knew his brothers wanted to interrupt with questions, yet they'd remained silent except for their tears.

Now all Alec's got left is the deep desire to pretend that his future isn't a giant Jenga tower, one wrong move from crumbling beyond repair. He doesn't have the energy for this right now, but, unfortunately for him, Theo is not paying attention.

"I don't even know how to prove to you that I mean it," Theo barrels on. "I think, no, I know, that I need therapy. And you'll have to be patient with me sometimes because I'm probably gonna screw up at some point. When that happens I might piss you off ,so you'll have to tell me. I don't want you to be afraid of me pushing you away again and—"

"Shut up," Alec says with as much energy as he can muster, before grabbing the call button from beside his hip and tossing it at Theo to get his attention.

Alec is so goddamn exhausted he wants to cry, but crying makes his ribs hurt and his face ache, and he's not sure there are any tears left, anyway. Everything hurts. *Everything.*

"Oh." Theo blinks. "Should I leave or?"

"Stay," Alec manages, glad at least his stupid arm isn't broken so he can hold it out, his fingers upturned in a wordless plea. Theo seems to understand, slipping his much larger hand over Alec's and cradling it safely. The last of Alec's fight goes out of him, exhaustion and pain taking over as he squeezes Theo's hand as tightly as he can, his grip only loosening when he finally passes out.

"YOU AWAKE?"

"Not by choice," Alec mutters, head pounding, ribs throbbing, and his skin sensitive to every movement he makes. As a result he lies very still, only opening his eyes once he's sure he's not going to vomit.

Last night was hell. The nurses had to ply him with Zofran for nausea and meds for the excruciating pain, which meant when his brothers had shown up at exactly eight in the morning for visiting hours, he'd been worn down and high as a kite. He can't actually remember what happened, but he's pretty sure the nurses warned everyone not to touch him too much, which is probably a good thing given his pain level, but also makes Alec want to scream.

All Alec wants is for Theo to throw his arms around him and hold him tightly, to hold on and never let go. He doesn't want Theo looking at him like he's made of glass, like he might break if Theo so much as breathes wrong. Exhaustion is etched in Theo's face, worry evident as his eyes roam over Alec as he tracks his every injury. When they land on Alec's leg, his entire face twists up in a way that makes Alec want to throw up.

"You know, if you keep looking at me like that, I'm gonna think you don't wanna be here."

"It's not that," Theo assures him, leaning over the bed until he's so close to Alec that if he closed the distance, he'd be lying on top of him. Alec's nervous system has been stripped raw and of all the things he wishes he could have right now, being crushed under Theo is at the top of the list. "I feel guilty. This is all my fault."

"Don't," Alec interrupts.

"Why, you going to tell me to shut up again?" The hint of a smile plays at Theo's mouth, and though it's small, it's enough to ease the knot of tension in Alec's stomach. "Or maybe you'll throw something at me again. Should I go find you something?"

Alec laughs, immediately regretting it when his ribs scream in protest. It takes a solid minute for him to regain his ability to speak through the pain. "Sorry, about last night. I was just—"

"Exhausted," Theo finishes.

"Yeah," Alec whispers.

"Pretty sure being run over by a car can do that. It's okay if you weren't ready to talk, or if you're still not today. Like I told Jason, I'm not going anywhere. Unless you ask me to. Otherwise, I'll be here."

"M'never gonna tell you to leave," Alec murmurs.

"That makes two of us," Theo says, letting his fingers brush some of the hair gently off Alec's forehead. It's the lightest of touches, but it soothes the raw, aching part of his sensory system desperate for contact.

"Where are my brothers?"

"They went to get food when you passed out. They let me come in while they were gone. I can call them if you'd rather they were here."

"No," Alec says, sliding his right hand towards the edge of the bed. "You. I want you."

Theo's jaw trembles as he reaches for Alec's hand, linking their fingers and bringing it to his mouth. He kisses the back of Alec's hand before pulling their joined fingers against his cheek. "I can't lose you, Alexander."

"M'not going anywhere. Literally. Can't even get up to piss."

The joke falls flat, wetness falling against the back of Alec's hand.

"Theodore."

"Don't leave me again," Theo chokes. "You can call me on my bullshit, demand we talk, do anything you want. Just don't walk away. Please."

He's never heard Theo sound so vulnerable, so afraid, and the knowledge that it's over Alec is something he's not sure he's ever going to get used to. His teenage fantasies used to involve moments like this. Well, minus the near-death experience and hospital thing. Back then, he would imagine Theo waking up one day and realizing he was in love with Alec, begging him to be with him. Those had been stories he told himself, born out of one-sided desire. This is something far different, and for all Alec dreamed about it, the truth is he doesn't want it. Not when it means Theo looks so pained.

All he wants, all he's ever wanted, is for Theo to be happy. The idea that his happiness might be with Alec is something he stopped dreaming about a long time ago.

"I won't leave," Alec promises. "I only left because it's what I thought you wanted."

"I don't think I've ever let myself think about what I wanted. Not really, not like this. But you leaving the other night was one of the worst experiences of my life."

"And here I thought me almost dying was."

He tries to smile, but Theo just lifts his gaze to Alec's with a pitiful frown. "Not funny, Alec."

"I have to entertain myself somehow," Alec sighs, pretty sure he's going to lose his goddamn mind being bedridden. It's been just over twenty-four hours, and while he technically might be in too much pain to get up, the fact that he isn't allowed to is fucking with him mentally. "Unless you wanted to give me a little bit of a show. Put those massive hands of yours somewhere, you know, forbidden. Now that would be very entertaining."

"Pretty sure the nurses might object."

"Spoilsport," Alec grumbles.

Theo shakes his head in fond exasperation. "Tell you what, I'll make you a deal."

"A deal?" Alec says, his entire face lighting up like the goddamn fourth of July.

"Yeah, a deal." He fixes his piercing blue eyes on Alec, intense and unblinking. Alec could drown in those eyes, wake up to those eyes, spend the rest of his life making sure they're full of happiness. "You do everything the nurses tell you to do—take your meds, follow orders and don't push yourself before your body is ready—and when you're finally back home, I'll give you a show. Any kind you want."

Alec doesn't even bother denying that pushing himself beyond what he's supposed to is exactly the kind of thing he was already considering. His desire to get better and get out of here is as all-consuming as his pain, and the fact that Theo knows him so well catches him by surprise. Instead, he focuses on the possible reward, willing to do anything to get it, including being a good patient.

"Theodore James, you have no idea what you're offering."

"On the contrary," Theo grins, lowering Alec's hand gently to the bed before leaning over Alec. His body is massive, blocking most of the harsh sunlight from the window. And for a few blissful seconds, Alec can pretend he's not in a hospital hooked up to IVs and heart monitors.

He's just a boy finally getting what he's always wanted. "I'll give you anything you want, Alexander."

"What if all I want is you?"

"Done," Theo answers, lowering his lips to Alec's in the barest of presses. He tastes like coffee, the familiar scent of his cologne making Alec's eyes water, because this isn't a daydream or a med-induced hallucination. Theo is really here, promising Alec the kind of future he was sure he could never have.

"I'm a greedy boy, Theodore. If you give yourself to me, there's no going back."

"Good."

"I mean it," Alec whispers, unsure when he started trembling. Never one to back down, Alec continues to push, needing to make sure Theo knows exactly what he's getting himself into. "I'm not easy. I'm loud and needy, and I don't share."

"I know," Theo grins, like all of that is a good thing.

"I'm a lot, Theo. I'm always going to be a lot. I don't know how to be less."

"Then don't be less, Alexander." Theo leans his forehead against Alec's, his breath warm and his scent soothing. "I'm not scared of you, not anymore. The only thing I'm scared of is losing you."

"That's never gonna happen," Alec croaks.

"Then we agree, I want you in all your needy, messy glory, and you want me in all my neurotic, anxious chaos."

"What a fucking pair," Alec sniffles, unsure why he's so close to crying when he's so happy. "I love you."

"Alec."

"I'm sorry, I have to say it. I can't hold it in, and it's okay if you don't say it back. I'm not going to ask you to promise anything before you're ready, but you have to know. It's always been you. You're it for me, Theodore. I love you with everything I have, and I always will."

"Thank you."

"What?" Alec blinks moisture clinging to his eyelashes.

"I said thank you. Thank you for loving me when I didn't deserve it, and seeing more in me than I saw in myself. Thank you for loving me when I didn't know what to do with it and loving me until I did. Thank you for loving me the way only you could."

"Oh." Alec's lips tremble and his heart aches, and he wishes there was a word for something beyond love, because that's what he feels for Theo.

"You're good for me, Alec. You're everything I need and all the things I never let myself want. I've never been in love, I don't know how. But you make me want to try. I can't give you those three words yet, but I can tell you if there was anyone I thought I could love, it would be you."

Alec cries in earnest, heavy tears of grief and joy that Theo wipes away with gentle hands and soft kisses. He murmurs promises against Alec's cheeks and lips, the kind that make Alec believe in forever. When the nurse comes in because of Alec's elevated heart rate, Theo has the decency to blush but remains at Alec's bedside, hand in Alec's as the nurses fuss and mark things down in his chart and give him more pain meds.

His brothers return by the time the meds kick in, his head spinning and the world going fuzzy. Not once does Theo leave, his hand firmly in place holding Alec's, even when Charlie glares at it. It's quiet at first, but then Jason says something that makes Andrew laugh and just like that, Charlie's expression loosens.

At some point, his parents arrive, leading to a tearful reunion and some difficult conversations. When they notice his and Theo's joined hands, Alec pretends to be in too much pain to partake in another conversation, choosing to focus on the way Theo's thumb smooths over the back of his hand while his parents move into the hallway for hushed conversations with his brothers. Their voices are low, drifting through the cracked door, and though Alec feels stripped raw in every way, there's a relief to finally have all of his secrets laid bare.

When Theo's lips press against his forehead, soft promises whispered against his temple, Alec gives in to his exhaustion and closes his eyes, his body aching but his heart lighter than it's been in years.

"YOU'RE BEING TOO NOISY."

"Me? You're the one stomping around like *La Chupacabra*."

"Is that like the boogeyman?"

"No. Yes. Maybe. Just shut up, or you'll wake him up. You're so noisy."

"You're both fucking noisy," Alec mutters, not needing to open his eyes to know who is in his room. He opens them anyway; his two best friends are a sight for sore eyes.

"Hey," Riley says with a smile that doesn't quite meet his eyes.

"You scared us, asshole." Antonio takes a deep breath, letting out a heavy exhale. He looks like he might cry. "Shit, you look—"

"Sexy as hell, I know." Alec cracks a smile that makes his cheeks ache. Despite being the one in the hospital bed, all he wants to do is make the worry on his friends' faces disappear. "It's okay to be jealous. Most people can't rock the hospital look as well as me. Or the bruises. It's a gift to wake up looking this good."

"Fucking idiot." Antonio shakes his head in fond exasperation and then sighs heavily. "I want to hug you, but all your family is in the hallway so we could have a few minutes, and they said, well Charlie said, if we hurt you he'd make sure security banned us."

"I'm pretty sure he was joking," Riley points out, but he does turn to look at the half-closed door. "Better safe than sorry, though."

"I want a hug," Alec pouts.

Riley moves first, angling his much larger body around Alec in a protective hold while Antonio moves around the other side of the bed to emulate. It's a bit awkward-looking for them and more of an air hug than a real one, but their unwavering presence fortifies Alec in a way only his best friends really can. When they pull back, they have the grace to pretend not to notice Alec wiping at his eyes. Maybe the car broke something in his brain, too. He's cried more in the last twenty-four hours than the last five years of his life combined, and he's pretty over feeling like a leaky faucet.

"So be honest, how much did you guys cry?" Alec asks, desperate for a narrative shift where he doesn't feel so out of control. "I bet you couldn't even sleep without me."

"How did you know the whole campus got together and held a crying vigil?" Riley deadpans. "We used up the entire supply of tissues at SLU."

"You two are so weird," Antonio snorts, but he's smiling the way he usually does when Alec and Riley are on their bullshit train.

"You love us," Riley grins, crossing his arms over his chest.

"Fuck knows why. You're both pains in my ass."

Antonio shoves his hand into his pocket and pulls something out, dangling it in front of Alec. "Here this is for you."

"Is that what I think it is?" Alec asks, turning his left hand palm up. The IV stings a little, but it's worth it when the cool plastic beads fall into his palm.

"If you're thinking 'wow, is this the most special and important piece of jewelry I'll ever get,' then yes," Riley smirks, reaching across the bed to add a second bracelet to Alec's palm.

He lifts them both, grinning at the chunky letter beads and colorful plastic ones. They're both blue—one a pale blue like the sky and the other dark, the word on both the same.

"We have matching ones," Riley says, tugging on the sleeve of his hoodie to reveal his own friendship bracelet in hot pink on his right wrist. Antonio copies, pushing his hoodie sleeves up to his elbows to reveal a red one.

"I can't believe you guys made these," Alec says, slipping both of them on his right wrist and thinking about that day he'd joked about making these all those weeks before. "You know I was teasing about these, right? You didn't have to make them, though I'm kind of glad you did."

"We had to do something to keep ourselves occupied yesterday," Riley replies. "Andrew is a goddamn warden, and refused to let us come see you."

"What Riley means is that he was pacing so much at our apartment, that he was going to wear a hole in the floor, so we all went to the craft store and got supplies."

"Who is we?"

"Hunter and Logan, obviously. They're coming by later. Andrew very strongly suggested we stagger who visited and when so as not to overwhelm you. And by strongly suggested, I mean he and Charlie are both kind of scary when they want to be." Antonio pulls a baggie out of the front of his hoodie pocket, dozens more friendship bracelets inside. "When I told the guys on the team what happened and what we were doing, they all came to our place and joined in."

"The guys on the team made me friendship bracelets," Alec mumbles, watching as Antonio pops open the baggie and sets it next to Alec's hip. He pulls the first one out, fingering the bright rainbow beads and the word team. The next one is red, with King and a 7. On it goes, each of them echoing Alec's association to the team, in what is probably supposed to make him feel better makes his hands sweat and his head throb while bile rises in his throat.

"Take them back," Alec says, shoving the baggie towards Antonio.

His eyebrows knit together in obvious confusion, and something in Alec he's been holding together breaks. He doesn't want to lose his best friend, all his friends. Aside from Riley and Hunter and Logan, his friends are the team. Or other athletes on campus. He's built his life around his identity as a soccer player, and it isn't until this moment that it occurs to Alec if he quits the team, he could lose them all.

"What's going on?" Antonio asks.

"Take the fucking bracelets," Alec begs, embarrassed by the desperation in his voice.

Antonio does what he asks, holding them between his hands. His eyes never leave Alec's face. "What's going on?"

"I'm not playing again," Alec grits out.

"Hey, you don't know that. Your parents said after your cast comes off you'll have a few months of PT, but me and the guys will come with you. We can train with you, get you back to normal, and then you can come back to the team."

"I'm not coming back, Antonio."

"You don't know that. They said—"

"I'm quitting," Alec says in a rush, those two little words leaving him feeling like he ran a marathon.

"But you love soccer," Antonio says, eyes wide. "We were gonna play in the MLS together. Playing profession-ally is what you've always wanted."

Alec shakes his head.

"I thought you loved it."

"I loved playing with you," Alec tells him, because that's the honest truth. "I love being part of a team, and I love the game. I always will. But playing at that level was making me miserable. It was making me hate the game and hate my body. The training and the stress and the pressure. I—I can't do it anymore. I don't want to be drafted and have my entire future be like that. I'm sorry. I'm so fucking sorry."

The silence stretches off for long seconds, broken by Antonio's soft, "I'm going to miss you."

Alec closes his eyes, swallowing down the urge to sob. His ribs wouldn't be able to handle it, nor would his heart. "I understand."

"Understand what?" Antonio presses.

"You're mad at me and don't want to be friends and—"

"*Dios mío*, you are the most dramatic fucker I've ever met," Antonio groans. "You are my family, Alec. You're not getting rid of me, ever. Who would be my best man when I marry Elsa? Hell, I think my *abuela* loves you more than she loves me. You're stuck with me. I won't lie to you, it sucks you won't be there, so yes I'm going to miss you on the field, but nothing is going to change our friendship. Besides, at least we can still graduate together, and oh my god, why do you look like you're going to throw up?"

"I hate my major, and I think I want to switch, which means I won't be able to graduate with you," Alec says so quickly the words jumble together. Maybe all he needed to start spilling his guts to everyone was to get hit by a car and stuck in a bed.

"Got any other life-changing secrets you wanna share?" Antonio sighs, dropping into the chair by Alec's bed and leaning against the railing. "Fuck."

"I'm sorry."

"If you apologize one more time, I'll kick you."

"No, you won't. You're scared of Andrew."

Antonio opens his mouth then shuts it. "Yeah, a little bit."

"So you don't hate me?"

"Nothing in the world could make me hate you," Antonio says seriously. "Which is amazing, considering how fucking difficult you are."

"Can we backtrack to the love fest? That was more fun."

"I love you," Riley offers.

"See, was that so hard?" Alec says. "Now if only the team were so easy. They're going to hate me."

"The team is going to miss you because you're a beast on the field, but all the guys want you to be happy. Well, maybe not Chaucer, but he can fuck off." Antonio lowers the friendship bracelets onto Alec's lap. "You're always going to be one of us, Alec. Even if you never play again, for SLU or anywhere else. You were a part of this team, the heart of it really, and nothing can change that."

"Don't make me cry, asshole. It hurts."

"Does it hurt being so pretty too?" Riley teases.

Alec smiles, flipping him off. "It does, actually. It's exhausting being this gorgeous."

"You should probably rest, then, from all that hard work being sexy."

Alec hums, perfectly aware of what his friends are doing and helpless to resist.

"Might close my eyes, just for a second."

"Gotta get that beauty sleep," Riley deadpans, playfully ruffling Alec's curls.

Antonio and Riley quietly start to bicker over what to put on the TV, letting Alec know they're not going anywhere anytime soon and giving him the freedom to relax. He only means to close his eyes for a few seconds, but the next time he opens them Antonio and Riley are gone, and Hunter and Logan appear. After they leave, the rest of Alec's team takes turns filing in. He strongly suspects Antonio talked to them because not one of the guys mentions Alec coming back to the team or quitting, avoiding the word soccer altogether. Most of his teammates take turns making sure Alec wears their bracelets, though, filling his room with crude jokes, raucous laughter and just enough hope for Alec to imagine one day everything might not feel so raw.

The hours tick by, yet the number of visitors never slows. In between friends and teammates, his family makes an appearance, as does Theo, each of them taking their leave when more of Alec's friends show up. By the time the sun has set and the announcement that visiting hours are almost over comes over the intercom system, Alec is exhausted in ways he didn't even know was possible. He's always been an extrovert, always felt exhilarated by being around people, but today took it out of him in unexpected ways and gave him a glimpse of how Theo must feel after social situations.

When Theo walks into the room with ten minutes to spare, there's a smile on his face and a familiar cup in his hand.

"Aren't you a sight for sore eyes." Alec manages a smile despite his bone-deep exhaustion.

"You saw me an hour ago," Theo says, but it doesn't escape Alec's notice that the tips of his ears—visible because the longest bits of his hair are pushed behind them—turn red. Alec tucks that away, deciding that while he's stuck in recovery mode, his new favorite game will be to see how much he can make his boyfriend blush.

Boyfriend. Fuck, Alec likes the sound of that.

"An entire hour, Theodore. That's forever. Get your ass over here and kiss me. Also is that a Sonic Coke? There are other more traditional ways to propose, but the answer is yes."

Theo's laughter is warm and rich as he crosses the room, dropping a kiss to Alec's forehead and then his lips. It's chaste, but satisfies something needy in Alec that longs to be reminded Theo really does want him. "Nice to know for future reference, all you want in a marriage proposal is a Coke."

He knows Theo is joking, but what Alec also knows is that he wasn't kidding when he told Theo that he was it for him. Without a doubt, Alec is going to marry this man. He knows it. He just needs to let Theo find his footing first and figure that out for himself, no matter how long it takes.

As long as Theo is his, he doesn't much care what word they use to define their relationship.

"Coke is one way. I also accept gold," Alec asserts, not about to pass up the opportunity to tease. If there's a little, or perhaps a lot, of truth to his words right now, no one needs to know yet. "Make sure it's engraved with something sentimental about how much you can't live without me. Oh, and flowers, lots of flowers—white dahlias with baby's breath. Probably a big party, too. On the beach."

"Anything else?" Theo grins, and the fact that he's not running away screaming from Alec joking about forever makes Alec's eyes burn.

"You," Alec says. "Maybe in a blue shirt."

"Blue shirt, white dahlias and gold. Got it."

"Don't forget the Coke," Alec says, voice quivering.

"Who could forget Coke?" Theo whispers, bringing the straw to Alec's lips. He takes a drink, little tingles of bliss flooding his nervous system at the first chug of the sweet, highly carbonated beverage.

"I love you."

Theo's eyes soften as he leans over to kiss Alec's nose and each of his cheeks before sitting back down. He links their fingers, then lifts their joined hands to his mouth, kissing the back of Alec's hand and each of his knuckles. His smile is easy and gentle. Theo might not be ready to say the words back, but Alec holds no doubts about the depth of Theo's feelings.

When the announcement comes that visiting hours are over, Theo lingers long enough a nurse has to kick him out. As he leaves, he promises to return tomorrow, a promise Alec knows Theo will keep. Theo will always come back to him. They will always come back to each other.

EPILOGUE
THEO

EARLY MORNING LIGHT filters through the curtains, casting a warm glow throughout the room and illuminating the sharp angles and soft curves of the beautiful man beside him. Even without Theo's glasses, looking at Alec is always a treat, from his bare legs and the curve of his equally bare ass to his sleep-tousled curls spilled all over his pillow. His pillow, in their bed, in what has become their house. Not that Theo had ever officially asked Alec to move in. What had started as convenience had organically grown into something else entirely.

After Alec's accident, he'd been unable to move back into his dorm on campus because of his extensive medical needs. Once his cast came off and physical therapy began, it became clear his college apartment with its cramped quarters and flights of stairs would be too much. Alec alternated between crashing at his parents' house and Theo's. Eventually, he'd spent more time at Theo's than his parents' and his stuff had started appearing. One day all his shoes were in Theo's closet and the next, his garage was full of soccer balls. A week later, Alec's most prized possessions lined the top of Theo's dresser next to his glasses and cologne. The last and most permanent had been when Alec's beloved blender had found its new home next to Theo's coffee pot.

While the shift from dating to living together had been surprisingly easy, the rest had been anything but. Alec's recovery and transition back to school had been fraught with pain and stress. After a prolonged break to recover both mentally and physically, Alec had eventually returned to classes in the spring, albeit with a shift in goals. He'd ultimately decided against switching his major and instead, with the help of his favorite academic advisor, devised a plan to take some needed prerequisites along with his required classes so that he could continue his education and eventually apply to a doctorate of physical therapy program.

It was amazing to watch Alec blossom, his exuberance for life and playful nature returning more every day. Which wasn't to say his recovery was easy. The months had been brutal and painful, and Theo had loved Alec more.

Love.

Just thinking about it makes Theo's belly swoop and his heart race. It's been a few months since he finally got the courage to say those three little words to Alec, after which Alec had flat-out sobbed, ugly snot-filled tears that soaked Theo's sweater. He'd been so beautiful with his teary eyes and soft lips, looking at Theo like being loved back was the greatest thing that had ever happened to him, when the truth was Alec was the best thing to ever happen to Theo. Alexander King was the light of his life, and Theo intended to spend every moment making sure Alec was as happy and loved as he deserved.

"You're thinking about me, aren't you?" Alec mumbles, pillow lines on his cheek visible when he rolls onto his side at the same time the automatic feeder in the kitchen dings, and Rio is off like a flash, bolting from their room.

"What makes you think that?" Theo asks, skimming his fingers over the exposed flat of Alec's tummy. He is almost always thinking about Alec, unless he's hyper-focused on a report at work, but sometimes admitting that out loud still makes Theo feel painfully vulnerable.

"Because it's a day that ends in Y," Alec replies easily. He throws both his arms overhead while his legs and back arch in a full body stretch. "Besides, who could wake up next to all this and not be starstruck."

"Your modesty never fails to astound." Theo laughs.

"Theodore, we've talked about this. Modesty has no place in this much perfection."

"You are perfect," Theo agrees, taking the opportunity to get on his knees to scoot closer so he can throw one leg over Alec's slim hips and straddle his body. For so long they'd have to be careful during moments like this, and while Theo had enjoyed every moment of that fragile intimacy, he's relieved to have Alec fully healed.

The days of uncertainty and pain are finally behind them, and there's nothing but joy and peace on Alec's face as he grins up at Theo like he hung the goddamn moon.

"Is this my birthday present?" Alec smirks, trailing his fingers over Theo's soft tummy before lowering them to wrap around Theo's dick, making Theo whimper. He's never going to tire of seeing Alec's long, delicate fingers with his freckle-covered knuckles stroking his cock. "You didn't even wrap it, but I accept."

"Oh, is it your birthday?" Theo gasps, struggling to think straight with Alec's teasing strokes taking him from half-hard to fully erect in seconds.

"If you forgot my birthday, I'm not going to suck your

cock," Alec says seriously, like that wouldn't be the world's largest punishment for himself. Still Theo plays along, delighting in this side of himself that Alec has pulled out. Not even when he was a teenager had he allowed himself to be so carefree, but Alec makes being alive, being in love, feel as easy as breathing.

"Well, we can't have that," Theo replies, reaching towards Alec's mouth. He drags a thumb over Alec's bottom lip, anticipation coiling around his heart when Alec's mouth falls open on a tiny whimper. Theo's not sure how he got so lucky as to have a boyfriend whose deepest desire is to wake up every morning and be allowed to suck Theo's dick. Sometimes it's hard and fast, and other times Alec's barely awake before he's opening his mouth and begging for it to be filled. On a few recent occasions, Alec's taken to doing nothing more than holding Theo's soft cock in his mouth, like just having it in there is perfect.

"Fuck, Theo."

"So needy," Theo whispers, pulling Alec's bottom lip down. "You want something, Alexander?"

"You know I do," Alec whines, his hands moving from Theo's length to his ass as Alec tries to physically move Theo up so he will sit on Alec's face. Eager to prolong the teasing just a moment more, he doesn't allow himself to be moved, earning him a pout.

"What did you want?" Theo asks, trying not to laugh. "Breakfast?"

"If by breakfast you mean your thick cock, then yes," Alec groans, fingers digging into Theo's ass. "Theodore, I swear if you don't sit on my goddamn face right now I'll... I'll—"

"You'll what, baby?" Theo presses his thumb into Alec's

mouth, his own dick leaking precome when Alec immediately sucks on his thumb.

Mouth full, Alec doesn't respond, but he does whine in the that low, needy way of his that he knows makes Theo feel insane. Playing it up with the sole purpose of making Theo crazy. Alec lets his eyes fall half-shut as he drags his tongue along the underside of Theo's thumb, a teasing imitation of what he plans to do to Theo. Unable to resist those sweet brown eyes and wanton expression, Theo crawls up Alec's body, hands braced on the headboard as he lowers himself over Alec's face.

"Happy fucking birthday to me." Alec grins, opening his mouth and making the world's most blissed out, desperate sound as Theo slips his cock inside.

No matter how many times they do this, Theo never gets used to how easily Alec swallows him down, the way Alec's hands roam over his ass and thighs like he might die if he stopped touching Theo. Somehow, despite the fact that Theo sets the pace as he fucks into Alec's mouth—Alec utterly at his mercy—it's Theo who feels completely powerless. No one has ever made sex this good, no one has ever made Theo feel so good.

The only person who has ever made anything feel this good is Alec. He's so warm and willing, and Theo's sleepy arousal brightens like the rising sun.

"Shit, your mouth," Theo moans, dropping his head between his shoulders so he can watch.

Alec hums happily while his fingers languidly massage up and down the backs of Theo's thighs as if he could spend all day sucking Theo. Which to be fair, he probably could. One day last month they'd done an experiment, and Alec had sucked him for damn near an hour before conceding his jaw ached, at which point he'd roll over and drooled into the pillow while Theo fucked him.

It would be a lie to say everything with Alec is easy. It's not. But it's worth it. It's so fucking worth it.

"You feel so good."

The praise earns him a squeeze, and Theo doesn't even dare blink, gaze riveted on the sweep of Alec's thick eyelashes and the moisture at the corner as they flutter shut. The softest of sighs escapes Alec, his grip slackening into something more like pets as he sucks Theo's cock like he really has been given a gift. The strip of sunlight streaks across the pillow, making Alec's curls seem to glow, like even the new day wants to bask in him.

Ridiculous as it might be after almost a year together, it still sends a thrill through Theo every time he remembers that Alec is his.

"I could come just like this, fill you with my load while you lie there and look pretty." Alec's moan makes it clear what he thinks of that idea, but then again, Theo's yet to find a version of sex Alec doesn't like. Likely because Theo knows what Alec's limits are. For as brash and wild as Alec can sometimes be, the truth is he's got a tender heart, and Theo has come to understand exactly how Alec loves sex.

Alec likes it close and needy, almost always face to face with lots of kissing and praise. Alec doesn't fuck, he makes love, and the difference isn't lost on Theo, who loses himself in the depth of that love every time he gets to feel Alec like this. There's something powerful about being trusted the way Alec trusts Theo, something that reaffirms their commitment every time they do this.

While Alec might not have been Theo's first, if he has anything to do about it, then Alec will be his last. Alec will be his forever.

"I'm so close," Theo whispers, reaching down to brush the hair from Alec's eyes.

They flutter open, his expression so unguarded and full of bliss that Theo can't hold back. He slips his fingers into Alec's curls and gives the softest of tugs to warn him, but as expected all Alec does is grip Theo's ass and urge him all the way down the back of his throat, swallowing Theo down. Boneless, high on post-coital bliss and eager to bring Alec with him, Theo drops down beside him on the bed and pulls him close. As expected, the second Theo's lips are on Alec's, he whimpers. Just a few lazy strokes and Alec's coming.

In the beginning, Theo used to be afraid of what might happen if the novelty wore off. He'd never been with the same person more than twice, had no idea what you were supposed to keep doing. Turns out that wasn't something he needed to worry about. He and Alec aren't reinventing the wheel, they're hardly adventurous by any means, yet sex with Alec is easily the most physically and emotionally satisfying thing Theo has ever experienced.

"Think I'm dead," Theo groans when they finally pull apart. He collapses on his back and stares at the ceiling. "You killed me."

"You're welcome," Alec says rather smugly, voice rough from the throat-fucking. His eyes are watery, lips red, and spit soaked. "I'll be here, well...as long as you'll have me."

He turns to look at Alec, heart catching in his throat. He looks so good in Theo's bed, in his home, in his heart. It's clear Alec is teasing, but Theo can't. Not about this.

"Forever," Theo whispers.

"You can't just ask a man to marry you after sex." Alec laughs, the sound dying down when Theo doesn't join in. "Theo?"

"I just...I love you."

"I love you, too." Alec cups Theo's cheek, his thumb stroking over the rise of Theo's cheekbones. His eyes are searching, unsure, but Theo's never been more certain of anything in his life.

"I don't want you to leave," Theo tells him, surprised by the way his voice shakes.

"I'm not going anywhere, Theodore. You can't even kick me out. You're stuck with me like a leech or something. Just try and get rid of me."

There was a hole in Theo's heart for so long, one he didn't even let Jason into. He'd been raised to shy away from any kind of affection that could lead to heartache, to never be vulnerable for fear of being weak. He's never been more vulnerable than he is now, but he doesn't feel weak. He feels strong. Loving Alec makes him strong.

"I'm serious."

"Me too," Alec says, face all scrunched up. "You literally can't get rid of me. I'm like an invasive plant or some shit. I'll just come back and—"

"Marry me," Theo blurts.

"Are you serious?" Alec whispers, voice so small Theo worries he's ruined this.

"I am. I didn't plan this. Or well, I did plan it, kind of...I have a ring, but I was going to wait. You said, um, you said dahlias and a blue shirt and a party, but I just looked at you right this moment and knew I couldn't go another second without asking you to be mine. Forever. I didn't think I was made to love anyone, but you barreled into my life and refused to let me get away with hiding anymore. I don't know how I got so lucky, but I know I won't let you go. I'll make you so happy, Alexander. I want to grow old with you and adopt so many pets we're outnumbered, and I want you to fill the fridge with Coke, and start every morning with those god-awful protein shakes, and I want you to be mine—today, tomorrow, forever. Please be my husband."

Quiet tears stain Alec's face, and he is so unnaturally quiet that Theo has no idea what to do. Alec is never quiet.

"Did I do it wrong?" Theo worries aloud. This is why he always plans things, but being with Alec means he keeps throwing plans out the window. "I should have waited until I could do it right with a party and—"

"Fuck the party," Alec sniffles, throwing his arms around Theo and pulling him down into a bruising hug. "The answer is yes, a million times yes. I'll marry you. Right now. Today."

"You've got a birthday party today," Theo reminds him, overcome with happiness. He reaches for Alec's hand, bringing it up to kiss the empty ring finger, hardly able to believe he gets to put something there so that everyone who looks at him will know who he belongs to.

"We could turn my party into a wedding, I bet."

Sometimes it's impossible to tell whether Alec is joking or not. If Theo's learned anything in the last ten months, it's that Alec is full of surprises.

"No shotgun weddings."

"Only shotgun proposals," Alec teases. "Don't pinch your face like that, I love it. Ten out of ten, best proposal ever. I sucked your dick so good you clearly couldn't let me go."

"That had nothing to do with it," Theo interjects. At Alec's raised eyebrow, he laughs. "Okay, I mean you are great at sucking cock, but that's not why I love you."

"Feel free to tell me why, in great detail." Alec folds his arms under his head. "I have all day."

"You don't have all day if you want to make your

appointment with Riley and Hunter. Unless you changed your mind about jumping out of a plane, because honestly that sounds absolutely horrible and very risky, and I support you changing your mind."

"You think everything is risky," Alec snorts, sitting up. He glances at the clock on the bedside table. "And no, I haven't changed my mind. I want to do this. I have to do this."

Much as Theo wishes he could talk Alec out of jumping out of a plane from ten thousand feet, he knows it really is something he has to do. After the accident and months of physical therapy, there'd been so many times Alec didn't trust his body. After a lifetime of feeling in control he'd felt anything but, and though he'd healed fine physically, there was still a mental block sometimes.

A few weeks ago, Riley suggested skydiving for Alec's birthday as a way to feel empowered and free, and Alec had jumped at the idea, eagerly roping Hunter into their plans. According to Alec, the only thing that would've made it perfect was if Antonio had been in the country to come with them, but since he was in Mexico for a few weeks before he started with his new team, it was just Riley, Logan, Hunter and Alec today.

Theo doesn't get the draw since you couldn't pay him to jump out of a plane; he only knows that it's important to Alec so he's staying quiet. He's also staying home, because if he had to watch Alec jump out of a plane, he'd probably pass out or have a panic attack. That and he has way too much to do to get ready for the party later.

"I guess I better shower, but only if you give me my ring, *fiancé*." The smile on Alec's face is bright enough to light up Theo's entire life. He really is devastatingly beautiful when he smiles.

"The ring," Theo echoes, rolling off the bed and shuffling to the dresser. He opens the top drawer, digging around until he finds a pair of black socks he never wears hidden in the back corner, unfolding them to reveal a small box that he carries back to the bed. Somehow even though Alec has already said yes, he can't help but feel nervous. He wants Alec to love it, to look at it on his finger and remember this moment, remember how precious he is.

"Well?" Alec's grinning, left hand outstretched.

Holding his breath, Theo opens the box, pulling out the delicate band. All gold, smooth except for the single blue topaz stone in the center. Proud of his steady hand, he slips the ring on Alec's finger, exhaling a heavy sigh of relief when it settles at the base in a perfect fit.

"It's beautiful." When Alec lifts his eyes to Theo's, he whispers, "Thank you."

"Everyone will know you're taken now." Theo lifts his hand, laying a single kiss atop the ring. "Forever."

"Theodore James, are you being possessive? You want me to get a shirt that says 'belongs to Theo' for when we go out? I will. Actually, that's a great idea."

"I don't think that's necessary," Theo chuckles, absolutely certain that Alec would in fact wear a shirt like that if he could. "Between you and me, I don't need to see you in a special shirt or ring to know you're mine. I feel it every time you look at me."

"Are you turning into a romantic, Theodore?"

"For you," Theo answers. "Anything for you."

"Anything?" Alec smirks.

"Anything except jumping out of a plane."

"Damn," Alec laughs as he slips out of bed, though not before dropping a kiss to Theo's head. "By the way, don't tell my brothers about the engagement when they come over later. I wanna do it. I wanna be here when they find out."

"Who says they're coming over? I don't have anything planned," Theo lies, wondering how on earth Alec figured out he's planning a surprise party. He's been so careful. Or at least he thought he had. Maybe he's not as good at hiding things from Alec as he thought.

"Uh-huh. Sure." Alec turns to look at Theo with a playful grin. "Whatever you say future husband of mine."

PAUSING to appreciate the difference a full day's work makes, Theo places his hands on his hips and surveys the small backyard. This morning it'd been in horrible shape, the last few months of Alec's recovery taking precedence over yard work. Even once he was better, there were far more important things to do, like spend every second with his pretty boyfriend, rather than worry about weeds and grass. Thankfully as soon as Alec left with Riley this morning, Jason came to help Theo tackle his problem. Together they mowed the lawn, pulled the weeds along the fence line, set up a few tables and chairs and rearranged and cleaned the patio furniture. Once that was done, Theo strung up a few new strings of white lights from the patio to the fence line in case the party went late, which knowing the King family, it would. Meanwhile, Jason built the new fire pit Theo bought. All in all, the yard looks amazing, and pride fills Theo's chest.

He's never thrown anyone a party before, not even Jason, since his family always handled that. It feels monumental somehow to realize that yet one more part of taking care of Alec, making him happy, is something he can do.

There's a responsibility there, and after months of therapy, that no longer feels like a burden but a privilege.

Watching the summer sun glint off the freshly cut grass, Theo can't help but smile, hoping Alec likes it all. When Alec had offhandedly mentioned wanting something small and cozy last month for his birthday, Theo took the idea and ran with it, eager to give him everything he wanted and more.

"Are you daydreaming about Alec?"

"No," Theo lies, turning to see Jason has returned from his trip to the recycling bin with a smirk.

"You're such a bad liar."

"Yeah, but we both know if I answered honestly it might incriminate me."

"I told you, you're allowed to talk about being in love. Just don't ever mention sex and my brother in the same sentence and we're good. As far as I'm concerned, he's still an innocent virginal baby."

Theo barks out a laugh, unable to picture Alec as innocent ever. "Whatever you say."

"I hate you," Jason grumbles. He's been a bit moody today, which is unusual given his normal positive disposition.

"You okay?"

"I'm fine," Jason sighs. "Ugh, you love Alec so much, don't you?"

"Uh, yes."

Jason groans loudly, covering his face. He mumbles something unintelligible, the words lost behind his big hands. When he drops his hands, his expression is still tight. "Sorry I've been a dick today. I'm so jealous."

Oh. *Oh.*

"Am I being a bad friend? Am I neglecting you? Maybe–"

"Stop." Jason holds up a hand, face pinched. "I'm fine, and I'm happy for you guys. I'm being a dick. It's just...ugh, I don't wanna talk about this today. Or ever, but especially not today. Raincheck?"

"Raincheck," Theo concedes. If Jason isn't ready to talk about it, then Theo isn't going to push. To his relief and surprise, dating Alec hadn't ruined his friendship with Jason, but he'd wondered if this might happen at some point. Even though he's made a concentrated effort to make sure they have bro time, it's been inevitable that some of that time involves Alec now. He thought Jason was cool with it, but maybe there's something else there. Either way, he's willing to be patient until Jason is ready to talk.

"You should probably shower," Theo says, offering Jason an escape since he looks like he ate a lemon. "You smell like you rolled around in the mud."

Jason lifts an arm and sniffs himself, grimacing. "Gross. I'm gonna head home and shower before the party, feed the dogs and take them for a quick walk. I'll be back in an hour and a half, is that good?"

"Sure, I'm pretty much done at this point. All I have to do after I shower is put out the tablecloths and flowers, and then the taco guy will be here at three to set up. Riley texted me earlier and said that he was going to take Alec out for lunch after their jump, so they're supposed to be here in—" he pauses to look at his watch. "Two hours, fuck."

"Calm down, Theo. You've got this. Everything is perfect. He's going to love it."

Jason squeezes Theo's shoulder, and when he releases it some of his tension fades. He's maybe been a little intense about the party today. While it's supposed to be low-key and simple, Theo's been deep in his anxious need to make it perfect.

"Pretty sure you could've bought him a shitty pizza and eaten on a picnic blanket on the overgrown grass, and Alec would have still been happy. He loves you so much, which is somehow amazing and gross all at once. I'm still not sure which is which. All I know is I've never seen either of you happier, and that makes me happy. So just relax, alright? You did good, Theo."

"Thanks," Theo says quietly, surprised at how much hearing that helps. Part of him itches to tell Jason right now about the engagement. Keeping the secret from him all day was brutal, the only thing that made Theo feel a little bit better about the entire thing is that Jason already knows about the ring and Theo's intention to propose; he just doesn't know it accidentally happened this morning. Not yet.

"I'm gonna take off," Jason announces. "See you."

Once Jason leaves, Theo hurries into the house to shower, scrubbing away the dirt and sweat. He takes the time for a close shave, eager to have Alec mouth the smooth skin later, like he always does when Theo is freshly shaved. Thoughts of Alec fill his mind while he dresses, spending more time than usual trying to tousle his hair and apply a generous amount of his favorite cologne Alec seems obsessed with. Once he's done, he heads to his closet, pulling on a pair of worn, faded jeans that are just this side of too tight and make Alec especially needy, along with a new blue sweater he bought last week for this very occasion. Most of his clothing leans towards earth tones, but there's something delightful about pulling on the bright blue sweater knowing it's going to be a beacon for Alec's attention.

It's odd to realize he spent his entire life avoiding being noticed, but with Alec he craves it, relishes in the other man's attention. Something about Alec's adoring gaze and handsy affection has turned Theo into a bit of attention whore, at least where Alec is involved.

By the time he's finished dressing, there's still over an hour until Jason and the taco guy arrive. Finding a taco guy who specialized in vegetarian options had been harder than Theo thought, and he'd had to hire one from Los Angeles, adding on a pretty penny to the travel expense, but it'll be worth it to see Alec devour his body weight in his favorite food.

Eager to make sure everything is ready by the time they arrive to set up, Theo hurries back into the yard, setting up the tablecloths and adding vases of white dahlias to each of the tables. Once he's done, it's hard not to notice that all of the white makes it look more like an engagement party than a birthday. Or maybe Theo's just got marriage on the brain.

Somehow, Theo had grown up believing that avoiding love would break a generational curse of abandonment and trauma. Thinking about Alec's tear-filled eyes as he'd let Theo slip the ring on his finger this morning, he understands the truth to be far different. Loving Alec, and letting himself be loved in return, is the bravest thing he's ever done.

"EVERYONE SHUT THE FUCK UP! He's coming," Jason yells, grabbing Theo's arm and tugging him back behind the door as if that will help.

Behind him is the rest of Alec's family. His parents came around to the idea of Theo and Alec together quickly once they saw how happy Alec was. To no one's surprise, the hardest to win over had been Charlie, who had been convinced for months that Theo was gonna freak out and break Alec's heart.

It'd been difficult at first, but Theo couldn't even be mad because he understood Charlie's distrust came from his deep need to protect Alec, especially after his accident. Thankfully he's come around since then, and the fact that he's here in Theo's home helping him throw Alec a surprise party is proof.

"Stop laughing," Jason yells at a group of Alec's old teammates piled on the couch. There's so many of them that Theo's half afraid it'll break under the weight, but the sight of so many people still here to celebrate Alec has his heart full. "He's walking up the path."

"Who turned Jason into a drill sergeant?" Charlie grumbles.

"Shut up," Jason snaps.

"Someone's an angry puppy," Charlie laughs. At Jason's frown, he continues. "Aw, is someone jealous it's not his birthday? Maybe—"

Andrew slaps a hand over Charlie's mouth to silence him, which is lucky because Jason's face has turned the exact same shade as a tomato, and it's anyone's guess whether that's anger or embarrassment. Theo makes a mental note to plan a bro date, just for them at some point in the coming weeks to check in with him.

Luckily they're spared further King sibling bickering by Alec's keys rattling in the front door, which everyone takes as their cue to finally be as quiet as possible while they wait.

Slowly the door swings open to reveal a smiling Alec with Riley and Hunter standing behind him. "Wow, a party! I am so surprised!" Alec announces dramatically. "So surprised."

"What the actual fuck are you wearing?" Charlie yells at the same time everyone else shouts *happy birthday*. Theo's eyes narrow as he focuses in on Alec's shirt, his own face now matching Jason's while Andrew starts to choke on his laughter. Alec's friends whistle and hoot, which makes Theo's face feel like it's on fire.

"Like my shirt, Theodore?" Alec saunters in wearing the same well-fitting black joggers he had on this morning, but instead of a loose cotton SLU tee, he's now wearing a pastel pink cropped t-shirt that says, *I love my daddy*. "It was a birthday present from Riley."

"You want to kill me, don't you?" Theo says. The question is rhetorical. The writing on the shirt might be ridiculous, but the way it fits makes Theo want to drag Alec into the bedroom and ignore the house full of people. The shirt is loose around his throat, his gold chain skimming sharp collar bones and the cut of the shirt showing off a sliver of his belly.

"Definitely not the little death I would choose," Alec smirks.

"How is it possible that he's gotten even more shameless?" Jason groans. "Theo, control your boyfriend."

"No one controls Alec," Theo replies.

At the exact same time, Alec holds up his hand. "*Fiancé.*"

The ring Theo put there this morning shimmers as Alec wiggles his fingers to show it off. Half a second passes before he is crushed in the world's loudest group hug, his friends laughing and cheering and asking a million questions. Theo takes a step back, surprised to find Alec's parents staring at him instead of waiting for a turn to hug Alec.

Alec's dad holds his hand out, but before Theo can shake it, Alec's mother pulls him into a hug. "You've always been part of this family, Theo. I hope you know that."

"Oh," Theo croaks, surprised to find he can't reply from the lump in his throat.

"You're a good boy. You'll take care of my son, I know you will." Then she says something that rocks Theo to the absolute core. "And he will take care of you, too. Both my boys happy? What more could a mother want?"

Theo is spared from blubbering on her shirt by Jason tapping on his mom's shoulder. "My turn."

As soon as Jason's mom steps aside, he grabs onto Theo, hugging him fiercely. "What happened to your plan? I thought you weren't proposing for a few months."

"Alec happened," Theo half-laughs, half-cries.

"Fucking Alec," Jason says, hugging him tighter. "I can't believe you're gonna legally be my brother."

"Brother," Theo croaks, unsure he can handle any more love.

"I just have one thing to say." Jason pulls back, holding onto Theo's shoulder with both hands. "If I hear any nonsense at your wedding about you marrying your best friend, I will interrupt that damn ceremony and call bullshit. I am the best friend, got it?"

"No one could ever replace you, Jason."

"Damn right they couldn't," Jason says before pulling Theo into another hug.

"Are we fighting over Theo? I want in," Alec says, grinning when Jason steps back to leave room for Alec, who folds himself into Theo's arms, pressing a kiss to the side of Theo's neck.

"There's no fighting over him," Jason says. "He was mine first."

Alec flips him off, but his smile remains easy. It's an ongoing thing between them, and Theo has realized it might never stop, but there's no bite from either of them so he's given up interjecting. Arguing is how they show their love, apparently.

"So how was jumping out of an airplane?" Theo asks once he's sure he's got Alec's attention.

"Fucking amazing," Alec says, "but so is this. Thank you."

"For the party?"

"For everything," Alec answers, arms tightening around Theo's waist. "I love you."

Theo drops his forehead to Alec's, breathing in the sweet scent of fresh air that clings to his sun-warmed skin. "I love you too."

"So, Theodore, are you ready for forever?"

"Never been more ready."

AFTERWORD

Thank you so much for reading Cross the Line. Publishing my debut novel is a dream come true. If you enjoyed it, I would love it if you'd leave a review on your favorite bookish site or share with friends. These kinds of recommendations and reviews mean everything to indie authors!

Rainbows, love and coffee,
    Lucky

Want more King brothers? Check out Jason's story in Make the Play here.

If you want to stay up to date with Lucky's writing and get a bonus story featuring Alec & Theo, be sure to join her mailing list.

ACKNOWLEDGMENTS

This book wouldn't have been possible without my two besties S & K. You both know who you are and your endless cheerleading and support got me through imposter syndrome, writer's block and everything in between. Thanks for believing in me even when I didn't believe in myself. Becoming a published writer has been a lifelong dream and while it took me a little while to get here, I made it because of you guys.

Thank you to my spouse who endured the most random questions (including giving me his native language perspective on the Spanish in one of the sex scenes) and my sensitivity readers Mel and Abigail who helped me ensure Alec's story was one of authenticity.

A massive thank you to BootyFeathers for the most gorgeous cover featuring Theo and Alec. You brought them to life and I couldn't be happier or more grateful.

Big thank you to my ARC team for reading the story and sharing it with the world. I appreciate you all. And a second thank you to the ARC readers who kindly helped me find and fix a few typos and formatting errors in the ARC stage so the final draft could be perfect. I appreciate you all so much.

And thank you to every reader who picks up this book, who carries these characters with you and who shares my words. I appreciate you.

ABOUT THE AUTHOR

Lucky writes character-driven, contemporary MM romance. Her debut novel CROSS THE LINE begins the "Kings of Heart" series, each book featuring one of four brothers on their sometimes messy, sometimes tender paths to happy ever after.

She's a millennial who grew up on fanfic, a lifelong West Coast resident, and a Canva Pro enthusiast. Queer and neurodivergent representation is deeply important to her as a member of both communities, and she loves exploring intersectional experiences through her fiction as a writer and a reader.

When she's not writing, her favorite things include drinking coffee, walking on the beach, staying up late to finish her latest read, and filling her house with rainbows.

Made in the USA
Columbia, SC
24 April 2025